I0630574

SKELOS

THE JOURNAL OF WEIRD FICTION AND DARK FANTASY

SKELOS

THE JOURNAL OF WEIRD FICTION AND DARK FANTASY

NUMBER 4   FALL 2020

Managing Editors

Mark Finn   Chris Gruber   Jeffrey Shanks

Poetry Editor: Frank Coffman

Contents

Short Fiction

Novelettes

Poetry

Essays

Artists

Front cover: Edmund Dulac (*The Alchemist*, 1910). *Back cover:* Alfred Kubin (*The Specimen*, ca. 1906). *Interior:* Gustave Doré (107, 141), Mike Dubisch (37), Victor Hugo (203), Rachel Kahn (91), Allen Koszowski (10, 11, 30, 50, 57, 192, 200), Mark Maddox (5), Jim Pitts (60, 66, 79), Michael H. Price (94–99), Andrea Rushing (109), Jeffrey Shanks (21, 33, 59, 87, 123, 162, 171, 179), Timothy Truman (157), George E. Turner (100), Bill Willingham (27)

Production

Design by Jeffrey Shanks and Mike Hunter. Copy editing by Chris Gruber, Mark Finn, Frank Coffman, Scott Cupp, Keith West, and Jeffrey Shanks.

SKELOS: THE JOURNAL OF WEIRD FICTION AND DARK FANTASY Volume 1, Number 4. ISBN-13: 978-0-9987010-4-2. Copyright © 2020 by Skelos Press, an imprint of Skelos Productions, LLC. Address: P. O. Box 20781, Tallahassee, FL 32316. All rights reserved. Nothing in this issue may be reprinted in whole or in part without the permission of the publisher and creator. All material in this issue is copyrighted to the respective creators. "Emperor of Dreams" is reprinted by permission of the Estate of Harold Hughesdon. Publisher assumes no responsibility for unsolicited submissions. *SKELOS* is published two times a year by Skelos Press. For more information on ordering or submissions please visit our website: www.skelospress.com.

Skelos logo design by Bryan "Mr. Zarono" Reagan.

SKULL SESSION

SKELOS: THE JOURNAL OF WEIRD FICTION AND DARK FANTASY
NUMBER 4   FALL 2020

Bill Crider, 1941–2018

I can't remember when I first met Bill Crider; I'm sure it was at either an Arma-dilloCon, in Austin, Texas, or an AggieCon, in College Station, Texas, and it was sometime in the mid to late 1990's, which may as well have been the Late Cretaceous Period for many people. All I know is that it feels like a lot longer than that.

Bill was known primarily as a mystery writer, but like every other Texas author I have ever known, he was known to stray and dabble whenever it suited him. His long-running series about Sheriff Dan Rhodes may be considered something of a "Texas Cozy" in that ironic way that we have of understating and exaggerating at the same time.

AggieCon was held on the campus of Texas A & M University, which is known for, among other things, its engineering program. The campus' interest in Science Fiction is said to have officially taken off during the original run of Star Trek in the mid–1960s. This student/fan-run convention was one of the many rites of passage for speculative fiction authors in Texas. One of the things that AggieCon used to offer to visiting SF authors and other questionable dignitaries was a tour of their Research Library and Archive, Cushing Library, which contains a vast array of science fiction, fantasy and related holdings. Naturally, I was interested (and who wouldn't be?)

On this particular Saturday morning, I showed up at the doorstep, along with two other people: Joe Lansdale and Bill Crider. It was just us, and as the then-curator Hal Hall gleefully showed us shelf upon shelf of rare books, manuscripts, and complete collections of expensive paperback originals, I followed Bill and Joe and watched as they walked up and down the aisle going, "Got it, got it, need it, read it, got it, need it, Oh Hell, I've never seen that, got it, got it . . ."

I thought I had a lot of books. I was wrong, so very, very wrong. Later, Bill and Rick Klaw and I went to Half-Price Books and ran a number on them, like con-men at a circus (which I guess we were), and then we all had a leisurely lunch at the Chinese Buffet. It was the first time we got to know each other and I found Bill to be a conversational delight, deeply read, and a long-time fan of movies with gorillas in them. Or, more specifically, movies with guys dressed as gorillas in them. He was the only other person I'd met (aside from Rick Klaw, who is as brain-damaged as me when it comes to things like this) that had seen *Ingagi*, a truly awful exploitational film starring Charlie Gemora as the eponymous albino gorilla.

And thus a friendship was forged over cheap Ace paperbacks, bad jungle action flicks, and fair-to-middling Sesame Chicken.

Over the years, Bill and I would fre-quently end up on panels together, usually (but not always) discussing gorillas in sci-ence fiction, apes in the cinema, or other frivolous topics. Afterward, we would end up in a larger group, talking about whatever the conversational drift sent our way. He was

good company, very funny, with an almost deprecating sense of humor, offset by the occasional zinger from the three-point line.

I learned a lot from Bill, in the arena of mysteries and mystery-writing, and also from his personal history. He knew I was a budding Howardist, interested in the life and works of Robert E. Howard, but I had to find out from someone else (it was very likely Scott Cupp) that Bill was actually a professor at Howard Payne University when the de Camps came to town on their research trip to write their biography of Robert E. Howard. It was Bill and Charlotte Laughlin, another Howard Payne professor, who greeted the de Camps (and of course, Bill knew who they were) and showed them around and had dinner with them, and I am certain that they were thrilled to meet someone, anyone, who knew who the hell they were after dealing with some of the less-talkative people in Cross Plains. Charlotte agreed to help them open a few doors that their genteel ways, ascot and smoking jacket, and walking stick could not. Charlotte (and Bill) spoke Texan. The de

Camps were, well . . .they were the de Camps. But that's another story.

Bill and I had long discussions about Robert E. Howard and also de Camp himself, and he chided me for taking a few unnecessary pot-shots at the Old Devil in my biography *Blood and Thunder: The Life and Art of Robert E. Howard*. I told him what I've said for years: I think de Camp was a heck of a cheerleader for Conan. I just wish he'd been nicer to Robert E. Howard. He readily agreed with me, but I never convinced him to throw de Camp under the bus. Bill was, at his core, a super gentleman and fan, and that was part of his charm.

A few years ago, during one of the long string of "Gorillas in SF" panels at ArmadilloCon, I brought out a copy of the cover to *Zeppelin Stories* #3. If you've never heard of that pulp before, I am not surprised; it was a specialized (some would say overly-so) pulp with stories grouped around a very narrow theme. It only lasted four issues, which shocks—shocks, I say—no one ever in the history of time. The magazine

would have been lost to the vagaries of pulp publishing history, except for the cover to *Zeppelin Stories* #3. It features a weirdly bucolic cover painting, showing the under-side of a zeppelin in the background, and a long rope ladder leading down to the fore-ground. At the end of this ladder is a man in a parka, swinging a giant wrench at what looks like an orangutan, hanging from the rungs. Next to this painting is the title: "The Gorilla of the Gas Bags, by Gil Brewer."

It's glorious. And it's very rare, so no one on the panel had ever read the story. I thought it would be cool for us to each tell our version of the story, as if we'd been handed the cover art and the title by the editor and told, "I need ten thousand words by the end of the day." Everyone had fun with their descriptions of what they would have written, but then Joe Lansdale, who was in the audience, decided to up the ante. He said to us, "What you

oughtta do is write that story. Y'all should all write it and sell it and we'll come back next year to read them. Hell, I'll do one."

Well, when Lansdale says something like that, you waste no time. There were only five of us on the panel, but somehow or another, every author in attendance was conscripted. The following year, we all gathered in a packed-to-the-gills meeting room to listen to each other's excerpts (because we couldn't have read the entire story, or we would have been there for hours) from our efforts. Scott Cupp, Bill Crider, Jayme Lynn Blaschke, Rhonda Eudaly, even Joe Lansdale, all read their pieces. Then it was my turn. I decided to write my story about a pair of International thieves named Smash and Grabbe. There was a double-cross, and then another double-cross, and a man impersonating a gorilla in a suit. I admit, I was playing to the audience. But when I read the part about the gorilla revealing his identity, I decided to have the rival be French, like Belloq, from Raiders of the Lost Ark. Only, I picked a different name.

"De Camp," Smash Gibson said, "the Gentleman Thief."

Bill smacked his hand down on the table in mock exasperation and said, "I knew you just couldn't resist!"

The very next year was difficult for me; I was going through some personal stuff, and I let some folks know that I might not be at my most effervescent and charming during the convention. Unsurprisingly, my friends rallied around me and kept me buoyed and cheered for the show, which was wonderful and helpful. Bill's contribution? Every time he saw me, he'd start singing, "Come on without, come on within, you've not seen nothing like the Mighty Finn . . ."

To this day, every time I hear Manfred Mann sing "The Mighty Quinn," I think of Bill. I miss him. We all do.

Mark Finn

Bill Crider and Me

I first met Bill Crider in about 1975 or 1976 at an AggieCon in College Station, Texas. I was selling paperbacks and he was crawling on the floor looking at trays of paperbacks that did not fit on the tabletop. While I was standing there, this short haired face looked up and asked "You got any Jim Thompson books down here?" As a matter of fact, I did and, at the princely sum of $3.00, he bought it. Bill had come in from Brownwood, roughly 200 miles to the west. We got talking about old paperbacks and *Paperback Quarterly*, a magazine edited by his friend Billy Lee, to which Bill was an occasional contributor. In fact, Billy was paperback diving on the floor there with Bill, though Bill got to the Jim Thompson book first.

The next year Bill was back and we talked more. We soon bonded over a love of old paperbacks and going to AggieCon. And AggieCon was where it happened. We soon were chatting late at night in the Serpentine Lounge (known of Phred) on the second floor of the Memorial Student Center. The discussions often included Joe Lansdale and Neal Barrett, Jr. and were the highlight of my convention going years. Sometimes the inimitable Judy would come around and her comments were as cogent as his. She would invariably fade about ten or eleven and we would continue. We did not need much sleep to continue to talk books. And who could forget the evening when the four of us ran into the "Mars Needs Chickens" idea and ran that sucker into the ground.

Around 1983 or 1984 (those years all run together), my work sent me to Brownwood and I visited the Crider home and library. Bill had just had his first novel published, a Nick Carter novel, *The Coyote Connection*, which was a collaboration with a friend. I was beginning to write then but had sold nothing. I showed him my story "One Fang" which I eventually sold (in 2006!)

When the Crider family moved to Alvin, Texas near Houston in the mid 1980's, it actually put them closer to me. I was in Houston regularly and when I was, I would call and we would do dinner and a trip to Half Price Books, which resembled a bombing run. We would go in and do an initial quick pass for the easy pickings. Then Bill and

Left to right: Bill Crider, Joe R. Lansdale, Scott Cupp (Photo courtsey of Keith West)

I would shop together and discuss what was still on the shelf. Because of his long time membership in DAPA-EM, a mystery amateur press association, Bill knew everyone in the field or knew someone who did. Those conversations were delightful when he'd say "This is a Harry Whittington novel" or Gil Brewer or Charles Williams, "and you need to read it." He was never wrong.

Once Bill began writing he became a force of nature, turning out more than 75 novels. I'm not quite sure exactly how many, there were some house names and ghost work involved, but it was a lot and it ranged all over the place. He did mystery series featuring Sheriff Dan Rhodes, Truman Smith, Carl Burns, and Sally Goode. He did young adult books (the Mike Gonzo series as well as *A Vampire Named Fred* and a Wishbone book, *Muttketeer*). He did some action adventure books, including the Nick Carter-mentioned above and entries in *The Tunnel Rats* and *MIA Hunter* series. There were regular and adult westerns. He worked with Willard Scott on two weatherman related mysteries.

But, mainly Bill was a fan of the writers he loved. He had a correspondence with Harry Whittington in the latter stages of Whittington's life. One day he came home to find a box of books Whittington had sent him. He went to BoucherCon each year for a long time to see friends and writers. He was excited when he got to meet Mickey Spillane. When I went to my first BoucherCon, he asked if there was anyone I really wanted to meet. I said Linda Barnes and Bill Pronzini. Within 15 minutes, both had been brought over to meet me. What a guy!

At one point, he and I talked about doing a young adult occult book for a series that was being solicited. About two months ago, I found that three page outline we had prepared. It wasn't bad, so I may tackle it at some point since the publisher obviously did not share our same vision.

Bill was also incredibly generous with his time. I called him many an evening and we spoke for a minimum of an hour each time, sometimes much longer. At a convention, all you had to do was say "Let's get a Dr Pepper!" (or "Mars Needs Chickens") and we would be off talking for what would seem like 15 minutes, but was in reality 3 hours. I miss that part the most. Frequently I travel long distances by car. He was one of my go to sources for entertainment when 200 miles of road beckoned and the radio was awful. I still get the urge to call when traveling and I have to remind myself that I just can't talk to him right now.

I never heard Bill speak badly about anyone. He was always polite. He was kind to men and animals, rescuing cats on a too frequent basis. Bill was one of a kind and that mold appears to have been broken or recalled. There just are not anymore like him these days. And we are the lesser for that.

Scott Cupp

Submission Guidelines:

We are NOT accepting unsolicited manuscripts at this time.

Skelos is interested in short fiction, poetry, and essays in the following genres: weird fiction, dark fantasy, horror, sword and sorcery, New Weird, and Slipstream, preferably flavored with one or more of the other genres. If you have a story, poem, or essay that you think might be a good fit, please query first.

Skelos pays one penny/word for stories and essays up to five thousand words long. For any story longer than the length listed, please query first. Skelos pays twenty-five cents a line for poems up to 60 lines long. For longer poems and prose poems, please query first.

Skelos wants material that exemplifies the above genres, not typifies them. Genre subversion, too, is always a good thing. Material can be graphic, as needed, but we are not interested in erotica, hardcore sex, or romance writing. Unless it's a brilliant sub-version of the genre that transcends the limitations inherent in the conventional form. Emphasis on brilliant. When in doubt, please query first. Send all queries regarding stories that meet the above criteria to SkelosPress@gmail.com. And please query first.

Advertising Rates

Skelos accepts appropriate advertising at the following rates:
Full Page - $100; Half Page - $60; Third Page $40; Quarter Page - $30
Email skelospress@gmail.com for details.

AMONG THE ANTHROPOPHAGAI

From *The Journals of Caleb Brown, Volume II*

Transcribed by Bill Crider

I met Caleb Brown in the year 2000, shortly before his 90th birthday. He was at that time living in a retirement home in Houston, and having read a memoir I'd written with a Houston private-eye named Clyde Wilson, he'd given me a call and asked me to pay him a visit. He said he wanted to talk about collaborating on a book much like the one I'd done with Wilson.

"You captured his voice quite well, I thought," Brown told me. "I'm hoping that you can do the same for me."

I mentioned that the book with Wilson had failed to find a major publisher and that it hadn't been a very lucrative venture. Brown brushed that objection aside. "I've accumulated quite a pile of money during my lifetime. I can pay you whatever you ask."

I liked the sound of that and named a figure and an advance.

"Fine," he said with never a quibble. I wished I'd asked for more. "Let's meet soon, and I'll have a check ready for you."

I met him a week later in his not unpleasant little room, which he'd decorated with photographs of himself at various stages of his life. I knew that if he hadn't faked them, he'd had some fine adventures, and I looked forward to hearing what he had to say.

After I introduced myself, he sized me up, as I did him. He was a thin but not frail old man with wispy white hair and faded blue eyes. He wore a spotless white shirt, neatly creased khakis, and highly polished black shoes. We chatted for a while, and he said that he was certain I was the writer he'd been looking for. He handed me a check, and after I'd folded it and put it in my shirt pocket, he launched into a wild tale of

what he and his friend Robert Hawkins had done one summer in Tibet some sixty-five years earlier. Luckily I'd brought along a small digital recorder, and I managed to get it all.

"How was that?" he asked me when he was finished.

"A bit hard to believe," I said.

He laughed. "Every word of it is true, and I have many such stories to tell. When can you come again?"

As I was still teaching at the time, I could meet with him only on weekends. Every Saturday for months, I'd drive to Houston, get out my recorder, and settle down to listen to his stories. Some were more fantastic than others, but they all involved Robert Hawkins in one way or another. I asked what had happened to Hawkins.

"He met the same end that we all shall meet, sooner or later. He was a bit older than I, and he's been gone for five years now. A fine fellow, fine fellow. I wish you could have met him."

I wished the same, but at least I'd met Brown and was getting to hear his tales. However, before I'd begun to transcribe them, he fell ill. He'd been fine when I saw him on Saturday, but I got a call from the home on Wednesday of the following week informing me that he had died peacefully in his sleep. In accordance with his wishes, his body had been transported to the medical school in Galveston where it would provide anatomy students something to study.

I transferred all the recorded material into my computer, and I have now transcribed a small portion of it, including the following harrowing tale, exactly as he told it to me.

My college chum Robert Hawkins was one of a certain breed of men for whom adventure was the breath of life. As for me, I much preferred sitting quietly in a comfortable chair with a good book and a glass of fine whiskey, yet for reasons I cannot explain, I often allowed myself to be drawn into Robert's schemes. So it was with his journey to the Impenetrable Forest of Bwindi.

"Really, Caleb, you must come with me," Robert said one day as we sipped an excellent Sumatran coffee in my study. Not everyone is attuned to the flavor, but both Robert and I enjoyed it. "It's the chance of a lifetime."

"If we survive," I said, setting my china cup in its saucer. "The danger and the horrors involved are something you never mention when you talk to me of your proposed adventures. Let me remind you of our journey to the lost city in the Sahara, and the terrible sunburn we both suffered, not to mention the severe dehydration. I felt much like a walking raisin. Not to mention being pursued by walking skeletons. I can still remember vividly the clicking of those dry bones."

Robert stood up. He was a bit over six feet tall and still possessed the athletic build of the halfback he had been at our beloved alma mater. (I am of a somewhat leaner and more esthetic mold.) Robert pushed back a shock of black hair and waved a hand to indicate the overstuffed bookshelves that lined the walls of the room.

"Look around us," he said. "What do you see?"

"I should think that is rather obvious," I told him. "Books. I see a great many books."

"No," he said. "What you see is life printed on musty pages rather than lived out in the open air. Life stifled between cardboard covers. Life with all the juice squeezed out."

"Not unlike me when I was crawling through the Sahara," I said.

"Bah." Robert was one of the few people I knew who actually said that. "You know very well that you enjoyed every minute of that adventure, including the skeletons, as fearful as they might have been at the time. And after all, how many men other than we two can say they have laid eyes on the remains of a lost colony of Atlantis?"

"Very few. I suspect that all the others are dead, as we very nearly were."

"Bah. Had we not lost the photographs and maps in that sandstorm, the place would be a veritable tourist paradise by now."

"Possibly," I said. "Or perhaps the tourists would all resemble raisins."

Robert gave me a grin and sat back down. "I can tell when you're joshing me, Caleb. You're as eager for this new adventure as I am."

"You are mistaken in your belief," I said. "The Impenetrable Forest of Bwindi holds nothing for me. Besides, how can you hope to penetrate it if it is impenetrable?"

He leaned forward. "I'm happy that you asked. It's really very simple. We'll travel by ship to Kenya and disembark in Mombasa, where I've arranged for a light plane to take us to Nairobi."

I held up a languid hand to interrupt him. "Perhaps I've misunderstood. Did you say that the arrangements had already been made?"

He had the grace to look sheepish. "I knew that you'd be persuaded, so things have indeed been arranged."

I dropped my hand. "But I have not been persuaded."

"Merely a matter of time."

"I see. Assuming that there are no landing strips in the impenetrable forest, what do we do upon reaching Nairobi?"

"There will be a Zeppelin awaiting us."

"A Zeppelin? Good lord, man, do you have no memory of the Hindenburg?"

The disaster had occurred only a year earlier. The memory of it was still fresh, aided by newspaper photographs and newsreel photography.

"Of course I remember, and I know better than to use hydrogen as a fuel. We'll be using helium. Completely safe. We'll travel in the Zeppelin from Nairobi to Uganda, the Pearl of Africa, floating high above the crystalline waters of Lake Victoria—"

I raised my hand a second time, and he gave me an inquiring look.

"I was just wondering," I said, "if you had taken memorizing the contents of The National Geographic as a hobby."

Again he looked sheepish, which he did very well, with a boyish grin that worked wonders with the ladies.

"I do get a bit carried away at times," he said.

"A bit," I agreed, lowering my hand. "Though I've heard that the waters of Lake Victoria are indeed crystalline."

"You're joshing me again."

"Perhaps. But do go on. You haven't explained how a Zeppelin can penetrate the impenetrable."

"It won't have to. You see, there is within the bounds of the forest a high plateau."

I did not ask how he knew of the plateau. He had sources of information all over the world. If he said the plateau was there, it was there.

"At that point," he continued, "we'll descend from the Zeppelin and proceed with our investigations."

"Of what, exactly?" I asked. "You have not yet even so much as alluded to the purpose of this journey into the heart of darkness."

"Speaking of alluding," he said, "I have read Mr. Conrad's tale. This will be nothing like that. Nothing at all."

"Naturally not," I said, but he appeared unwithered by my sarcasm. "We are traveling by air, whereas Marlow was on the great river."

"Thus will our hardships be fewer."

"Of course. But what of our purpose in making this flight? You still have not mentioned it."

"The forest is an amazing place," he said. "It has survived unchanged since Africa's last Ice Age, more than twelve thousand years ago."

"Remarkable. Do bring me some photographs. Try not to lose them this time."

"There is more than just the forest," he said, and paused.

I waited.

"Perhaps we will see the African Green Broadbill. Two hundred species of butterflies. An amazing variety of toads."

"That's the National Geographic again," I said. "I am not going around the world to see birds or butterflies. And especially not to see toads. You'll have to do better."

"It wouldn't be entirely around the world. Just a large part of it."

"Are you going to get to the point, or not?"

"There are also the gorillas," he said. "Mountain gorillas. We might see one of the great silverbacks."

"That's more like it," I said, "yet somehow I don't think we've arrived at the heart of the matter."

Robert sighed. "Very well. I'll tell you. But you must promise not to tell anyone else. If we make the discovery I hope for, we'll be famous far beyond our lifetimes."

"Ah. What more could a man ask?"

"That's enough joshing," he said. "This is a serious matter. We will be seeking the anthropophagai."

"Cannibals? We could find them in much more accessible places. That is, if we cared to look for them, which I most certainly do not. I appreciate the meat that sticks to my bones, and I'd like for it to remain there."

"Not just any cannibals," he said. "These are the creatures Othello described, the ones 'whose heads do grow below their shoulders.'"

"That would be the Blemmyes," I said.

"And they are a different matter entirely. Your research is lacking. Shakespeare did not mean that the anthropophagai's heads were in such a position. You can see that from the phrasing of the sentence in Othello, act one, scene three."

Robert grinned. "If anyone knows about how unreliable the phrasing of a Shakespearean sentence is, you are that man." He pointed to a shelf just to my right and a bit higher than my head. "Is there not a small monograph on that shelf that discusses the 'good' and 'bad' quartos of Shakespeare's works, with emphasis on the fact that in some cases, many, in fact, we can never be sure of the exact word that Shakespeare used? Didn't you point out that one of the great controversies of Hamlet is over whether Hamlet said 'sullied' or 'solid' and that we can never be certain which one Shakespeare intended?"

I gave a negligent shrug. "I suppose the monograph is there."

"And who was its author? Someone named Caleb Brown, I believe."

"Very well. You have me there. Perhaps Shakespeare did indeed mean that the anthropophagai and the cannibals were one and the same. Or not. That really proves nothing."

"Perhaps not. I'm not talking about Shakespeare, however. I'm talking about Othello himself. Shakespeare based his Moor on a real person, as I have discovered by a full year of research through many a dusty tome and manuscript. Othello did indeed mean what I have said, and he saw the apthropophagai. Believe me, Caleb, for of this I am sure. And he saw them in the Impenetrable Forest of Bwindi."

I gave Robert an incredulous look, but he was not bothered.

"I'll prove it to you," he said, and with that he picked up a leather briefcase that he had placed by his chair at the beginning of our conversation. He produced certain papers and photographs of manuscripts that did indeed convince me of the truth of his state-

ments about Othello, though I remained a bit skeptical of the anthropophagai.

"He was making them up to impress Desdemona," I said.

"No," Robert said. "He was not. Herodotus wrote of them, as did Pliny. They are real, and we will find them."

"And then they will have us for lunch."

"Not if we're careful," Robert said.

"As we always are. Like that time on the Upper Amazon—"

"Never mind the Amazon. What happened there could never happen again. I promise you that."

Of course I didn't believe him, and I put up another good hour of protestation, but in the end he won me over.

Which is how, some months later, I came to be clinging to a rope ladder just a few feet above a jungle plateau in the Impenetrable Forest of Bwindi.

The view was incredible indeed, and I could but wonder how Othello had managed to make his way through the dense forest. As far as I could see in all directions, the world was green. Some trees towered above the rest, but even the occasional gaps among them were covered with the thickest of vines, ferns, and blooming flowers. A river gleamed like a silver ribbon in the distance, and verdant hills rose all around us.

"You'll have to let go of the ladder," Robert called. He was standing a good fifteen yards away. "The Zeppelin will be leaving at any second."

I reluctantly released my hold on the ladder and dropped lightly to the ground. Above me a crewman pulled up the ladder, and the Zeppelin rose slowly, a majestic sight in the clear blue sky. I watched until it turned back in the direction of Nairobi, from whence it would return in exactly five days if all went according to plan. It would return sooner if we called for it on the radio. Hoping that we would have no need to call, I joined Robert and the others.

One of them was Doctor Wilberforce Obote. The British ruled Uganda, which explains Wilberforce's first name. He was a professor of anthropology from Makerere University with an interest in evolutionary anthropology. While he was even more skeptical of Robert's claims that I was, he couldn't resist the opportunity to be in on the discovery, if one were to be made. Robert wanted him along to lend a bit of scholarly respectability to our small expedition.

"Not that I'm slighting you," he said to me when he told me that Wilberforce would be coming along. "But your association with me is well known, and some might suspect that we were in cahoots."

I told him that if he planned on doing any cahooting, I was returning home. He accused me of joshing.

The other two members of our party were James and John Wamala, twin brothers and graduate students in Dr. Obote's department, though they looked more like members of a professional rugby team. They were stocky and powerfully built, and Obote had chosen them because he felt they would be able to stand up to the rigors of the journey and to help us carry our burdens, which consisted of tents, camera equipment, food, a field radio, and weapons, which consisted of five M1 rifles with extra clips and five Colt M1911 pistols. Robert and I wore the pistols in holsters strapped to our waists, but the others preferred not to go armed.

"We might not need the weapons," Robert had said as we planned our expedition, "but when meeting an unknown species like the anthropophagai, it's best to be prepared."

"Yes," I said. "Considering that they are cannibals."

"Not entirely," he said. "They couldn't exist if they lived only on the flesh of their kind. They are doubtless perfectly content with

small animals and such as long as nothing else presents itself. And their enemies, of course. I suspect that they do eat their enemies."

"And who would those be?"

"Primarily the mountain gorillas, I assume. They would be natural antagonists for the anthropophagai."

"As would we," I said.

"Perhaps. Perhaps not. That's one thing we'll find out."

"I can hardly wait."

"You'll have to," he said.

And now, here we were, standing on a windy plateau, high above the impenetrable forest with not a single representative of the anthropophagai in sight.

"This is quite exhilarating," Obote said. "I can easily imagine that no human being before us has set foot on this plateau."

The forest was protected by the government, and I was surprised that Robert had received permission to land on the plateau. If it came to it, he was not above paying bribes, as he did not mind drawing on his ample inheritance for such exigencies.

"Too bad we can't stay here," I said.

It would have been nice to camp in that spot. The vegetation was sparse, no snakes crawled about, no stinging or biting insects swarmed in the crisp air. But we had to go down into the forest if we wanted to see the fauna, which is why we were there in the first place.

While Robert went to scout out a way down, I sat on one of the packs and listened to Obote tell his students about the wonders that we might soon be seeing.

"No one has ever been this far inside the forest," he said. Robert must not have mentioned Othello to him. "Thus no one knows for sure what sort of creatures might live here. Oh, there have been excursions into the outer edges, and there have been glimpses of several kinds of beasts and birds, including the mountain gorillas, but no one knows how many of the gorillas there might be or what other apes might reside within this realm."

"Are the anthropophagai a branch of the hominidae?" I asked.

James Mawala laughed. I knew it was James because he had a scar on his forehead, the result of a tussle with his brother when they were small boys. There was no rancor between the two about the incident, which was, after all, nothing more than boyish high spirits.

"You must forgive James," Obote said. "He and John do not believe in the existence of the anthropophagai."

We had discussed this on the trip to the plateau, and I knew that the twins had little faith that we would see anything so unusual as men whose heads grew beneath their shoulders.

"But you do," I said.

"Not entirely, but let me put it this way: No one has ever been into this part of the forest before, so no one can say what we might find. As for the anthropophagai, if they do exist, it is quite possible that they are more like the great apes than like us. Evolution has taken strange turns before, as with the neanderthal. It may have taken another in the forest."

"The neanderthals did not last long," James said, "and they are no longer around. They all died long ago."

"True," Obote said. "At least as far as we know. One might well be living in an alley somewhere, however, without our knowledge. It's possible. We cannot say that we know for sure. What is certain, however, is that we do not know is the names of all the things that might live in the forest below us. The anthropophagai might be among them."

"Whatever might be there," Robert said, returning to us, "we're about to find out. I've located a way down that might not be too difficult for us."

We shouldered our packs and followed Robert to the edge of the plateau. While there was no trail, there was at least a break in the vegetation. It did not appear to extend for any great distance.

"Once we get into the trees, we'll need to do some hacking," Robert said. "Have your machetes handy."

Each of us had an eighteen-inch machete attached to the outside of our packs. They had been sharpened and honed to a fine edge in Nairobi.

"Ready?" Robert said.

Without awaiting an answer, he started down, and the rest of us followed.

The plateau was about a mile above sea level, and the temperature had been pleasant. As we worked our way lower, the temperature rose. The job of hacking through the vegetation was a grueling one. Mahogany trees towered above us, and thick vines dropped from them. Other sorts of vines covered the ground and often tripped us up. I fell more than once, as did Obote. Robert, James and John were more nimble and managed to keep their feet, though occasionally they had to grab hold of the hanging vines to keep from tumbling to the forest floor.

I felt that James and John did well not to laugh at my clumsiness, though the monkeys that surrounded us made no attempt to hold in their own laughter. At least I assumed it was laughter. It certainly sounded that way to me.

Obote was fascinated by the monkeys, of which there were many. I am no expert, but I easily recognized the black-and-white mantled guereza, several varieties of guenon, and the baboons. They were around us and above us, constantly moving and chittering. Or laughing. Of them all, what especially caught Obote's attention was the chimpanzees.

"In no other place in Africa do the chimpanzees and mountain gorillas exist together," he said. "It would be wonderful to know if they compete for the same foods or nesting sites. I must return here and do a complete study."

I wished him well in that possibility, but as for me, I would be happy never to return. After only a few hours the humidity, the vines, the noise of the monkeys, and the heat were beginning to make me wish I had never let Robert talk me into this foolhardy expedition.

Another thing that made me uncomfortable was the feeling that we were being watched.

"Entirely possible," Robert said when I mentioned it to him. "The mountain gorillas are shy, and they're experts at blending into the foliage to hide themselves. Also, they can climb quite well and quite high. They might be a hundred feet up in the trees. If they were, we'd never know it."

That was all right with me. The way I felt, I didn't care to encounter any big apes who might not be friendly toward us.

We pushed on until I was near collapse, which was typical of any journey with Robert. He always assumed that everyone was as fit as he, and everyone was forced to keep up with him. James and John had no problem doing so. Obote and I were another story.

After what seemed days but must have been only four or five hours, Obote made a discovery that warranted a halt. I had no idea what it was, but I was quite happy to collapse with my back against the trunk of a small tree while the others began to photograph whatever Obote found so fascinating.

I could not see anything from where I was, but that fact didn't bother me at all. I found my eyes closing, and I was almost asleep when I felt something drop onto my shoulder. I hoped it was only a lizard or some other harmless denizen of the forest, but that was not the case as I learned when it extended its head for a look around. Out of the corner of my eye I could see it clearly. It was thin, thin as a pencil, and brownish green. I had no doubt that it was a Forest Vine Snake.

Now I am not one to panic at the sight of a serpent, like some people I have known. One young professor whom I had met, Jones, I believe his name was, disliked them intensely, and I had warned him that he should never let his fear overcome him when in the field. I've often wondered what became of him.

At any rate, I emphatically did not panic, though I knew the snake to be venomous and knew that its bite was occasionally fatal. Instead I calmly called out for Robert to join me at the tree.

"There's no need to shriek," Robert said as he got near me. "You're scaring the monkeys."

"I was not shrieking," I whispered. "I was whispering."

"Do you know there's a snake on your shoulder?"

"Really?"

"Really. It's looking right at me."

"Do you think you might remove it?"

"I don't want to scare it. Those things are poisonous."

Sweat ran down my face and neck and into my shirt. "Do tell."

By now Obote and the twins were looking on, albeit from a safe distance. I hoped I was providing them with decent entertainment, and judging from the grins on the faces of James and John, I must have been.

"I suppose the snake is making you nervous, perched there as he is," Robert said.

"Not at all," I told him. "I'm quite comfortable."

"I'm sure you are, but nevertheless I'll remove him."

Robert's machete moved with such speed that it was only a blur in front of my face. It came so close to my nose that I felt the breeze as it went by, but I did not flinch. The snake's head and body parted company, with the head landing beside me and the rest falling behind me. There was very little blood. As I said, it was quite a skinny snake.

Robert cleaned the specks of blood off his machete with a piece of cloth he had stuck in his belt. When he was done, he put down a hand and helped me to my feet, not that I was shaky or needed assistance. And yet if I had, there would have been no shame in it. Even the mountain gorilla is said to be fearful of serpents.

"Let's walk over to that tree where Obote is," he said. "You should take a look at what he's found."

I obliged him, as I didn't feel sleepy any longer. In fact, I was wide awake and glad to be that way, though I was not as impressed with Obote's find as he seemed to be. It appeared to be nothing more than a pair of sticks stripped of the bark.

"Look at the ends of the sticks," Obote said. "They're slightly pointed. They were deliberately shaped that way."

"And listen," John said. "What do you hear?"

I listened and heard a slight buzzing noise above me.

"Bees?" I said.

"Very good," James said. "And now do you see about the sticks?"

"I suppose you're going to tell me that something made those sticks to get to the honey."

"Indeed," Obote said. He was quite excited. "Chimpanzees, beyond a doubt. Making tools. This is a significant discovery. By itself, it justifies this expedition. Who knows what other wonders we shall find?"

The sticks had already been photographed in situ, and now James took them and packed them away securely while his brother watched.

"In fact," Obote said, "this discovery may well signal that other animal residents here are much farther along the evolutionary path than might be expected."

I wasn't sure I liked the sound of that. Big apes with superior intelligence? And what about the men whose heads did grow beneath their shoulders? I felt a chill creep down my spine.

Once the sticks were packed away, we re-

sumed our wandering. Obote and the twins could hardly contain their delight in picking up spoor samples and such for later examination under laboratory conditions. I was less delighted than they, but I was happy that just as it was growing dark, we came upon a shallow stream by which we could camp for the night. We unpacked our tents and set up camp. The twins started a small fire, so we had coffee along with our beans and sausage. After that, we slept. I did not dream of snakes.

We struck camp the next morning and followed the stream. Obote was sure that we would find signs of the mountain gorillas, which he was eager to see.

"They are a dying breed," he explained. "At least in other parts of Africa. No one can say how many of them might be here in this particular forest. I believe there are many. No one hunts them here, and there are no threats from without or within."

I thought of the anthropophagai, but said nothing until later, when we came across a troubling find. James was in the lead, and when he called out, I could hear a tremor in his voice.

What he had found was a pile of bones picked clean of their flesh and left near a tree. They appeared to me to be human bones, but Obote said they were not.

"They are the bones of a mountain gorilla," he announced after looking them over.

I mentioned the fact that he'd told us the forest held no natural enemies of the gorilla. And that the bones did not look as if they'd been beside the tree for very long.

"Odd," he said, "but perhaps the animal died of natural causes and lay here until the flesh was gone."

It didn't look that way to me, nor did it to Robert, who said, "Look more carefully at the bones. They appear to have been gnawed." He pointed at one of the bones. "See here? And here?"

I cannot speak for the others, but I was a

bit spooked by this. Perhaps more than a bit. I said, "Could this be the work of the anthropophagai?"

"There are other animals for them to eat," Robert said. "The monkeys, and a few feline species. The giant apes would be much more of a challenge."

His statement did not make me feel any better, and I loosened my .45 in its holster. The others must have been as nervous as I, since they immediately removed their pistols from their packs and strapped them on. Even Robert, who I was convinced had frigid water in his veins instead of blood, looked a tad wary.

We pressed on, leaving the bones where they lay. Whereas we had been rather casual about our travels, we were now watchful, each of us looking right and left as we went, though seeing anything in the forest was next to impossible. We also listened. The chattering of the monkeys and the calls of the birds were a comfort to me, as I knew they would vacate the area if there was any danger.

Our walking was made somewhat easier by the course of the stream. Though the plants grew right up to the edge of it, they were not as thick as they were only a short distance away, and we were able to make good time. In the late afternoon we were able to make out a high hill that appeared to be directly in front of us and about a mile away. Robert and Obote were eager to explore it, so we went toward it.

We had not gone far before James made another discovery. Leading away from the stream was a path. There was no question of it. Branches had been broken from the trees, and the ground cover was worn away. To me, this sight was even more disturbing than the pile of bones, for if there was a path, someone had made it, someone who lived in the forest, the forest where no one was supposed to live. Except for the anthropophagai, who now seemed suddenly very much a reality to me. I do not think I had truly believed in them

until that moment.

Robert, of course, was excited beyond measure, as was Obote, and nothing would do but that we follow the path, even though I expressed my misgivings in the strongest terms. I believe that James and John, who had scoffed at the idea of the anthropophagai, were now believers as well. They glanced uneasily from side to side as we traveled the path, occasionally coming to an abrupt halt as a monkey screeched nearby or a bird called overhead.

We saw no footprints in the path, but that meant nothing. The way had been worn smooth from long travel, and the ground was packed hard. As we got farther from the stream, we saw other paths that branched off from the one we were on. I thought we might explore one of those, but Robert was convinced that we were on the main trail.

"It's the one that goes to the source of water," he said. "If we follow it, we might come to a habitation of some sort."

"That is exactly what worries me," I said Robert laughed.

"I am not joshing," I said, but Robert paid me no mind and went on up the path.

I could only follow.

We had not gone much farther along the path when the forest grew quiet. It was a gradual thing. First the bird calls grew fewer and the cries of the monkeys came from farther away. Soon the calls had ceased altogether, and the cries were so faint and far that they might as well have ceased.

Robert, who was leading our little column, stopped, as did we all. Now it was not only James and John who were apprehensive. The heat and humidity settled upon us and breathing became difficult.

"Do you see anything?" I asked from the rear of the column.

"Nothing," Robert said. "Though I think

something must be up ahead of us."

He had his pistol in his hand, as did we all, even Obote, who I was certain had only a vague idea of how to fire it.

I remembered the feeling of being watched that I had experienced earlier. It returned stronger than before, but perhaps it was the result of the power of suggestion.

Or so I thought until the silence was broken by a terrible howling and crashing of branches.

Out of the forest on both sides of us burst the anthropophagai.

They were not men. I am not sure what they were, though they bore a strong resemblance to the great apes, with shaggy brown hair and long, powerful arms. Their heads, which did indeed grow beneath their shoulders, were hairless and resembled skulls more than the heads of any living thing. Their teeth were sharp, and pointed fangs gleamed at the corners of their wide-stretched mouths.

I did not count their numbers at the time. All I knew was that they far outnumbered us, and, though it shames me to admit it, I turned and ran back down the path as fast as I could. I had not gone far before I tripped over my own feet and fell.

I rolled off the path into the vegetation and lay there panting, my pistol pointed in front of me. Over the rasping of my breath, I could hear the firing of pistols, the screams of the anthropophagai, and, finally, their bellows of triumph. Then all grew quiet again.

I do not know how long I lay there, expecting at every second the appearance of one of the horrible creatures. When none of them came, I finally got to my feet and peered back up the path. I saw no one, so I walked back to see if anyone had survived.

Blood spattered the green ferns and leaves. Quite a bit of blood. Bits of clothing lay nearby, and everyone's pack had been torn away and ripped apart. Camping equipment, rifles, food, and cooking utensils lay scattered all around.

The field radio was there, all intact. It took me only minutes to get it set up and working. I put in a call as soon as I did and informed the captain that he was to return at once to the plateau and to wait for us to arrive.

"Something awful has happened," I told him, not bothering to explain further. "It is urgent that you return."

Before he could question me, I shut down the radio and looked around once more. None of the anthropophagai were to be seen, either dead or alive. I have no idea why they had not come after me when I fled. Perhaps they had never even seen me, being intent on their attack and then distracted by gunshots. Surely some of them had been killed or wounded, but if so they had left with their companions or been carried away.

I had no doubts about what would happen to Robert and the others if I did not intervene. The bones of the ape were all the proof that was needed. The anthropophagai might not have eaten men for many years, perhaps not since Othello's time, but men were now on the menu once again.

The birds began to resume their calling, and the monkeys chittered away once more. I took two of the rifles and extra ammunition, along with a couple of pistols that I stuck in my belt. The rifles had slings, so I was able to hang them from my shoulders. Thus burdened, I went to look for the others. All along the path I saw great splotches of blood, and I could only hope that some of them remained alive and that I could do something to rescue them.

Shortly I came to the base of the hill. The path lay upward, winding through the trees, and I followed it, hoping that the anthropophagai would be too occupied with their prisoners to think of looking for another one.

I came at length to a wide bend in the path, and I heard something ahead. I paused to listen and heard such sounds as I hope never to hear again: the rending of flesh, bones being torn from their sockets, the sounds of mastication, the cries of anthropophagai delight at tasting the sweetness of human flesh.

I unslung the rifles and laid them on the ground, placing the pistols beside them. I knew that if he had been beside me, Obote would have begged me to spare at least one specimen, but I planned to kill as many as I could, and all of them if possible, that is if any of my party was still alive. If not, I would steal quietly away.

Moving as close as I dared, I pushed aside a frond and peered out. The sight of mutilated bodies turned my stomach, though not as much as the sight of the anthropophagai, their hair now matted with blood and their skeletal faces smeared with it. They had dismembered James and John and now sat feasting on their remains. One of the creatures waved an arm in the air as it gnawed on a leg. Another contemplated James's head as Hamlet had gazed at the skull of Yorick.

Robert and Obote lay nearby, either dead or unconscious, I knew not which.

As I watched, one of the anthropophagai rose and moved to Obote's prone form. The creatures had not sated themselves on James and John and were now preparing to eat Obote. I retrieved one of the rifles, and though I was trembling with rage, disgust, and fear, I steadied myself as best I could.

The creature had its back to me, and I could of course not see its head, only the wide shoulders and back. I had no idea where or even if it might have a vulnerable spot. I decided that it hardly mattered. I had no choice but to fire. I pulled the trigger.

The bullet tore into the back of the beast and out the other side. A scream began and was cut off at once. The bullet had, by sheerist luck, exploded the creature's head. The other anthropophagai danced and gibbered in surprise and horror.

At the sound of the shot, Robert leapt up and ran toward me. He had been feigning unconsciousness, and as he burst through the branches, I tossed him the rifle and began fir-

ing with my pistol. Obote had not moved.

"Obote's dead," Robert said. "We have to get out of here."

That sounded like a capital idea to me. Robert snatched up the other rifle, I grabbed a pistol, and we ran through the forest, whipped by branches but hardly noticing. Vines tried to trip us, but we maintained our balance out of sheer desperation, as the anthropophagai had recovered from their surprise at my attack and were close behind us, proceeding with eerie snuffling and wild outcries.

It was already late in the afternoon, and I knew we could not travel at night without losing our way. I stopped at the site of the massacre and picked up a flashlight. Robert did the same, and we continued our flight. We came to the stream.

"Follow me," Robert said, splashing into the water.

I did not question him. I ran into the water after him, hoping that we would not drown. There was no danger of that, as it turned out. The stream was quite shallow, and we were across in a moment. When we reached the other side, Robert slid to the ground and turned to the stream. I followed suit. The anthropophagai had arrived at the opposite bank.

They appeared hesitant to cross the stream, though they must have known where we were. They gestured and made guttural sounds that approximated speech. I looked at Robert, and when he looked back, I raised the pistol. He shook his head. For some reason he did not want to open fire. I knew it could not be sympathy for the anthropophagai, not after what had occurred, but I did not argue. Robert always had his reasons, and they were usually good ones.

We lay where we were for at last half an hour while the creatures chattered. It appeared that they were arguing, but I could not be sure. Since I had nothing else to do, I counted them. There were ten. Finally some sort of agreement must have been reached, if argument it was, and they turned and walked back into the forest.

Robert and I lay still and quiet for another half hour. Darkness was sifting through the trees, and the calls of birds and animals seemed to take on a drowsy quality. I ventured a whisper to Robert.

"Why not kill them?" I asked.

"Because that may be all of them that there are. We can't be responsible for their extinction."

Frankly, I did not care in the least if the beasts were wiped from the face of the earth, and while I could understand Robert's reasoning, I tried to change his mind.

"We would never have to tell anyone that they are here," I said. "No one would ever know."

"No one may ever know, anyway. We have no photographs. All we have is our word."

It was the Sahara expedition all over again. "How will we explain the loss of Obote, James, and John."

"Men are lost all the time in the jungles. There will be some trouble, maybe even an inquiry, but it will be all right in the end."

I wished I shared his confidence. "Why did the anthropophagai not come after us?"

"The water. I had a feeling they might fear it, considering their stench. They've never washed in their lives."

"Surely they must drink."

"I saw gourds back there. They must dip from the stream. Very carefully, I assume."

Not that any of that mattered. "We must get back to the plateau. I called on the radio for the Zeppelin. It should be here by tomorrow."

"Travel in darkness will be difficult," Robert said. "However, the moonlight will help us as long as we stick to the stream. I hope the flashlight batteries hold out after that."

"They are Eveready."

"I hope so."

"Are you joshing me, Robert?"

"Not a bit." He stood up. "We have to cross back over the stream and find the path we cut through the forest. We'll have to travel fast, running much of the time. Are you up to it?"

"I am ever ready," I said.

Robert did not laugh.

We were able to make fair time along the stream bank without crossing over, so we went that way for several miles. At that point Robert decided it was best to return to the other side. The dark water was silvered by the moonlight, and I hoped it was no deeper than it had been at our original crossing.

Such proved to be the case, and we crossed without difficulty. It took us several minutes to pick up the trail we had hacked through the forest, but we found it and began to run again, or at least to jog. Even with the flashlights it was difficult at best and I was beginning to feel the strain of all that I had seen and done that day. Somehow I carried on, though keeping up with Robert was difficult. Had I not known better, I would have thought he had rested for days.

As morning neared, I was close to collapse. Robert encouraged me by telling me that the plateau was only a bit farther along. I believe he told me that at least five different times, but the last time it proved to be the truth. I was elated, but only for a moment, for that was when we learned that the anthropophagai were more intelligent that we had thought. Although they had not crossed the stream, they had somehow figured out that we would have to do so to get back to our path. They must have tracked us through the night, and just at dawn was breaking, they attacked.

This time they did not rush us from the side of the path but dropped down from the trees in front, on the sides, and in back. Their cries as they descended made my neck hair stand to attention.

Their attack had to have been planned, and they had given us nowhere to run. They stood hopping around us as if gloating at our situation, the pale skull-like faces of their oddly positioned heads gleaming in the early light, their mouths hanging open with slaver dripping from their pointed teeth.

If only we had killed them at the stream. But this was no time for recriminations, and it was no time to worry about extinction of a species. Though I had been tempted more than once to throw aside the pistols because of their weight, I had not, and Robert still carried his rifle.

"Clear the path," Robert said, and we opened fire, Robert appearing to have no concerns related to extinction.

That the anthropophagai were intelligent creatures I did not doubt, but they had only slight acquaintance with our weapons, and again the shock of seeing their fellows fall with burst heads sent them into a frenzy of fear and excitement. They screamed and gibbered in confusion. Taking advantage of their momentary disarray, Robert and I burst through them and along the way we had cleared to the plateau.

We reached it and began the ascent. I fell twice, but Robert helped me to my feet each time, practically dragging me along. The only thing that kept me going was the screams of the beasts as they pursued us. And then the sight of the Zeppelin hanging in the sky, the morning sunlight glowing on its side. Even more thrilling than the airship itself was the rope ladder that dangled beneath it in easy reach of the ground, if only we could get to it.

We arrived at the plateau with the anthropophagai close behind. If they had been afraid before, all their fear was gone now. They leapt after us with odd cries that actually gave me the strength to run faster.

It was not enough. One of the beasts, swifter than the others, reached me. His long arm swung out and he grabbed my arm, his huge hand easily encircling the biceps. I turned and shot him in the face. His head exploded in a haze of blood, and I was free and running. I believe I had never run faster.

Robert reached the ladder, but he did not ascend. He turned and began to fire his rifle, killing two of the anthropophagai. The others jumped over them and came on.

"You go ahead," I shouted to Robert. "I'm right behind you."

Robert slung the rifle over his shoulder and began the ascent. He was nearly to the gondola when I reached the ladder, and as I tossed away my .45 and took hold of the rungs, the Zeppelin started to climb, as did I. A feeling of relief washed over me.

But it was a false relief. I was not safe yet. One of the anthropophagai leapt so high that I thought he must have wings. He caught hold of the rungs and clung to the ladder above me. He seemed to cackle with delight as he kicked me in the face.

I lost my grip on the ladder and fell backward. Only by grabbing the beast's loathsome fur was I able to keep from falling. He hooked an arm over one of the rungs and swung at me with the other arm.

I ducked my head, and he missed. As he prepared to swing again, I looked up and saw Robert descending the ladder. He carried a pistol in one hand.

I could think of only one way to save myself. Or die somewhere other than the creature's foul embrace. I let go of its fur and dropped.

As I passed the feet of the beast, I caught hold of the bottom rung. My arms were almost pulled from their sockets, but I held on. Looking down, I saw that the Zeppelin had continued to rise. We were at least a hundred yards above the plateau. Below us the remaining anthropophagai danced in frustration and rage.

Above me I heard two shots in rapid succession. Then came a third, and the odious beast fell away from the ladder, limp in death, its head destroyed by the bullets Robert had fired.

I had not the strength to pull myself back

onto the ladder, nor was there any way for Robert to help me. I considered letting go, but I was not going to give myself to the anthropophagai. I did not plan to feed their foul appetites even if I were dead.

"Hang on," Robert called as he started back up the ladder. "Hang on."

I hung on, and the ladder was hauled up, ever so slowly. My fingers were numb, but I did not release my hold. Eventually, after what seemed hours, I was pulled into the gondola, safe this time at last.

As Robert predicted, there was some trouble in Nairobi, and while no one believed our story, the crew of the Zeppelin vouched for the existence of the anthrophphagai. Or for some such creatures, for even with binoculars they could not be absolutely certain that they were not seeing overgrown mountain gorillas.

And perhaps that is all the anthropophagai were, though I did not believe it. I knew what I had seen.

Neither Robert nor I ever returned to the Impenetrable Forest of Bwindi. Others entered it and even explored many parts of it, though no one came upon the anthropophagai. It is my belief that they withdrew into some deep fastness, or that their reduced numbers spelled the doom of their species. There were already so few of them that they were well on the way to extinction, perhaps for lack of food.

Yet the great silverbacks remain small in number. They are in today's terms an endangered species. Why can they not reproduce in sufficient numbers? Or do they reproduce only to provide food for the anthropophagai?

It is something I have often wondered about, but it is not something I will ever know.

Saddle up for ADVENTURE with Heroic Fantasy Quarterly! Check out our current issue and archives online at heroicfantasyquarterly.com

HEROIC FANTASY QUARTERLY .COM

CORNER TABLE IN THE BACK

Written and Illustrated by Bill Willingham

"I'm required to pay the full price in advance?" Lan said. He was young and had a nervous look about him—understandable, given the circumstances.

"That's how it's done," Waterhearth said. She'd given him something close to her real name, having settled on it as the name she'd use to begin building her reputation in the world of men. Waterhearth was a direct trans-literation of her Deep Lodge name Kelkellan, which cannot be revealed to those outside of her lodge. In Sark, perhaps the bright world's most universal tongue, kel becomes water and kellan could be anything from dwelling, to rampart, to hearth. "It's best for you that way too, since it removes the requirement we meet again, after the deed is done. Safer all around. But you're worried I'll simply take your money and run off without doing the work."

He didn't answer aloud and didn't need to. His expression told the tale.

"It's a legitimate concern," she said. "There are many swindlers who pretend to my profession. They tend not to last long though. Word gets around. Names and faces are remembered. When we find such deceivers we tend to remove them from the playing field."

"You kill them?" Lan said.

"It's in our best interest to weed our own garden."

The tavern was called The Bull and Goose. It was a sprawling stone and wood basement under a low ceiling. Overhead was a manufactory where fabrics were dyed and warehoused. The tavern floor was mostly wood planks, worn smooth by years of countless feet, and built on many levels, more the product of uncertain digging than artful design. There were few windows, high on the walls inside but barely ground level outside. Because of the dyes used above them, the tavern smelled of strong chemicals, along with the more customary odors of yeast, wood oils, sweat and spilled alcohol.

Lan and Watherhearth occupied a corner table in the back of the room. Still looking skeptical, Lan fetched a pouch from his belt and poured its contents of six golden stags on the table. She took note of his hands which had the small burns and scars common to one who works in a tannery. So at least that much of his story was true.

She scooped up the coins almost as fast as they'd appeared.

"Best not to flash gold in a neighborhood where even a penny purse is dear," she said.

Waterhearth drained her glass. She stood up from her seat.

"Have I taken your last coin," she said, "or can you stand us another round?" She'd been drinking mead, while Lan drank the house's cheapest ale.

"I have drinking money," he said. "The living I make may be frugal, but I can pay my way. The gold is—it was something extra."

"I meant no offense," she said. "If you'll excuse me then, I need to visit the garderobe." She left him at the table. Many glances, heavy with speculation, followed her as she navigated the room, winding frictionless through the crowd.

She was gone long enough that Lan began to wonder if she'd be back, or if his initial instincts were accurate. The barmaid had brought her new drink, which sat untouched and unattended on the table, like an accusation. Then she returned, fresh and smiling, sitting again. Lan hoped the shadows of their corner were deep enough to hide the flush of guilt he immediately felt for doubting her.

She tasted her mead.

"They must have tapped a new keg," she said. "This tastes different. Subtle, but—I don't know. My father was the expert in our clan. With a single sip of mead he could tell you what flowers the bees made their nectar from. Often as not he could name the month in which the nectar was harvested."

Lan looked miserable. He wanted to get their ugly business concluded, so he could flee home, but found himself at a loss as to how he might steer the conversation back to the subject. She helped him then by asking, "Where were we?"

"I had a thought about how you might contact him," he said. "If you were to simply visit his shop, I'm certain he would offer you a job on the spot. That's how my Ewa, my wife, fell into his hands. She had a few years of school and wanted parchment to practice her letters. That's what he does. He makes parchment. His shop is just next door."

"I know," Waterheart said. "You told me."

"It's why I chose to meet you here, so that I can show you his place, when we leave."

"No need," she said. "You described him and his shop in detail."

They were surrounded by the sounds of

more than a dozen nearby conversations, most at a volume buttressed by strong drink. The sounds formed an almost physical wall around them, creating a barrier of privacy nearly as functional as if the room were silent.

"My wife is—was—pretty," Lan said. "And in hindsight that's why he offered her the position in his shop. The pay he promised was too much. I see that now. But at the time it seemed a godsend. We made such plans. In a year we could've moved to a better home, in a safer neighborhood. Maybe even north of The Market."

"He expected things other than a day's work in return for a day's pay," she said.

"Exactly so. At first it seemed legitimate work—hard work, which argued to justify the good pay. She learned to frame the skin and rub pumice powder into it, to smooth it out for the pen. She'd mix the calcium compounds into paste. He'd take over from there, doing the more delicate treatments. But he'd promised to eventually teach her that part too. And since she had her cyphers, he was beginning to let her treat with customers as well."

"I'm not sure I need to know all of this," she said.

"That's how he got his hooks into her," Lan said. "He gave her ever more responsibility, causing her to have to work later and later into an evening. Until one night she didn't come home at all. I went to find her, of course, sooner than he expected. At first he claimed she'd gone hours earlier, but I searched against his protests. Her body was still in the back. In the workroom."

Waterhearth started to protest again, but realized the young man was intent on telling his story.

"I guess we have time," she said.

"What?"

"Never mind. Go on."

"Do you know what he did next?" Lan said. "When I discovered her, I expected violence from him, but instead he got quiet.

Stopped protesting altogether. He simply said, 'She wouldn't stop fighting me,' as if that excused him. Then he put the gold stags in my hand to pay me for my loss. To make us even."

"Ah," Waterhouse said. "I see now what you meant about the six coins being extra money."

"They're a corruption. A sin against every goodness. I wouldn't consider using them for anything else, except to purchase his death."

"The city watch was of no help," she said, as a statement rather than question.

"Not in this part of the city. So I began to ask around. If justice couldn't be had, vengeance would have to do."

"Same thing where this sort of incident is concerned," Waterhearth said. "For reasons beyond my understanding, the rich in your world tend to purchase their policing indirectly, perhaps to maintain the illusion of keeping their hands clean. But it's actually a remarkably inefficient system. Personal revenge bought on a case-by-case basis is less costly in the long run."

She finished her glass and began to look for a barmaid to refill it. He hadn't touched much of the same cow-horned flagon of ale he'd nursed since they first sat down. His fingers drew absent diagrams in the condensation on the outside of the cup.

"If you were to appear as a customer," he said, "I'm confident he'd make the same offer to you as he did to Ewa. You're pretty and have an exotic look to you. He'd take notice of it."

"I infiltrate his life through his business," she said. He didn't notice the indulgent smile that had grown on her lips.

"And when he tries to—when he makes his move—"

"I strike."

"He won't expect it. If you've the skills you claim, you're certain to prevail. And you'll have a justification for killing him anyone would excuse."

"You've thought this through," she said. "Only one problem though. That's much too much work for so few coins."

"I don't understand," he said. "It's all I have. You agreed to the price."

"Yes I did," she said. "And for no extra cost I'll add an education. You didn't have enough to hire me or someone like me, but I came cheap because this is my first job. At the moment the need to build experience and a reputation transcends the need for more reasonable pay. For six stags you don't get an accomplished and sophisticated assassin, who'll take days, or even weeks, to carefully insinuate himself into a victim's life. You don't get complex scenarios and cover stories. All you get is a quick act of thuggery."

"Then what do you plan to do?" he said.

"I don't plan anything. I already did it."

"What?"

"When I excused myself a few minutes ago, I walked over to Gerdon's Parchment Shop, entered, gutted him like a trout, and returned here."

"But—"

"Quick as can be. I was prepared to have to kick the door in, but it was unlocked. For all of his sins, the man wasn't afraid to put in late hours at his trade."

"But—"

"Calm down, Lan. Take a drink."

He did.

When he could speak again he said, "What do we do now? What do I do?" He looked around, guiltily, expecting to see a thousand accusing eyes directed his way. Those who did look seemed only intent on stealing glances at his companion.

"Relax," she said. "No one knows what happened yet. No one noticed me, because I didn't act suspiciously. I didn't slink from shadow to shadow, or hide my features behind a dark cloak. There aren't cadres of spies keeping a record of who comes and goes from an unremarkable local parchment shop."

"But they'll know sooner or later," Lan said. "Someone will find him."

"Sooner or later. If it's later, no one will ever know who did it. If it's sooner, anyone who remembers you at all will know you spent the entire evening here in the company of an unusually striking woman. Don't think me vain. I'm not bragging, mind you, but stating a fact. Men have been looking at me all evening. You're a nice young fellow, Lan. Pleasant company. And I'm feeling good about finally taking the first step in establishing myself in what I hope to be a long and prosperous career. Good enough to help you establish the alibi you almost certainly won't need, for no extra charge."

"I didn't expect it to happen this way. So soon. I don't know what to do next."

She put a hand over his trembling one, willing calmness into him.

"Sit and pass the time. If someone discovers the foul murder before we close this place out, we'll join those who rush out to gawp and marvel at the sight, exactly as innocent folks would do. Otherwise we'll part ways come the dawn. You can go sleep the day away, to return to your normal life when it seems good to do so. In the meantime, we've agreeable mead to drink and hours of conversation before anyone even thinks about clearing us out of here. Why don't you tell me about Ewa before things turned bad. What was she like?

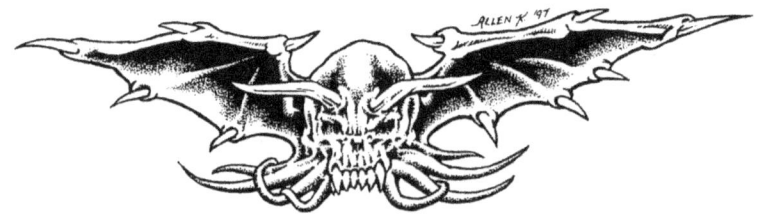

THE WHITE TRASH BLACK WIZARD

By Chad Hensley

Wears faded heavy metal t-shirts, Emperor and Iron Maiden his favorite bands.

His hair is always dyed black, pulled back in a ponytail.

Dangling down to his ass,

Armies of tiny muscular, multi-headed demons

Wage war amongst the greasy, grizzled strands.

Always bare foot, his feet stained the color of asphalt

Hover millimeters above the ground.

Over-sized beach shorts hang just below bony knees,

Day-glow tattoos of big-breasted succubi swirling around his legs and ankles.

Pulling free from the prison of his flesh, the dragon-winged vixens spring to life

When he's feeling lonely or just to fuck

With the neighbors when they complain the music is too loud.

Thick, dark circles ring his severely sunken eyes like Stonehenge

And he always smells of burning cannabis.

Giant horse flies with human mouths, wide drunken grins on their faces,

Buzz awkwardly around his head but never land.

Strange protruding rings with sparkling gems

(minute forms struggling deep inside as if to break free)

Set in miniature platinum baby skulls

Cover his thin, gnarled fingers, nails painted polished black, of course.

He pretends he's descended from Norwegian frost giant vampires

Because it sounds better than the backwoods of Metairie, Louisiana.

THE GHOST STONES OF MTHURA

By Peter Rawlik

Illustrated by Mike Dubisch

Common wisdom says that the light envelopes, the starships comprised of condensed photons, grant the Nug Soth access to Twenty Eight Galaxies, but the science-wizards of that ancient race know a secret truth, that there is a twenty-ninth, an ancient gray cluster of dead stars. Its true name is lost to time, but those who study the skies refer to it as Q'yth, the Midden Stars, though those astronomers who turn their lenses toward that portion of the sky are few, and these are prone to inscribing sigils of protection in the air when that dread name is invoked.

It was to this place that Buo, the archhierophant of the Nug Soth, had charged the wizard Zkauba to travel. All the champions of Yaddith had been summoned home and beneath the gaze of Buo and his councilors the latest atrocity was revealed. The burrowing Dholes, which had for centuries made a habit of violating the brooding chambers, had in a concerted effort, undermined the very foundations of Ocsic, a city on the southern continent. Without warning, the entire metropolis had been swallowed up into an abyssal grave. With it were lost all the inhabitants, young and old, wizened and unbirthed, as well as the great archives of ancient knowledge and learning that were housed there amidst titanic statues and towering minarets dedicated to the memory of the magnificence of the Nug Soth.

It was with this disaster that Buo and his minions rallied the brave and the bold to a fever. For eons the Nug Soth had searched for a way to end the depredations of the Dholes, but to no avail. There was a reason for this, a secret reason, a secret that the wizard Zkauba had learned, but it had driven him mad, and forced his retreat into the recesses of his own brain. None of the other championed heroes suspected the truth, though Zkauba had reasoned that Buo and his council also knew, and thus they accepted their assignments without question. They were dispatched throughout the twenty-eight galaxies in their light envelopes on yet another mission to seek weapons and spells and sigils that might finally protect the Nug Soth from the hungers and machinations of the abhorrent Dholes. Into the sky they flew, their ships catching the solar winds and propelling them beyond the seven suns about which Yaddith orbited, until they reached the point beyond the gravitational sphere where they could engage the Yhnngrr Engines and slip beneath the ether upon which the galaxies themselves float.

It was to Q'yth that Zkauba had been assigned, and when that had been announced a low murmur had passed amongst the gathered masses. No others were assigned to travel to that haunted cluster of dying stars, for there was rumored to be only one world worth traveling to, a world where none dared go, though none would say why. Mthura was a world on the edge of the galaxy itself; a place rumored to be the last depository of the knowledge that snuffed out the stars of Q'yth. In the memory of all who still lived on Yaddith, none could recall any who had visited Mthura, and the archives themselves only hinted that a few necromancers had once dared to travel there, never to return.

None suspected when that terrible charge was accepted that it was not Zkauba who reached out for it, but rather something alien that had wormed its way inside his prosaic brain. How a man of Earth had been whisked across time and space and forced to occupy the body of Zkauba is another story, one that I have recorded before. Nor shall I waste time retelling how I learned the secret of the Nug Soth, solved the Riddle of Thaqqualah, and in the process drove Zkauba mad. The body of the Wizard-Scientist Zkauba had been usurped, and it was I, Randolph Carter, who had in his body responded to Buo's call, and it was I who accepted the charge to travel to Mthura, Randolph Carter, who had secretly proclaimed himself the Warlock of Yaddith!

There are other stories I could tell, of Stronti and Shaggai and even of Tond, but that is not what I wish to write of this day. This day, on these metallic amber pages, I shall record my journey to Mthura, what I learned there, and what happened next. It is I suppose my apology, my testament, perhaps my way of seeking absolution for what I have done. I came to Mthura searching for wisdom, for knowledge. I found only the dead, and worse.

My journey to Mthura was indirect, and I spent days circling the galaxy of Q'yth, studying it, playing the lenses and organs of the light envelope across its sickly visage. The stars of the Q'yth are ancient, primordial things and have long since decayed to the point where the only light they emit is pale, gray and slow. They are cold, collapsing things, so weak that they can no longer bind

planets to themselves. Thus the few worlds that remain wander in queer orbits through dying star fields, the dust of collapsed worlds, and the ashes of dead civilizations. Mthura's orbit is perpendicular to what remains of its ancient home galaxy, arcing deep into the void between star clusters. It was here that I found Mthura; just where the star charts on the seventeenth Tablet of Nhing said it would be, in the darkness of abyssal space, bathed in the sallow light of a dying galaxy.

Mthura was as gray and desolate as the galaxy it was once part of. It hung in the inky black of the night, a sickly thing with little atmosphere. There were no signs of life, nothing blue, or green, or red on the surface. Only a single tower rising from the surface and extending into space suggested that there once was or might still be anything sentient on Mthura. I spread the sails of my light envelope and tacked toward the tip of the tower. An iris portal spun open, beckoning me to enter. I complied, gliding in and settling the great tesseract onto the deck as the portal closed behind it and atmosphere filled the chamber.

As I waited I equipped myself. I donned my armor, encasing all six limbs in protections that were both mystic and physical in nature. I checked my chainsword, and the crystals that powered and supplemented my defenses and wards. The ceramics felt cool against my rugose skin. If it was one thing that the Nug Soth knew, it was how to craft the weapons of war and the defenses against them. The pommel of the sword felt good in my upper right claw, as did the gauntlets that graced my other three limbs. Even the boots that wrapped around my feet and legs were not only comfortable but also capable of terrible feats, both offensive and defensive.

As the portal to my own ship opened, a great light in one of the chamber walls sputtered to life. A doorframe appeared and above it, written in ancient hieroglyphics in the language of the Progenitors, a single word. As with all such words there were meanings, and inflections and things implied but not spoken, still the meaning was clear and the easiest of all translations was the English lychgate, the entryway through which a corpse is carried into a cemetery. Though I will admit that there were certain inflections in the language that even Zkauba's memories and knowledge could not explain. I use the word "lich" for its old meaning of a corpse, but human language is insufficient here, there was a tone of distaste and of something malevolent and infectious. In one symbol, that might be described as little more than a stray punctuation mark, there was a suggestion of what men might refer to as the undead, but again language fails here. The symbol was similar to that used for the reanimated but was subtly different. Whatever was done in this place, on Mthura, it was not for the dead, it was not for the undead, but rather for something else entirely.

The lychgate opened and from it crept forth a wizened thing draped in robes. It wasn't any species I could identify, but Zkauba's memories suggested that it was a servitor, a construct made out of living tissue, to carry out specific tasks, the word Tethlaoth, bubbled to the surface of our shared brain. It slouched toward me, harshly breathing with each labored step. As it came closer the stench of the thing became overwhelming and I gagged as it lowered its cowl and revealed the confused mass of eyes and ears that it called a face.

When it finally spoke, it was all I could to keep from retching. "Tek thelli'tek the'melli az." When I didn't respond it spoke again, "Tek thelli'tek the'melli az." It took me a moment to process, it had been eons since anyone had heard this language spoken, but using Zkauba's memories and knowledge, I stumbled through the translation knowing that the sound "az" was related to memorials for the dead. "Give me the cenotaph."

It took a second or two for my mouth to stumble through the response, and I am sure my words were poor, but they did the job. "I have no cenotaph to give. I have come seeking knowledge." I made sure to use the same word he had used, but I had no idea what a cenotaph was.

The Tethlaoth whined in frustration. "The lychgate is for the acceptance of cenotaphs. Visitors are not allowed through the lychgate."

My mind raced; the servitor before me seemed adamant. "I have come seeking assistance."

"The lychgate is for the acceptance of cenotaphs. Visitors are not allowed through the lychgate."

It wasn't a thing to be reasoned with. It may have looked like a living thing, but it wasn't, it was just a machine, and it responded only the way it had been taught. Visitors were not allowed through the lychgate. Something in my mind clicked, and in an instant I knew how to circumvent the servitor. "I am not a visitor."

The servitor stretched its neck, and its eyes widened. "Are you a Mortician?" Once again, Mortician wasn't the proper term, but it embodied the concept, a concept that would take paragraphs to explain, and even now I am not sure that I fully understand it. I could have just as easily translated it as "management" or "controller".

I confirmed his statement, "I am the Mortician. Will you let me through the lychgate?"

The creature bowed, almost prostrated himself before me. I ignored him and marched toward the gate. The creature folded its cowl back over itself and fell into step behind me. The gate shimmered as we went through and in a single step we weren't on the tip of the tower anymore, but on the surface of the planet itself. It was a cold world with little atmosphere. There was no sun, but the gray Q'yth galaxy that hung in the sky bathed the landscape in a weak gloom. Hard radiation permeated the thin air. If it weren't for

my armor I would have been dead in seconds.

All around me were stones. I was in a forest of graves. They were of all sizes and shapes, some towering pillars; others little bigger than my hand, but all of them were made from the same material, a kind of gray-green stone, and all of them carved with names written in the ancient language of the Progenitors. I was standing in the middle of a world of graves; even the pathways upon which I was walking were paved with head-stones.

"How many bodies are buried here?" I said aloud, not really expecting an answer.

"There are no bodies buried here." The voice of the Tethlaoth whispered through the receiver in my helmet. "There are over three vigitillion cenotaphs accumulated here." The slave-thing made a queer sound. "You should know this, you are the Mortician."

"Mortician?" The voice was weak and slow, but the source was clear, one of the stones was speaking. "Have you finally come for us Mortician?"

In an instant I knew where I was and what I was looking at. Even amongst the Nug Soth there were still tales of intrepid wanderers who had found and spoken to Ghost Stones. Where they came from and what they were was never revealed, but all the tales followed the same pattern: someone finds a stone which then proceeds to seduce the finder with promises of wealth, or power, or knowledge. A quest is undertaken and the promise fulfilled, but always with a macabre twist ending that resulted in the death of the unfortunate finder.

And I was standing in a field, an entire world of them.

The Tethlaoth whined again. "You are not a Mortician, you do not belong here." It reared up and threw its cloak clear. Any semblance of pretense was over, and the full terror of the thing was revealed. It was an amorphous thing, in places transparent, and in others solid and fearsome. Tendrils of insubstantial mist spiraled through space towards me their tips full of claws and gnashing maws of curved and ferocious teeth. I spun the chain sword out of its sheath slicing through the nearest appendages. With my lower hands I formed the signs and sigils that would cast up a shield and block any further assaults.

Or so I had hoped. The Tethlaoth refused to cooperate. Instead of being stopped by the shield it phased out of this world and into the

spaces between, rendering my shield useless. The creature impaled itself on my sword, allowing the circulating blades to tear into its flesh and send gore into the air and covering the nearby stones with chunks of alien flesh and the strange protoplasmic fluid that was held within. It squirmed down the blade screaming as it clawed toward me. I charged one of my gauntlets with energy drawn from the inbetween space itself and drove my fist into the creature's interior. It whimpered as I punched through to the other side of the soft fleshy matter. More gore exploded out as the creature shifted back into the inbetween, but the grasp I had on its guts kept it from escaping. It was pinned into the substance of our universe, like an insect on a mounting board.

It screamed at me, tried to claw at me, but where the mystical shield failed, the ceramic armor did its job. I punched up with another fist, this time into the head. My fingers, my claws dug around, followed the thick strands of protoplasm that it used as nerves. There was a bundle of something, of soft tissue with strands moving in and out of it. It wasn't really a brain, but it functioned as one and crushing it brought the struggle to an end. The creature died, and crumbled into a lump of inanimate jelly and viscous slime. Then the world exploded.

Suddenly I was on the ground, my mind overwhelmed by the explosion of knowledge that suddenly filled my head. The Tethlaoth wasn't really a person, it didn't have memories, but it did have information. It knew what the cenotaphs, the ghost stones, were, and what Mthura was for as well. By crushing that small pseudo-brain I released all that knowledge, and it rushed into my head like a wave of light.

Looking out at the viscera covered stones, I knew that they were more than just grave markers, they were ancient technology that preserved the memories and personality of a sentient being within a crystalline matrix that was nearly indestructible, and powered by an ethereal link to the heart of a star. All around me, the shattered bits of servitor, ancient biotechnology, were seeping into the stones, slowly being absorbed.

Over the course of millennia the use of cenotaphs spread. It crept from culture to culture, from world to world, from system to system, and became endemic throughout the galaxy. The cenotaphs were not alive, but nor were they dead, they were the Necrophiles, the Loved Dead. They were cherished and honored by those who knew them. They became treasures, advisors, leaders, and they ushered in a golden age of enlightenment for an entire galaxy.

That age was short lived.

Something stirred in the vast garden of stones. It shifted and creaked. I could hear stone grating against stone. Something electric was in the air, great sparks of blue lightning arced from stone to stone. Two technologies that were never meant to meet were suddenly meshing, integrating, learning how to accommodate one another. There was something shuddering out there in the labyrinth of stones, something going through the pain of being born, or reborn. A throat made of gravel screamed, cried out in agony.

Even with only choosing the wisest, the most learned, or the most talented, the number of minds that were converted into cenotaphs—Az—quickly outnumbered the living. In the process an empire was created where the living served the not dead. Great ethereal networks of energy and communications were fabricated. To power these webs of undead minds the stars themselves were enslaved. There were wars, the living against the dead and their allies. But as the living fell, the ranks and genius of the Az grew. How does one wage a war against an enemy that can recruit from the dead?

The screaming in the garden subsided. Stones were falling, falling into place, linking into a polycrystalline latticework. Tendrils of linked stone swirled into existence, as did bulwarks of great stelae crashed together forming into cyclopean megaliths that shifted and groaned into a new kind of life. The stones were falling into place.

The Az fell from power the same way they rose, slowly and at their own hands. There were plots—grave plots within plots, which set ancient Az against the younger. Prison worlds, Mthura, were created, where the lesser Az could be held. The wars were terrible and the death toll amongst the living caught in the middle was immense. Those living that could, found ways to flee in vast fleets of ships that braved the gulf between galaxies. Those that remained were too few and too sparsely populated to be of service to the Az for long. A whole galaxy was abandoned by the living, and left for the dead, for the Az, and thus Q'yth, the Midden, came into being.

"MORTICIAN!" The voice of the dead, of the Az, of the cenotaph roared across the surface of Mthura. "Mortician, you should not have come for us." All around me the stones had formed into monstrous creatures, like homunculi or perhaps the Golems of the Hebrews. "We should not go quietly into the void. And the death of the Tethlaoth, the caretaker, supplies us with the means to oppose you." They were of myriad shapes, nightmares of claws and tentacles, of talons and tendrils, of thrashing limbs and gnashing teeth, but each part was not of flesh or bone, but rather of crystalline stone, of cenotaphs of infinite variety assembled into patchwork monsters. They stumbled toward me, their stone feet and paws gathering up their brethren with each clumsy step.

There had to be Caretakers, constructs to take in new additions, and make sure the prison worlds were cared for. It wasn't thought necessary to provide any security, the Conquerors couldn't think of anyone who would want to come to Mthura. That had been unfathomable eons ago, and in time Q'yth grew older and colder and greyer. Eventually, the Conquerors themselves vanished from the dead galaxy, and all that was left behind were their relics, their cold and barren worlds, places like Mthura, and their Caretakers.

And the Morticians. The Caretakers didn't know much about the Morticians, neither did the Az, but both knew that when they came, it meant the end of their existence. They were creatures of age and power, whose sole purpose was to find the remaining Az and bring about their final dispensation.

And I had tried to pass myself off as a Mortician, the embodiment of everything that the Az feared, and had struggled to avoid while entire species had evolved, flourished, and died. I had masqueraded as the embodiment of mortality, was it any surprise that they had risen up in fear to oppose me?

I stumbled to my feet, my sword smashing through stone monsters forming just beyond my reach. Rock trolls fell beneath my blade, shattering into dust as the chain sword, enchanted with Elder magics, ground through their component cenotaphs. They weren't as indestructible as they had thought, or perhaps age or the conglomeration had made them vulnerable. Whatever the case, they fell before my weapons like winter wheat before the reaping scythe.

A small squadron of simian things took up a position before me, buying time for the others to complete their transformation. It was a transparent strategy but effective. Two of them rushed me, drawing the attention of my blades, while two more aimed for my midsection, where my gauntleted fist fended them off. The last went for my head, wrapping an arm around my helmet, and trying desperately to pull it free. They may have thought of me as a Mortician, but they still recognized that if my armor came off I would be exposed to the near vacuum that Mthura called an atmosphere. With a free claw I traced a sigil of protection into the air and reinforced my armor and shields, repelling the stone simians. They flew back through the air and crashed against a selection of their brethren, shattering into pieces. But the pieces didn't fall, they

adhered themselves to the other stones and became incorporated into new more complex constructs.

Behind me a dragon roared.

It was an eerie sound, not unlike the high-pitched tinkling of glass bottles magnified through some alien amplifier. The source was a titanic thing, I call it a dragon, but it was nothing like those of human myth. Like the body I wore, it drew characteristics from a variety of species. Three great serpentine heads were counterbalanced by two tails, that all sat atop a thick gold-scaled body carried by two elephantine legs. It was inspired I suppose by some terrifying primordial creature drawn from the memory of one of those interred here. Great perfunctory wings graced its back supported by massive ribs of vermillion. It was all for show of course, meant to terrify me, to distract me, as the legions of cenotaphs bound themselves into something more.

The beast reared up, why it bothered was unknown to me, for the thing was easily five times my size and could have simply trampled me. Instead, one of its mouths opened and a weird arcing shaft of electric energy exploded out pounding me with tremendous force. I was thrown backwards, my armor and weapons all sounding alarms as their various systems failed. I limped to my feet, the armor was sluggish, the power cells nearly drained. I couldn't take another hit like that. By my estimation I couldn't take another hit at all. I was nearly powerless as I watched the second head rear up to strike. I diverted what little energies I had into the armor and dashed toward the tower entrance. The beast's bolt impacted just behind me and the ensuing explosion catapulted me forward. I used the momentum to my advantage, twisting my body so that I glided into the shimmering lychgate that would take me back to the pinnacle of the reception tower. In the blink of an eye, I was miles above Mthura in the docking bay where my ship waited.

I limped forward and signaled the light envelope to prepare to leave. The entryway dilated open and the engines powered up. Behind me the lychgate sparked and something made of stone tried to climb through. A clawed tentacle whipped out and searched to find something to grab hold of. When it failed, it hooked itself on to the frame itself, but the structure was insufficient, and collapsed under the added weight. Its mechanics broken, the gate became unstable, gouts of liquid proto-matter suddenly bulged out and then collapsed. The lychgate ate itself, consumed itself and then collapsed into a single spark of light. It was a torch, a beacon so bright that even through the filters of my helmet it hurt my eyes. It burned bright and hot, scorching everything within its reach, and that reach was expanding, growing as the very air itself caught flame. As I fled toward my ship my arms and armor felt that heat and were scorched by it. Even the skin of my light envelope blistered as the collapsed lychgate exploded outward and devoured the tower that once held it.

My ship moved through space, urged on by my panic and fear. I tuned my lenses back towards Mthura. Any pretense of being something else was cast aside. Mthura, or, more specifically, the cenotaphs of Mthura, the fallen Az of the galaxy known as Q'yth were becoming something else. The golems, the creatures constructed from the Az, the Ghost Stones of Mthura, were being consolidated, absorbed, not unlike the process that had destroyed the lychgate. But here instead of being a sudden bright and burning light, there was only darkness, a palpable evil forming from matter and becoming something else.

As I left the system, fleeing not only Mthura but Q'yth as well, I saw the terrifying horrific thing that was growing there, spreading, and consuming the planet and the tower that stood there. The Az and all the energy nearby had coalesced into a single crystalline formation that floated where once Mthura had been. It was a terrifying thing to look at, with angles that were all wrong, that opened into obtuse spaces and acute dimensions beyond those understood by even the Nug Soth. It hurt even my mind to look at what was happening there, but I was compelled to. For I wanted to see, needed to see, as the Az made Mthura the center of a new network of great tendrils that reached out into the dying galaxy of Q'yth. Ethereal conduits were spun and grey star after grey star was linked into a new and terrifying web. As galaxies go, there wasn't much energy left in Q'yth, but the Az, or whatever they had become were determined to drain it dry, to turn grey stars black, and to draw sustenance from the very collapse of an entire galaxy.

The light ship sailed on, and eventually moved beyond where even the strongest of enhanced lenses could still focus on the place where Mthura once was. I shuddered and went about repairing my armor and weapons, hoping that I would never again have to see the ghost stones of Mthura or what they had become, or what they would someday become. Once they had been men, or things not unlike men, but they had become something else. Time and power and fear had set them on a course of metamorphosis, and I had been a catalyst, an impetus for their final transformation. They were no longer the Az; I could not call them that anymore. So I gave them a new name, my right I suppose, after all it was I and I alone who witnessed the birth of the singular and crystalline thing that devoured the galaxy that spawned it.

I called it Q'yth-Az, which I suppose is as good a name as any for the monstrous thing that now stalks the stars, and the places between the stars, and haunts my memories with its hideous crystalline nature.

For Scott David Aniolowski

DREAMS OF SALT

By Cynthia Ward

Illustrated by Allen Koszowski

Above the Pacific, 1985

Abigail Derby hadn't had a nightmare since the years following her father's overdose. But what else could she call the dream that took her on the Hawaiian Airlines flight to Honolulu? It woke her with a cry.

Her seatmate removed Walkman headphones in a spray of Cocteau Twins and looked at her with concern. "Bad dream?"

Flushing, Abby replied reflexively. "Just weird, Nalani."

Nalani Kealoha knew about Abby's old nightmares; they'd been together since '67, when they were UC-Berkeley freshmen and Abby would wake screaming.

Nalani placed her hand on Abby's. The gesture drew a look from the man sitting across the aisle. The women ignored him. At least the stranger wasn't accusing them of "shoving your lifestyle down my throat."

"What did you dream?" Nalani asked her partner softly.

"I'm swimming through an underwater city," Abby murmured. "It's built against an immense coral reef, and schools of bright tropical fish are swimming everywhere. I can see everything clearly, even though I'm so deep in the ocean there's hardly any light. The buildings look vaguely Roman or Greek, but they're much bigger than a real ancient building. They're not marble, like you'd expect. I think they're black lava."

"Sounds intriguing, actually."

"I suppose." Abby repressed a shiver. "The city's magnificent—but I'm feeling weird as I swim through it. Maybe because it looks totally empty, except for the fish and me. But it feels like there are—people of some sort, watching me from inside the buildings. I can't see them—can't even see their eyes when I look at the windows. But I know they're not actually *people*."

That was one reason she was disturbed. Another was the lines and angles of the dream-buildings. They were subtly off, unsettling Abby in a way she couldn't articulate.

Nalani's hand tightened on hers.

"The weird feeling gets stronger when I see this—statue," she continued. "It's a religious idol, I guess." She was no judge; like Nalani, she'd been an atheist since childhood. "The thing is huge—makes me look like a minnow. It's also made of marble. Which makes no sense in a lava city."

Nalani smiled gently. "Dreams never make sense."

"The idol doesn't. It has a nude woman's torso—curvy and strong—and a woman's neck, but the neck has gills. The head is ugly and hairless and earless, and the face—if you ignore the long, sharp teeth, it's the face of a striped bass."

"You're right," Nalani said. "That's a weird dream."

"It gets weirder." Abby shifted to ease her hips and knees. They ached most of the time now, and she was barely thirty-five. "The idol's got webbed fingers and toes," she said, "and it's crouching on muscular legs. I realize they're giant frog legs, and wake up."

Nalani curled her fingers around Abby's. "I'm sorry you had such a creepy dream."

Abby didn't tell Nalani this wasn't her first

creepy dream. She'd been approaching the submerged city every night since her birthday, a month back. She never saw her dream-self the way you normally do, from outside, like you'd view yourself on TV.

She did see her dream-hands. They were clawed and webbed and greenish-gray. With every dream, they brought her closer to the dream-city. But she'd never reached it—until this mid-air dream.

She didn't tell Nalani the idol's obtruding marble fish-eyes seemed familiar. Partly, this was because Abby's father used to take her fishing as a child in Massachusetts, and she'd seen plenty of fish. But the eyes were also familiar in some eerie, *déjà-vu* way she couldn't identify.

She didn't tell Nalani the word she spoke underwater, just before waking. It made no sense, even in context.

"Mother?"

It was disturbing. But it wasn't what roused her. She didn't wake until the idol spoke silently inside her head:

Do you think yourself mortal?

As the Aloha Airlines island-hopper began its descent to Lihue Airport on Kauai, Nalani gestured at the window. "Those are the forbidden islands."

"'Forbidden islands'?"

Abby leaned past Nalani to look through the Plexiglas. As she discerned two small islands to the west, her stomach constricted with a ridiculous thought. *The dream-city is waiting for me there.*

"Why 'forbidden'?"

Nalani smiled. "I suppose it sounds like a Stephen King novel."

Abby glanced at a lurid British paperback, titled *Books of Blood*, tented on Nalani's knee. Abby didn't share her lover's taste for horror. She got her fill in childhood, when her father went irreversibly insane.

"The forbidden islands aren't as exciting as they sound," Nalani told her. "Outsiders purchased Niihau and Lahalahai from the Kingdom of Hawaii in the 1860s. A Scotswoman bought Niihau and an Englishman bought Lahalahai, but they both closed their islands to visitors."

"Which got the 'forbidden' label started?"

"I guess so. Niihau's not sealed off, though—people commute there from Kauai, the closest of the 'big islands.'" Nalani's expression turned thoughtful. "I haven't heard of anyone commuting between Lahalahai and Kauai. Or moving, either, besides my mother." She twisted the thin silver band on the ring finger of her left hand. "That's why my father joined the navy, I think. His family didn't approve of his bride being from Lahalahai."

Her explanation of the estrangement was news to Abby. Was it also why Nalani's parents weren't flying out from San Diego for the Kealoha family reunion? Abby had assumed they weren't attending because she and Nalani were. Nalani's parents became born-again Baptists when she was a teen; and they hadn't spoken to their only child or her partner since the young women moved to San Francisco and came out in the '70s.

Abby would have preferred to skip the Kealoha family reunion. If Nalani's paternal relatives didn't already know their mainland kinswoman had a girlfriend, they would once Nalani showed up with her longtime female roommate. With the exception of Nalani's parents, Abby had never met any of her lover's relatives; she'd never even been to Hawaii. She wasn't reassured by Nalani's description of her father's family as mostly full-blooded Hawaiian and very traditional.

Nalani sensed her partner's mood. "The reunion's one day," she reminded Abby. "We have the rest of the week to ourselves."

There was no need to discuss Nalani's implication. They used to commute together to their biochem jobs at Palo Alto drug firms, until Abby accepted a research position at an East Bay biotech start-up a year ago. Now, she often slept in her office.

Time to put the conversation back on track. "Did your mother ever say anything about her home island?"

"Only that she was glad to get away from Lahalahai."

Abby shook her head. But she couldn't shake the notion of the dream-city, waiting for her in deep waters off Lahalahai.

The dream-city, and the monstrous idol.

Abby discarded blouse and skirt and undergarments on her path to the bathroom. She was intent on showering away the hours of canned air and cigarette smoke. Reaching for an earring, she faced the mirror.

"Jesus Christ!"

Nalani stepped into the bathroom of their "vacation condo," a mid-tier hotel room with a tiny kitchenette. "What's wrong?"

Abby made no response. Her eyes were fixed on the mirror. She'd learned why the dream-idol's protuberant eyes looked so familiar.

She said, "I just noticed how old I'm getting."

In the span of glass, Nalani still wore her travel clothes. She stepped behind Abby and wrapped her arms around her partner's waist. The women were built very differently—Nalani was Junoesque, Abby petite—but Nalani was barely an inch taller.

Meeting Abby's gaze in the mirror, she smiled. "Who's the sexy couple?" She rested her chin on Abby's shoulder. "Thirty-five isn't old."

"It's the halfway point, at best," Abby muttered, "when your mother and father both died young."

Her observation wasn't strictly fair. Any links between genes and breast cancer, which killed Abby's mother, were hypothetical,

while her father's death was the result of accidental Thorazine over-sedation. But Nalani got the point.

"You know genetics aren't destiny." Her lips brushed Abby's ear. "Isn't that why you work in biotech?"

When Abby didn't respond, Nalani lightly stroked her lover's bare belly. In the reflection, Abby saw the plain silver ring she'd given Nalani in '68, when they pledged their commitment to one another. Nalani's lovely brown skin reminded Abby how much she disliked her own milky pallor.

"I don't see any signs of age here," Nalani murmured, tensing her fingers on Abby's stomach. "Still tight." She slid one hand upward to cup a small breast. "Still firm."

Abby exhaled in exasperation. "Look at my eyes. They're starting to look ancient. Bulging, and—and—baggy!"

Nalani studied her lover's mirror eyes. "They seem a little bigger." She sang a line from the chorus to "Bette Davis Eyes" in her off-key soprano, then said, "You've always had eyes like Bette Davis. Is it so bad if the resemblance continues when we're no longer seventeen? They're still beautif—"

"Getting old is bad," Abby said. "My eyes are getting difficult to shut. My neck is getting wrinkles. My knees and hips ache like an old woman's. Not to mention, my hair is starting to fall out."

"I'm sorry," Nalani said softly. "Of course you don't like those changes. But your doctor's prescribed Naprosyn, and—"

"—there are worse problems'?" Abby said. "Of course there are. But—Jesus, Nalani. I'm too young for alopecia or arthritis."

Nalani tightened her embrace in an attempt to reassure. "I know, love," she murmured. "But life is change. We don't look like we did when we met. In thirty years—twenty years, ten—we won't look like we do now. Life consists of cycles. We live, we die, we return in new forms—"

"Worm food. Tree roots."

"Abby—"

"You know there's nothing more." Abby rapped the cultured marble countertop with a knuckle. "This world's the only one we get. So how can you be so goddam calm about dying?"

Holding her reflected gaze, Nalani rested her head against Abby's.

"The cycle of creation and destruction is as old as life." Nalani spoke quietly. "It's not likely to change any time soon. Why get upset about something that's beyond our control?"

"We're finally in a position to do something about death," Abby said. "Why do you think I left a secure job at Syntex to join a biotech start-up in Fremont? Because Gerongenex is devoted to the science of life extension."

Nalani didn't say anything.

"Of course you don't approve of that, either," Abby said.

The women had always disagreed about whether to rage against the dying of the light. The disagreement was friendly, the concern remote, when the term "life extension technology" meant wishful thinking. But they were no longer in their twenties, and genetic engineering was no longer just a concept.

"Why should we accept death by aging?" Abby asked. "Death by disease is no less 'natural.'" Her voice was rising. "Yet you get vaccines, and work for a drug delivery company, and don't seem happy that AIDS sends us to a funeral every weekend."

"Of course we should fight disease and suffering." Nalani sounded tired suddenly. "I just mean—" She took a breath. "If older generations don't die, the planet will become too overcrowded to sustain life. Please, Abby, let's not fight. We're in Hawaii." She smiled. She'd never been good at staying upset. "What would be the best thing to do in paradise?"

"Right now," Abby said, "it's take a shower."

Raising her hands to an earring, she fo-

cused on her reflection. She stilled, a frisson undulating unpleasantly up her back. She finally knew what was bothering her about her eyes. They'd changed the way her father's did, right before he lost his mind.

Flamboyant fish darted past Abby as she tried to swim away. No matter how she twisted, she always ended up turned in the same direction. She always found herself facing the idol.

The marble lips parted.

Daughter. The idol's voice was silent, yet it resounded through the ocean and through Abby's body; and there was nothing human about it. *Welcome to your new home.*

I'm not moving to Hawaii—I'm not your daughter—

You're a Deep One.

What? Abby thought. *Who are you?*

The idol's voice shook Abby's body so she feared she'd shatter like crystal.

I'm Mother Hydra.

She'd never heard the name before, yet it was familiar.

Silently, she cried, *Why do you disturb my dreams?*

The soundless voice answered. *You need never die.*

Abby woke weeping.

Eucalyptus branches striped the rented Accord in sliding shadows. Cheap speakers spilled a trebly "Raspberry Beret." Nalani was driving, so she also steered the radio dial.

Tilting her head to see over her sunglasses, she glanced at Abby. "I wish you'd tell me about your dream this morning."

"Why?" Abby glared through her Ray-Bans. "Discussing my last weird dream caused another. I can learn from experience."

She turned up the radio, though she didn't

share Nalani's taste for contemporary music. She preferred the old jazz and pop standards and Broadway show tunes. They were in Hawaii; why couldn't the radio play something from *South Pacific*?

When the couple arrived at Poipu Beach, Abby found white sands and cerulean waves and tall palms and roast pig and other Hawaiian touches, including a great-aunt of Nalani's who welcomed them each with a fragrant fresh-flower lei around the neck and an almost-kiss on the cheek.

For the most part, however, the Kealoha family reunion could be mistaken for a mainland beach party, right down to the stone-washed button-fly 501s and the Sanyo boombox blasting "We Are the World." There were even a few same-sex pairs in suggestive proximity, and an older native guy who attracted no particular notice, despite wearing a muu-muu dress and women's jewelry and standing very close to the man at his side. Abby appreciated the Kealohas' casual acceptance when Nalani introduced Abby as her partner, but their reaction only strengthened Abby's impression of crossing half the Pacific Ocean to end up on a California beach.

Never comfortable with strangers or crowds, Abby drank Primo beer from a red Solo cup while Nalani's relatives filled them in on recent family history. When she couldn't make herself listen to one more story, Abby excused herself ("I've never gone swimming in Hawaii before").

The water proved quite pleasant for the first Saturday of October. Like bathwater, Abby thought. Even in July, the ocean in northern California was unpleasantly chilly. Maybe exercise in the tropical sea would ease her aching joints.

When she emerged, her knees and hips felt worse, her skin was the color of a cooked lobster, and her beer buzz was gone. Nalani was engrossed in conversation with one of her aunts. Abby turned and headed to the punch bowl ("no rum in our mai tai, we use

home-made okolehao"). Settling under the palm where she and Nalani had left their beach towels, she slid on her aviator shades, then squeezed out a palmful of Coppertone sunscreen and applied a fresh coat to her stinging skin.

Abby was a lightweight, and the local liquor was potent. Within a few sips, the skin of her skull was too tight, and a remote numbness limned the edges of her palms. A few more sips, and she found herself addressing near-strangers when the person in a dress and his—her—companion walked by.

"I have to confess." Abby gestured a little too broadly with her plastic punch cup. "I didn't think traditional Hawaiians would be so—accepting of people like us."

The one in a dress ("Kaleo on my birth certificate, but call me Carlotta") smiled at Abby. "The Kealohas value ohana."

Abby recognized the Hawaiian word. Nalani had told her it meant family, but with connotations of a closely interwoven, mutually supportive extended family. At the time, Abby had assumed that if the clan excluded Nalani's mother, the Kealohas must mean "family" in the same way that Nalani's born-again parents meant "family values."

Carlotta was still talking. "The Kealoha family keeps to the old ways, and the Hawaiian mahu tradition is ancient." Observing Abby's puzzled expression, Carlotta added, "I'm mahu."

"Sure." Abby had never heard this word before. She would have thought it meant transsexual, transvestite, or drag queen, if Carlotta were wearing falsies or otherwise trying to obscure a male body.

"In most parts of Hawaii, the word's become an insult," Carlotta said. "That's why Mark and I moved to Molokai." She pronounced the island's name in four syllables, like Nalani did. "We're just part of the community there. I suppose we'd also be accepted on Niihau. Maybe Lahalahai, too."

"You'd move there? I thought your family didn't approve of Nalani's father marrying someone from Lahalahai."

Mark answered Abby as if she weren't indiscreet with inebriation. "They believe a ridiculous old superstition."

Carlotta gave Mark a look, then told Abby, "A Polynesian legend says fish people live in the deep waters off Lahalahai."

"'Fish people'?" Abby shuddered, though she knew she shouldn't. It was just a coincidence. "Mermaids?"

Carlotta shook her head. She and Mark were in their fifties or sixties, but Carlotta's hair was black, and even longer and more lush than Nalani's. It would fill Abby with envy even if her own hair wasn't thinning.

"Not mermaids," Carlotta told Abby. "They're more like scaly humans with the heads of fish."

"And the legs and webbed paws of frogs," Mark added, shaking his head.

Coincidences happen all the time, Abby reminded herself, and took a generous gulp of okolehao. We only notice the coincidences that seem meaningful.

"In the old language," Carlotta told Abby, "they're called keiki o ka ia—children of the fish."

Mark said, "Sometimes they're called moanahune—it means sea people." He smiled sardonically. "More or less."

Abby said, "I don't see why an old legend about sea creatures would make Hawaiians shun people from Lahalahai."

"They're avoided because—" Carlotta paused, as if choosing her words "—they're said to interbreed with the fish people."

The words stirred a long-forgotten memory: a walk home from kindergarten, the daughter of a Miskatonic University librarian shouting at Abby. "Your daddy's the son of the fish woman from Innsmouth!"

Abby's long-dead grandmother had been born in the abandoned fishing port of Innsmouth, but why a fourth-grader would shout at her about it, five-year-old Abby couldn't

imagine.

The older girl smiled nastily and spoke again. "She was a fishy witch and she took over your grandfather's mind."

When Abby asked her father what the girl was talking about, she was spanked for repeating a ridiculous rumor and ordered to forget it ("Some people have no respect for the dead, but you will"). She didn't achieve enlightenment until she overheard the next-door neighbor entertaining guests in his back yard. His story, Abby would not forget.

"Dr. Derby's childhood was tragic," the neighbor said. "His father—Edward Derby, Sr.—developed a case of split personality after he murdered his wife. His best friend decided Derby, Sr. was possessed by the murdered wife, and killed him."

Peeping through a knothole in the fence, Abby saw the neighbor's guests. They looked shocked. Their host's lips twitched. He rinsed away his smile with gin and tonic.

"The couple's little boy was packed off to a great-aunt in Cambridge for raising," he continued. "Don't know why Derby, Jr. didn't stay there—he married a girl from an old Boston family and got his degrees from Harvard—but he became an economics professor at Miskatonic. Now he's taking a position at San Jose State. Can't say I'm surprised."

Abby realized her memories were affecting her expression when Carlotta's lover spoke to her reassuringly.

"The moanahune are lolo rubbish, yah? But the legend gets even crazier. It says, unless they're killed, the fish people live forever."

Abby stared. "They're immortal?"

"So the old tales say," Carlotta replied neutrally.

Abby's laugh was brittle. "Unbelievable."

Mark's guffaw drowned "Money for Nothing" on the boombox. "Of course it's unbelievable," he said. "But it's the reason an old Englishman named H. Phillips Newcomb bought the island of Lahalahai. He wanted to inject the immortality of the Deep Ones—that's what he called the fish people—into his descendants."

You're a Deep One.

Abby had difficulty speaking through the sudden tightness of her throat. "'Deep Ones'?"

"They're supposed to live deep in the ocean," Mark said. "Nobody lived on Lahalahai in those days, even though it's always had the best fishing. The old haole got the island for a song." He laughed. "Newcomb wanted to make money off fishing and agriculture, but he had to pay people to move there—Micronesians and Melanesians and Asians, mostly. Polynesians steer clear to this day." He smiled cynically. "Hard to believe anyone buys this nonsense in 1985, isn't it?"

Carlotta tossed her lover a scowl. "'There are more things in heaven and earth, Horatio—'"

"I thought Nalani was a native Hawaiian," Abby said.

Mark said, "Her father is."

Carlotta quickly added, "Some Hawaiians did move to Lahalahai." She smiled at Abby. "Anyone looking at Nalani would see she's pure Polynesian."

"She doesn't look like she's got moanahune ancestors," Mark said. He gave Abby a mordant smile. "You do."

Far below the waves, Abby faced the idol. *Mother Hydra.* The thought was like a tape loop. *Mother Hydra. Mother Hydra.*

Why did the thought sound like an invocation?

The loop snapped when color flushed across the enormous white limbs and torso and head, marble turning to scaled hide. The torso assumed the hue of bass-belly from throat to mons. Elsewhere, the hide gained a silver-blue mackerel shimmer.

Now the fish-face was mobile. Alive. Even

in such an immense head, the bulging eyes were oversized. On the humanoid neck, the bald head turned like a horse's, to examine Abby with one lidless fish-eye. Iridescent gold, it dwarfed Abby. The head tilted closer, and the vast round pupil seemed a black cave mouth, looming to swallow her.

Abby opened her mouth to cry out.

Ocean rushed in. She writhed, silenced, panicked, sure she'd drown. Then the water flowed out through unexpected gill slits in the sides of her neck.

Muscles flexed sinuously along the massive arms. With unexpected speed, the webbed hands closed around Abby. Cupped together, they trapped her like a tadpole. She could see past the fingers, but not slip between them.

Daughter. The silent voice set Abby's head to aching. *Deep One, you will never survive the flight back. You must complete your transformation.*

Abby pushed, but the gelid fingers were as unyielding as jail bars.

Mother Hydra will hasten your change, said the inhuman voice, *and you shall live forever in Y'ha-lahai.*

A fingertip settled on the back of Abby's skull, forcing her head down as easily as she'd thumb-mash a gnat.

The nipple was flesh, but no warmer than granite pried from wintry Maine soil. It shouldn't have fit, but Abby's mouth widened to encompass the nipple. Fluid as cold as ice-melt flooded her mouth.

The taste and texture suggested the liquefied remains of long-dead fish. Abby wanted to vomit. Yet she couldn't stop drinking.

"Aaaah!"

"Abby?" Nalani's voice was followed by the click of a lamp switch. "Dear God, why does it smell like a working dock in here?" She approached the bathroom, where her lover stood naked. "Abby, are you all r—oh, my God my God my God—"

Abby turned from the mirror.

Nalani's complexion grayed. She backed away, her hands rising to her mouth. Wordless sounds escaped.

When her back struck the bedroom's far wall, she found her voice. "Wh—where'd you get a Halloween costume?"

Abby's webbed fingers pulled on her head, without effect. Her voice was an inhuman croak. "No costume."

"Jesus." Nalani's voice was vibrating, perhaps because she was shaking. "We need to get you to a doctor."

"The pain's gone. I'm all better," Abby said. "Does illness cause this?"

She flexed long, green-gray legs that jutted like a frog's, and crossed ten feet of floor in a bound.

An old Englishman named H. Phillips Newcomb bought the island of Lahalahai. He wanted to inject the immortality of the Deep Ones—that's what he called the fish people—into his descendants. Unless they're killed, the fish people live forever.

Shoving her face close to Nalani's, Abby said, "I'm not ill. I've become what I should be." She didn't blink. Her eyelids were gone. "I'm what my father should have been," she said. "I won't let them lock me up and kill me, too."

Nalani pressed herself back against the wall. One eyelid twitched. "What?" Her voice was nearly unintelligible. "I don't understand."

Your daddy's the son of the fish woman from Innsmouth! said the librarian's daughter in Arkham. *She was a fishy witch and she took over your grandfather's mind.*

Abby's laughter might have been crockery shattering. "I've gained my heritage as a Deep One," she told her lover. "I'm ocean-dwelling and immortal."

Nalani reached for the bedside telephone.

Abby's hand was faster now, and more impervious to pain.

The receiver nearly struck Nalani's head as the telephone flew out of her reach. The gray cord snapped near the wall jack. The phone gave off a ring as it struck the hardwood floor. Claw marks scored the off-white plastic.

Trembling, Nalani faced her lover. "If you're okay, Abby," she whispered, "the doctor will give you a clean bill of health. We'll know there's nothing to worry about. Now—" reaching for her lover "—let's go to the hos—"

"You're not listening!" Abby's hand snapped forward again, to close on her lover's neck. She raised the robust woman without strain and shook her. "Pay attention, Nalani. I'm not going anywhere except the ocean. I'm one of the Deep Ones."

Nalani had shut up, which was what Abby wanted, but she gave her lover another shake for emphasis as her voice rose to a crescendo.

"Life is a cycle of life and death? I always knew that was bullshit, and I was right. I'm going to live forever."

When she released Nalani, Abby was surprised by her lover's boneless collapse. She frowned, or tried to; her brow muscles proved inflexible. She spoke in a soft, puzzled voice.

"Nalani?"

Her lover lay motionless on the floor, reddish-purple marks darkening on her throat.

"Nalani, are you all right?"

The prone woman didn't stir. Abby tried to press her fingertips to Nalani's wrist, but her claws interfered. She pressed her exposed eardrum to Nalani's breast. She could hear the rustle of fronds on banana trees and coconut palms, the rising notes of rain, despite the closed window and humming air conditioner. Finally, she heard Nalani's heart-beat.

Abby gathered Nalani to her breast and rocked her. Abby's eyes ached. She couldn't cry any more.

As the rain grew heavier, the roof resonated like a great drum-skin. The wind came in gusts and fronds thrashed and tore. A tree fell with a groan and the ground juddered.

Stillness had descended when Abby rose

and laid Nalani on the bed. She didn't stir as Abby straightened the limbs, brushed a fingertip over the bruised throat. Abby lowered her head to hear the rhythm of Nalani's heart.

"Human life is so brief," Abby whispered. "Nalani's mother was from a place like Innsmouth." An exhalation shook her. "Why couldn't Nalani be like me?"

A siren woke distantly, startling Abby. The walls of the room were thin enough to hear the TVs in the adjoining rooms. Had someone heard her shouting and called the police?

Turning her head sideways, she studied Nalani more closely with one eye.

"The cops might not think it's an accident." She firmed her jaw, the rows of sharp teeth fitting neatly together. "I'm not going to be killed because some ignorant mortal thinks I'm a monster."

The condo door opened directly outside. Where the clouds were breaking, the sky showed more stars than Abby had ever imagined. The waning moon seemed sun-bright as it shone on the empty lawn and iron-fenced swimming pool. Raindrops made the close-cropped grass a field of diamonds.

The hotel grounds were deserted. To the east, a few crabs scuttled on the narrow sand beach. The low surf muttered. The siren moaned, closer this time, and fell silent again.

The air was sweet with cut grass and night-blooming flowers and rain-soaked earth and a thousand other scents. All were clear and distinct. They were so powerful, they almost made Abby dizzy.

West of the hotel complex, the fallen palm tree pointed to undeveloped acreage. Every tree was sharp as sheared tin. A bullfrog's *rrrr-um* swelled sporadically and the shadows breathed the scent of fresh water.

Abby returned her attention to the ocean. *You shall live forever in Y'ha-lahai.*

Abby moved toward the beach. Behind her, bullfrogs set up a rhythmic thrumming. The chorus assaulted her ears like punk rock.

She wasn't surprised to see a figure rise from the ocean, enormous and alive and streaming, her arm extended, the open palm waiting.

Abigail Derby leaped.

ALL-NEW SWORDS & SORCERY FICTION

Tales From The MAGICIAN'S SKULL

GOODMAN PUBLICATIONS GP

WIELAND:
CHARLES BROCKDEN BROWN'S
AMERICAN HORROR STORY

By Karen Joan Kohoutek

One of the writers mentioned in H.P. Lovecraft's influential work *Supernatural Horror in Literature* is American author Charles Brockden Brown, whose writing is unfortunately neglected today. Perhaps his most important novel, described by Lovecraft as his "most famous," is *Wieland; or, The Transformation: An American Tale* (1798). As the first full-fledged American Gothic novel, it has an important place in the history of weird fiction.

In his introduction to the Penguin edition of the novel, critic Jay Fliegelman calls it "the first published novel by the first native-born American author to make a profession of, and a living by, writing" (vii). Brown, who died in 1810, was a clear literary predecessor to Nathanial Hawthorne and Edgar Allan Poe (born in 1804 and 1809, respectively), particularly in their more Gothic modes, and also of Herman Melville, who wasn't born until 1819.

Fliegelman notes that these three important figures from American literature were "all readers of Brown" (vii), making him more influential than one might think from popular contemporary knowledge of his works. He was an important influence outside the United States as well, with Carwin "a character who would influence Mary Shelley (an admirer of Brown) on the eve of her writing *Frankenstein*" (Fliegelman xx).

Shelley's journal shows her reading *Wieland* in 1815 (47), and her letters contain an account of borrowing an 1815 biography of Brown, about whom she says "what a delightful person he seems to have been" (498, 499). When a friend visited America in 1826, Mary Shelley wrote to him that "I should be very melancholy if I were going there," but added "it produced one man whom I am sure I should have liked—the author of *Wieland*" (402).

At the same time, scholars agree that Brown was influenced by the philosophical fiction of Shelly's father, William Godwin. In his book *Mary Shelley's Frankenstein: Tracing the Myth*, Christopher Small writes that Brown's work, while "owing much to Godwin" as an influence, also acted as a "mediator between him and Mary Shelley" (91), stating decisively that Brown was "one of her favorite authors" (91–92).

Brown was born into a Quaker family in 1771, and *Wieland* is set in the period leading up to the American Revolution. His family suffered during that war when his pacifist father was branded a traitor (Fliegelman xiii–xiv), which may account in part for the tone of the novel's setting. The peaceful village, the idyllic natural settings, and the open, educated society, full of high moral feeling, offers a picture not often associated with this tumultuous period. It has an Edenic quality, and the introduction of a serpent comes

Engraved by I.R.Forrest from a Miniature by William Dunlap in 1806

Charles Brockden Brown (1771–1810)

with the pivotal character of Carwin, who has come from Europe, the old world, and pushes the ideal of personal independence to the point of recklessness and criminality.

Wieland is something of a tough sell for modern readers, with its earnest, often pedantic style, but the central situation is very compelling. It depicts a wealthy, educated family, whose warm social circle and relatively complacent lives are disrupted by uncanny experiences, the apparently inexplicable nature of which leads to madness and tragedy.

The novel begins with the narrator, Clara Wieland, retelling her family's story to an unnamed friend, in a calm but bleak mood of deep fatalism that will continue for much of the book: "Fate has done its worst. Henceforth, I am callous to misfortune" (Brown 5). In happier times, she and her brother lived on neighboring estates in an idyllic spot in Pennsylvania. Her brother, Theodore, married Clara's best friend and started a family; the wife's brother Henry Pleyel is Theodore's best friend; and Clara is secretly in love with Pleyel. All of this makes the group particularly tightly-knit, and they spend much of their time together discussing literature and philosophy in an outdoor temple on the property.

An acquaintance, a drifter named Carwin,

53

is introduced to their social circle around the same time that strange events start to happen. Wieland hears his wife's voice calling a warning to him, at a time when the family swears she was nowhere nearby. Clara has a terrifying experience when she overhears men inside her room, plotting her murder. Then, most damningly, Pleyel seems to hear a conversation between Clara and Carwin, which leads him to believe the two are involved both sexually and criminally.

In time, unsettled by these uncanny events, Wieland thinks he's heard the voice of God, asking him to make an Abraham-like sacrifice. He murders his wife and children, along with a young woman who lives with them as a ward and becomes obsessed with finishing the job by killing his sister. She, in turn, blames Carwin for the tragedy, since he has revealed a skill at ventriloquism, which he used against the family, first simply "suggested by the momentary exigence," and then, after "some daemon of mischief seized me" (Brown 229, 230), against Clara in an outright plot.

Throughout the novel, Brown doesn't give us what we expect from a narrator. Clara's understanding isn't necessarily accurate, since she has only partial knowledge of events, and much of the information comes from the villain, who she knows not to fully trust. The intimate insight into her life, though, gives a different picture of a single woman's life in the 1770s than we might expect to find. Clara has independent wealth, lives by herself because she is "desirous of administering a fund, and regulating a household, of my own" (24), and frequently entertains Henry, the close male friend oblivious to her feelings for him, as a guest in her home, with no one concerned about a chaperone.

When she first hears the apparent threat in her own home, Clara muses, "I was habitually indifferent to all the causes of fear, by which the majority are afflicted. I entertained no apprehension of either ghosts or robbers. Our

security had never been molested by either, and I made use of no means to prevent or counterwork their machinations" (64). Confident in the power of rational thought, she had always been "a stranger even to that terror which is pleasing" (52). She has no way of knowing that this very commonsense self-sufficiency is what inspires Carwin to harass her, in order "to put this courage to the test. A woman capable of recollection in danger, of warding off groundless panics, of discerning the true mode of proceeding, and profiting by her best resources, is a prodigy. I was desirous of ascertaining whether you were such an one" (230).

Despite her independence, Clara is constrained by the gender-based conventions of her time in one important respect: when it comes to her feelings for Pleyel, propriety dictates her behavior, and she insists that "I must not speak ... he must be prompted to avow himself" (90). Looking back later on her emotional suffering, she will realize that these "scruples were preposterous and criminal," and "bred in all hearts, by a perverse and vicious education" (91). It would have been better to "deal with him explicitly, and assure him of the truth" (94), even if society considered it unseemly for a woman to declare her love. Unfortunately, she was unable to summon this kind of courage until the experience of true horror put it into perspective.

While Carwin is a malicious force in the lives of the Wielands and Pleyels, he frames his behavior in terms the modern world would call unintended consequences, as he deftly admits his involvement, but refuses to take responsibility. "I have acted, but my actions have possibly effected more than I designed" (223), he says, and "I intended no ill; but my folly, indirectly and remotely, may have caused it ... I have handled a tool of wonderful efficacy without malignant intentions, but without caution" (223–224, 225–226).

Confronted by Clara, Carwin confesses his crimes, but swears to the end that he never suggested murder, or used his skill against Wieland during the time the latter thought he heard the voice of God: "surely my malignant stars had not made me the cause of her death; yet had I not rashly set in motion a machine, over whose progress I had no control" (246). If that's true, then the origin of the voice lies within Wieland, either through mental illness or a previously unacknowledged capacity for violence.

Whatever the means, Wieland's breakdown seems clearly linked to his encounter with the other inexplicable voices, for which Carwin was responsible. When he had impossibly heard his wife calling to him, Wieland had said, "If my ear was not deceived, it was her voice" (37), and the question of whether to murder his family later rests on whether his ear is deceived in discerning the voice of God.

It is as if his rational self has become unhinged by the encounter with a mystery outside any clearly rational explanation, which acts as a catalyst, releasing his own murderous impulses. Faced with the inexplicable, Wieland's rationality falls apart. Describing a nightmare, Clara had said that "there are means by which we are able to distinguish a substance from a shadow, a reality from the phantom of a dream" (Brown 99), and it is this ability that her brother seems to have lost, with terrible results.

While the family largely brushed off this early strange experience, since there are "twenty suppositions" that might explain it (41), its possible effect on her brother preyed on Clara's mind. "The will is the tool of understanding, which must fashion its conclusions on the notices of sense. If the senses be depraved, it is impossible to calculate the evils that may flow from the consequent deductions of understanding" (39). In their reliance on pragmatism and rationality to explain the world, the Wielands seem particularly American, and they are vulnerable when Carwin sets out to "test the age of reason's faith in itself (Fliegelman ix).

Among the peculiarities for modern readers, Brown's narrative insists on the importance of characters who don't properly appear in the novel. These include a European woman Pleyel had been romantically involved with, whose existence leads to all sorts of complications. More prominently, one of Wieland's victims is Louisa Conway, their young ward. Her family history is told in great detail, and Clara emphasizes her feelings for this girl, "whom I loved with so ineffable a passion" (179). She "cannot do justice to the attractions of this girl," for whom the family feels an "unspeakable fondness," and a concern that "almost exceeded the bounds of discretion" (30).

Despite all this, Louisa never speaks, and is only mentioned, in passing, as existing in the background of scenes where the group gathers, rendering this whole plot thread very odd, especially since it ends so grotesquely, with Clara unable to give her dead friend a sentimental kiss of farewell. "Such had been the merciless blow that destroyed her, that not a *lineament remained*!" (179, italics and exclamation point in the text)

Brown based the novel at least in part on a real-life "Murder Committed by Mr. J---- Y----, upon his Family, in December, A.D. 1781" (Clark 168). Both the fictional and historical fathers "made confessions of guilt, both protested their innocence of a conscious desire to commit such awful crimes, and both acted according to what they thought was the Divine Will." Also, "the sister was in each case attacked," but survived (ibid).

In Clark's analysis, Brown transformed the true-crime facts to present a meditation on "frail, ignorant, selfish, superstitious man," and offer "a sermon against credulity" (168). Interestingly, the central situation has survived to take contemporary forms. While Wieland, with his religious instinct and sense of duty, is very different from *The Shining*'s Jack Torrance, both are driven to murder their families at the urging of voices that seem to them completely apart from themselves, and in both books, the characters fear mysterious and inexplicable happenings, but their closest family members, who should be a source of security, turn out to be the real threat against them.

Lovecraft wrote authoritatively about Brown in *Supernatural Horror in Literature*, even though he read little of his work, and seems to have based his opinions on a relatively small sample. In his letters to R. H. Barlow, Lovecraft admitted his limited knowledge of Brown's fiction: "So you've read '*Wieland; or, The Transformation*?' I never had a chance to get hold of the entire book, but possess part of it in the 'Lock & Key Library.' I'd like to see the whole thing, as well as other efforts by Charles Brockden Brown. Charlie seems rather a difficult bird to locate" (Lovecraft *Fortunate Floridian* 193).

Lovecraft had previously mentioned to his aunt that "I find much valuable material in that 10-volume red-bound 'Lock & Key Library' of strange tales which I picked up during my 1922 N.Y. trip" (*Lovecraft Letters from New York* 274).

The excerpt from *Wieland* appears in Volume 9, and from the text, one can see that Lovecraft had access to a severely truncated version of the novel. The first fifty-some pages are omitted completely, which include the novel's first apparently supernatural encounter, a significant episode, and the Wieland family's entire tragic history, in which their father was the victim of spontaneous human combustion (Brown 57).

Peculiarly, this abridgement also omits the novel's most dramatic incident: Clara's discovery of her murdered family, and the ensuing confrontation with the brother who killed them. The Lock and Key version ends on what is page 266 in the Penguin edition, where the novel continues until page 278, with the revelation that Clara and Pleyel reunite and wind up happily married. That fact,

along with the mood of moral reflection, meditating on how all their troubles could have been avoided if they had been more vigilant, gives the novel's actual ending a different tone than the bleak, despairing conclusion of the abridgement, where Clara looks for "only quick deliverance from life and all the ills that attend it" (Brown 266).

Julian Hawthorne, editor of the edition read by Lovecraft, unreservedly describes *Wieland* as "the first American novel," and says "its author was soon recognized as the earliest American novelist" (222), so that information was available to Lovecraft in his critique. It's possible that Hawthorne's other opinions influenced Lovecraft as well. He stated that *Wieland*'s flaws lie in its "improbability, morbidness, and a style often too elevated." At the same time, he praises Brown for his "downright originality," and says that in the weird, "he has been surpassed by few writers save Edgar Allan Poe" (ibid).

Lovecraft states in *Supernatural Horror in Literature* that, despite its hinging on "a lame ventriloquial explanation," Brown's work is filled with "an uncanny atmospheric power which gives his horrors a frightful vitality" (29). Comparing Brown to his contemporary, the trend-selling Gothic writer Ann Radcliffe (now most well-known to the general public from Jane Austen's *Northanger Abbey*), Lovecraft seems to approve the American writer's "choosing modern American scenes for his mysteries," rather than stereotypical Gothic settings (ibid).

A bit of early metafiction appears in Wieland when, just before the first experience of the seeming supernatural which is going to violently disrupt their lives, Wieland and Pleyel talk about classical literature, and discuss the fact that "to make the picture of a single family a model from which to sketch the condition of a nation, was absurd" (Brown 34). At the same time, the very subtitle "An American Tale" suggests some desire to sketch the condition of a nation. In

1709, Brown even sent a copy of the novel to Thomas Jefferson, who wrote a polite note of acknowledgement in return, although, "it is not known" if he ever actually read it (Clark 163, 164).

In the family tree of American weird fiction, Brown is clearly the patriarch, and his most significant work deserves to be more widely read. Despite the archaism of his style, *Wieland* remains an absorbing account of the complexity of human minds and human interactions.

Works Cited

Brown, Charles Brocken. *Wieland and Memoirs of Carwin the Biloquist.* New York: Penguin, 1991.

Clark, David L. *Charles Brockden Brown: Pioneer Voice of America.* Durham, N.C: Duke University Press, 1952.

Fliegelman, Jay. Introduction. *Wieland and Memoirs of Carwin the Biloquist,* by Charles Brockden Brown, Penguin, 1991, pp, vii–xlii.

Hawthorne, Julian. *The Lock and Key Library: The Most Interesting Stories of All Nations.* Vol. 9. New York: Review of reviews Co, 1909.

Lovecraft, H.P. *Supernatural Horror in Literature.* New York: Dover, 1973.

Lovecraft, H P, S T. Joshi, and David E. Schultz. *Letters from New York.* San Francisco & Portland, Or.: Night Shade Books, 2005.

Shelley, Mary, and Betty T. Bennett. *The Letters of Mary Wollstonecraft Shelley*: Vol. III. Baltimore: Johns Hopkins University Press, 1988.

Shelley, Mary W, and Frederick L. Jones. *Mary Shelley's Journal.* Norman: University of Oklahoma Press, 1981.

Small, Christopher. *Mary Shelley's Frankenstein: Tracing the Myth.* Pittsburgh: University of Pittsburgh Press, 1973.

EVE. AWAKENING.

(AFTER MARY SHELLEY)

By Shannon Connor Winward

I ought to be
thy Adam.

moonlight.
hands.
knots black.

Alive.

her feet.
oh. Him.
shards of glass.

his hair.
snow.
shadow.

cringing, broken.
mirror.
open door.

ocean's roar.
she wants.

waves.
make her.

forget.
undo her.
falter.
   ing.

quench her.
rage.
wash.
  Blood.

but.
the shadow.
comes.
love in me
the likes of which you
can scarcely imagine
in.

out there.
sea moan.
cold.

wind.
evil.
impatient.

born.
screaming.
like she.

wants.
to scream.
like she.
would. scream.

if.
They had.
given her.
a tongue.

REVENGE OF THE SORCERER

An Elak of Atlantis Story
By Adrian Cole

Illustrated by Jim Pitts

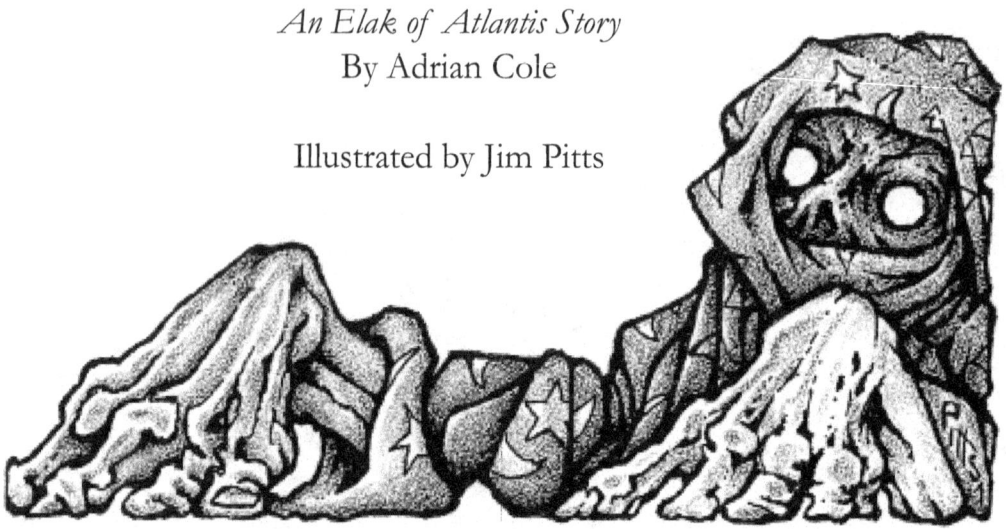

Chapter One: A Gift for the Pirate's Daughter

Kazraan considered himself as good a pirate thief as anyone; few of his fellow cutthroats would have argued with him. His bloody career had won him many a prize but he had decided the time was ripe for greater promotion. He had his own ship, the *Vagabond*, and it had won him a worthy reputation among the red-handed brethren of the Eastern Islands and beyond, the waters controlled by Atlantis. The royal navies of the capital had brought many a freebooter to task, but Kazraan was too quick for the sailors of the young king, Elak.

What better way for Kazraan to advance himself than to win Shiveeri, the daughter of the pirate overlord, Amaal the Black, that one-eyed killer who ruled his own fleet with a ferocity and determination that had made him the terror of the seas, and which had made his citadel, Zeranga, an impregnable

fortress, as powerful as those of other nations who did not bow to the Atlantean throne. The larger independent island states paid deference to Elak's empire, rather than risk war and probably absorption into the empire; Zeranga was for the most part treated in the same way. Sooner or later, though, Elak was bound to launch a full-blooded assault on the pirate stronghold. Amaal was too stubborn and crazed to sue for peace. He would bring the pirate brethren to defeat and slavery before agreeing to a treaty. Kazraan, a much younger man than the grizzled pirate leader, saw opportunities in capitulation with an empire that was growing stronger under its new monarch.

Kazraan gripped his sword tightly and moved through the dense jungle foliage, climbing to the heights of this island, following instructions given to him by the old priest, who had died cursing this Isle of Bones, on which many of his own followers had come to a bitter end over the years. Kazraan would risk much to win the hand of Shiveeri. Here, at the heart of the island, among the ghost-hung ruins of a temple older than memory, there was said to be an idol, with twin jewels for eyes—jewels of such dazzling beauty and possessed of such magical powers, that they would bestow upon anyone who claimed them the powers of a demi-god.

What a gift they would make for the magnificent daughter of Amaal, Shiveeri the hell-cat, the she-fiend, and the most wondrous of women. Few of the pirates did not lust after her, but none dared risk either her cutting tongue or the light blade she used so effectively. She had sliced up many an overzealous would-be suitor in the pirate crews, as ferocious and terrifying a fighter as any of them. No man had yet bedded her, nor would they until she willed it, with or without her father's blessing. The jewels, however, thought Kazraan—now that may be a different matter. If he could procure them for her, surely her cold heart would melt, at least enough for him to win favour.

If she chose him for her mate, his future was secured. He would be Amaal's right arm, and indeed, with Amaal having no other offspring to oppose him, Kazraan could become first in line to rule the pirates, with Shiveeri beside him. He tried not to think of the pleasures it would bring him as he clambered over the crest of another ridge. There was a strong moon tonight and by its rich glow he studied the land falling away before him. As promised, there was a path, narrow and overgrown. A goat would have struggled to use it, but Kazraan was patient and cautious, moving along and down the face of a huge cliff, dropping towards the darkness below, where the jungle had smothered old ruins.

The moonlight picked out shapes in a way that daylight might not have, and Kazraan discerned the unnatural angles of stone buildings, even though they were richly hung with vegetation. He found the one that he had been told of, a huge dome, the roof of what

had once been a temple to gods long discredited. Carefully he climbed out onto its lower rim, using the ivy to pull himself up through broken sections and leaning spars. Here the roof was so ravaged by time that he could climb no higher. However, looking into the darkness, he could see various long tendrils of vine or creeper, limned in moonlight, offering the way downward. He grinned, gripping his blade in his teeth. There was none as agile as he when it came to swinging up into the rigging of a ship, and quickly he grabbed a vine and lowered himself.

It was a long drop, but there was sufficient moonlight dappling the floor for him to see his surroundings. Tall fingers of stone, possibly statues, reared up on either side; he had to wade through sticky pools and heaped, decaying leaves. What he sought, he knew, was at the very centre of the temple. As he squeezed between thick tresses of more vine and cold statue, he sensed light up ahead, unnatural, too bright for moonlight. Like a predator, lithe and silent, he slipped through to the last stone and hid behind it. He found himself on the upper edge of a small amphitheatre, steps curving around it, falling away from his place of concealment.

What he saw both amazed and excited him. There was a gathering of armed warriors here. He did not recognise them—all were clad in thick cloaks sewn with bright feathers, and they wore masks, the fixed expressions of which were demonic and unnerving, the acolytes of some unknown god of the island. Kazraan shuddered at the thought. Did its disciples still flourish here, in secret? Who were these people?

They had a high priest, for the one raised above them on a small stepped area, wore an elaborate garment, rattling with gold and jewels, a suit that would itself have fetched a fortune among the pirate traders. The being pointed with a silver rod at the altar in the centre of the clearing and as Kazraan watched, something rose up from below ground, as though a tomb were delivering its contents to the outer world. Darkness cloaked the shape that was stretched out on the rising slab, which seemed human in form, but far larger than a man. A grotesque statue, perhaps.

The high priest pulled aside his robes and held out two objects that made Kazraan gasp anew. The jewels! The huge, scarlet jewels he had come here to pilfer! There they were, and light shone from within them, as though, like organs, they beat with living energy.

That light focused itself into a radiant beam, searching the darkness above the arena, probing like a finger until it struck the stone behind which Kazraan hid. At once the stone dissolved and Kazraan felt himself gripped by fingers of ice, deep to the bone. He was dragged, completely unable to resist, out to the lip of the arena and then down over its broken steps. The acolytes moved to one side as Kazraan, writhing and twisting uselessly, was flung under the altar stone. He could not move a muscle, his eyes gazing up at whatever was on the stone. He could feel intense waves of something execrable and intensely evil, and a smell that almost overpowered him. Blood! The stones were stained with it.

He heard the voice of the high priest, invoking the old gods and calling upon one of them. Kazraan recognised the name of an ancient, cursed sorcerer, Quazzir-Rahan—these gathered acolytes meant to bring the fiend back into this world. The sudden blaze of scarlet light—from the jewels, Kazraan knew—infused the thing on the altar and the massive being began to quiver with life. One huge foot shifted as the colossus clambered from its deeply weathered sarcophagus.

Kazraan's last thought before the terrible pain began was that he was the sacrifice, the means by which this horror would again stride the world.

Chapter Two: The Bone Citadel

The Atlantean galley hove to at the mouth of the wide inlet, the oarsmen lifting their long blades, pausing to draw breath, while up in the prow of the sleek vessel, the captain studied the coastal greenery of the island. Behind the mass of jungle, steep, forbidding mountains reared up against the backdrop of a troubled sky, where racing thunderheads presaged the coming of a storm.

"What place is this?" said the young man at the captain's shoulder. He was tall, slender but well-muscled, with a gaze as keen as any eagle's.

"It is the Isle of Bones, sire," said the captain, studying the features of the young Atlantean king. The latter had proven more than once to be a warrior of remarkable skill and agility, perhaps a little tempestuous and incautious for his own good, but his people loved a man who led by example. He was here, on this expedition, much against the wishes of his Council, who forever worried about the risks the king took in administering to his empire. It was well known that Elak preferred an adventurer's life to that of court, but short of providing him with enough troops and sailors to protect his back, there was little they could do to rein him in.

"The principal township is Golgundir, sire, at the far end of yon inlet. Word reached us that the *Sea Eagle* docked there before she was lost."

"Take us in," said Elak. "Anchor offshore. I'll have the men alerted for action. If this is an ambush, we'll be well prepared."

Another figure stirred beside him. In contrast to the king, the man was less tall, but far bulkier, his ample weight suggesting sluggishness and probably a general disinterest in activity, but those who knew him understood well his own skill with a sword and the deceptive energy housed in that bulky frame. Lycon snorted, glaring at the far shore.

"I've a nose for treachery," he said. "And

right now, it's telling me to keep well away from that place. Furthermore, there's a storm brewing. If we're to be caught, better to ride it out on the waves than in that sinister place."

Elak clapped his friend on the shoulders and grinned. "These eastern islands are full of terrors for you, Lycon, since we fell foul of Doom Island and its horrors a while back. Will you avoid setting foot on them for the rest of your days?"

"By Bel, I'd rather be a poor sailor than a good meal for a tribe of savage cannibals, Elak. That place is called the Isle of Bones for good reason."

Elak turned to the captain. "What do you know of this place, Galtuus? I thought the rumours about cannibalism were merely spread to keep unwanted travellers at bay."

"Golgundir is a trading port, sire. If there are cannibals hereabouts, they live up in the mountains. At worst they come down periodically to trade. We may not receive the warmest of greetings in the town, but our company would certainly deter any hostile moves."

"Tell that to the missing crew of the *Sea Eagle*," snapped Lycon.

"Where do you think she is?" Elak asked the captain.

"Perhaps the people of Golgundir can tell us," said Galtuus.

With the storm drawing ever closer, promising to be no minor event, it was decided to steer the galley into port, in spite of Lycon's growing misgivings. Elak put his faith in the two hundred and fifty warriors his ship held—each of them had been hand-picked by his commanders as the best available in the service of the king. The missing *Sea Eagle* had been a much smaller ship, with far fewer men, so may have been more susceptible to an attack.

Golgundir had a deep water harbour, with enough draught to take the Atlantean war galley. Word came down from the lookout that there was very little activity in the port. Elak, puzzled, insisted on shinning up the rigging

to take a clearer look for himself, his warriors below grinning to each other, although Galtuus' unease was clear to read.

Elak studied Golgundir's cramped streets from the masthead. They were indeed almost deserted, and he wondered if the townsfolk had simply taken cover on seeing the war galley. Yet there was an atmosphere about the place, an undoubted air of weirdness, something indefinable and sinister. Sorcery, Elak wondered. It would be a brave opponent of the Empire who dared set up a trap for him and his men, though. Perhaps the inhabitants had abandoned the town, for fear of the Empire's strength.

As Elak watched the buildings on the quayside, he saw several figures materialise. None of them seemed to be armed, and they waited quietly. Beyond the buildings, jungles and mountain peaks, the storm clouds rolled in, dark and boiling, an enormous tide.

"Take us in!" Elak called to the captain and the galley moved forward sleekly, soon tying up on the quay.

The men who had come here as a reception committee were a ragged bunch, surly and economical with words. They accorded minimal respect to Galtuus as he disembarked with a handful of warriors. Elak and Lycon stepped ashore, the latter watching every window for signs of a threat, his hand firmly grasping his sword hilt.

One of the townsmen, a scruffy individual whose face and bare arms were laced with strange tattoos and whose ears were hung with bright gold rings, inclined his head in a sleepy bow. "Men of Empire are always welcome," he said mechanically.

"We'll rest here while the storm passes," said Galtuus. "Can you provide for us? You'll be well paid."

"Of course," said the man. His fellows, looking no less like vagrants, all bowed. They glanced at Elak, and although the king had made no effort to announce himself—nor would he—they clearly understood he must be a person of some importance. Quietly they led the way to the first of the inns, while behind them the sailors attended to the safe berthing of their ship, as the first huge droplets of rain splattered the quay.

Chapter Three: Dark Alliance

Seated around the huge table, eating meagre fare and drinking beer that Lycon pronounced volubly to be watered down seal's piss, Elak and his immediate bodyguard heard the growl of thunder overhead and the incessant beating of rain on the slated roof.

"What do you know of our ship, the *Sea Eagle*?" Galtuus asked of the seated trio of men who were spokesmen for the port.

"Only that she berthed for one night, sire," said the first of them, his eyes never still, his whole manner one of unease, as though he would bolt at the first opportunity. "Like you, her men fed here, slept for a short while, leaving with the dawn."

"You watched the ship leave the inlet?" said Lycon impatiently.

"Aye, master. She took to the open sea. There was a sea fog that day. Unusual for the season, but there is a cold current running in from the east."

Elak considered the man's words quietly. He knew that the crew of the *Sea Eagle*, some hundred men, had all been fine seamen and the kind of warriors he'd want in a difficult situation. If they had been involved in a fight, it would have taken a powerful enemy to defeat them, much less remove all sign of them or their ship. They had been escorting one of Elak's principal commanders, Dannovas, a fierce but disciplined warrior whose loyalty to the throne was unquestioned, to a secret rendezvous with agents of the pirate warlord, Amaal the Black. The pirate and Elak had been conducting clandestine negotiations, which were intended to result in an unprecedented treaty; this was to have been sealed by a marriage between Dannovas and Amaal's

notorious daughter, Shiveeri. Elak grinned to himself whenever he thought of the girl, whom he had seen only once—but by Bel she had created an impression! Dannovas was putting his head into the mouth of a mountain lioness!

Whether the girl had any interest in having Dannovas for a husband, Elak could not say, but she stood to gain much from the alliance with the Empire, so the thinking was that she would play along. Dannovas would be a worthy catch for her—he was a fine man, an excellent warrior, and of course, he enjoyed considerable Atlantean wealth. That, most of all, would appeal to a pirate wench.

However, all this careful planning and bargaining, which had been going on for several months, trying Elak's patience to the limit, was now jeopardised by the loss of the *Sea Eagle*, Dannovas and his crew. The situation had been exacerbated by some of Elak's councillors grumbling from the beginning about the foolhardiness of trusting pirates and the likelihood of betrayals and other skulduggery. Elak had to admit now that there was a possibility that Amaal had deceived him, but his gut feeling was that there was far more to this. The reason for the secrecy surrounding the negotiations was that Amaal knew full well that not all of the pirate leaders were in favour of an alliance with the Empire. They knew it would bring restrictions on their practices and limit the prizes they could win on the open seas.

If Elak had sent out a small fleet to search for Dannovas, he knew that the world would immediately learn of all the subterfuge and private wheeling and dealing. To avoid that, he had set out in his single ship, crewed with elite warriors, donning an alias for himself and Lycon. He was not well known in Atlantis—and even less so beyond its immediate waters—so he had been confident of maintaining the deceit on this voyage. His prime suspicion was that rival pirates, who sought to oust Amaal and rule the freebooters in his stead, were behind whatever perfidy had taken place. Sadly, Dannovas may be lost.

Elak's thoughts were broken as Lycon gripped his arm gently. "By the Nine Hells, Elak, we'll learn nothing from these dolts. Not unless you want me to have them taken outside and hung up over the waters of the bay, with the threat of using them for shark bait if they don't—"

"They're frightened of something, my friend. Us, of course, but more than that. They have to live in these pirate waters. If they've been threatened already, they'll cling to their silence. I'm sure you'll have better opportunities to use your sword before this affair is done. Let's get some rest and hope the storm blows itself out in the night."

Back in the ship they bedded down for the night, but the young king was restless and could not sleep. Thunder rolled incessantly overhead, the rain lashing the ship, which tossed up and down at her moorings. Lycon would have slept ashore, but he'd drunk enough of the local beer to render him unconscious as soon as he hit his bunk, murderous storm or no. Elak grinned at the sprawled shape and slipped out of the cabin and up under a deck awning. His guards were beside him in moments, anxious to protect him.

"The outer sea is as dangerous as anything I've seen before, sire" said Haruk, master of the night watch. "And this inlet is little better. 'Tis unnatural."

"Sorcery, you think?"

The watchman grunted, and the king knew he'd prodded a nerve. The islands in this part of the empire were notorious for witchery and deviltry. He was only sorry he hadn't brought the druid, Dalan, with them. He was always useful in such situations, but he'd been needed back at court, keeping an eye on the various inevitable intrigues.

Elak studied the waves rolling in from beyond the inlet's mouth to the harbour, churning around the ship. It was as though each wave was bulging with sea life, shapes

that swelled it, a small army of elemental creatures, determined to bring havoc to the sailors. The noise was deafening, sea and sky both, as the rain hammered down.

"See! There!" shouted one of the watch. Elak and Haruk both craned their necks to get a view over the rail. Out in the inlet, the waters swirled in a huge vortex, a whirlpool that revolved so quickly it flung up debris from the sea's bottom, exposing a long length of muddy bed. Abruptly a huge shape burst up from the muck, an immense, worm-like creature thrice as long as the galley and twice its size. The blunt, serpent-like head nosed forward, scenting the ship, intent on attacking it.

The assault was so rapid that the sailors had no time to prepare for it. Elak watched in horror as the monster reared up, its eyes blazing with unnatural, hellish light, its mouth opening to reveal row upon row of jagged teeth, as the creature poised to crash down across the bow of the galley.

Chapter Four: Death From the Sea

As Elak and his men leapt aside, jammed up against the ship's rail, they felt the rancid breath of the huge sea beast as the thing came down with devastating force across the bow of the ship, smashing planks and timbers, allowing a huge wave to break over them. They were swept over the rail in an instant and Elak felt the cold clutch of the churning seas. The danger for him now was of being crushed between the ship and the harbourside, and he dived as deep as he dared in the pitch black murk.

Something thumped into him, possibly another of the sailors, tumbled and twisted in the watery chaos, and for a moment the king felt himself pinned against cold rocks and clinging weed. He kicked out in desperation and moved forward along the bottom of the harbour wall until his lungs reached bursting

point and he was forced to break surface. He took a deep lungful of air and dove again, arrowing away from the nightmare behind him. Twice more he surfaced and dived until another great wave lashed in and swept him up like a doll, flinging him over the quay.

The lower streets of the port were inundated by the continuing advance of the sea, whipped up by the storm's seemingly superhuman purpose, as though half the demons in hell had amassed to fuel it. Elak was utterly powerless to prevent himself from being tossed about, almost knocked unconscious. Several times he tried to get to his feet, only to have them sucked out from under him by the swirling current. He was dragged backwards, towards the quay repeatedly, barely able to grip the wall of a building and prevent himself from being dragged out into the watery chaos once more. He rolled over and fought his way upright, grabbing at a doorway and using it to gain some respite.

He looked towards the ship, only to behold disaster. The huge sea worm had crashed down upon it more than once, wrecking it, driving whole sections underwater, twisting so violently that the oars were snapped like matchwood, the masts ripped down and snapped. The last of the men who had been on board were desperately trying to find a way ashore, but the combination of rolling deck and hammering waves was too much for them and one by one they were hurtled into the merciless foam.

Elak saw with horror that the sea beast had sucked up a number of victims, opening its pink-lined mouth to devour them whole. How many men could have survived this dreadful assault? He clung to the door as another wave lashed him; his fingers were tugged free as he felt himself again swept far up the street, thumped against its narrow walls. As the water receded, he got to his knees, retching, eventually managing to get beyond the deeper water. He staggered further upwards, fighting the driving rain, until he reached firmer ground.

There were other survivors around him, and he saw Haruk and a few of his watch. They came to him, exhausted, relieved to see their king was alive.

"I fear the ship is lost," Haruk gasped, his face white in the dim light of the alley.

"What of those who were on board?" said Elak. "Are we the only survivors?"

No one answered and they feared the worst. Elak felt a deep stab of sorrow – Lycon! Gods, had he perished in this catastrophe?

Lights from beyond the alley snared his attention and he saw a group of men, robed and cowled against the unflagging storm, all carrying blazing firebrands that defied the rain. They wound down from the higher streets in a silent procession. Their leader came to Elak. He wore a mask, as though he might be the priest of some secret cult, these robed beings the acolytes. A bizarre, scarlet light shone from within the eyes of the mask, eerie and somehow not human.

"Keep away from the harbour," said the man. "If there are survivors, we will find them." He said no more, waving his party down towards the quay, where the heaving seas were showing signs of calming at last. Elak followed with his men, but they kept their distance, fearing another driving wave. They could see the robed beings lining the harbour, their brands held high. In that garish light, the mangled wreckage of the ship was clearly visible, tossed this way and that, out on the waters. The destruction had been total.

At first it seemed that the huge sea beast had returned to the deeps, but abruptly the waters burst aside to reveal that terrible head once more and it swung upwards and readied to crash down on the robed gathering. However, the men swung their torches in blazing arcs, their voices lifting in a combined chant. Elak realised uneasily that the sea beast was responding, its head weaving to and fro, as though the creature was entranced.

"By Ishtar," growled Haruk. "They have power over that thing!"

Elak nodded. His unease grew. This whole business was beginning to seem contrived. The sea beast sank back into the sea, disappearing. The waves no longer raged, and overhead the storm clouds moved away, the rain easing.

"Search every street for survivors!" Elak shouted. "And have the harbour scoured— see if there are any men left in the water."

His sailors were quick to respond and Elak joined the search himself, his guts knotted. It was not long before the first bodies were pulled from the waterlogged streets —some men had been killed, either drowned or battered to death by the violence of the waves against walls and buildings, but others, mercifully, were yet alive. Coughing and spluttering they stumbled back to life.

Elak found Lycon, buried under a smashed cart that contained countless sacks of grain, some of which had split and disgorged their contents across the muddied street. Elak and two of his men dragged Lycon's inert form from the debris and rolled him over onto his back. For a moment Elak was certain that his companion of so many years was dead, but the huge form quivered and emptied itself of a mixture of beer and ocean, presently cursing as roundly and imaginatively as he had ever done.

"Not much wrong with him," Elak said to his men, though their laughter was strained.

Lycon rose unsteadily to his feet, gripping the broken cartwheel for support. "Gods of the pits! That was some nightmare." He gazed about him. "This is not the cabin—"

"No," said Elak.

"And I'm soaking wet! What in damnation— ?"

"Get yourself dry, old friend. Time for explanations later."

"What demented realm is this?" Lycon pointed to one of the buildings. "Who builds a house from such things?"

Puzzled, Elak turned to see what had caught Lycon's eye. It was only then that he noted the partial construction of the nearest building. It was bricked, but other things had been used in its making. They were unmistakably bones. Many bones. And they were clearly recognisable as human.

Chapter Five: Fangs in the Night

The search of the surrounding streets did not take Elak's men long. They gathered around the young monarch, faces drawn, spirits ebbing like the tide in the night. There were, all told, little more than thirty survivors out of the entire crew. They had all managed somehow to retain their arms, but it was poor consolation given the huge losses.

"I like not these hooded creatures," said Haruk, pulling Elak to one side. "They controlled that beast from the sea. You saw how easily they directed it back out into the waters. You heard them chanting. Perhaps they summoned it, too."

Another sailor stood alongside them. "Sire, I was atop the mast when the ship was smitten. I was thrown into the sea and cast up in the streets by the waves. But before I fell, I saw much of the sea bed the storm had opened up to view. I saw—I saw—ships, sire! Many broken ships. I thought one of them was—the *Sea Eagle*, the ship of Dannovas."

Elak cursed. "We must quit this place. We go upwards to higher ground."

Another of his men called out, pointing to the lower streets. "They follow!" The man indicated more of the hooded inhabitants, who appeared to have grown in numbers. They were moving as one, it seemed with a menacing purpose. Elak led his men upwards to the last of the streets to where the silent jungles of the mountain's lower reaches awaited them. However, there were more blurred shapes lurking up there and it was evident a fresh trap awaited the Altanteans.

Lycon drew his sword and snarled a fresh curse. "If it's a fight these scum want, let's get at them!"

Elak had his men form a close, wedge-shaped unit and cautiously they moved up the incline. They were soon beyond the last houses and overhead a curved splinter of moon shed the barest of light on the land-scape. Shapes detached from the jungle, four-legged creatures that loped downhill and whose fangs gleamed. Their heads were more human than animal, as if these horrors had once enjoyed a more human form. No longer! The eyes of the beast-things gleamed with scarlet hell-fire light as Elak's men echoed the snarls of their assailants and they drove for-ward, fuelled by a thirst for revenge. Man and beast clashed furiously and swords flashed in the moonlight, blood spraying as steel bit into flesh and fang tore at Elak's faithful.

The sailors, well drilled and organised, sliced through the heart of the things that howled and slavered at them, huge, wolf-like beasts that seemed to have been spawned in some demonic underworld, minions of dark and terrible sorcery. Lycon roared as he de-capitated three of the horrors, and Elak was equally as deadly with his rapier, plucking out the eyes of the foe and slashing open their throats.

Yet it was an unequal contest. It was as though the sailors had stumbled on a nest of the beasts, who came on in wave after wave, encouraged by the hooded shapes that kept themselves at the periphery of the carnage, silently directing affairs. Elak and his men were driven back, towards another arm of the jungle. There was a brief lull as the huge hounds of the night gathered themselves for a concerted assault that would surely be the end of the Atlanteans.

A lone voice broke the stillness, calling from the undergrowth.

Elak strained his eyes against the dark, but he could see a young man there, clothed roughly, waving to him. "This way," the youth called. "There is a way here."

"Another trap," growled Lycon.

Elak waved one of the sailors over to the youth. "Go—carefully."

The sailors closed around their king, pre-paring to sell their lives dearly as the things above them began the slow creep forward they knew would be the prelude to the final attack. Several more Altanteans had fallen and it could only be a matter of time before they were all torn apart.

"There is a path," called the scout.

"We'll risk it," said Elak and led his men into the spur of jungle. He heard a unified howl of fury behind him as the hounds bounded forward. In moments he and the last of his men were swallowed by the thick jungle walls, winding and twisting through the tunnel-like curves of the narrow path-way. They had gone some distance into the jungle's humid embrace when a shout went up from the rear of the column. The hounds had not followed.

"Well," said Lycon, wiping thick blood from his sword on a robe already sodden and ripped. "Either they fear this place, or they've herded us into it."

"We're alive, old friend," said Elak, with a grin. He felt no warmth, though, trying to set aside his horror at the death of so many of his men. Someone would pay for this, he swore.

Ahead of them the path debouched into a more open area where the rampant jungle had drawn back, as though its tendrils and vines wormed their way around the space, re-pelled by it. There were stones here, heaped randomly, but others suggested ruins, ancient and rotting, a place long forgotten and dis-used. Haruk faced the king with a fresh look of unease. He had discovered more bones, many of them, and countless skulls, piled high in pyramids. This was a place of death, a midden.

Elak had their young rescuer brought be-fore him. Scrawny, wide-eyed with fear, the youth fell before Elak and pressed his head to the ground. "Spare me, master!" he cried.

Elak knelt down and lifted the boy's head. "Who are you, and what is this place?"

"I am Sharferim, sire. An orphan of Golgundir. For years my people worshipped the gods of the islands and gave them many sacrifices. This is one of many shrines on the Isle of Bones." Once the boy started talking, his words tumbled out of him like a stream. "That was long in our past. Peace came at last and we traded with the pirates. These old shrines fell into ruin. No one visits them anymore. Now a new terror has arisen in the heart of the mountains. A terrible being has been resurrected. The people of Golgundir have been corrupted, sire. Things from the darkness have taken them and enslaved their minds. My own parents were killed. I escaped and live as I can on the mountain. Our city is overrun. Only the ancient places of bone are sanctuary for us now. You will not be attacked here."

"What of the sea beast that destroyed my ship?" said Elak.

"Since the sorcerer has risen, such things have come to plague the islands and the seas. No one is safe from this plague."

"Sorcerer?" said Lycon. "Who is he? What brought him to this remote place?"

"He is said to be very ancient, sire. Banished centuries ago from Atlantis. Chained by powerful magic under the earth, for he is indestructible. Now he is awake."

Chapter Six : Pirate Plunder

"Does this sorcerer have a name?" said Lycon.

Sharferim lowered his voice, barely above a whisper. "Quazzir-Rahan."

"By the Nine Hells!" Lycon gasped. "That's a name from a hundred years past."

Elak nodded, his face grave. "He grew to power when my grandfather, then the prince,

was young. As an old man, he told me of the time of the great sorcerer and the plot he hatched to try to take control of the throne of Atlantis through his manipulations and intrigues. A being of frightful power, who almost brought ruin on the Empire."

"Wasn't he destroyed?" said Lycon.

"Banished and chained up with sorcery that even the Council of the city were afraid of. Taken to a remote island and thrust deep under the earth, surrounded by magics that were thought to be unbreakable."

"This island?" said Lycon.

"The location was kept secret. But this could well be it." Elak turned to the youth. "You say he has risen, Sharferim. How is that so? Who could have undone the sorcery that bound him? The powers that were used were beyond the comprehension of even the most accomplished of mages."

"It is whispered among my people, sire, that two magnificent jewels were found in a treasure hoard that was lost since the days of the lizard warriors. The jewels contain powers from the dawn of man. They have fallen into the hands of worshippers of Quazzir-Rahan and it is these objects that have renewed his life and raised him."

Elak again nodded. "What are these jewels?"

"I have heard it said that they are serpent's eyes, sire," said the youth. "From a great creature, once slain by the sorcery of lost eons. A servant of the snake-god, Set."

Lycon gasped. "This is evil news of the worst kind, Elak. Such things should never reach the light of day. If Quazzir-Rahan has possession of the jewels—"

"He has them," said Sharferim. "They are his eyes now."

"Yes, I understand," said Elak. "The eyes of the sea beast and those of the creatures that have attacked us, all of them were infused with power—the commanding will of the sorcerer. We must find him and destroy him."

"Elak—I will always be the first to stand with you in a fight," said Lycon, "but surely we are too ill-equipped for such a contest! We are no more than two dozen strong. We must go back to Atlantis and bring a fleet, and as many mages as we can muster. Quazzir-Rahan will have powers beyond imagining."

"Indeed," said Elak. "Your head overrules my heart in this. Very well. Sharferim, can you help us get away? We need a ship or at least passage on one."

The youth scowled. "I would not trust my people, sire. They would attack you again—too many have fallen under the spell of the sorcerer. I know of only one other way off the island. Below us are the old caves. They riddle the island like holes in cheese. I know my way through them. I can take you down to the place where the pirates store their treasure."

"Oh-ho!" said Lycon, a rare smile cracking his features. "What is this?"

"The Isle of Bones is shunned by most," Sharferim went on. "The pirates have therefore made it a safe haven, and use some of the great sea caves north east of the island. They are there now, with a ship."

Elak glanced at Lycon. "We could seek their help, but it would be a dangerous game. Who are these pirates? Who rules them?" he asked the youth.

"I never go close to them, sire. They would take me and make me work on their ship."

Elak and his men discussed their situation. The young king listened to the men, many of whom were veterans and whose opinions he respected. They knew they could speak their mind to him. After a while it was agreed—they would go in search of the pirates and review their position then. If it came to it, they would attempt to take the ship. Lycon grinned, evidently more than willing to fight.

Sharferim led them to an old stone building and through a partially collapsed door that opened down into darkness and steps that dropped dizzily away. Several firebrands were lit and soon the party was descending into the gloom, a place of weirdly sculpted rock and disused tunnels, as though the men were worming their way through a mausoleum from another age. They glimpsed old, crumbling statues, representations of creatures and deities long forgotten, glad of the sepulchral silence.

It was a long time before they were able to discard the last of the firebrands and see by the light that filtered in from overhead and the fissures that led up to the surface. Day had broken, and from ahead the men could hear the whisper of the sea as waves rolled in and broke on the rocks of the caves. The place was labyrinthine, but Sharferim knew his way around every stone and weed-hung rock. Without his help, Elak and his men would have become hopelessly lost.

"If you climb along this ledge," said the youth, "you will come to a rough quay. The ship is moored some way along it. I dare not come with you."

"We'll protect you," Elak promised him.

Still Sharferim demurred. "My place is here. If you need me again, I will aid you." With that he slipped away, lithe as a sea otter; the darkness of the inner cave soon took him.

Elak drew his rapier and grinned at Lycon. "Let's see what awaits us."

Stealthily the party moved along the narrow ledge, the waters of the cave gurgling beneath them. The daylight grew stronger and in its glow they could see the wide, high mouth of the cavern. Silhouetted against the early morning light, a small pirate craft bobbed on the sluggish tide. Voices came from the ship, laughter, curses, and sounds of men working, fetching and carrying. Elak sent two of his men to scout, waiting in the rocks for their return.

A while later the men reported back. "A small craft, sire. Unloading a cargo of casks that probably contain wine. The ship is no bigger than a small galley, with no more than fifty oars. A coastal vessel, not for use on the high seas."

"Probably serving a larger ship moored out in deeper water," said Lycon. "How many men?"

"Maybe seventy, no more than that."

Lycon grinned wolfishly. "Good odds."

Elak chuckled. "They'll be fighting men, for sure. Even so, they may be willing to talk. Come; let's see what they're made of."

The sailors formed their usual wedge-shaped unit, protecting Elak, and he took them along the quay, prepared for hostility if it should arise. In a moment one of the pirates gave the alarm and a score or more were on the quay, various weapons gleaming in the morning sun. Their leader, a sun-scorched fellow with broken teeth and a glare that would have cracked a rock open, stood, arms folded aggressively, his men quickly falling in beside him, primed for the violent protection of their plunder.

Chapter Seven: Lord of the Seas

Elak motioned for his men to keep their weapons at their sides, although Lycon was like a caged beast, eager to surge forward.

"You're on the wrong island," growled the pirate spokesman, deliberately spitting his contempt.

Elak went closer, lowering his voice. "I daresay. But we are the king's men."

"You're a long way from Atlantis."

"And would return to it, with all speed."

"Why are you here?"

"Shipwrecked in last night's storm, and attacked by a sea serpent at Golgundir. There are some evil forces at work on this island."

The pirate grimaced. "Aye, that's true."

"My men are well trained in warfare. If it's a fight you want, we'll give it to you. But there'll be few left standing if we do, on either side I suspect."

The pirate stiffened. However, he was weighing the situation up, knowing that a fight would indeed mean casualties, perhaps

more than he would have liked. "So what do you want, king's man?"

"To return to our own islands. Safe passage. We'll work for our keep."

The pirate grinned. "A strange alliance, but then, these are strange times. There's sorcery unleashed in these waters. No man is safe. Wait here." He turned abruptly and went to speak to his men. A group of them gathered around him.

Elak went back to Lycon and Haruk and explained what he had said. Lycon shook his head, fearing treachery, although Haruk seemed less volatile.

"They'll be wary of attacking king's men, especially with a treaty in the offing. And they'll know about Amaal's dealings with you, sire, even if they didn't recognise you."

After a while the pirate came back to Elak. "I am Jarrood. An independent trader and no enemy to Atlantis. We'll get you across to Mallomas, an island where Atlantean ships regularly dock. It's a day's journey. Have your men eaten? We've food enough, if they want it."

"Thank you," said Elak. "You'll be well rewarded. I'm Kellomor, commander in the army of Elak, the king." They did not shake hands, but for now the air between them was seemingly untroubled. Elak's men were quickly assembled and took their place on the small pirate galley, where they were fed, true to Jarrood's word. His free traders ate from the same hot food the cook had prepared, so no one feared being poisoned; the tension that had thickened the air when the two parties first met eased considerably.

Lycon, however, remained like a cat on hot tiles, never far from Elak's side. He'd been offered wine, but for once declined. "I'll be glad when we reach Mallomas, Elak. These dogs would eat their own mothers if the need arose."

"They don't want a fight, my friend. They know a good fighting man when they see one."

The morning passed without incident and Elak's sailors lent their own seamanship to the skills of the pirates and a curious camaraderie began to grow. The sea, Elak thought, is a great leveller. It was a hot day, the sea calm, the ship working the current across the deep water divide between the islands, and for a while the events back on the Isle of Bones receded, although the young king yet mourned the loss of so many of his men.

Sometime after the sun had passed its zenith, a sail was spotted out on the gently rocking waters, and then several others. Elak was aware all too soon that the ships were not from his own navy. More pirates, a small fleet in fact.

"We're not going to be able to outrun them," Jarrood told him, although he could hardly suppress a broken grin. "They'll cut us off long before we reach land."

"I know that sail," said Lycon. "A black eagle insignia with crossed blades beneath it."

"Amaal," said Elak. "Let me do the talking, but have the men told discreetly to be ready. He will know me. We may be potential allies, but out here, Ishtar alone knows how he will react at having me at his mercy." He turned to Jarrood. "You serve Amaal? You are bound to him?"

"Of course. Few of the lesser captains in these waters stand against him. Not if they want to live!"

Soon afterwards the small galley was surrounded by several larger pirate galleys, and Elak knew he and his men were to be presented to the ship of their ruler. Clearly it had been Jarrood's intention all along. Such things were to be expected. Lines were thrown across the two ships and Jarrood indicated to Elak and Lycon that they should go over to Amaal's craft. Its sides were lined with numerous sea veterans, warriors armed to the teeth, their faces lit up with grim smiles, like sharks awaiting feeding time.

Elak stepped on to the deck and was met by two burly ruffians, who bowed low, probably mockingly. "Welcome to the *Sea Bitch*,"

said one of them. "A pleasure it is to have men of the great Atlantean kingdom aboard."

"Thank you," said Elak. "I should remind you that, as the king's men, we enjoy the protection of the lord of Atlantis, even here."

There were chuckles and a few bursts of laughter among the assembled crew, but Elak ignored them.

Another figure pushed through the men and stood brazenly before the two Atlanteans. He was a huge fellow of some sixty years and wore fine clothes and a thick belt with three fat cutlasses thrust into it. His skin was burned a deep bronze, his single eye blazing in the sunlight as he fixed its wild stare upon Elak.

"As my guest, Elak, king of Atlantis, you are under my protection. Whatever fate befalls you will, believe me, be at my behest. You are, of course, very welcome." Amaal the Black bowed low.

"I trust that the good work our ambassadors have achieved in preparing the treaty between us goes well with you."

Amaal nodded slowly. "It heartens me to see you have come in person. I think, however, there are other matters of concern. Come; let us go to my private quarters. Your men will be perfectly safe—for now."

Elak and Lycon followed the huge pirate down into the belly of the warship. Amaal had had food and drink prepared, but both Atlanteans took sparingly of it.

"You are seeking Dannovas," said Amaal, eager to cut to the bone of matters. "I awaited his ship eagerly. My daughter, Shiveeri, was also very keen to see the *Sea Eagle* enter our port. It never arrived, as you will know, Elak."

"Whatever powers have risen on the Isle of Bones played their evil part in that. I fear Dannovas is lost."

"Almost certainly. There is worse news," said the pirate lord, his face wreathed in suppressed anger and something more—sorrow perhaps. "Shiveeri has been abducted. That creature on the Isle of Bones has taken her."

Chapter Eight: Blood in the Surf

Elak paced the narrow cabin restlessly, face clouded with frustration and anger. "It's far too dangerous, Amaal! I've lost over three hundred men on this venture. I have to go back to Cyrena and tell their families. Then I need my entire navy here! You cannot risk sending your fleet in. Quazzir-Rahan will unleash the same terrible powers that slaughtered my men!"

"You think I will stand by and let him persecute my only child!"

Lycon waited for the two men to pause for breath. It was obvious they were getting close to coming to blows over the strategy for Shiveeri's rescue. "There is another way," he said.

Both men turned to him, Amaal's single eye gleaming, his body quivering with all the pent-up fury an enraged father could summon. "What way?"

"Elak is right—a full-on attack would mean chaos. There's no time for us to return to Atlantis and bring a fleet. But perhaps a small unit of men, say two score, could slip in under the defences of the sorcerer's acolytes, without being detected. A swift, direct stroke."

Amaal seemed ready to protest, but weighed Lycon's words for a moment. "It would be unexpected. Quazzir-Rahan would be watching for a fleet, an invasion."

"That's why he's done this," said Elak. "To bring you to him."

"So that he could crush me," Amaal nodded.

"Send the fleet in so far," said Elak. "A subterfuge, to draw the attention of the sorcerer. Stay beyond the inner shores of the island. Long enough for a small party to land. Where would be the worst, most hazardous place to do it?"

Amaal grunted. "Obviously—Shark Point. The northern tip of The Isle of Bones. The tidal rip there is deadly and the rocks are infested with seals. Sharks patrol the waters ceaselessly, able to fill their bellies with seal meat whenever they're hungry, which is always."

"So there's no reason, "said Lycon, "for the sorcerer to have the point watched."

"Only a madman would try to land a boat there," said Amaal. "That, or a desperate man."

"My men are the best seamen in Atlantis," said Elak. "They like a challenge."

Amaal laughed. "Indeed? You think they'd be a match for my corsairs! Hah! We must put this to the test."

Elak held out his hand and the two men gripped each other, nodding. Lycon felt a pang of relief, although the idea of shark infested waters swirling around the fangs of a northern cape did not appeal to him. He'd need an entire keg of wine before he took to the seas there.

By late afternoon Amaal's fleet had reached the seas around the Isle of Bones. A stiff breeze had sprung up and the ships bobbed in the increasingly choppy waters. Each had a lookout, studying the sea for any sign of attack from below, monsters such as the creature which had struck Elak's ship at Golgundir. It seemed, however, as though the being on the Isle of Bones was biding its time. The sun slowly dipped in the west and the sea darkened.

Elak, Lycon, Amaal and some two score men, a mixture of Elak's remaining sailors and the best of Amaal's pirates, boarded a small craft. The oars were manned, the mast lowered. By the last daylight, they rowed swiftly for the island's northernmost point; there were no indications they had been discovered. The dark bulk of the island reared up east of them, smothered in a deep, cloying darkness.

The moon was obscured by thickening clouds, and the air smelled of rain, another storm flowing in from the deeper ocean to the east. Elak prayed to his gods that it did not break too early. Their task at Shark's Point would be hellish enough without a storm to contend with. As they rowed ever closer, the northern waters swirled and churned, currents intersecting, producing eddies and whirlpools that threatened to drag the craft down into the depths.

Shark's Point loomed, a fist of cliffs and sharp rocks, etched in the grim, grey light. Waves crashed over the promontory's lower edge, sheets of foam hurled skywards by the impact. The seas surged, rising and falling, creating deep troughs, broken up by the profusion of rocks, and the wind's strength intensified, ripping in from the east. The small craft steadied itself, the oarsmen straining every muscle to keep it afloat. Above the cliffs, the land appeared to be desolate, devoid of life; there seemed no suggestion of a watch there.

Numerous seals had been seen during the late day, the creatures oblivious to the tempestuous environment, and there were shark fins out in the waters from time to time, a reminder that the predators were here, another obstacle to success. Amaal and Elak chose their strongest swimmers, and six men were readied for the first attempt to land. Smeared from head to foot in thick seal grease to protect them from the icy waters, the men dived into the maelstrom that now surrounded the craft, swimming with powerful strokes to the first of the rocks, each of them with a thin, strong rope tied around their waists. If even one of them could fix a line to the shore, it would be a beginning.

Lycon swore profusely, certain that at least three of the men had gone under the creaming surf, never to rise up again, snatched, almost certainly by the waiting sharks. There would be blood in the water now, and that could only mean more of the horrors to contend with. At least two of the swimmers did make it across to the rocks, though, and both made busy affixing their ropes to solid land. There were cheers from the crew as the men

waved, but of the other four, there was no further sign. Four ropes were hauled back into the ship, their ends severed, testament to the worst of the crews' fears. Two ropes ran from the ship's low mast to the shore.

Amaal insisted on being one of the first to swing out over the crashing seas, thick blade clenched in his teeth, huge hands gripping the rope as he dangled. Spume swatted at him, but the old warrior defied the elements and his men—and Elak's—roared encouragement. Elak followed, and as he hovered mid-passage, he looked down into the pink maw of a huge shark, its row upon row of teeth rising as the powerful creature snapped at his dangling legs. Elak swung up, barely avoiding being dragged to a bloody doom. He knew, however, the massive engine of destruction would try for him again and it was a question of who tired the quickest. He feared that it would not be the shark.

Chapter Nine: Under the Temple of Blood

"Ishtar!"cried Lycon, seeing the predicament of the king. Instinctively he snatched up one of the spears that the pirate landing party had brought to the rail. Drawing back his arm, the big Atlantean hurled the missile with all his considerable strength and the men around him gasped as it tore unerringly through the air and ripped into the head of the shark, just below its eye. Blood spurted and the creature tumbled back into the waters, thrashing madly about. Within moments a dozen of its fellows slammed into it, ripping and shredding.

Elak swung across the boiling, bloody cauldron, fingers numbing so he thought he must surely drop and be torn limb from limb, but he reached the shore, where Amaal dragged him to safety. "Gods!" Elak laughed. "I never knew Lycon could use a spear."

Lycon waved, himself surprised at the accuracy of his cast. His wide grin faded, however, as he realised it was his turn to cross, the sailors behind him waiting for him to do so. Praying to as many gods as he could put a name to, the big man gripped the rope and swung out over the foaming maelstrom. His weight brought him within inches of the feasting sharks and he kicked out in desperation, feeling something solid give way. His burly arms swung with amazing dexterity, and roared on by the two lots of men, he reached the shore. The ship rocked and twisted, but the ropes held, and at last all the landing party was safely across.

"That was the easy part," Elak said. "Let's hope no one's seen us."

"Not here," said Amaal. "Seals and gulls—even the sorcerer wouldn't send men to such an inaccessible place."

They moved slowly across the rocks and up the steep cliffs, hampered by the darkness and stone made slippery by the constant drizzle. When they reached the top, a treeless, empty terrain, they moved more swiftly, hugging the ground. The early strains of dawn tainted the eastern skies and they knew they would have to find cover soon.

Ahead of them, a scout called for help and was quickly answered as two of the party joined him. Moments later they brought back a struggling, clawing bundle of humanity. Amaal raised his curved blade and lifted the chin of the captive. "Who are you, and who do you serve?"

Elak put a restraining hand on the huge pirate's arm. "I know this youth. Sharferim! Why are you here?"

"I was watching the seas. I saw your ships, and then your single craft. These are dangerous cliffs and not far from here there are many servants of darkness. You are entering a trap."

Elak signalled for the men to release the youth. "I can help you," said Sharferim. "There are more caves below. You can hide in them by daylight. Otherwise the sorcerer's servants will find you. They would outnum-

ber you by many."

Elak explained to Amaal who the youth was and, somewhat begrudgingly, the pirate agreed to Sharferim taking them to a haven underground. The youth found a wide fissure in the rocks. The sea could be heard crashing and swirling below. Sharferim insisted it was safe; after a while the scouts pronounced it so. The party slid down into darkness but found themselves in a labyrinth of tall caves winding further into the cliffs. Brands were lit as Amaal and Elak rested their men.

"Better a surprise attack by night," said the pirate.

Elak nodded. "Sharferim, do you know the old ruins where the sorcerer has his lair? Can you describe them?"

"Yes, sire. It was a huge temple, but mostly now the walls are collapsed. The central area has been cleared and the sarcophagus has been raised from the tomb beneath it. I have not dared to look upon Quazzir-Rahan. He is brought up from his prison for a brief time each lunar cycle. His servants feed him—blood. Slowly his powers are returning, getting stronger each time he is fed. Soon he will walk free of his chains."

"Sacrifices!" said Lycon. "By the Nine Hells, it is why Shiveeri has been taken."

Amaal swore crudely. "When will the demon walk again?" he snapped at the youth.

"The servants are amassing. It will be soon."

"Then we go tonight," said Amaal.

Elak nodded. "Take us as close to the temple as we can get without being detected," he told Sharferim. "Tell me every detail. Amaal, one of us must assume overall command. We have to coordinate our attack."

The pirate's one eye studied Elak and for a moment it seemed the huge seaman would insist that he lead. "You think I might allow my emotions to diminish my judgement in battle? Perhaps you are right, Elak. Very well, you lead. But I warn you—if there is any danger of my daughter suffering at the hands of this creature, I will raise the demons of hell against him!"

They spent a good part of the day going over a plan of attack, with Sharferim doing his utmost to describe the temple area and every rock, statue and fallen wall within it. The day dragged, and nerves were becoming fraught. A few petty arguments broke out among the men, but both Amaal and Elak silenced them. As night drew on again, the tension had become a palpable force, all of them coiled like serpents eager to strike.

Sharferim guided them through the narrowing caves, explaining there were drains within the temple complex, some of which had not fallen into complete disrepair. They could just be the means to unleashing the shock tactics Elak and Amaal had in mind. The youth led the men like a rat guiding a pack, now stooping in the narrow confines of the old, dried drains, all of them listening out for sounds around them, wondering if the creaking of the stones and the flurries of dust would presage a fall-in. There were whisperings here, like the breath of ghosts, but Sharferim said it would be rodents and other underground creatures.

Lycon felt his throat constricting with fear, dry as a desert, his bulk not suited to this desperate crawl through dimly lit workings. Amaal, an even bigger man, was equally as on edge, his face dripping with sweat.

Sharferim reached a point where several drains led off from the main channel. These, he said, circumvented the main temple area. The men would have to split up. "There are grilles set in the floor above the drains. Open them carefully and you should be able to enter the edges of the temple."

They split into four groups, led by Elak, Lycon, Amaal and Kasim, another pirate, respectively. As they moved along one of the drains, Elak saw a number of narrow pipes feeding into the drain. Each of them was stained, and there was a distinct smell about them, the growing stench of decay, a charnel

reek. The floor was stained and slippery. Elak did not want to dwell on what fluids ran from these pipes. Overhead he heard sounds, voices raised in a rhythmic ululation, the voices, he guessed, of the gathered acolytes of the sorcerer.

Soon, with all of the intruders in position, it would be time to begin the bloody work.

Chapter Ten: The Eyes of the Sorcerer

Elak positioned himself under a grille, his shoulders pressed up against it as he listened to the gathering in the chamber above. Satisfied no one overhead was close, he strained and felt the shifting of the old metal. It was lightweight, but had been fitted in place and overgrown with weeds for many years. Nevertheless it gave. Gradually he eased it upward until he could slide it aside, preparing himself for any sudden attack. None came. The chanting grew in volume as Elak pulled himself up into the shadows, which danced in wavering light from a score of braziers set around the large chamber.

He kept low to the ground and waved up the next of his men. There were a number of crumbling pillars, thicker than a man, ringing the chamber and the curved roof was mostly fallen in, the place open to the night sky. As he slipped behind one of these pillars, Elak studied the nearby darkness for any sign of guards, but the acolytes were gathered at the heart of the chamber, their attention fixed on proceedings there. Slowly his men came up from the drain and spread out along a section of the chamber's rim. Elak couldn't see far around the circumference but had to assume that Amaal, Lycon and the others had all similarly taken up their positions, ringing the chamber.

What he could see, however, made his blood run colder in his veins. In the centre of the chamber, raised up on a rectangular block of ancient, pitted stone, rested a sarcophagus, peppered with glyphs and sigils from a remote age, intermingled with bizarre, carved creatures and demonic, leering faces. Stretched out on this was a figure, a man-shaped body and yet one that was far taller and larger. It was wrapped around in black robes, tight to the skin, as though the being had been embalmed. Silver and gold accoutrements attached to the clothing, the head of which was also wrapped in black cloth. Around this prone being, a hundred or more of its acolytes stood in rapt attention, hands raised to the heavens, themselves attired in ceremonial robes, bejewelled and hung with golden chains.

It would have been a disturbing sight on its own, but what was chained beneath the sarcophagus made Elak's hackles rise. Several men, all recognisable as either Atlanteans or pirates, were slumped there, including the missing Dannovas. Their bodies were shrunken, almost desiccated. All had been slain, blood running freely from severed throats—sacrificial blood, which some of the acolytes were collecting in silver libation bowls. They took these up to the inert figure and emptied their contents over it. As the blood saturated the wrappings of the prone form, steam rose from it until the whole body shuddered into slow life.

One of the figures beneath the sarcophagus was alive. Chained, standing defiantly, a young woman struggled and cursed, her limbs gleaming in the torchlight, her lips pulled back in a feral snarl.

Shiveeri! Elak recognised her. She was to be the last victim, her death the climax of this grotesque ceremony.

Beyond the head of the body on the slab—it could be none other than Quazzir-Rahan himself—the high priest called for a cessation of the chanting. At once a deep silence fell. The darkness of the night overhead pressed in, like a listening, approving god.

"It is time!" called the priest. "Once again we wake our master from the long slumber

of his imprisonment, to right the evils done to him! Tonight he is made whole again. The process will be completed. He will wake, he will walk, and he will live on, freed from his chains—freed to extract his vengeance upon the world that cheated him of his glory!"

From his robes, the priest took two glittering jewels, scarlet orbs the size of apples. Elak had never seen their like before. Their light dazzled, pulsing with a living energy that held him momentarily rigid. Elak knew his companions, sailor and pirate alike, would be equally as entranced by that coruscating power, transfixed. The priest leaned over the comatose sorcerer and bent to its head, lowering the twin jewels. In a moment the huge being stirred, then lifted its bulbous head. Those jewels had become its eyes, as if a great statue had suddenly been imbued with life. It swung its thick legs from the sarcophagus and stood erect, towering over the girl.

"A last sacrifice!" called the priest as the acolytes roared their approval. "Her blood will fully rejuvenate Quazzir-Rahan."

Shiveeri snarled her fury like a huge cat, tugging at her chains, her arms stretched as if they would snap with the effort. As the shape of the sorcerer bent, something tore through the air, which was suddenly filled with shouts and the battle roars of Elak's companions. The sorcerer's head snapped back and for a moment the huge being stumbled. Elak could see the back end of a spear, jutting from just below the sorcerer's throat. It had ripped through the being, but only slowed him, and no blood gushed from the wound. It was enough to galvanise Elak, and he charged forward. Before any of the acolytes could gather their wits, he cut several down and reached the sarcophagus. Now they closed in, howling with fury as he leapt up the lower steps beside Shiveeri.

Quazzir-Rahan emitted a snarl, a deep-throated curse, his wide mouth opening to reveal teeth that reminded Elak of the sharks he had so recently evaded. Elak thrust his rapier hard at the left jewel in the sorcerer's head, avoiding looking into its baleful, scarlet glow. Light fizzed and something crackled like lightning.

Pandemonium had broken out in the chamber. The acolytes, finally alert, cast aside their robes and pulled out their swords, defending themselves desperately. Initially the Atlanteans and pirates cut into them and slaughtered a dozen or more before the fighting became even more furious. Amaal used his wide, curved blade to hew his way toward his daughter, while Lycon and Haruk spearheaded similar drives towards the sorcerer.

Elak dodged a ferocious swipe from the huge fist of Quazzir-Rahan, whose balance had been damaged by the loss of its eye, which had fallen to the stone floor and rolled aside. The high priest rushed at Elak, a long dagger held aloft, but the young king was too lithe for his robed assailant and his rapier opened the man's throat from ear to ear, toppling him over the sarcophagus. Elak whirled about and again attacked the sorcerer, avoiding looking at the remaining blazing eye as he tried to slice into the muscles that held it in place.

Behind him he heard Amaal roaring his defiance at the cluster of acolytes who tried to bring him down, blood showering them all as the pirate made his way to his daughter's side. When he reached her, his blade scythed through her chains and she was freed, immediately taking up a fallen sword and plunging into the acolytes as violently and bloodily as any other. Although Elak's men were outnumbered, they fought with such fire and fury that the acolytes were cut to pieces, three falling for every Atlantean or pirate they cut down.

Amaal saw the fallen jewel, its still blazing light, and brought his weapon down upon it. There was a crack like thunder as the blade disintegrated, but the jewel was similarly blasted into dust. As it did so, the sorcerer again stumbled, his power evidently diminished, dropping to one knee as if the blow had landed on him. Elak was quick to dart in, his rapier again flicking out like a serpent's tongue. It tore into the sorcerer's exposed flesh and cut out the second jewel. Like the first, it fell to the floor. Elak stepped back as the nightmare figure groped blindly for him. He heard Quazzir-Rahan cursing Atlantis and all her sons, swearing vengeance yet.

Lycon had carved a bloody path to the steps. He brought his sword down with all the power he could muster. It chopped deep into the sorcerer's neck and the head sprung out into the affray, the huge body collapsing, a black, oily ichor gushing from the severed neck. Elak stood back to back with Shiveeri, fighting off other waves of acolytes, but as the sorcerer stiffened, the last of its stolen life stilled, their efforts weakened with Quazzir-Rahan's passing. As one, they threw aside their weapons and knelt in surrender. The conflict was over.

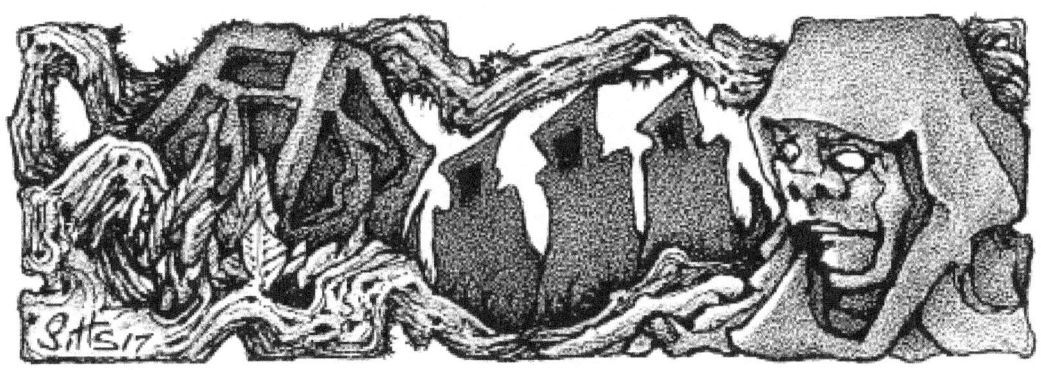

Amaal laughed long and loud and crushed his daughter to him. Elak counted his own men—barely a dozen were left alive. Lycon sagged, his face dripping with sweat.

"That's the second time I've seen you hurl a spear," Elak told him. "You have the arm of a god."

"Beginner's luck," said Lycon. "By Ishtar, I am thirsty!"

Near to him, Amaal bent down and picked something up. It was the second jewel, though its colours were dimming. The pirate ruler examined it, apparently bemused. "Why should I, Amaal the Black, not enjoy the power of the gods!"

"Father—no!" cried Shiveeri, realising what was happening.

Something evil had poured itself into Amaal, perhaps the dregs of the fallen sorcerer. Before anyone could prevent him, Amaal pulled away his eye patch and pushed the jewel into his empty eye socket.

Both Elak and Shiveeri cried out in alarm, rushing forward, but too late to stop the sudden flash of light. They all staggered back, knocked aside by the release of terrible power. Amaal roared as though his head was on fire and tore at the air with his hands, as if beset by all the demons in hell. Abruptly he fell back and landed among the heaped dead.

Shiveeri was first to him, but she knew at once her father was dead. Lycon ripped the spear from the dead sorcerer and used its point to pluck out the jewel from Amaal's face—a face that had melted. Lycon dropped the jewel on to the stone floor. The big man tore a stone free from the steps, raised it on high and brought it crashing down on the jewel, pulverising it.

"The power of Quazzir-Rahan is broken," said Elak. "The people of this island, and of all those here in the East are free of his yolk." He looked at the pirates, all of whom were aghast at the dreadful end of their ruler. "You have a new ruler—a queen," said Elak.

Slowly he eased Shiveeri to her feet. Her face was streaked with tears, her skin slick with the blood of those she had killed, yet an iron resolution shone from her eyes. She nodded and her men hailed her as one.

"I am proud to call you ally," Elak told her.

"We will give honour to you and your men," she said. "From this day, we are brothers and sisters in blood."

Elak nodded. It would bring peace closer in these eastern waters. Yet the price in men had been high. Atlantis would mourn their passing for a long while. The burden of rule was growing heavier and he felt the days of his youth slipping away, replaced by something new. Like Lycon, he really needed a flagon of wine.

WHETSTONE

whetstonemag.blogspot.com
NEW SWORD AND SORCERY!

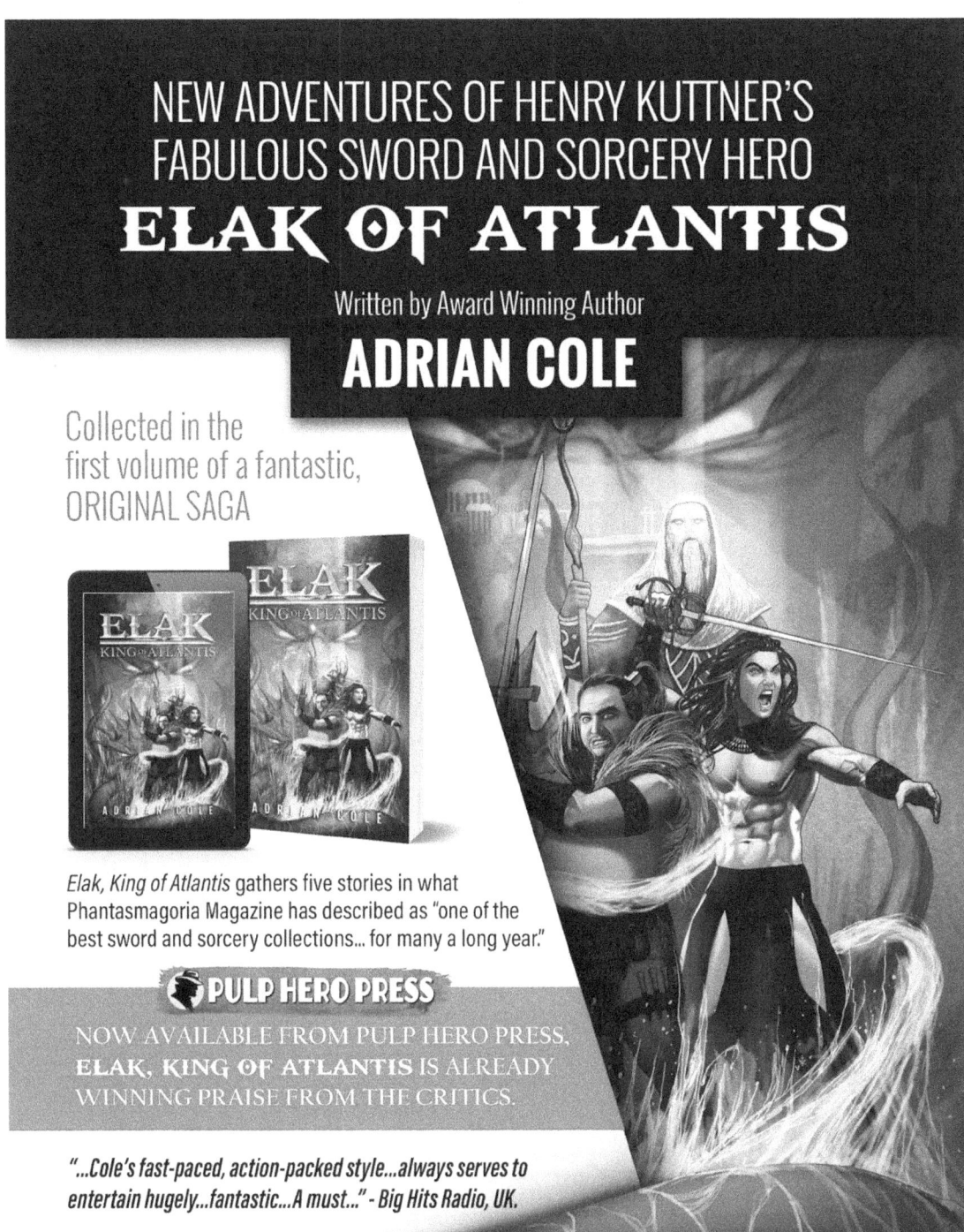

NEW ADVENTURES OF HENRY KUTTNER'S
FABULOUS SWORD AND SORCERY HERO

ELAK OF ATLANTIS

Written by Award Winning Author

ADRIAN COLE

Collected in the
first volume of a fantastic,
ORIGINAL SAGA

Elak, King of Atlantis gathers five stories in what
Phantasmagoria Magazine has described as "one of the
best sword and sorcery collections... for many a long year."

PULP HERO PRESS

NOW AVAILABLE FROM PULP HERO PRESS,
ELAK, KING OF ATLANTIS IS ALREADY
WINNING PRAISE FROM THE CRITICS.

*"...Cole's fast-paced, action-packed style...always serves to
entertain hugely...fantastic...A must..." - Big Hits Radio, UK.*

BORN IN STRANGE SHADOW

By Charles R Rutledge

"Either he was born in strange shadow, or he'd found a way to open the forbidden gate."
—H.P. Lovecraft *Pickman's Model*

Boston PD Detective Mallory Lee was on her way home when the car radio crackled. A uniformed officer telling dispatch he'd found a child wandering around Copp's Hill Terrace. A girl, maybe six or seven, and possibly in shock. Lee wasn't five minutes from the park, and going in the wrong direction but at the words 'lost child' her stomach clenched. Not her department, of course. But she still put the blue light on and made a U-turn back toward Copp's Hill.

Copp's Hill Terrace was a small park between Commercial and Charter streets in the North End. A set of granite steps led up to the terrace which overlooked the mouth of the Mystic River. On the Charter street side the terrace faced Copp's Hill Burying Ground, the city's second oldest graveyard.

When Lee got to Charter Street she found a burly uniformed officer who she didn't know sitting on a bench with a small girl. Lee showed her badge and said, "I'm Detective Lee. How's it going?"

The uniform, whose name tag read Carlson, shook his head. "She hasn't spoken, Detective. Some tourists saw her wandering around near the trees over there and flagged me down."

"Has children's services been notified?"

"Yeah, they got a case worker on the way."

Lee knelt down in front of the girl. She had pale blonde hair and enormous eyes. Her face was devoid of expression. Lee said, "Can you tell me your name, honey? Mine's Mallory."

The girl looked at her, but said nothing. Behind Lee the street lamps blinked on as twilight gathered. October had been mild in Boston but there was a chill in the air now as November moved in.

"See?" Carlson said. "I've been talking to her but she doesn't answer."

Lee stood up. "I wonder what happened. Her dress collar is torn, but otherwise she looks okay. Where did you say the people found her?"

Carlson pointed over Lee's shoulder. "Near those trees at the edge of the terrace, past that mailbox. I had a look around, Detective, I didn't see anything."

"I'll take a look just in case."

As Lee started away she felt a tug at the hem of her coat and a small voice said, "Don't go. The dog men will get you."

Lee glanced at Carlson who shrugged. Lee crouched back down and said. "Dog men? What do you mean, sweetie?"

Tears formed at the edges of the girl's eyes but she said, "The dog men got mommy and daddy and Katie."

"Katie is your sister?"

The girl nodded. "They took them all. One of them grabbed me but I ran away." Her hand strayed to her torn collar.

Lee said, "Can you tell me your name?"

"Becca."

"Okay, Becca. Some men with a dog took your family?"

Becca shook her head. "Not men with a

dog. Men like dogs. Big mean dogs."

Lee was trying to grasp what the child meant. Maybe men wearing masks. She said, "Were the men by the trees over there where you were found?"

Another head shake. Becca pointed across the street to the burying ground. "We were over there. The dog men came out of the ground and took mommy."

Lee looked over toward the graveyard. There was a gate almost directly across from where they stood. She said, "Did you come through that gate when you ran away, Becca?"

"Yes. I was afraid and I ran."

"You did right, honey. Now I'm going to go over there and look for your mom and dad. You stay here with officer Carlson until I come back."

Lee was still crouched down and Becca suddenly threw her arms around Lee's neck. Becca said, "They'll get you. They'll get you too."

Lee had forgotten the feel of small arms. She hadn't let herself remember. Not after what had happened to Derek. No. She wasn't going there. She pushed those thoughts away and slid her own arms around the child. "No they won't. I promise."

"You want me to call this in?" Carlson said. "Sounds like this could be gang related."

Lee gently disengaged herself from the child and stood. "Yeah, get a couple of units out here. At the least they can help me look around. And Carlson, if the child services people come for Becca, find out where they take her. I'll want to follow up."

"Sure thing, Detective. Watch yourself."

It was full dark as Lee crossed the street and approached the gate to the Burying Ground. She rummaged in her bag for her Mag-lite. She could still see by the glow of the streetlights but she wanted to be ready. She wished she could have asked Becca more questions but felt that she had probably pushed the girl as far as she safely could. Becca was definitely in shock.

Lee stepped through the gate and took one of the paths that led among the tombstones. The burying ground really wasn't that large and Lee didn't think anyone would be hiding there. But whoever had taken Becca's family might have crossed the graveyard and gone out the other side on Hull Street. And they might have left some sign. Lee turned the flashlight on and began scanning the area.

She didn't know what she was looking for exactly. The burying ground was a popular spot for tourists. Lee could imagine someone trying to rob visitors or shake them down, but why would anybody try and abduct a family of four in the middle of the North End? She kept playing the light around, looking for some sign of disturbance on the ground.

The ground.

Becca had said the men had come out of the ground. When she was a kid, Lee had heard rumors that there had once been a network of tunnels under Copp's hill, but she wasn't sure how much of that was urban legend. And hadn't she read that the recent work on the 'Big Dig' had turned up abandoned subway tunnels and other old excavations?

Out of her peripheral vision, Lee thought she saw movement. A flash of something pale against the darkness over to her left, near one of the red brick walls of a bank of buildings that separated the burying ground from the streets beyond. Lee shined her light toward the buildings but saw nothing. She went toward the buildings, letting her right hand fall to the butt of the Glock 9mm on her hip.

She played the flashlight beam along the foundation of the building closest to Charter Street. A square of darkness yawned near the corner of the foundation. Lee edged up. An old iron hatch of some sort was leaning against the wall near the opening. She moved closer so that she could shine the light into the hole. It was a shaft, lined with concrete, which was obviously of considerable age. There were iron rungs set into one wall.

What to do? The probability was the shaft

led to an old maintenance tunnel of some sort, or to a storm drain. The smart thing to do would be to wait for backup to arrive. Going down into the tunnel would be a bad idea.

Then Lee heard someone scream. It was faint and far away, but it was definitely rising from the depths. Shaking her head and cursing, Lee bent down and began to descend the iron rungs. She held the Mag-lite in her teeth until she reached the bottom of the shaft. Then she stood for a moment, shining the light around her.

The tunnel was obviously very old. It was lined with red brick and the ceiling was arched. Old bricks, rusted metal fuse boxes, and other, unidentifiable bits of debris were strewn across the floor. Lee guessed that the tunnel was part of the city's original electrical grid, long since abandoned.

A thick, sour scent assaulted Lee's nostrils. Decomposition mixed with something worse. Now she definitely wanted to wait for backup. Then she spotted a small, red, tennis shoe. That had to belong to Becca's sister, Katie.

"Shit," Lee said. She gritted her teeth, focused the flashlight beam ahead into the blackness, and started down the tunnel. Her footsteps echoed on the old concrete floor. She noted that the dust on the floor was recently scuffed and disturbed, but it also showed evidence of considerable traffic, so she couldn't be sure how recent the marks of passage were.

She came to what looked like some sort of junction box. Massive and ancient conduit tubes ran off in all directions. Most were cracked and broken and wires splayed from the breaks in the tubes. The tunnel split in two directions at this point, but Lee had little trouble discerning in which direction her quarry had gone. She turned right.

The smell was worse here, and she felt her feet crunching on something on the floor. Lee pointed the flashlight down. The floor of the tunnel was littered with bones.

"Jesus!" Lee said, stepping backwards automatically.

She focused the light on the bones and bent down for a closer look. These weren't animal bones. Lee had recently been preparing for the exams for the homicide division. She knew human bones when she saw them. And they didn't belong to any of the old graves above her. These were fairly new.

Despite the stench in the tunnel, Lee took a deep breath and pushed it out, fighting back the urge to panic. What the hell had she walked into? A serial killer's lair? Her first impulse was to run, but then she remembered Becca's family. They were still down there.

Lee froze in place as she heard a sound behind her. A low, rumbling growl like some big dogs made. Lee pushed the paralysis of fear aside. She slapped the flashlight into her left hand and drew the Glock with her right as she spun.

What could only be described as a monster crouched on the floor in the flashlight's glare. It was roughly man shaped, with bluish white skin spotted with what looked like mold. But it wasn't human. It had elongated hands and feet, both tipped with claws.

And its face. Oh Jesus, it's face. Red eyes. A long snout like a wolf's. A wide mouth filled with sharp teeth. Here was one of Becca's dog men in the horrible, deathly pale flesh.

Lee didn't wait for the thing to attack. She leveled the Glock and put three rounds into the creature's torso. The thing gave a startled yelp, but it rose from its crouch and lurched forward. Lee backpedaled, still firing. The thing growled and snarled until one round caught it high on the side of the head, blowing out part of its skull and spraying the old brick of the tunnel with dark blood.

Lee was breathing hard and her heart felt like it was trying to escape her chest. What was that thing? What had she walked into? It was a goddamn monster. In the middle of Boston.

She heard a scrabbling noise and looked

up to see two pair of red eyes in the darkness beyond the fallen creature. Jesus, there were more of them. And they can see in the dark, she realized. She brought the flashlight up, hoping it might blind them for a second or two, and wished she hadn't. If anything, they were bigger and uglier than the one she had shot.

She lined up between the eyes of one of them and fired. The thing moved at the last second and the shot hit it in the shoulder. Both beasts howled and came forward. Lee's next shot took one of them through the eye, and then the Glock clicked on empty. The remaining creature slammed into her and she fell, feeling the sharp bones on the tunnel floor as the thing's weight settled on her.

Lee struggled to breathe as the wind was pushed from her lungs by the impact. This close, the reek of the monster was almost unbearable. She could feel the animal heat of the thing as its breath washed over her face.

"Get the fuck off of me!" She said as she swung the Glock upwards, striking the thing in the head. The creature snarled and grabbed her wrist, making her grunt in pain. Its strength was incredible.

And then the creature's head exploded and Lee was almost deafened by a gunshot close to her ear. Hot blood spurted across Lee's face and she scrambled backwards, kicking the dead weight off her body.

Lee had lost the Mag-lite but it had fallen close by and a tall, slender man was framed in the circle of light it threw. He had a big .45 automatic in one hand and a flashlight in the other.

"Are you injured?" The man said. "Can you get up?"

"Watch me," said Lee, hauling herself to her feet. "And whoever you are, thanks."

"You're welcome, but we need to get moving. There are more of the ghouls on the way."

"The what?"

"Ghouls. Come with me. Do you have another magazine for your Glock?"

"One more." Lee dug into her bag and brought out her backup clip. She changed the magazines out and put a round in the chamber.

The man said, "The ghouls are between us and the way you came in. I know another way out."

"Who are you, mister?"

"Hardly the time for introductions. Come this way quickly."

"Wait, I need to know…"

But Lee was talking to the man's back. He had turned and started down the tunnel. There was something strapped across the man's narrow back. A slender black cylinder about three feet long.

The man was receding into the darkness quickly and Lee Hurried to catch up. She said, "Listen, there's a family down here."

"Yes," the man said over his shoulder. "Father, mother, and daughter. The father's dead. We'll try and save the other two but we need to get clear of the group of ghouls who are stalking you before we do anything else."

"Stalking me? What about you?"

"They didn't know I was here until I shot the one that you were wrestling with."

Who the hell was this guy? Up ahead there was a break in one of the walls. A dark, ragged hole. The man said, "Through here, and don't talk anymore until I say it's okay. The ghouls have very acute hearing."

Lee didn't like being told to keep her mouth shut, but the guy seemed to know what he was doing. She turned sideways and ducked through the narrow hole in the brick wall. She kept the beam of her flashlight pointed down so as not to trip over debris on the tunnel floor.

The man went another hundred yards or so and stopped in front of a big wooden door. He tried the heavy old handle but the door didn't budge. The man put his hand against the door's old fashioned keyhole and mumbled something that sounded like Latin. Then he tried the door again and it opened with an ominous creak.

The man went through the door and motioned for Lee to follow. Lee shrugged and stepped into the darkness. The man closed the door behind them and mumbled something else. The glow of the flashlights showed a small room with rough-hewn stone walls.

"We can talk here," the man said in a normal voice. "I've warded the door against sound and the ghouls can't open it now."

Warded? What was this guy going on about?

"You keep calling them ghouls?" Lee said.

"That's what they are. Carnivorous, ravenous creatures who prefer human flesh. They normally like it ripe, but deprived of rotting meat, they'll take fresh kill."

"That's crazy."

"It is and it's going to get worse."

"What do you mean?"

"The ghouls are coming up from tunnels below. They've been dormant for years, but somehow they've escaped the wards that kept them out of Copp's Hill. I became aware of their return a few days ago and came to Boston to see what I could do."

"Look, I don't mean to be rude, since you saved my life and all, but who the fuck are you?"

The man smiled. "My name is Carter Decamp. I'm something of a specialist in matters of this sort."

"Of what sort?"

"Of the occult and supernatural."

"That's crazy."

"So you said. And yet here we are. We don't have much time, Detective. Yes I saw your badge. I have to find out how the ghouls escaped the mystic wards that were put here in the twenties to keep them out, and if possible save the woman and her daughter who haven't been devoured yet. You can help me, or you can stay out of my way."

Lee took a long look at Decamp's face in the eerie glow from the flashlights. He didn't look like a nut job and she hadn't caught any

of the body language 'tells' she usually spotted when people were lying. Decamp believed what he was saying.

"You said the father was already dead."

"I came across what was left of him as I was examining the tunnels. I heard the ghouls talking about the mother and child. They were taking them deeper into the tunnels."

"These things can talk?"

"Not in a language you'd understand, but yes, they can communicate."

"Okay. I'll help you. I don't necessarily believe all this about ghouls but there are two people in danger."

"Excellent. May I know your name?"

"Sorry. I'm Mallory Lee."

"Nice to meet you, Mallory. Here's the plan. We need to go deeper in the tunnels to find the mother and child and to hopefully discover the origins of the breach the ghouls are coming through. Keep your weapon handy, but don't fire unless you absolutely have to. The noise will bring more ghouls."

"Might be hard to get past them without shooting some."

Decamp had already holstered his .45. He reached over his back to the black cylinder and drew forth a long, slender blade. "I'll use this to try and clear our way."

"A sword? Seriously, Decamp? It took half a clip to put one of those things down."

Decamp said, "The sword has special properties. It will get the job done."

Decamp did the thing with the door again. Before he could open it, Lee said, "Where are we, anyway?"

"This? The sub-basement of a house on Salem Street. It was sealed off years ago and the current owners don't even know it's here. Believe it or not, it was once used by smugglers. The tunnel beyond the door used to run down to the river. That end is sealed as well."

"You've got an odd way of talking, Decamp. Almost like you're lecturing."

"An unfortunate affectation. I used to be

an English professor."

"English professor. Right."

Decamp opened the door and stepped out, sword at the ready. Lee followed, holding the Glock in ready position. She preferred to use both hands when using the weapon, but she had put in plenty of practice on the range shooting one handed. Anyone who'd been in a firefight could tell you that there wasn't a lot of aiming, anyway. Point and shoot and move.

Decamp turned right and started down yet another tunnel. Lee wondered how he knew where he was going in this maze. Maybe he didn't.

They had gone a few hundred yards when two ghouls came lurching out of the shadows. Lee brought the Glock up but Decamp lunged forward. The tip of the slender blade ripped through the throat of one of the ghouls and blood splashed on the floor. The second ghoul swung one clawed hand at Decamp, only to see that hand go spinning away, severed by the sword. With an almost casual flourish, Decamp sent the ghoul's head after the hand.

"Good God," Lee said. "Forget I doubted you and the pig-sticker."

Decamp nodded. "We go left here and that will take us to part of the abandoned subway system. That's where we'll find the woman and her daughter, I think."

"They've got to be terrified," said Lee.

"As long as they're still alive. As I told you, the ghouls are ravenous after lying dormant in the earth."

"How long can they live like that?"

"No one knows. The nature and origins of ghouls have never been fully determined. They almost overran this part of Boston in 1923, led by a changeling named Pickman. My friend Kharrn stopped them. I wish he was with us now."

"He's still alive?"

"Yes and quite spry for a man of his years. But I couldn't locate him. He moves around a lot. Now, we'd best not talk anymore until we see what the situation is in the subway tunnels."

"Let me ask one question then. How are you navigating down here?"

"I studied old city maps. And I'd been scouting for a few hours. I was almost at this point when I heard the ghouls saying a human had come down the access shaft near the burying grounds."

"And you hurried up to save me."

"I thought it prudent."

"I'm glad you did."

Decamp inclined his head, almost a small bow, which Lee found oddly charming in this weird situation. Then he turned and started along the tunnel and she followed. As before, Lee used the light to check the tunnel floor. There were more bones in this area.

After they had walked for a while, Decamp stopped and held up one hand. In a whisper he said, "We'd better turn off the lights. We're near the opening to the subway tunnel."

"How will we see?"

"There should be some light where they congregate. Not all of them can see in total darkness."

Decamp switched off his flashlight. Lee didn't relish the idea of being down there in the dark where one or more of those things could come upon them unseen, but Decamp had been right so far. She thumbed the light off.

For a few harrowing moments, that seemed longer, there was total blackness. Then, as her eye adjusted, she became aware of a faint flickering light emanating from a break in the wall just ahead of them. Firelight.

Decamp waited another few moments, then moved up to the opening and peered around the corner. He motioned for Lee to join him. She eased up, setting her feet down cautiously so as not to step on any bones that might snap, then leaned forward so she could look into the chamber beyond.

The subway tunnel was huge, probably some sort of switching point which could house more than one train. A bonfire was set up in the middle of it and there were at least a dozen ghouls in the chamber. Not far from the fire Lee could make out two small, pale forms lying on the ground. Becca's mother and sister.

"Jesus," Lee said. "How the hell are we going to get them out of there?"

Decamp said, "It may not be possible, Mallory. You see that big hole on the floor? That's where they're coming from. My first priority is to repair the wards that keep them out of the surface world."

Lee grabbed Decamp's arm. "We are not leaving that woman and that little girl down here, Decamp. We're not."

Decamp turned toward her and even in the darkness she could feel the intensity of his gaze. He said, "You lost someone, didn't you?"

How could he know? "My son. Derek. He disappeared from his school's playground three years ago. I never found out what happened to him."

"I'm sorry."

"Thank you. But yeah, we have to find a way to save Becca's mother and sister."

"Don't think me cold, Mallory. But if I don't reseal those wards, many people will die. Still, I'll do what I can."

"Fair enough. What can I do to help you?"

Decamp took the .45 from its holster and offered it to Lee. "I need a few minutes to look at that opening in the floor. Keep the ghouls off of me as long as you can. There are seven rounds left in the .45 and you have a full magazine in your Glock."

Lee said, "I hope that's enough."

"It will have to be. Let's go."

Decamp stepped through the crack in the wall. Lee entered right behind him, just in time to see a wave of the pale creature swarm over Decamp. She saw the blade flash and two creatures fall, but then Decamp went down under a mass of the ghouls and the sword went spinning away. Lee started firing as the group turned to her, and though she had the satisfaction of seeing a snarling face disintegrate, she too was quickly overwhelmed.

The damn things had set a trap. Or maybe they had figured she and Decamp would try and save Becca's mother and sister, and they had waited just inside the entrance to the chamber. In any case, she and Decamp were royally screwed. Lee had often heard the phrase 'her blood ran cold', but until now she had never known what it meant. These things didn't just want to kill her. They wanted to eat her. She had lost her place on the food chain.

The ghouls dragged Lee across the floor toward the fire. They were chattering among themselves, though she, of course, had no idea what they were saying. Maybe discussing recipes.

She looked over to where Decamp hung limp between two ghouls who were holding him. The mob of ghouls had given him a thorough beating and there was a cut above one eye. He appeared to be unconscious, but at least he was breathing.

When they reached the fire, Lee saw that Becca's mom and Katie were also still breathing, though neither was moving. She hoped they had just passed out from shock and terror.

Which gave Lee an idea. She sagged in the grip of her two captors as if she had fainted. The two ghouls muttered for a moment, then they dragged Lee over to where the two captives lay and dropped her on the ground. They still didn't release Decamp but they probably considered him the greater threat.

Lee considered her options. Both guns and Decamp's sword were too far away. She had a backup gun in her bag, but it was a snub nose .38, which probably wouldn't do more than piss the ghouls off. Still, it was better than nothing.

The ghouls had gathered around Decamp and were studying him. They lifted his arms and prodded his chest. One of them said something and the others laughed. They laughed. How close to human were they?

With the ghoul's attention on Decamp, Lee slowly slid her hand into her bag. One of the ghouls that was holding Decamp released his grip and held Decamp's arm out to one side. The ghoul opened his mouth wide. Hell, he was going to bite Decamp's arm off.

Lee slid the gun out of the bag. She rolled to her back and pointed the weapon at the ghoul who was about to chow down on Decamp. A snub nose wasn't accurate beyond a few feet but it was all she had. Hoping that none of the ghouls would look her way, she took careful aim. With any luck, she'd at least get him in the head.

And then Decamp moved. He jerked his arm free and jammed his fingers into the eyes of the ghoul who had been about to bite him. The creature howled and clutched at its face. One of the ghouls was still holding Decamp. The slender man stepped closer to the creature, then reversed direction, pivoted, and did some sort of judo throw, sending the ghoul careening into the closest of its brothers.

Another ghoul lunged at Decamp and Lee fired. The bullet caught the ghoul in the forehead and it went down. Decamp, meanwhile, jammed both fists into the pockets of his coat and came out with handfuls of dust. He cast the dust at the group of ghouls around him and said something in that weird language he had used before. The dust burst into flame and the ghouls were suddenly running around screeching in agony.

Decamp sprinted toward where he had lost his sword. Lee got to her feet and started after him. Her Glock was still mostly full. But as she moved forward, something caught the collar of her coat and jerked her backwards. Lee turned and found the grinning face of a ghoul mere inches away. She jammed the barrel of the .38 under the thing's jaw and pulled the trigger twice. The ghoul's head snapped back and brain matter flew. Lee was running before the thing hit the ground.

Decamp scooped up the sword just as two ghouls caught up with him. He lunged forward in a picture perfect fencer's stance and the blade passed through the heart of one of the ghouls. The other roared and tried to tackle Decamp but he sidestepped like a toreador and slit the thing's throat.

Lee found the Glock and snatched it from the ground. She was firing as she turned and one ghoul fell, but then she saw something that almost stopped her heart. Two of the ghouls, rather than pursuing Lee and Decamp, had instead picked up Katie and her mother and were hurrying toward the hole in the floor.

"Oh no you Goddamn don't," Lee said, heading toward the hole. "Decamp!"

Decamp turned toward Lee and saw what the two ghouls were doing. He began moving to intercept them. But there were a half dozen or so other ghouls left and they were also heading toward the hole.

Lee fired the Glock as she ran, but her shot went wide. The ghoul carrying Katie was moving the quickest and had almost reached the hole. Lee couldn't risk a shot so she made a dive at the ghoul's legs, hitting the creature with her shoulder. The ghoul fell and Katie rolled away. Lee could only hope the girl was okay. She got up on her knees and shot the ghoul twice through the head as it tried to rise. Then she scrambled toward the fallen child.

The ghoul carrying the mother was on the lip of the hole when Decamp came from the other direction. Long legs churning, he vaulted the hole and kicked the ghoul, sending the creature staggering back. Decamp ran the creature through and caught the mother before her head could hit the ground. Decamp stood ready with the sword, but the few remaining ghouls seemed to have had all they wanted of their human foes. They dropped into the hole and vanished into blackness.

Decamp said, "I hope that's all of them. Watch my back while I do what needs to be done."

Lee nodded. She was sitting on the cold floor with one arm around Katie. The girl whimpered softly but didn't awaken. That was probably good.

As Lee watched, Decamp made a slow circuit around the hole, speaking again in that weird Latin-like language and occasionally making a mark on the ground with the tip of his sword. For the first time, Lee noted that the sword's edge glittered oddly, as if shot through with silver.

Finally Decamp said, "That's it. I've repaired the forbidding wards that were placed here in the twenties and I've added to them. I can only surmise that they had gradually lost their potency over the years."

"I have no idea what you're talking about," Lee said.

Decamp grinned. "That's quite all right, Mallory."

"But where did they go?"

"Back to the dark where I hope they'll go dormant again. But they can't come back here."

"What if they come out somewhere else?"

"I'll be watching."

"I guess that will have to do," Lee said. "Do you really think that was all of the ghouls in these tunnels?"

"I think it likely, but I'll come back and make sure. Right now we need to see to these two."

Lee looked down at Katie. Without realizing it, she had pulled the child close. "How will we get them out of here?"

Decamp had gone to one knee and was examining Katie's mom. He said, "She seems all right physically. As far as getting them back to the surface, I think you'll have help. Listen."

Lee was still for a moment and then she heard voices calling. "Great. Now backup arrives. And what do you mean, I'll have help. What about you?"

Decamp said, "It would be better for my purposes if I weren't mentioned in any report you made."

"I owe you my life, so I'll do what I can, but how will I explain all this?"

"The bodies of the ghouls will be all the evidence you need. However, the powers that be will most likely hush all this up."

Lee gestured at the chamber around her. "Do you really think they can?"

Decamp said, "They've done it before. Now, if you'll excuse me, I think I'd best take my leave. Your fellow officers are getting close."

"I'm letting you go, Decamp, but I want more answers. How can I reach you?"

"I'll reach you. You can count on that."

And with that, Carter Decamp turned and faded into the shadows. Katie stirred again in Lee's arms and Lee stroked the child's hair and made reassuring noises as she had once made to another child.

BY CROM!

By Rachel Kahn

COURTEOUS KING JAMIE

By Matthew Gregory Lewis

Illustrated by George E. Turner & Michael H. Price

The pedigree of this presentation is as circuitous and tangled as the poetastery itself is archaically direct and uncomplicated. The original illustrator, here, George E. Turner, had as a schoolboy in Texas studied the lyrical grotesqueries of Matthew Gregory Lewis (author of *The Monk*), among many additional such purveyors of Gothic horrors and drolleries. George carried the interest on along into college. At a curiously progressive provincial institution, West Texas State Normal School, during 1947–1948, George found the senior professor of English, Dr. A. Kirk Knott, to be "as devoted a champion of the ghastlier fare as I ever was," as Turner told it.

"Kind of validated the interest, in a sense, to find that the Chief Egghead was attuned to the horrors, too," George added. "Helped matters, as well, that Dr. Knott looked as though he could've stepped out of a Lovecraft story — gaunt, with a shock of white hair and a piercing gaze – every bit the part of some faculty member from Miskatonic U."

While studying at the Art Institute of Chicago during 1949–1950, Turner found his literary interests enforced further by a friendship with classmate Gahan Wilson. They made a ritual of illustrating favorite pieces of Gothic prose and poesy, more for the exercise than in search of any marketplace. George made "Monk" Lewis's "Courteous King Jamie" a springboard for one such piece. That drawing (which forms the closing page of the present package) first saw print in 1953 in an amateur publication called *FaNews*.

By the early 1950s, Turner had put his Art Institute degree to practical use as a newspaper illustrator and designer in Texas. He was still holding forth in that newsroom in 1968, when I joined the paper as a college-kid cub reporter. Our mutual interests prompted a brotherly bond, generational gulfs be damned, and by the early 1970s George and I had begun working together on such books as his *The Making of King Kong* (1975) and a first volume of our collaborative Forgotten Horrors genre-study series. While researching this chapter or that in his labyrinth of file cabinets, George and I chanced upon the issue of *FaNews* containing "Courteous King Jamie."

"Feh!" George said. "Now, there's a drawing that should never've seen print!"

"Looks good to me," I answered. "Kind of reminds me of Virgil Finlay."

"Finlay, schminlay!" George grumped. "Damned piece gives Lewis' whole punchline away!" (The moronic conceit of the "Spoiler Alert" had yet to be invented in 1975. George would never've tolerated any such nonsense, in any event.)

"Well, I like the thing," I said. "And I

think it'd make a great capper for a new presentation of the poem."

"Hmph…"

We left it at that, then, for the longest damned old time, and then around 1998 George 'phoned from his newer digs in Los Angeles to ask if I'd still like to do an illustrated presentation of "Courteous King Jamie." Why, of course.

"I'll get crackin' on the art," he said, "and you can handle the lettering."

And so he did, although the project was sidelined amidships by more urgent commercial deadlines for the both of us. Most of the art that graces the pages following was left unfinished upon George's unexpected death in 1999. I have finished these pieces and performed a restoration upon the 1953 Turner drawing "that should've never seen print." (Sez who?)

— Michael H. Price

Matthew Gregory "Monk" Lewis (1775–1818)

· MATTHEW GREGORY LEWIS ·

Courteous King Jamie

Courteous King Jamie is gone to the wood,
The fattest Buck to find;
He chased the deer, and he chased the roe,
Till his friends were left behind.

He hunted o'er moss and moor,
And over hill and down,
Till he came to a ruined Hunting-Hall
'Twas seven miles from town.

He entered up the Hunting-Hall,
To make him Goodly Cheer,
For of all the herds in the Good Green Wood,
He had slain the Fairest Deer.

He sat him down, with food and rest
His courage to restore;
When a Rising Wind was heard to sigh,
And an earthquake rock'd the floor.

And darkness co'ered the Hunting-Hall,
Where he sat, all at his meat;
The Grey Dogs, haowling, left their food,
And crept to Jamie's feet.

And louder haowl'd the Rising Storm,
And burst the fastened door,
And in there came a Grisly Ghost,
Loud stamping 'pon the floor.

Her head touched the roof-tree of the hoose,
Her waist, a child could span;
I wot, the look of her hollow eye
Would have scared the bravest man.

Her locks, like snakes; her teeth, like stakes,
And her breath had a Brimstone Smell
I nothing know that she seemed to be,
But the Devil, just come from Hell!

"Some meat! Some meat! King Jamie,
"Some meat, now gi'e to me!"
"And to what meat in this hoose, Lady,
"Shall ye not welcome be?"
"Oh! Ye must kill your Berry-Brown Steed,
"And sairve him up to me!"

King Jamie killed his Berry-Brown Steed,
Though it caused him Mickle Caire;
The Ghost ate up both Flesh and Bone,
Left naught but hooves and haire.

"Mair meat! Mair meat! King Jamie,
"Mair meat, now gi'e to me!"
"And to what meat in this hoose, lady,
"Shall ye not welcome be?"
"Oh! ye must kill your Good Greyhounds!
"They'll taste most daintily."

King Jamie killed his Good Greyhounds,
Though 't made his hairt to fail;
The Ghost ate them all up, one by one,
Left naught but ears and tail.

"A bed! A bed! King Jamie,
"Now, make a bed for me!"
"And to what bed in this hoose, lady,
"Shall ye not welcome be?"
"Oh! Ye must pull the Heather So Green,
"And make a Bed So Soft for me!"

King Jamie pull'd the Heather So Green,
And made for the Ghost a bed,
And o'er the heather, with courtesy rare,
His plaid hath he daintily spread.

"Now, swear! Now, swear! King Jamie,
"To take me for your bride;"
"Now, Heaven forbid!" King Jamie said,
"That e'er the like betide,
That the Devil so Foul, just come from Hell,
"Should stretch him by my side."

"Now, fye! Now, fye! King Jamie,
"I swear by the Holy Tree,
"I am no Devil, or Evil Thing,
"Howe'er foul I be.

"Then yield! Then yield! King Jamie,
"And take my Bridegroom's Place,
"For shame shall light on the Dastard Knight,
"Who refuses a Lady's Grace."

Then quoth King Jamie, with a groan,
For his heart was big with care,
"It shall ne'er be said that King Jamie
Denied a lady's prayer."

So he laid him by the foul Thing's side,
And piteously he moaned;
She pressed his hand, and he shuddered!
She kissed his lips, and he groaned!

When day was come, and night was gone,
And the sun shone through the hall,
The fairest Lady that e'er was seen,
Lay 'tween him and the wall.

"Oh! Well is me!" King Jamie cried,
"How long will your beauty stay?"
Then out and spake that lady fair,
"E'en till my Dying Day.

"For I was witch'd to a Ghastly Shape,
All by my Step-Dame's skill,
'Til could I alight 'pon a Courteous Knight
Who'd allow me all my will."

—From Tales of Wonder, *written and collected by*
Matthew Gregory Lewis. London; 1801

ༀ ༀ ༀ

The source is a folkloric recitation. Wrote Lewis: "I have altered and added so much ..., that I might almost claim it for my own."

Lewis (1775–1818), a novelist and dramatist of the British Commonwealth, was popularly known as Monk Lewis, in light of of the success of his Gothic novel of 1796, *The Monk*.

Whilst in service with the British Embassy in the Hague, Lewis produced the romance *Ambrosio, or The Monk*, whose provocative nature inspired an outcry for censorship. Lord Byron would write of "Wonder-working Lewis... Even Satan's self with thee might dread to dwell, and in thy skull discern a deeper hell."

THE MOST FRIGHTENING STORY IN THE WORLD

By Amanda DeWees

I dressed as if I were going for a run. It was early morning, with dew still on the grass, and I didn't pass a single car in this residential neighborhood.

At a quick walk, I cut through a few back yards. They held nothing but weeds, rusty swing sets, and one sleepy Sheltie who did no more than raise her head when I passed. When I met up with the couple at the dead end as arranged, they were dressed as if for the office.

"Can you climb a ladder in those heels?" I asked the woman.

Both of them looked unsettled, whether by me or by the circumstances I had no idea. Maybe they hadn't expected a grad student in a ponytail and English Beat t-shirt.

"Just what is this place you're taking us to?" she challenged.

I shrugged. She'd see it soon enough. "Follow me."

I led them downhill, following a track worn into the grass. The woman grabbed her husband's arm to steady herself. I expected her to take off her ridiculously high heels, but she seemed determined not to, and it wouldn't be my fault if she turned her ankle.

The wide grassy slope was edged with pines on two sides. Eventually it would abut the back side of another street of houses, but we weren't going that far. Just where the ground leveled out I signaled for them to slow. It was easy to miss, by design, but there was the round metal lid set into the ground like the hatch of a submarine.

Leaning down, I grasped the wheel and tried to turn it. It was stiff, and the man reached down to help. Between the two of us, it soon loosened, and I was able to raise the hatch.

"In you go," I said.

The woman peered down the metal shaft. Metal rungs were bolted to the side, leading straight down into darkness, and her eyes widened. "We have to climb down?"

"You don't have to, no. It was your choice to come here. I'm only the guide." Still she hesitated, and I started to lose patience. "Go or don't go, whatever you want. But your money won't be refunded."

She bit her lip, then wrenched off first one shoe, then the other. From the red soles I guessed they were Louboutins, which meant they were probably worth as much as I earned in a month as a teaching assistant. She set them down by the lip of the opening, placing them carefully upright. If she had been wearing hose I'd have warned her that she'd find the rungs too slippery, but she wasn't. Maybe pantyhose were out of style.

"I'll be right behind you," her husband told her reassuringly, and she darted one last skeptical look toward me before stepping into the shaft.

I was the last to descend. When I stepped down from the last rung, Josh was already doing the security check.

"Turn out your pockets, please," he was saying. His face was sallow under the amber bulb that lit the anteroom. "Any electronic or recording devices?"

"The instructions said not to bring our

phones," the husband said. He put a wallet and a set of keys into the tray Josh held out.

"No phones, cameras, flash drives, anything of that sort," Josh confirmed.

"Why not?" the woman asked. Evidently she was the half of the couple that liked to challenge and resist, while her husband was the peacemaker. Fine, I supposed, as long as it worked for them.

For a moment I wondered who they were, but I shook the curiosity off. Better for all of us not to know each other's names.

"Did he write it?" the husband whispered to me, indicating Josh.

I shook my head. "We've never been told," I said aloud.

Josh began to pat them down for hidden devices. He was ex-military, and it showed in the efficiency of his movements. "No copies can be removed from the premises."

"But we'll remember what we read," the wife said. "What's to prevent us from just writing it down from memory when we leave?"

Josh and I exchanged wry grins. She was hardly the first to suggest that . . . when they arrived. No one suggested it when they left.

"We'll take that chance" was all he said. "You're clean. Follow me."

That was where my part ended. Josh led them to a metal door, punched some numbers into the keypad, and ushered them through. Just before the door closed behind them he gave me a little nod of dismissal.

I didn't want to wait down there in the dark, so I climbed back up to the surface. Birds were starting to sing busily. I thought about the psychology paper I had coming up while I did some stretches. Climbing up and down got my calf muscles bunched up, and

I'd be taking another party down later today.

Maybe twenty minutes later I heard the couple climbing up the metal rungs. As each of them breasted the entrance I took their hands and helped them out.

There were traces of tears on the woman's face. The man looked pale.

"Did you read it?" I asked, although there was no need.

The man just gave me a startled look. He didn't seem quite together yet. But the woman's eyes flashed at me. "Have you?" she demanded.

I couldn't help but smile. They always asked me that. Do I look that dumb? I wanted to say, but that would have implied that they were, and no one rich enough to afford this field trip wanted their choices judged by some grad student. Instead I said, "I'm happier not reading it."

"You're smart," said the man, and his voice was unsteady. "Don't ever read it."

"I won't."

"Why do you do this?" the woman cried suddenly. "Why not destroy it?"

That shocked me. "It has to be read," I said.

"Why?"

"It just . . . it has to. Stories die when they aren't read."

I waited for her to say This one should die, as some did. Sometimes they even got violent.

But she didn't say it. She just turned away.

They started back up the hill. The woman's hand reached out and clutched her husband's.

"Ma'am," I called after them. "You forgot your shoes."

They didn't look back.

DRACULA'S DESCENDENT

AN INTERVIEW WITH DACRE STOKER

By Anthony Taylor

Dacre Stoker is a dashing looking fellow in his fifties who happens to be related to the most famous horror author of all time. A descendant of *Dracula* author Bram Stoker, Dacre runs the Stoker Family Estate, coaches tennis, and is himself an author (with Ian Holt) of *Dracula, The Undead* (McMillan & Sons, 2014). In addition, he hosts travel events and tours to the Romanian locations mentioned in *Dracula*, and gives live presentations about his famous ancestor in a program called Stoker on Stoker. His staunch efforts to keep Bram's name in the public eye have created a buzz for his next book and other upcoming projects. We're happy to speak with him here for *Skelos*.

Anthony Taylor: What are your earliest memories of *Dracula*?

Dacre Stoker: I remember watching the Famous Vampire Hunters movie when I was about 12 at boarding school. Then I finally read *Dracula* when I was in College in 1979.

AT: What were your first impressions of the novel?

DS: At first *Dracula* was a hard read for me, quite slow moving, the epistolary style was not easy and the dialects by some of the characters were difficult to follow. However, at about the half-way point I was hooked and had a hard time putting it down.

AT: When did you find out Bram Stoker was your Great Grand Uncle?

DS: As a child growing up in Montreal at the age of 9 I noticed some old books on our bookshelf, written by Bram Stoker. My father then explained our connection. His grandfather was Bram Stoker's youngest brother George Stoker.

AT: Were you teased mercilessly in school when your friends found out?

DS: It wasn't too bad, but close to Halloween my friends did joke about the potential risks of trick or treating at the Stoker household. Believe me our home did not resemble the Addams family or the Munsters' houses.

AT: What is your favorite Dracula film?

DS: It's a toss up between the fairly recent 1992 (Francis Ford) Coppola movie and the good old 1931 Todd Browning version with Bela Lugosi.

AT: When did you realize that Bram's legacy was your birthright and that you wanted to carry it forward?

DS: It really wasn't until 2004 when Ian Holt contacted me and asked if I would be interested in co-writing a sequel did I decide to jump in and learn as much as I possibly could about my famous relative and his writing. Ian was looking for a member of the Stoker family to get involved in his project to write a sequel to *Dracula*.

AT: What was the working process like with the two of you?

DS: I have now collaborated with two different authors, Ian Holt on *Dracula the Un-Dead*, and JD Barker on *Dracul*. Both stories and co-authors were very different, I needed to adapt my writing style in each case in order to contribute in a productive manner.

Ian had the idea (from a screenplay he had written) to give Count Dracula a chance to represent his side of the story. By 2004 we felt that most *Dracula* fans identified with the Dracula character as a vampire version of the historic Vlad Dracula III as he has been depicted in most movies. So we decided to continue Bram's work but to develop all of the surviving (*Dracula*) characters so the reader could actually learn much more about them; where did they come from, how they knew each other, some of their personal issues. We obviously did the same with Count Dracula; we did not set out to make him good, we wanted to give him a backstory and fill in details of what Vlad the Impaler would be like if he was a vampire. It took us a while to settle on the final outline for the story. Ian had a basic premise that served as the backbone of the story, so everything stemmed from there. We constantly bounced ideas off of each other as we wrote our separate parts of the book. I did a lot of research into Bram's writing of *Dracula* as well as finding a lot of information about Bram's personal life. This helped tremendously as I was able to contribute by writing sections of the book pertaining to Bram Stoker and Detective Cotford, a character who Bram originally slated to appear in *Dracula*.

In writing *Dracul* I provided JD with the framework for our story based on a lot of historic research that I had done not only about Bram's life but alos about his writing of *Dracula*. We shared ideas about how to best tell our story, we decided on the epistolary style, similar to how Bram wrote *Dracula*. I submitted JD with blocks of text, some he would use and some he would not, in the end we decided it was best to have his voice be the consistent one as he was the more seasoned author. I was very happy with the end result; JD was a pleasure to work with.

AT: Your latest book, *Dracul* how does it fit in with the legacy of *Dracula*?

DS: JD Barker and I have written a prequel to *Dracula*, an historical based work of fiction entitled *Dracul*. Our story chronicles Bram Stoker's life and that of his family while he was growing up in Ireland, as well as certain personal experiences that lead to him writing *Dracula* as a warning to the world that vampires were in fact rea. *Dracul* was the number 1 bestselling hardcover horror novel in the UK in 2018 and it was a Horror Writers Association finalist for Superior Achievement in a novel in 2018. Paramount studios has purchased an option for the film rights.

AT: What's the most surprising thing you've found out about Bram in your family research?

DS: I found that I share a lot of similar qualities with Bram. Organized, and detailed oriented, but at the same time we love to dream up stories based on things going on around us.

AT: How did you become involved in giving tours of Dracula sites in Romania?

DS: I started working on a travel guide to places associated with both Vlad Dracula III and Count Dracula and the novel. On my first research trip I realized how beautiful Romania is and how much there is to experience when one delves into the locations associated with the life and times of Vlad Dracula III and also the towns villages where the action was set in Bram's famous novel. Even though he never went there the research that Bram did was very thorough and accurate. It seemed the right thing to do to partner with Romania Treasures Travel and help them lead tours.

AT: Who is the Bram Stoker Estate, and what do they represent?

DS: The Bram Stoker Estate is made up of two of Bram's direct descendants, I manage the estate for my cousins. Our mission is to inspire and facilitate research and interest in all things pertaining to Bram Stoker and his family. To protect and promote Bram's Intellectual Property through trademarks and licensing worldwide.

AT: What does the name Stoker mean to you beyond the obvious, and how is the estate working to keep it relevant in the culture?

DS: We are constantly exploring opportunities to market and sell items that portray Bram Stoker in his desired likeness. It is our family name and Bram's reputation, so we are very keen to protect it. We're also working on various projects related to providing educational and entertaining information about Bram Stoker to fans and the public.

AT: Why does *Dracula* thrive even now, a hundred and twenty years after it's publication?

DS: *Dracula* is a very complex book, people go back and read it many times… it can be a slow read but it has many deep complex issues to be sorted out on many levels. Many of today's vampire and werewolf stories, movies, and TV shows were inspired by the same central theme that *Dracula* was, existing superstitions and folklore. People in many cultures believed these supernatural stories told hundreds of years ago, they are deeply etched in many peoples' history. Fundamentally, *Dracula* is a story about what makes us human . . . and what makes us inhuman.

THE NIGHT ANGEL

By Will Murray

I saw a dark shape against the night,
Borne along in endless flight.

Each eve at this time, he glides on past,
I often wonder how long he'll last.

Flying from unknown foes that follow,
From what vengeful, volcanic Apollo?

Wither goes this moon-watched soul?
Is eternal night his only goal?

Is he the spirit of the lunar loom,
Or a vampire, fleeing fiery doom?

His staring eyes are redly barren pits,
Behind which, unknown terror flits.

Through the lightless centuries he's flown,
Will his fate ever be known?

His face is an arctic waste,
A mask of cold white paste.

Of what distant, dim-lit worlds could he tell?
What fears that eternal nights cannot quell?

What future has a fleeing man,
Whose mad flight allows no time to plan?

Each night he passes without a sound,
Toward what fell destiny is he bound?

Perhaps he pays the price for immortality,
Moonlit eons in which to flee,
A relentless, sun-spawned eternity.

Moon of darkness,
Moon of trust,
Even angels come to dust.

RISEN

By Milton J. Davis

Illustrated by Andrea Rushing

Part One

It was as if the sun knew Maona Durobe's day of decision had come. The golden star rose with a brilliance confirming its strength, its intensity radiating through the thick curtains as if the windows of Durobe's expansive bedroom were uncovered. The eighth child of Kidama Yigo Durobe rose with its summons, rubbing his eyes then stretching his well muscled arms upward as if in praise. It had taken him longer than usual to sleep the night before, yet his awakening was urgent. The day had come; his duty could no longer be avoided. He would face his brother and challenge him for the right to gain the Stool after the passing of their father. It was likely he would not survive the week.

His servant and bodyguard, Mona, rose from his mat at the foot of Maona's bed then hurried from the room to fetch Maona's breakfast. No sooner had the servant exited did Jukundu, his djele, enter the room. The dark-skinned man shared his ever present smile as he strummed his kora.

"Go away, Jukundu," he said. "It's too early."

"Not on a fateful day as today," Jukundu replied. "This is an auspicious day, a day that must be remembered from beginning to end. I feel a great song that needs to be sung."

"Then pay attention to my words now," Maona said. "For you are not accompanying me to Karago's compound."

Jukundu's mouth fell open. Maona walked by the stunned djele to his wardrobe. Normally he would wait until Gboli arrived to assist him, but this was a day that he did not want the attention her station required.

"What do you mean I'm not going?" Jukundu finally said. "I am your djele!"

"It is true," Maona said. "But this is one time I don't wish the truth to be recited. My life should end with lies."

Jukundu looked insulted.

"The Traores do not deal in lies. We are the greatest djeles of Joba, some say of the entire Hadal. The Durobes pay well for our services, which is why I can't understand why you don't want me to accompany you."

Maona chose a pair of loose lavender pants.

"Yes, the Traores are excellent and expensive djeles and I am honored you chose to record my song. But I will not be responsible for your death."

Jukundu swallowed. "My death?"

Maona pulled his waist string tight then tied it.

"It is highly likely Karago will not take my challenge well. If that happens I can't guarantee your safety. Since you are not a fighter like your brethren and my bodyguards hate you, you will remain here. I won't have your death debt come out of my treasury."

"I am insulted!" Jukundu exclaimed.

"I don't care," Maona replied.

Mona entered the room with his breakfast

tray. Gboli followed him, elegantly dressed as always. Her hand flew to her mouth as she gasped upon seeing him.

"*Melda!* What are you doing?"

"I'm dressing myself," Maona replied.

"Stop this instant!" she said

Maona cut his eyes at Gboli and she quickly fell to the floor, touching her forehead to the tiles.

"Forgive my tone, Melda," she said.

Maona continued to search his closet for a proper shirt. Gboli rose from the floor then approached him carefully.

"Please, Melda, allow me to do which is my duty," she said.

Maona stepped aside then strolled to his tray where his breakfast waited. He silently scolded himself for embarrassing Gboli. It was her duty to oversee his wardrobe. He had dishonored her by doing so. He would have to apologize to her once he returned from Karago's compound.

He frowned when Jukundu took a seat beside him.

"It is done," he said before the djele could open his mouth. "There is nothing left to discuss."

"What have I done to anger you?" Jukundu said.

Maona placed down his fork.

"You've done nothing and I am not angry. This is a meeting that best goes unobserved."

Jukundu looked puzzled for a moment. Then his eyes widened.

"You wish to tell this story the way you see fit."

Maona smiled. "Exactly."

"There is no honesty in what you propose," Jukundu said.

Maona chewed his mango before answering.

"This is not a matter of honesty. It's a matter of influence. I am Karago's strongest rival. Meeting with him is only formality. Karago has no contact with our siblings or those of lineage. He stays holed up in his citadel gathering warriors around him hoping to take the title of Kidama by force. He doesn't understand the ways of politics."

Jukundu was about to reply when his eyes strayed. Maona turned to see a figure standing in the doorway of his room draped in a cloak and hood that obscured its face. Mona charged toward the woman, his short sword drawn.

"Who are you?" he demanded. "How did you..."

"Mona, stop," Maona said. "Everyone leave us."

Mona sheathed his sword then exited the room, glaring at the figure before leaving. Gboli left the room as well, careful not to contact the stranger. Jukundu remained seated, a curious glint in his eyes.

"You too, Jukundu," Maona said.

Jukundu's mouth dropped open.

"Melda! Surely you don't expect me to leave at such a mysterious moment! This must be remembered!"

"Leave, Jukundu," Maona said.

Jukundu shot to his feet then stormed from the room. Maona looked at the figure then motioned.

"I told you never to come here Turhaas," he said.

"You are not my master," the figure said, a deep female voice emitting from the hood. Slender hands reached up and pulled back the hood, revealing her beautiful ebony face. She glided into the room then took the seat Jukundu had occupied. Those slender hands brushed against Maona's cheeks and he was aroused.

"Not now," he said weakly.

"If not now, when?" she replied.

Maona fought to focus. He knew well the shapely body shifting under the layers of fabric. He's crossed the line with the sonchai too many times to claim innocence of her ways. But she did not control him.

"Did you bring what I asked for?" he said, his voice more forceful.

"Of course," Turhaas said, undeterred by his formal tone. "Let me give it to you."

Turhaas lifted her robes high, exposing her shapely and well muscled tattooed legs. She pushed aside his tray table with her hip then straddled him. Reaching into her robes about her neck she took out a talisman bag which she draped onto Maona's perspiring shoulders. She leaned in as she lowered the talisman then pressed her full lips against his. Maona opened his mouth, letting her tongue inside. Something hard passed between them, an object that burst into a cascade of flavor and sensations. The talisman grew hot against his chest, somehow merging with that which she had passed into his mouth. His arms circled around her waist; for a brief moment a feeling passed between them that was more intense than any lovemaking they'd experienced. When Turhaas pulled her lips away from him he felt as if he'd been laid upon a cloud.

"There," she said. "It is done."

Maona looked confounded. "What? What is done? We've barely begun."

Turhaas pressed her hips against him before dismounting.

"As you said, not now. I gave you the protection you asked. Your brother will not be able to harm you."

Maona felt for the talisman against his chest then remembered the object passed into his mouth.

"Why must you pass on your skills to me this way?" he asked. "Do you share yourself with the others you serve?"

Turhaas's smile faded, replaced by a stern countenance that concerned Maona. He reached absently for a sword that was not there. Turhaas noticed his gesture and her smile returned.

"How I dispense my skills are not your concern," she answered. "Be grateful that I choose to serve you more intimately. The closer the relationship between a sonchai and whom she serves, the stronger the nyama.

Besides, you pay me well enough now that I serve no other."

She sauntered to the door before turning to face him again.

"I wish you well on your task. I'll pour libations to my ancestors in hopes of your safe return."

"Hope?" Maona said. "I thought you said I was protected."

"You are," she replied. "But you are not the only Durobe with a sonchai. If your meeting comes to a confrontation we will see which one of us is strongest. Goodbye, Melda."

Turhaas left his room in a swirl of robes and scents. Soon afterwards his servants entered. Mona was the first to his side.

"Did she harm you?" he asked.

Maona laughed. "No. Summon additional guards to stand watch outside my room. I want no more unexpected intrusions."

"It's not as if they could stop her," Jukundu said as he entered. "Her nyama is strong. I know Turhaas and her family. You would do well to be wary of her."

"Your advice is a bit late," Maona replied.

Gboli was the last to return. She tipped to the wardrobe, waiting patiently for Maona to finish his meal. After washing his food down with a glass of mango juice he stood then stretched. Whatever Turhaas had given him infused him energy he normally didn't experience so early. He strode to the wardrobe where Gboli quickly began redressing him. Her choices were far better than his; he was reminded of why she was chosen for such a task.

"Now you look like a Kidama," she said proudly.

Maona looked at her with narrow eyes and she quickly stepped away.

"What have you heard, Gboli?" he asked.

"Nothing, Melba!" she answered. "I only…"

"Don't lie to me," Maona replied.

Gboli prostrated before him for the second time.

"Forgive me, Melba!" she whimpered. "There is talk among the guards that you go to challenge your brother for inheritance."

"That talk goes no further than you, do you understand?"

Gboli pressed her face harder against the floor.

"Yes, Melba. I understand. Please forgive me!"

"Leave me," he said.

Gboli scurried from the room, tears in her eyes. Jukundu watched her leave then shrugged.

"She is a weak one," he commented. "Yet she loves you fiercely."

"She's made a terrible choice," Maona replied.

Mona appeared at his door with his guards. The warriors were resplendent in their bright red leather armor and helmets, each holding a thick broadleaf tipped spear in their right hands and their elliptical shields bearing his adinkra in their left hands.

"Come Jukundu," Maona said.

His guards made way as he and the djele strode together down the hallway to the spiral stairs which descended into the foyer of the grand palace. The door guards held the door open as they passed through, both bowing their heads and touching their foreheads in acknowledgement of his rank. The horses waited for them; Maona's stable boy helped him mount his horse as the others mounted theirs.

Jukundu was at his boots, a pleading look in his eyes.

"Melda, I beseech you one last time! Let me accompany you!"

"No," Maona replied. "I will tell you all you need to know when I return."

He snapped the reins of his horse and the beast pivoted toward the compound gates. Maona nodded to the ranking guard and the man took his place at the vanguards. The drummers signaled the gate with a rapid ca-

dence and the iron and wood portal opened. The drummers' cadence slowed to a steady rhythm and Maona and his entourage galloped away. They rode for most of the day, taking respites when needed. That evening they settled in a small village resting on the border of Maona's lands, enjoying the hospitality of the village chief and the elders. The chief offered Maona his home which Maona accepted; his men were housed in a nearby compound usually reserved for special ceremonies.

The next day they set out beyond his borders after a morning feast that included a roasted bull and dancers. The chief spent much time attempting to convince Maona to consider one of his daughters for marriage. Maona politely refused. He was familiar with the chief's bloodline and knew any children born by his daughter would not be eligible for Kidama. The woman was quite beautiful and seemed interested in the match, but Maona held his ground. Seeking suitable wives and presenting himself as a suitable husband was not his focus. He had much more serious things on his mind during this journey.

That afternoon they crossed into the lands controlled by his brother, his adinkra visible on the border totems. A wave of nervousness swept Maona. It could all end here on the road, he and his guards overwhelmed by a superior force sent to make sure their meeting never took place. Their deaths would be blamed on bandits most likely; no one would believe it, but they would accept it. Once again the thought that what he was doing was folly crossed his mind but he shook it away. Their country depended on protocol to exist; he was sure Karago would meet with him to hear his claim before any hostilities began. It has always been thus; it would always be.

The narrow road they traversed widened toward the end of the day into an extensive highway bordered by carved stone. This was a sign of Karago's wealth that he could line his thoroughfare with such extravagance. After a few more miles the hard-packed mud gave way to gravel, then to paver brick. The hooves of their mounts clattered against the stone, striking a rhythm that infused a sense of confidence into the riders. Maona himself was affected, sitting higher in his saddle as they approached the outer villages of Karago's realm. Only merchants shared the road and the occasional curious farmer. After another brief respite to replenish their water and supplies, they continued their processional to Karago's compound. It was dusk before it came into view, its towers the first to make their appearance as they protruded over the hill studded horizon. By dark the towers glowed with welcoming fires burning within their uppermost rooms, a sign that Maona's entourage had been acknowledged and would be received. The tension that consumed the party since their departure eased upon seeing the wavering signal; at least the meeting would be peaceful.

Maona sat alone in his road tent, enjoying a meal of the local game and fruit. Now that they were in Karago's realm they would take their time covering the final miles to his brother's compound. It was important that he approached in the right way, displaying his rank while not being so arrogant as to give an impression of confrontation. He had chosen carefully the number of warriors that accompanied him and had personally overseen the gifts he would offer Karago for allowing him to meet. He was the eldest and deserved the honor Maona planned to show him. But once the proper rituals were observed, their meeting would become much more intense.

"Melda, may I enter?" a voice asked.

"Come," Maona said as he nodded.

His tent flapped open and Mona stepped inside. His personal bodyguard was covered in full warrior regalia, much unlike his wardrobe in Maona's compound.

"Melda Karago sends a messenger," he said.

Maona signaled for the messenger to en-

ter.

Mona exited the tent then returned with Karago's messenger. Maona smiled when the woman entered. This was no ordinary messenger; his brother had sent one of his elite Ntmapuwe warriors to greet him. The woman's black hair displayed the complex cornrow pattern of the Ntmapuwe, the blood red tips brushing the back of her neck. A leather and iron breastplate covered her torso, her muscled arms exposed with golden torcs punctuated by stylized leopard heads circling her biceps and wrists. A wide leather pleated skirt fell from her belted waist to just below her knees, hiding her well muscled thighs but exposing thick calves. On her feet were the infamous Ntmapuwe war boots, supple leather boots with sharpened steel edged toes. Maona's guards had relieved her of her shield, short sword, war club and spear, but that made no difference. She was just as deadly empty-handed as she was armed.

The woman prostrated before him, sprinkling dirt on her head before rising.

"Welcome, Melda Maona Traore," she said. "I am Ekuva Malungo, First Hand of Melda Karago. I welcome you to his compound. Is there anything you need to make your visit more comfortable?"

"I have all that I need, First Hand," Maona replied. "Tell my brother I am grateful for his offer. I assume our meeting is still scheduled for tomorrow at first light?"

"I cannot say, Melda," Ekuva replied. "Melda Karago is a very busy man. Much is demanded of one as great as he."

Maona smirked. "You can save your boasting, First Hand. Karago is my brother. I know his truth."

A flash of anger filled the First Hand's eyes. Maona considered summoning his guards to throw her out, but he would not waste good warriors for a veiled insult.

"Again, we welcome you," the warrior said, her voice more restrained. "If you see that you have any need, please send a messenger. My Melda awaits your audience."

The Ntmapuwe spun about then marched out of Maona's tent, shoving the flap aside before Mona could open it. Mona snarled after her then turned to Maona.

"You must be careful tomorrow," he said. "We are not welcomed here."

"I know," Maona replied. "But this is just a visit. I will meet my brother, state my intentions then leave. He knows better than to go beyond this. The Elders would deny him lineage otherwise."

Mona frowned. "The Elders. They are old. I don't trust anyone that will not stand with a weapon."

"Watch yourself," Maona replied. "The Elders' wisdom is irreproachable. Now go and make sure our visitor arrives at Karago's compound safely."

Mona prostrated then left the tent as Maona sat to finish his meal. Even he couldn't deny that this meeting would not be ordinary. Karago would have to follow protocol, he mused. To do anything otherwise would damage his reputation among the Elders, which was already precarious due to his insular and vulgar nature. A sip of palm wine soothed his uneasiness. He was being too cautious. They would meet, he would issue his challenge before witnesses then he would go home. Nothing would or could play out before their mother's death. That was the way it would be; that was the way it had always been.

Maona slept easy that night, sung to sleep by the sounds of the bush. He was awakened by Mona, who stood guard as he washed and donned his ceremonial robes. He exited his tent to an encouraging sight; Karago had sent him an escort. Ekuva led her horse to him, handing the reins to a wary Mona before prostrating.

"Good morning, Melda," she said. "I hope this day finds you in good spirits."

"It does," Maona replied.

"Melda Karago is anxious to meet with

you. He has sent us to provide your protection along the route."

"Is his realm so unruly that one must be guarded to travel only a few lengths to his compound?" Mona said.

Ekuva's eyes narrowed as she looked at Mona.

"My Melda wishes his brother to have the best protection," she replied.

"I have no time for rivalries," Maona said, even though the situation amused him. Mona and his guards had no reason to feel threatened by the Ntmapuwe. They were formidable in their own right and were protected by the strongest talisman Maona could afford. He walked between the two to his mount.

"Come," he said. "The two of you will ride with me."

"I am honored," Ekuva said.

Mona huffed. "You should be."

Maona and his entourage rode through Karago's town in silence save for the clatter of horse shoes against stone. No drummers preceded them, which suited Maona. He did not want this meeting with Karago to be remembered as a gaudy parade. As they neared Maona was reminded of the strength of the compound. Thick walls rose from the soil four times the height of a tall man. A wide gate of solid ironwood formed the entrance, raised by two winches attached to the gate with chains. They rode into a wide open courtyard bordered by low mud brick buildings which housed Karago's servants and guards. In the center of the compound stood Karago's palace, a three level square building with its own wall punctuated on each corner by round towers. A dome capped the third level, housing the private residence of Karago and his wives. Their meeting would take place on the second level.

The gates to Karago's home opened and an army of servants spilled forth. They assisted Maona and the others from their horses then whisked the beasts off to the nearby stable. One of the servants, a short broad man with a full beard and a golden cap approached Maona. Ekuva acknowledged the man with a deep bow, signaling that he was someone of importance.

The man prostrated before Maona.

"Melda Maona Traore, it is an honor to finally meet you," the man said. "I am Caungula, palace master of Karago. My Melda has spoken highly of you."

"I'm sure he has," Maona said. "Does he wait for me?"

"Yes," Caungula replied. "I will take you to him."

"Proceed," Maona said.

Caungula's face became heavy. "There is one thing, Melda Maona. Melda Karago wishes that you come alone."

"No," Mona blurted. His outburst was met by a glare from Caungula and Ekuva. Maona raised his hand to cut off any exchange between the three.

"Will my brother be alone as well?" he asked.

"Yes, Melda," Caungula replied. "He wishes this to be a private meeting."

"But his Ntmapuwe will be stationed outside our meeting, am I correct?"

"Of course," Caungula said.

"Then my guards will accompany me to the meeting room and join the Ntmapuwe," Maona said.

"As you wish, Melda," Caungula replied.

"Then let us go," Maona said.

They entered Karago's palace. Even Maona, raised among the opulence of the lineage families was impressed. The wide atrium floor consisted of granite tiles painted with epic figures of ancestors past, the walls covered with elaborate patterned carpets representing all the families of note. Karago was making his palace a place to be visited by dignitaries throughout the Hadal, anticipating his ascension even though their mother was far from relinquishing the stool. Maona would have something to say about that.

They reached the spiral stairway to the second level. Caugula took a step, and then looked back at Maona as if to say something, but Maona's stern gaze silenced him. He proceeded up the stairs, Maona and the others following. As they reached the top of the stairs they entered a short hallway punctuated by closed double doors with gilded handles. Two Ntmapuwe stood on either side of the door, armed with swords and shields. Maona's guards took position beside them, cutting glances at their adversaries. Caugula ambled to the doors, gripping the handles. Maona stood behind him as he opened the doors.

Karago's meeting room was as simple as his atrium was elaborate. His brother sat on a plain wooden stool wearing a crimson robe trimmed with golden threads. The hilt of his jyamba glittered at his waist, as did Maona's. If there was to be a confrontation between them, it would be with the blades. His head was shaved, another pretentious gesture. Maona was glad he had come to confront his brother; he was taking too many liberties hidden away in his compound.

"Leave us," his brother said with his soft voice. Caugula prostrated then walked backwards from the room, closing the doors behind him. Maona proceeded to the empty stool before his brother, sweeping his robe aside before sitting.

"Maona, it is good to see you," Karago said.

Maona smirked. "Is it?"

Karago responded with a smile.

"Yes it is. It is not often that my siblings visit me. Sometimes I miss your company."

"Sometimes?"

Karago's smile faded. "Our circumstances prevent us from being close. You know this."

Maona nodded. "That is true. I thank you for your courteous welcome. You did not have to be so kind."

"No I didn't," Karago said.

"I have come to…"

"I know why you have come," Karago

said. "Half of the Hadal knows as well and it is not their business. What right do you have to challenge what is mine?"

"I have the right as a child of our parents and the blood that flows through my veins," Maona replied.

"I am eldest," Karago countered.

"That is no guarantee to Kidama," Maona said. "It is the Elders and the Ancestors that make the choice."

"And they have always chosen the eldest." Karago's eyes narrowed. "Always."

Maona stood and began to pace. "And what will you do for Joba, Karago?"

"You have no right to ask me that," Karago replied.

"I have the right as your successor to know your intentions," Maona shot back.

"I will do as those before me have done," Karago said. "I will maintain the traditions. I will honor our ancestors. I will serve the people. Most of all, I will maintain the peace between us and our neighbors."

The last statement was aimed directly at Maona. He grinned at his brother.

"So we will conform to the rules of complacency while our rivals scheme for our demise."

"You have no proof of this," Karago said.

"What proof do I need? You know as well as I do what every Kidama in the Hadal dreams of."

"Not every Kidama," Karago replied.

Maona's disappointment in his brother surfaced on his face.

"No, not every Kidama."

"You would ruin us," Karago said. "You would see our young men and women murdered for your pride. The harvest would die in the fields while you attempt to fulfill a dream, if there would be a harvest at all. Because who would plant it? Old men, women and children? The people do not want war. They wish peace, as do I."

"It is not the people's place to tell us what they want."

Karago closed his eyes. "Do what you wish, Maona. Present your argument to the Elders. Let them decide. If you came here hoping to convince me to step aside you wasted your time. I will do no such thing."

"I didn't expect you to," Maona replied. "I am fulfilling my obligation as your brother."

"And you've done so."

Karago stood, indicating that their meeting was over.

"I have prepared lodging for you within my compound. There will be a feast in your honor this evening. I hope you understand if I do not attend."

"Thank you for your generosity," Maona said. "Despite my challenge."

Karago nodded.

"Goodbye, brother. May your journey home be safe."

Maona stood then approached his brother. They hugged, and then Maona turned and left the room. The meeting had gone as he had expected; direct and to the point. Karago was not a verbose man, nor was he. He would return to his compound for a week's rest then journey to Jakada, the home city of the Elders. There he would make his case to succeed his mother's rule.

The 'celebration' in his honor was a tepid affair, the dancers and servers performing their duties and not much more. Maona was happy when it was over; giving him and his entourage a chance to get some much needed rest. The next morning they broke camp without fanfare and began the journey back to Maona's compound. He was right not to let Jukundu accompany him. With the exception of the journey there was not much to tell. That afternoon they stopped to eat and replenish their supplies at a local market, much to the delight of the merchants. Maona was generous with his spending, hoping to leave an impression that would serve him once he became Kidama. Yes, he would become Kidama, for he would be like his father and his mother before him, seeking to make Joba the land it was meant to be, a land of proud warriors and prosperous subjects. Karago's fear would be pushed aside, and the others would follow him because of his strength. There could be no other outcome. There would not be.

Dusk found the entourage entering the bush. Maona fought to stay awake as the rhythm of his horse lulled him into drowsiness. Mona rode beside him, every diligent.

"Mona, ride forward and let the vanguard know we will stop at the next clearing and camp for the night."

Mona nodded his head then kicked his horse into a gallop. Another bodyguard quickly took his position, a wide grin on his face.

"Melda, I am honored to be chosen to accompany you on this journey," the guard said. "My family has served you…"

The man jerked as an arrow pierced from his throat. Maona moved instinctively, jumping from his mount and using its broad body for protection. His bodyguards did the same, forming a ring around him with their horses, their swords drawn. He heard Mona's voice shouting over the confusion.

"Archers! Form ranks and return fire!"

Mona's voice was drowned out by the cries of the horses as they were pummeled with arrows. Maona jumped away as his horse fell at him. Many of his bodyguards were not as lucky, their mounts fell on top of them, pinning them to the ground. Maona took out his sword as his attackers converged. He was not fooled by the ragged clothing and nondescript weapons; these were Ntmapuwe. They'd disguised themselves just in case anyone was witness to his murder, but he was sure they scoured the area of any potential witnesses before they attacked. His surviving guards rushed to meet them with two remaining beside him lest one of the assassins broke through. The guards were beaten back closer to him as the attackers numbers increased. Maona was not afraid. If he died

this day he would die as a warrior and one day the truth of his demise would be sung. He tightened his grip on his sword and waited.

A spear flashed through the protection. Maona had no time to block it. It shattered just before striking him, splinters and bits of metal flying in every direction. He laughed; Turhaas's talisman worked well. His relief was short-lived; his bodyguards lay on the ground, wounded by the shrapnel. An assassin charged toward him with another spear ready to throw but she was shoved aside by one of her companions, one whose eyes revealed who she was despite her covered face.

"Ekuva," Maona said. "So he sent you to deliver the death blow. Come then, see if you are worthy."

Ekuva attacked. As expected she was skillful, but so was Maona. He parried her every move with a skill beyond most Kidama, for Maona was a true warrior. Those blows that slipped by his guard were deflected by Turhaas's nyama, much to Ekuva's frustration. Although she was not able to wound him, Maona found it just as difficult to inflict damage to her. The few cuts he managed to make were annoying at the most.

Ekuva readied herself for another attack when she looked suddenly to her left. A horse slammed into her a moment later, sending her sprawling to the ground. Maona looked up to see Mona on his horse accompanied by two archers. In his bodyguard's hands were the reins of an unmounted horse. Maona needed no urging; he climbed onto the horse and together they rode toward the bush, Maona and Mona slashing down on their attackers, the archers firing into the assassins attempting to block their path. Soon they were clear, riding hard down the narrow trail. Maona pulled his horse beside Mona.

"We must leave the road," he shouted. "It will be too easy to follow us."

"We must return to the compound," Mona replied.

Maona shook his head. "We must leave

the road. I know a different route."

Maona took the lead. They followed the road for another span then dismounted and led their horses into the dense bush. He had no intentions of returning to his compound. Karago had declared war against him. It was time for his siblings to choose sides. When he felt they were far enough from the road he signaled for a halt. He addressed the archers first.

"Ride back to the compound. Tell everyone to prepare for attack, a siege most likely. Confirm that everyone believes I am in the compound as well."

Maona took off one of his rings and gave it to the archers.

"This will make sure that your words are true. Stay in the bush until you are sure you're not being followed."

The archers dismounted then prostrated before Maona and Mona. They mounted then rode off.

"Are they good warriors?" Maona asked.

"Among the best," Mona replied. "Melda, where are we going?"

"To gather allies," Maona replied.

"Do we have time? I suspect Melda Karago has planned this assassination for quite some time. He would not do such a thing unless he felt he had support among your siblings."

"Among our siblings, no. Among the Elders, yes. We ride to Melda Moke's compound."

Moke's compound was the closest to Karago. She was not one of Maona's closest siblings, but she was also not fond of Karago. The word of an assassination attempt would put all the siblings on edge; if it happened to one, it would happen to another. The journey took longer than normal since they stuck to the bush, but soon the sight of Moke's modest compound and surrounding villages came to view. Maona and Mona rode the narrow road to the compound, exhausted yet relieved. Rest and safety lay ahead.

The compound gates opened and the welcoming entourage galloped to them. To his surprise Moke was among them. Her guards surrounded them; when Moke came to him her expression made him worry.

"Brother," she said. "It is good to see you alive."

A chill ran through Maona.

"You knew?"

Moke nodded. "Yes. So do the others."

Maona took a quick assessment of his situation. He and Mona were completely surrounded. The weakest link in the circle was his sister. His hand fell to his hilt.

"No Maona," she warned. "I did not come here to finish what Karago started. I don't agree with his methods, but his words are true. You have no right to challenge his ascension."

"I can't believe you're siding with him!" Maona said.

"I am not taking Karago's side," Maona replied. "I'm siding with tradition. True, I dislike Karago but his rule will not be one of concern. He doesn't seek glory like you do but he will not harm the Kidamalands either. We have always ruled with strength and patience."

"This is not acceptable," Maona said.

"It has to be." Moke gave Maona a sympathetic smile.

"You must accept this, brother. The others will join Karago in seeking your death if you don't. I want no part of it."

"So you will not support me?"

"No, I won't."

"Then the Ancestors curse you!"

Shock took over Moke's face.

"Why would you curse me so after I have tried to help you?"

"Curse you all!" he said. "If I have to fight him I'll do so on my own! As soon as I return to my compound…"

Moke looked away when he mentioned his stronghold.

"No," he said.

"I'm sorry, Maona."

He turned his horse away and kicked it to a full gallop. Moke's guards cleared his way. For eight days he and Mona rode in silence, pushing themselves and their horses to the limit. They took the main road, oblivious to whatever ambushes that might occur. Any hope Maona harbored left him as he saw the smoke rising in the distance. They reached the crest of a nearby hill and the truth was revealed. The fire that had been set had long burned out. His compound lay in smoldering ruins, as did the surrounding villages.

"By the ancestors," Mona whispered.

Maona could not speak, his voice silenced by despair and anger.

"Come, we must search for survivors!" Mona said.

Maona did not move.

"Melda!"

Maona turned his mount around. Karago had destroyed him. He had let his confidence blind him; he had underestimated his brother.

"Melda!"

Maona did not look back. He would ride south into the bush beyond the Pem River. It was said that when a Kidama failed his people, the Elders would give him a choice; kill himself or cross the Pem, which was sure death as well. Maona, a Kidama in his mind only, chose to cross the river. To do so would leave no trace of him or his shame.

"Now there's a song for you to sing if you are still alive, Jukundu," he said aloud. "Quite a song indeed."

To be continued. . .

The **CROMCAST**

...A podcast for the barbarian at heart!

Find us on iTunes, Stitcher, or your favorite podcatcher.

thecromcast.blogspot.com
thecromcast@gmail.com
@thecromcast

UNDER THE BLOOD

By Darrell Z. Grizzle

I asked Daddy once why our church doesn't have any windows. It's a plain cinder block building with a small cross on top of the roof. Doesn't look like any other churches in the holler. Daddy said we keep to ourselves because it's nobody's business how we worship the Lord. He said there are some folks who don't take kindly to those who speak in tongues and take up serpents, and maybe it's just best if they never find out.

I've never done any snakehandling myself. Daddy says I have to wait till I'm 13 years old, the age of accountability, when I can get baptized and officially join the church. I got saved when I was 5, so if I die before I'm baptized I know I'll go to heaven. My friend Billy said he'd wait till he's 13 to get saved and baptized both. I always worried about that, like he might not make it to heaven if he died before he was saved. But Daddy says children are under the blood of Jesus and they don't go to hell if they die before the age of accountability. Daddy is the pastor so I reckon he knows best.

Billy always said he'd be a healer when he grew up and that he already had the gift. I'd seen him bring two small animals back to life, a possum and a redbird. When the possum came back to life it ran off into the woods. But the black cat who lives down by the creek had killed the redbird and torn off one of its wings, so when it came back to life it couldn't fly away, and the black cat got it again.

I hated it when Billy threw rocks at my bedroom window at night. I was always afraid Daddy would hear. I still remember the night I looked out the window and saw Billy waving up at me with a shovel in one hand and a crowbar and a flashlight in the other. I motioned for him to shush and I came downstairs and out into the backyard. Billy whispered, "Grab a shovel."

"What for?" I whispered back, heading toward the toolshed.

"I want to see if we can heal something bigger than a possum. Let's go to the graveyard." I started to say no, but Billy was already heading that way, so I followed him. The moon was full and bright and we didn't really need his flashlight.

I followed Billy to the grave of Deacon Turner, who'd died the week before. "What are we doing?" I asked, still whispering, although we were a good quarter-mile from our houses.

"Mr. Turner was a deacon at church," said Billy, "so I bet he would have enough faith to resurrect and be healed."

"But I thought it was the healer who had to have faith, not the one being healed," I said, no longer whispering. "That possum and that redbird didn't have any faith."

"No, but Jesus said 'thy faith hath made thee whole.' I reckon if one don't have faith, the other one will do. But if both have faith—and if you and me do too—that's three times the faith. We can do this."

"Do what? Bring Deacon Turner back to life? He's already in his grave!"

"Just have faith, John Mark. Faith like a

mustard seed. That's all I ask. And help me dig him up."

We started digging and Billy started praying as we dug. He got louder and more out of breath as he commanded health and healing and newness of life into Deacon Turner's body in the name of Jesus Christ. He quoted the King James Bible, "And ye shall know that I am the Lord, when I have opened your graves, O my people, and brought you up out of your graves!" By the time we reached the coffin and pulled it up beside the dug-up grave, sweat was running down both our faces.

"What's that?" I said sharply. "Sounds like—a scratching or something." We both listened closely at the simple pine coffin and sure enough, there was a scratching noise coming from inside it. Then there was a sound like someone gasping for breath.

"He's alive! He's trying to get out!" I yelled.

Billy took the crowbar and tried to prise open the lid. He couldn't get it open and finally took the crowbar and hit the top of the coffin several times. The crowbar smashed through the lid of the coffin, splintering the wood and lodging in Deacon Turner's face. I screamed and stepped backwards when the deacon let out a loud cry of pain. His eyes were open and they looked wild and frantic.

Deacon Turner struggled to sit up in the coffin and he was still wheezing, like he was dying, not coming back to life. He looked like a madman. He was trying to speak but he couldn't catch his breath. He reached out one arm like he was going to grab me but I jerked away.

I started crying and shouted, "We've got to go get our parents! They'll know what to do!"

"No!" yelled Billy. "We can't just leave him like this! He can't get his breath!"

"Well maybe you need to pray harder or something! He looks like he's dying all over again!"

Billy laid his hands on Deacon Turner's shoulder. "By the blood of Jesus Christ I command you to breathe and be healed!"

Deacon Turner swung around, knocking Billy's hand off his shoulder. Billy jerked back and then he started to cry too. Deacon Turner struggled to get out of his coffin, then collapsed in a dead faint. He was perfectly still. I rolled him over and it looked liked he was dead again, with a look of horror frozen on his face.

Billy and I grabbed our shovels and ran all the way home. We got to my house first and Billy grabbed me by the shoulders. "We can't tell anyone about this! They won't understand and they'll blame us for doing it wrong."

"But what will we do about Deacon Turner?"

"We'll get up early and go bury him again, before anybody can find him."

I wanted to say we needed to go bury him now but no way did I want to go back to the graveyard that night. I nodded, "OK." Billy went home and I put the shovel back in Daddy's tool shed, then snuck back into my bedroom and pulled the covers up over my head and cried most of the night.

Next morning I got up early and started to sneak out but Daddy was already up, drinking coffee at the kitchen table and reading his big Scofield Bible. He smiled at me and asked, "What are you doing up so early, John Mark?"

"I, uh, I got a test this morning and wanted to do some more studying."

"I reckon that's what I'm doing too, studying. But studying the Word, not a schoolbook."

I poured myself a bowl and cereal and sat down. "Do you believe if we have enough faith we can bring the dead back to life?"

"Of course. That's what it says in the Bible."

"Have you ever seen someone brought back to life?"

"No, I've never seen it myself, but I know it happens. We sponsor missionaries who've seen it happen, out on the mission field. Why do you ask?"

"Oh, I was just reading the Book of Acts last night and wondered what it would be like to see that for myself."

He reached out and tussled my hair. "I'm glad I raised a son who studies the Word. You'll make a fine man of God some day."

I didn't feel like a fine man of God. I felt like I'd done something wrong but I couldn't figure out why. I was hoping Billy had gotten out to the graveyard that morning to re-bury Deacon Turner, but I soon found out he hadn't.

Billy's dad came knocking at the door. Daddy looked surprised to see him. "What brings you over so early, Brother Jonathan? Come in and have some coffee."

"I'm afraid I've got some horrible news, Preacher. Someone desecrated a grave last night in the church cemetery."

"What?" Daddy sank down into the kitchen chair in surprise.

"Someone dug up Deacon Turner's grave and dragged his body out into the kudzu behind the church. It's a horrible sight. The po–lice are already out there." Billy's dad said "police" like "PO–leece."

Daddy looked angry and confused. "Who would do something like that to the grave of a deacon?"

"I don't know. The po–lice said his widow is the one who found the grave all dug up, early this morning. She had a breakdown and had to be taken to the hospital and given medication. They called me because I'm the caretaker of the graveyard, and I wanted you to know before I tell the other deacons."

"I appreciate that, Jonathan. I'll come on over to the graveyard and see if I can be of any assistance."

"We need to get him buried again but we can't touch anything till the po–lice finish their investigation."

"We might need to keep watch over the graveyard at night in case these hooligans want to desecrate any other graves. My beloved wife is buried out there." He nodded towards me. "John Mark's mom."

"My wife is a nervous wreck right now, all upset about the desecration. If you have the time, I'm sure she'd appreciate a visit from the pastor this morning."

"Of course," Daddy said, as Billy's dad said goodbye. Daddy was gathering up the keys to his truck, along with his big leather-bound Bible. I asked if I could come along. "School don't start for another couple of hours," I said.

He looked at me like he was about to say no, then he changed his mind. "You're only a year and a half away from the age of accountability. I reckon you're old enough to see what kind of evil deeds happen in this world sometimes. But you stay in the truck, OK?"

"OK, Daddy. I will." Evil deeds. He thought what Billy and I had done was evil deeds. A chill went down my spine.

All four patrol cars from the sheriff's office were out at the graveyard, lights flashing. Yellow crime scene tape surrounded the grave as well as a narrow path to the kudzu-covered woods out back. Daddy got out of the truck, his Bible in hand, and walked over to his friend Mack, who was a deputy. I rolled down my window I could hear. "This is a dark day, Pastor," Mack said to Daddy. "We've never had a crime like this in the county before."

"What happened?" asked Daddy.

"Someone dug up the grave of Deacon Turner, then busted open his coffin and dragged his body out." I looked over at the grave and could see the coffin's top had splintered into two big pieces when I'd prised it open with the shovel.

Mack was still talking. "Whoever did it dragged the body along the ground instead of carrying it. The coroner says it almost looks like Deacon Turner crawled his way into the kudzu."

"This doesn't make any sense. Who would do this kind of thing?"

"The sheriff has already called the state bureau of investigation. They've got a special officer who works occult and satanic crimes. I never ever thought we'd need to call him." He said again, "This is a dark day."

I wanted to tell them it was just me and Billy trying to do what the Bible says believers can do. But I knew we'd be in trouble and maybe even taken to juvenile hall if I said anything.

Mack reached out and grabbed Daddy's shoulder. "I want you know, Pastor, me and the missus will be in church Sunday. I know we don't make it every Sunday when I have to work, but if this kind of occult activity is going on in our community, we all need to make sure we're right with the Lord."

Daddy nodded his head in agreement. "I appreciate that, Mack. I look forward to seeing you and the wife in church Sunday morning."

We stayed for almost an hour, me in the truck, Daddy offering to help in anyway he could. The sheriff's deputies looked nervous and scared, like the dug-up grave was something dark and evil, and several told Daddy they were grateful for his presence—and for the Bible he carried—as they worked the crime scene.

At school that morning I pulled Billy aside and told him, in whispers, what I'd seen. "We can't tell anyone we did it," I said. "They've got a special agent from the state coming out because they think this is occult and satanic. They might arrest us and take us to juvenile hall."

Billy looked frightened and nodded his head. "If they found Deacon Turner in the kudzu, that means he was still alive when we

left and he crawled out there himself. I feel horrible. We left that poor man to die when we might could've saved him." I felt sick to my stomach. I'd learned CPR in school but didn't even think to use it when Deacon Turner was gasping for breath.

Billy told me he had gotten up early and gone to the graveyard with his shovel, hoping to re-bury Deacon Turner before anyone found the dug-up grave. But he said the Widow Turner was already there and she was screaming like a madwoman. She ran off towards her home, and Billy hid in the woods until he could sneak back home.

While he was in the woods he'd found the black cat that lives down by the creek. The cat was dead. Billy's voice was trembling as he told me what happened. "I laid hands on it and prayed and it came back to life, but it had the devil in its eyes and it started attacking me." He pulled up his shirt and showed me the deep red scratch marks on his chest and stomach. "I tried to get away but it kept coming after me. I finally grabbed the shovel and got it off me. It ran away then, off towards the graveyard."

I didn't know what to say to that. I felt awful. I felt like I was going to throw up.

After school I was doing homework at the kitchen table when Deputy Mack dropped by. Daddy invited him into the kitchen and poured him some sweet ice tea. Mack glanced at me and Daddy told him it was OK to talk about the crime scene in front of me.

Mack drew a deep breath and said, "It gets worse, Pastor. The occult and satanic specialist came out this afternoon. He found the dead body of a cat on top of a nearby grave. The specialist thinks it was some kind of ritual sacrifice. Whatever occult group did this, they probably offered the cat as a sacrifice before they dug up Deacon Turner's grave."

I gasped out loud and dropped my pencil.

Daddy looked over at me and said, "Son, I think you'd better finish your homework upstairs."

"Yes sir," I said. I grabbed my books and my papers and went to my room.

I kept thinking about how they all kept using the words occult and satanic and I wanted to tell them no, it was just me and Billy. Actually, it was just Billy, not me. Billy had brought Deacon Turner back to life, as well as the black cat. For the first time I started to wonder if maybe the grownups were right and maybe Billy actually was occult and satanic. He was my best friend and went to church regular but I couldn't help but wonder.

I didn't see Billy at school the next day. When I got home, Daddy was at the kitchen table again, and he looked up at me with a face full of worry and I think even fear. "John Mark, we need to talk." He scooted one of the chairs out from the table with his foot and motioned for me to sit down. I did.

"Son, your friend Billy broke down and confessed to digging up the grave. Some kind of nonsense about wanting to pray Deacon Turner back to life, to see if he could do it. He disrespected the Lord's work by being prideful and treating it like it was a game or a prank. Did you know anything about what Billy was doing?"

For a split second I thought about lying and saying no. If Daddy was asking me, that meant Billy hadn't mentioned my name when he told the story. Or maybe he did, and Daddy was just testing me to see if I'd be honest or not. Regardless, I just couldn't bring myself to lie to Daddy, not when he had that worried look on his face. "Yes sir," I said. "I was with him when he dug up the grave."

"I thought as much. You go on up to your room while I figure out what I need to do." I hurried up the stairs and stayed in my room for the rest of the night. Daddy didn't call me down for dinner, and I didn't dare to leave my room.

The next morning, Saturday, Daddy told me that he and the deacons had called an emergency meeting at church for three o'clock that afternoon. A service of deliverance. I asked him if I could go to it. He looked at me for a long minute before he said, "Yes. You're part of all this, so it's only right you be there. But I want you to sit quietly and not interrupt anything."

"Yes sir," I said, as I hungrily dug into breakfast.

There were about a dozen folks at the deliverance meeting. All the deacons of the church were there, including Billy's dad, along with some of their wives. Deputy Mack was there too, in uniform, his gun in its holster. I was surprised to see Evangelist Harold Week, who lived several states away. He usually only visited our church once a year, in the summertime, to hold weeklong revival services. He looked like he had driven all night to be there. His eyes were dark and his hairpiece, which did a poor job of disguising the fact that he was bald, was a little bit lop-sided.

I heard Evangelist Week whisper to Daddy, "Why is a deputy here?" Daddy whispered back, "That's Mack. He's a good friend and a faithful member of the church." Evangelist Peak nodded but he still looked concerned.

Daddy went up front and addressed the congregation. "We all know why we're here. I hope you've all fortified yourselves with prayer. We got a mighty task ahead of us." He turned to one of the deacons and asked, "Brother Peppers, will you lead us in singing Power in the Blood?"

There was no piano player but Deacon Peppers started singing and we all joined in, raising our voices high.

Would you be free from the burden of sin?

There's power in the blood, power in the blood.

Would you o'er evil a victory win?

There's wonderful power in the blood.

We sang all four verses, then Daddy nodded at Billy's dad and said, "OK, Jonathan, bring Billy in."

Deacon Jonathan went into the small side room and came out with Billy, who had his eyes cast down at the floor as his dad walked him to the front of the church. They stood with Daddy in front of the communion table that stood in front of the pulpit. "This Do In Remembrance Of Me" was carved into the front of the wooden table. To the side of the pulpit and table were altar rails. Daddy laid his hand on Billy's shoulder and said, "Are you ready to be delivered?" Billy looked up at Daddy and said "Yes sir, I am," then cast his eyes down at the floor again. I could see Billy had been crying.

Daddy looked out at the small congregation. "We are honored to have Evangelist Harold Week with us today. I'd like to invite Brother Harold to start us off with a word of prayer."

The evangelist came up front and put one hand on Billy's shoulder. With the other hand he lifted his large leather-bound Bible into the air as he prayed. "We thank you, Heavenly Father, for the good heart of this boy. He's a good boy, Lord, but he got led astray by Satan and presumed to do things only your ordained ministers can do." There were shouts of "Amen!" from the small assembly as he prayed. "This boy knows your Word, but he's young and he doesn't know how to rightly divide it. We know that your Word says even the Devil can cite Scripture for his purpose." I knew from school that Shakespeare said that, not the Bible, but no way was I going to interrupt this prayer, even though it was beginning to frighten me. Billy was trembling now, and tears were rolling down both cheeks. I'd never been frightened by prayer in church before.

The evangelist went on as the amens rose louder from those assembled. Some of the deacons were speaking in tongues. Shout-ing in tongues. The evangelist continued his prayer. "We come before your heavenly throne, Our Father, and ask that you deliver this boy from the evil spirit that has deceived him. We cast out the demon of deception and presumption. By the Blood of Jesus Christ and in his holy name we cast you out, evil spirit!"

Billy started to convulse as the evangelist prayed on. I could hear a low guttural sound, like a growl, coming deep from Billy's throat. He had a wild look in his eyes, like a trapped feral cat. I looked around at the deacons and others who were praying loudly with the evangelist, and I was shocked to see the same wild look in their eyes.

The praying continued as Billy pitched backward, the convulsions knocking him off his feet. As he fell, Billy's daddy caught him and laid him gently to the ground, but Billy's shirt had come up as he fell and we could see the deep red scratches the cat had given him. "Look!" shouted the evangelist. "The demon is trying to come out!" I could tell Billy had not told anyone else about the scratches because Billy's dad's eyes widened in fear. The praying got louder as everyone crowded around and continued shouting for the demon to BE GONE in Jesus' name.

I stood still, confused, not knowing whether to join in the prayer or run away, until Billy started making a choking sound. "He's choking on his tongue!" I shouted. "We need to clear his mouth and give him CPR!"

Daddy broke free of the assembly and grabbed me roughly by the collar and shouted at me, "Go home! It was a mistake to let you be here!" I looked in Daddy's eyes and saw the same wild look I'd seen in Billy's eyes. I looked over at Billy and saw that he was no longer choking but his eyes were wide with terror and confusion. I looked down at my pants as I realized I had peed myself. I ran out the door of the church in horror and shame. I didn't stop running till I got home and ran to my room. I threw off my pants, which were soaking wet, and collapsed into bed and sobbed into my pillow until I fell asleep.

Hours later, I woke up when Daddy put his hand on my shoulder, nudging me awake. I could tell it was the middle of the night because it was pitch dark outside the bedroom window. "I'm afraid Billy didn't make it," Daddy said. I looked at him in confusion, not knowing what he meant. He went on. "He wasn't delivered from evil. His body is down at the county morgue." I just stared at Daddy, not knowing what to say. Daddy got up and left the room. I lay in bed for a long minute before I realized I wasn't breathing, then I gasped again, this time for air.

Billy's funeral was two days later, on the opposite side of the cemetery from Deacon Turner's grave, which had been restored with a fresh mound of earth when his body had been reburied. The funeral was a somber affair. About fifty people—all the members of our small congregation, plus some of Billy's school friends and their parents—gathered round the casket. Most of the folks there didn't know about the service of deliverance at the church. The county coroner had listed Billy's cause of death as a seizure.

Daddy said a few words and quoted some Bible verses. He said Billy was a good boy who'd be missed by everyone who knew him. He said Billy was young and had not yet reached the age of accountability, so he was in heaven now. He was "under the blood." Some of the people nodded their heads in agreement, but I could tell that some of the

church members didn't agree and were wondering if Billy was in heaven or hell. I found myself hating those folks as Billy's coffin was lowered into his grave.

After the funeral Billy's dad walked over to me and said he had a bag of things he thought Billy would want me to have, since I was his best friend. I looked in the bag and saw Billy's favorite toy Army men and the model starship he'd been so proud of putting together. I said "Thank you, sir," to Billy's dad, although I didn't feel like saying anything to anybody.

That night I went out to the graveyard and put the starship and the Army men on Billy's grave, where the headstone would go when the stonemason had it ready. The smell of freshly dug earth was still strong, and the caretakers had left their four shovels near the grave. I wondered if they had intentionally left the shovels in the form of a cross, or if that was just how they'd left them. The cemetery was silent except for a hoot owl, off in the distance. I sat down by the grave and I let myself cry.

I didn't mean to cry so loudly, but I guess I needed to let it all out. I cried so hard I got short of breath. As I tried to calm myself down, I heard it. A scratching noise. Coming from Billy's grave. I leaned closer to see if I'd heard what I thought I had heard. The scratching noise got louder, then changed into a knock. Billy was knocking on the lid of his casket. From inside the casket. I leaped backwards, not knowing what to do.

Those four shovels gleamed in the moonlight. The knocking grew louder.

I grabbed one of the shovels, and I started to dig.

INTRODUCTION TO DONALD WANDREI'S "THE EMPEROR OF DREAMS"

By Scott Connors

Readers of the *Overland Monthly*, a San Francisco literary magazine founded by Bret Harte in 1868, may have found the following editorial preface to an article in the December 1926 issue damning by faint praise:

"This may be a little too much of praise of Clark Ashton Smith, but at least it will bring comment and that is what we want," said George Sterling when he brought this article into our office for the December issue. (380)

The story of how this essay came to be written and published, along with the subsequent debate between Sterling and his one-time protégé Smith, may illuminate the aesthetic rift that had opened between them and also elucidate his subsequent embrace of the weird tale as an art form.

Donald Albert Wandrei (1908–1987) began corresponding with H. P. Lovecraft almost precisely two years after he began to exchange letters with Clark Ashton Smith. We often speak of the Lovecraft Circle, as if HPL were a massive celestial object whose immense gravitational field captured lesser writers and transformed them into mere satellites, mere footnotes in his biography or volume of his letters. Yet three of Lovecraft's closest friends—Samuel Loveman, George Kirk, and Wandrei—only entered into his life after their friendships with Smith. Bearing this in mind, it might be more accurate to speak of HPL and CAS as forming a binary star system.

Donald Albert Wandrei (1908-1987)

The summer of 1924 was a critical time for Wandrei's intellectual development. "In three months," he wrote to Lovecraft, "the summer I read 'Ebony and Crystal' and [Arthur Machen's] 'The Hill of Dreams'—my ideas underwent a complete revolution, and I walked to the opposite side of the fence, changing from a half-materialistic scientist to a romanticist and idealist and aesthete" (*Mysteries* 81). Wandrei described his discovery of Clark Ashton Smith and its impact upon him in his posthumously published mainstream novel *Invisible Sun*. Wandrei's protagonist, Drew, discovers a pulp magazine, obviously inspired by *Weird Tales*, and is impressed by its cover, which "instantly reminded him of a nightmare he had once experienced" (257). As he peruses the magazine, Drew "chanced[1] upon reference to a book of 'mad, strange, haunted' verse by a California poet" (258). This was Smith's collection *Ebony and Crystal: Poems in Verse and Prose*.[2] After ordering the book, Drew was disappointed at its shoddy production values.[3]

But Drew read on, and the book became a living empire through which he wandered. A magic casement had opened. The familiar world passed away. In its place rose a kingdom of fantasy and glory, of haunted pools and alien spires. The wind sang to him and the sea gave up its secrets. The opulence of the *Arabian Nights* unfolded; ornate decorations were scrolled upon these leaves. It was poetry that ached with the burden of a wonderful vision that life must always fall short of. It was the cry of a dead man. ... These were not songs for the many, or lyrics for the few. They were the language of hierophants, couched in cryptical symbols. Often they were so cryptic as to be meaningless; but often, too, they were instinct with magic. They were a sorcery breathed by only witches and read by neophytes alone. They were ebony and crystal. (258–259)

Soon Wandrei was putting his money where his mouth was: when Smith was experiencing difficulty in finding a publisher willing to bring out his next poetry collection, *Sandalwood*, Wandrei offered to subsidize half of the printing costs from his own pocket.[4] *Sandalwood* appeared in late 1925, with Sterling using his contacts among the San Francisco newspapers to arrange for reviews, and its 250 copy edition was the only one of Smith's self-published books that he ever saw go out of print.

Wandrei was at this time a student at the University of Minnesota and a staff writer for the *Minnesota Review*. He conceived of writing

a series of monographs on neglected imaginative writers such as Park Barnitz, author of the exquisite poetry collection *The Book of Jade* (1901). I know of only two such that he completed: "Arthur Machen and *The Hill of Dreams*" (*Minnesota Review Spring* 1926), and "The Emperor of Dreams," the piece under discussion here. Wandrei sent his tribute to Smith that summer. Smith was appreciative of it, writing to Wandrei that "Portions of it are prose-poetry" (*SL* 88). At the same time, he recognized that it was the product of a young man's enthusiasm:

> I think you were wise to "tone down" superlative adjectives, and I have no fault to find with the alterations. The whole paper seems excellent to me. As to bettering it, I fear I have no suggestions that would be worth offering. More criticism and less eulogy would make the paper more acceptable to editors and readers. However, you wanted to express your own "reaction" (which doesn't seem to include fault-finding!) as clearly and sincerely as possible. And it seems to me that you have done this. (*SL* 89)

Smith had shown the essay to both Lovecraft and Sterling. Lovecraft was more than receptive to Wandrei's praises:

> I was very glad to hear from you, & to receive the critique I have so long been anxious to see. The latter is really very just & acute in its analysis of your work, but as you say may meet editorial opposition because of its tone of youthful effervescence & colourful rhapsody. I imagine that Wandrei must be rather a young chap—though possessed of a fund of imagery & command of language which will serve him well when he has learnt the lessons of restraint & austerity of form which come with later life. I certainly wish he could get the review into print somewhere, though I know the process is none too easy. What is Wandrei, anyway? That is, what does he write, & what are his general literary bearings? I am interested

in anyone as genuinely sensitive to the fantastic as he. (*SL* II.76–77)

When Smith first mentioned Wandrei's essay to Sterling, he wrote that "I appreciate the article, but fear he'll have a hard time getting it published except at his own expense" (*SU* 276). When CAS first mentioned Wandrei's essay, Sterling replied "If your St. Paul friend can't get his appreciation printed, have him send it to me, and I'll get it in the *Overland*, if it's not too long" (*SU* 276). Sterling was at this time on the editorial staff of the *Overland Monthly*, for which he wrote a monthly column, "Rhymes and Reactions." He had already used his editorial influence to place one of Smith first experiments in the weird tale, the extended prose poem "The Abominations of Yondo," in the magazine; it was published in the April 1926 issue, where it "evoked many loud, lugubrious and indignant howls from the readers" (*SL* 255).[5] After Wandrei unsuccessfully submitted "The Emperor of Dreams" to the *Bookman* and to the *Nation*, he sent the manuscript to Sterling.

It is at this point that Sterling, hearkening back to his own career, raised concerns about the fervor of Wandrei's praises:

A matter has come up that worries me. Your friend Wandrei has sent me an essay on your poetry, perhaps with the intention of having it in some magazine. That would be impossible in any eastern one, for he is evidently a pretty man, with a young man's unbridled enthusiasms, and has heaped such extravagant praises on you as not a combination of Shakespear (sic), Coleridge and Keats could merit. So his adulation would awaken only derision in editorial bosoms, and laughter in readers', if published. I remember what I got in the case of "A Wine of Wizardry."[6]

However, if you don't mind the incredulity of lesser poets, I can have the essay run in the *Overland*, very probably. It would at least attract much attention to your work, and in itself is well-written, however open to argument some

of its eulogies may be. Let me know your wishes, and they shall be complied with. Heaven knows you get little enough credit for your exquisite work, and if this will wake folks up, all the better (*SU* 280).

Sterling said much the same in his letter to Wandrei:

Enthusiastic as I am over much of Clark's work, I can hardly, as I have written him, rise to your heights of esthetic worship. ... you are sincere in all that you've written here, and written well, and I see no reason why the article shouldn't find publication, if you don't mind a certain amount of laughter over your hyper-enthusiasm—and it won't all come from the morons, either. The essay will attract attention to Clark's work and promote its sale, whether or not you find anyone to agree with you; and attention is what he needs and, oddly enough, seems to desire (Sterling to Wandrei, 26 October 1926).

Smith granted the validity of Sterling's concerns, but came to Wandrei's defense—and, indirectly, his own.

[Wandrei]'s a strange fellow, but is much more critical than you imagine. I don't know just how young he is; but it's only fair to say that there are men of middle-age (enough of them for a jury, almost!) who would back him up in his contention that my eventual place will be a very high one. He doesn't really contend that I am greater than certain other poets, and the excess of his essay is more in the manner than in the substance. Doubtful though I am, myself, I think that the people who will laugh at him are fools, and are deaf and blind to all the lessons of literary history. Literary tastes and standards are in a state of perpetual flux, and the narrow, hidebound "humanism" of the present may seem absurd in some future age (*SU* 282).

Sterling apparently sensed that he had inadvertently wounded Clark's ego, but his attempt to salve his younger colleague's feelings opened up an old wound: "[it] is disquieting to observe that the whole intellectual (including of course the esthetic) trend is increasingly against admiration of the daemonic, the supernatural. Such elements now seem only to awaken smiles, as being childish in their nature and no part of the future vision of the race" (*SU* 283).

Sterling had expressed similar sentiments when Smith sent him "The Abominations of Yondo," stating that "All highbrows think the 'Yondo' material outworn and childish. The demonic is done for, for the present, so far as our contemporaries go, and imagination must seek other fields" (*SU* 263). This is hardly a sentiment that one would expect from the poet who wrote "The blue-eyed vampire, sated at her feast, / Smiles bloodily against the leprous moon" (Sterling 152). But in the years since he first penned those lines in "A Wine of Wizardry," Sterling's self-confidence began to waver before repeated attacks on his work by critics such as Harriet Monroe. As he grew older, Sterling was befriended by writers, such as Theodore Dreiser and H. L. Mencken, who were hardly advocates of the type of Romantic or Symbolist fantasy that had first drawn Smith to the older poet's work. Always the social creature, he began to embrace viewpoints that he once viewed with disfavor: "I still can't stomach [Walt Whitman] except in very brief passages. Yet I must admit that W. is great, for the whole intellectual consensus of opinion so judges" (*SU* 267).

It appears as if Sterling had been won over by the New Humanists, a critical movement led by Harvard professor Irving Babbitt (who was a mentor of T. S. Eliot). They stressed the human elements of experience over supernatural and attacked Romanticism for its embrace of individualism and emotionalism. Babbitt taught that literature was most "vital" when it was subordinate to the affirmation of

"a general nature, a core of normal experience" that was open to most normal people. (27) Sterling expressed this shift in his aesthetic views in a 1925 letter to Smith wherein he wrote "As one grows older, one takes pleasure in writing things that have a vital value, a human relationship, as apart from 'the literature of escape'" (*SU* 260).[7] He elaborated on this to Wandrei:

> It is an odd phenomenon that Clark should have hit so squarely your ultimate tastes in poetry, and fortunate for him, since all poets need adherents. I hope I too am his admirer, but really am unable to rank him as high as you do. We need have, however, no quarrel in this matter, though I've a notion you'll "smile a little sadly" at the enthusiasms of your article, when you're fifty. The point is that beauty plus life is greater than beauty plus death. It is the difference between a "mummy swathed in splendors" and a girl dancing naked in sunshine or moonlight, the difference between my "Wine of Wizardry" and the "Eve of St. Agnes" or "Dolores." Of course if you wish to set yourself against the whole world in the matter, including all other poets, it's "up to you." (Sterling to Wandrei, 9 November 1926)

Smith had by this time grown confident enough in his views that he was not willing to defer automatically to the elder poet's opinion and was able to defend his positions. In response to Sterling's statement that "the whole intellectual ... trend is increasingly against admiration of the daemonic, the supernatural," Smith asserted that "Anything that the human imagination can conceive of becomes thereby a part of life, and poetry such as mine, properly considered, is not an 'escape', but an extension" (*SU* 282–83). He sarcastically suggested that Sterling write an essay on "The Americanization of Intellect," and wrote one himself "In Defense of Imaginative Poetry"[8]

By this time both Smith and Sterling understood the futility of argument. Sterling insisted that he had "no quarrel with imaginative poetry, for as Bierce has said, imagination is poetry, or poetry imagination. I'd merely want that imagination turned on such themes as have some relation to life, some vital significance, as in Adonis, the Eve of St. Agnes, Ulysses, Delores, and many other great poems I could specify. I've no quarrel with such poems as my 'Wine' and your 'Hashish Eater,' but cannot rank them as high as those I've mentioned" (*SU* 285).

Sterling wrote the above in his last letter to Smith, which was dated November 9,

1926. One week later, Sterling opened an envelope marked "Peace" that he had carried in his pocket for many years and partook of the cyanide therein. Many theories have been suggested for his motivation to end his life, but this episode suggests that a misplaced despair over his life's work being insignificant may have played a role in it. Wandrei's essay appeared in the December 1926 issue of the *Overland Monthly*, but the grief over Sterling's death overwhelmed any controversy over Smith's merits that it might otherwise have generated.

Notes:

1. Misprinted as "changed" in *Dead Titans Waken! Invisible Sun* (258)

2. In a 1959 memoir, "Lovecraft in Providence," Wandrei states that his correspondence with HPL began when he wrote him seeking Smith's address after reading his praise for the Californian in a letter to *Weird Tales* (303). (This would have been HPL's first letter to *WT*, in the October 1923 issue, wherein he referred to "the California poet of horror, madness and morbid beauty".) However, the correspondence published in *Mysteries of Time and Spirit* clearly establishes that HPL's first letter to Wandrei was dated 11 December 1926.

3. The book's printer, the Auburn Journal newspaper, omitted end papers when sending the book to the binder, which does detract substantially from its appearance, proving the old adage about not judging a book by its cover to be true in at least this instance.

4. Sterling had found a publisher willing to take a chance on Smith's collection: George Steele Seymour, of The Bookfellows (a Chicago literary society that had published Sterling's dramatic poem *Truth* in 1923) indicated a willingness to bring out a slender edition of Smith's poetry, but would not be able to undertake its printing for approximately a year. Wandrei's offer meant that Smith would not have to wait, but I cannot help but wonder if the stigma of self-publication impeded critical reception of CAS' collection. Seymour later published a substantial selection of Smith's poems in the May 1927 issue of the *Step Ladder*, the Bookfellows' house organ.

5. Sterling had also arranged for two poems by Frank Belknap Long, with whom he was also in correspondence, to appear in the *Overland Monthly*.

6. When "A Wine of Wizardry" was first published in the September 1907 issue of the Hearst *Cosmopolitan*, it was accompanied by an enthusiastic article by Ambrose Bierce, "A Poet and His Poem," which aroused a great deal of controversy and accusations of favoritism directed against both Sterling and his mentor. Sterling was also very careful in his advocacy of Smith not to allow any appearance of such "log-rolling."

7. See Scott Connors, "Gesturing Toward the Infinite." In *The Freedom of Fantastic Things: Selected Criticism on Clark Ashton Smith*. Ed. Scott Connors (New York: Hippocampus Press, 2006): 180–194.

8. A manuscript for this was catalogued as part of Smith's papers at the John Hay Library of Brown University, but it has apparently been misfiled.

Works Cited

Babbitt, Irving. *Rousseau and Romanticism*. New York: Meridian, 1955.

Lovecraft, H. P. *Selected Letters 1925–1929*. Ed. August Derleth and Donald Wandrei. Sauk City, WI: Arkham House, 1968. (*SL* II)

Smith, Clark Ashton. *Selected Letters of Clark Ashton Smith*. Ed. David E. Schultz and Scott Connors. Sauk City, WI: Arkham House, 2003. (*SL*)

—. and George Sterling. *The Shadow of the Unattained: The Letters of George Sterling and Clark Ashton Smith*. Ed. David E. Schultz and S. T. Joshi. New York: Hippocampus Press, 2005. (*SU*)

Sterling, George. Two letters to Donald Wandrei, dated October 23, 1926 and November 9, 1926. Mss, Bancroft Library Special Collections, University of California at Berkeley.

—. "A Wine of Wizardry." In *The Thirst of Satan: Poems of Fantasy and Terror*. Ed. S. T. Joshi. New York: Hippocampus Press, 2003. 145–152.

Wandrei, Donald. "Arthur Machen and The Hill of Dreams." *Studies in Weird Fiction* No. 15 (Summer 1994): 27–30.

—. *Dead Titans, Waken! Invisible Sun: Two Novels*. Ed. S. T. Joshi. Lakewood, CO: Centipede Press, 2011.

—. "The Emperor of Dreams." *Overland Monthly* 84, No. 12 (December 1926): 380–81, 407, 409.

—. "Lovecraft in Providence." (1959) Rpt in *Lovecraft Remembered*. Ed. Peter Cannon. Sauk City, WI: Arkham House, 1998. 303–317.

— and H. P. Lovecraft. *Mysteries of Time and Spirit: The Letters of H. P. Lovecraft and Donald Wandrei*. Ed. S. T. Joshi and David E. Schultz. San Francisco: Night Shade Books, 2002.

MONTY HAUL

A 5th edition 'zine with a 1st edition vibe.

"This stuff is great, and it will add depth and interest to your world."
-Ben G.

AVAILABLE NOW AT DriveThruRPG.com

EMPEROR OF DREAMS

By Donald A. Wandrei

"This may be a little too much of praise of Clark Ashton Smith, but at least it will bring comment and that is what we want," said George Sterling when we brought this article into our office for the December issue.

In 1912 there came from the press of A. M. Robertson, in San Francisco, a slender book of poems. Had that volume come from a well-known writer, it would have ranked him with the immortals. Had it come from a rising author, it would have spread his fame far and wide. It came from neither. It was little advertised, for it had no financial backing and the author had neither influential friends nor acquaintances among those who determine what the public may read. No attempt was made to popularize it. The book shortly passed from sight, almost unknown save to a few fortunate people who possessed copies. The book was, "The Star-Treader and Other Poems;" its author, Clark Ashton Smith, a young poet, not yet twenty, who had already dreamed and dared to dream as few men have in a lifetime. That book of poems is one of the great contributions to American literature. It contains some of our finest pure poetry, some of our best imaginative lyrics. A few of them would now be famous, had they been written by a Keats or Shelley, and a cause of laurels. The critics have ignored the volume. The literary pontiffs have passed it over. Today, not many persons know it, even by title. Yet the same critics decry the anaemic state of American letters, its lack of enduring works. A genius—in the true, not abused,

sense—appears, his eyes on the other side of eternity, his poems of eternity, his work the kind that endures. He is unnoticed. He is given no encouragement. American poetry is still anaemic.

A thousand years hence, when the people of that distant time survey the accumulated mass of all literature, they will place high up on the roll of honor the name, Clark Ashton Smith; and looking backward, they will ask why the world of that age long ago did not appreciate him when it had him. Perhaps this is as it ought to be. The man of letters should be the possession of those who do appreciate him. It is not given to ordinary man to walk with the gods; nor, when it is so given, does he usually avail himself of the opportunity unless he is one of that group which is the justification of himself, the cornerstone of the arts, and the prophet of immortality.

A poet can not live on visions, on dreams, on a prospect of future fame. He must live on something more material. And one can not write when it is necessary to earn a sustenance. Perhaps this was the reason that ten years elapsed before another book appeared under the poet's name. Or perhaps it was the neglect, popular, which is of little importance, and critical, which may be of the greatest importance, given his first book. Or perhaps the dreamer lived in his own realm, indifferent to ephemeral external life, writing seldom and then mainly for his own pleasure. Or perhaps . . . One trembles at the thought. "Ebony and Crystal" was published in 1922.

Its fate is akin to that of "The Star-Treader." Not many persons know it. Those who do regard it as worshippers a sanctum sanctorum, as connoisseurs a rare tapestry, as jewellers a priceless pearl. (I have since been informed that the silence was due to the destruction of imperfect poems, and to ill-health. It is hard to believe this statement in a day when the least is treasured by those whose best is mediocre. But it explains the uniform excellence of his work, the lack of a single weak poem.)

There is no place in contemporary prose and poetry for genius.

Was "Ebony and Crystal" worth the labor of ten years? It is a larger volume than the first and contains twice as many poems, one hundred and fourteen against fifty-five. Did eleven poems a year, and those not of unusual length, with one exception, justify the author a place among the front-rank poets? If fame is the criterion, no. If excellence, yes. "Ebony and Crystal" is the finest volume of pure poetry that has appeared in America since the opening of the twentieth century, perhaps the finest since the time of Edgar Allan Poe. Not until its publication did any of our poets approach him in imaginative power. "Ebony and Crystal" belongs on that shelf with Poe, Coleridge, Blake, Shelley, Baudelaire. In that group where each is coequally supreme, he may justly take his place.

Imagination is his god, beauty his ideal; his poems are an offering to both. He is the poet of the infinite, the envoy of eternity, the amanuensis of beauty. For even as beauty was deity to Keats and Shelley, so it is to him, and in its praise has he written. But he has not celebrated it as an abstract term or an aesthetic quality, but as a more tangible substance. He has constructed entire worlds of his own and filled them with creations of his own fancy. And his beauty has thus crossed the boundary between that which is mortal and that which is immortal, and has become the beauty of strange stars and distant lands, of jewels and cypresses and moons, of flaming suns and comets, of marble palaces, of fabled realms and wonders, of gods, and daemons, and sorcery. Time and Space have been his servants, the universe his domain; with the stars his steeds and the heavens his tramping ground, he has wandered in realms afar; and he has found there a wondrous beauty and a strange fear, the goal of his early dreams and the enchanted road to greater, all manner of things illusory and fantastical.

Some of his poems are like shadowed gold; some are like flame-encircled ebony; some are crystal-clear and pure; others are as unearthly starshine. One is coldly wrought in marble; another is curiously carved in jade; there are a few glittering diamonds; and there are many rubies and emeralds aflame, glowing with a secret fire. Here and there may be found a poppy-flower, an orchid from the hotbed of Hell, the whisper of an eldritch wind, a breath from the burning sands of regions infernal. The wizard calls, and at his imperious summons come genie, witch, and daemon to open the portal to the haunted realms of faery; and their wonder is transmuted so that those who can open the door may listen to the murmuring waters of Acheron, or watch the passing of a phantom throng; and the fen-fires gleam; and the slow mists arise; and heavy perfumes, and poisons, and dank odors fill the air. A marble palace rises in the dusk, a treasure-house of gold, and ebony, and ivory; soft lutes play within; fair women, passionless and passionate, wander in the corridors; silks and tapestries adorn the walls, and fuming censers burn a rare incense. And fabulous demogorgon and hippogriff guard the golden gateway to the hoarded wealth. The sky is black. But now and again white comets blaze, or suns of green, or crimson, of purple, flame across the firmament with silver moons. The sky is burning. Stars hurtle to destruction or waste away. All mysteries are uncurtained. One may watch a landscape of the moon, the seas of Saturn, the sunken fanes of old Atlantis, wars and wonders on some distant star.

There is no place in the poetry of Clark Ashton Smith for the conventional, the trite, the outworn. It is useless to search his work for offerings to popular desire. Some authors pander to the public taste; their books may have a huge sale, but die with the author. Some writers have skill and ability but desire wealth or immediate fame; their work has not so great a popularity but endures longer. A very few have what is called "genius." They write primarily for themselves, or with a certain small group of people who know literature in mind. They are artists, word artists; and they fashion their prose or poetry with care and labor. They are seldom appreciated in their lifetime, and never have widespread popularity, but the highest minds of every age enjoy their work. These are ones who speak to us across the ages, who will speak across the ages to come. It is to this class that Clark Ashton Smith belongs. One will examine his poems in vain for the commonplaces that have so largely crept into our literature; and by so much as he has avoided ephemeral and written of immortal things, by so much the longer will his work endure.

II

"The Star-Treader" was his earliest volume, and it shows the effects of imagination in its first exuberance. Stars and suns and comets parade in all their majesty; Chaos. Infinity, and "the eldritch dark" are ever present; and the wonder, the inexplicable mystery of the Universe form the background of the book. It was then that the young poet wrote "The Song of a Comet;" it was then that he fashioned "The Song of the Stars;" and from his pen came "The Wind and the Moon." Of the fixed forms, the sonnet was his favorite, and nearly a third of the poems have its form. In most of them he strove to obtain single, dominant effects, to limn one unforgettable scene, as in "The Last Night," "The Medusa

of the Skies," and "Averted Malefice." Occasionally, he was content with a single quatrain, or a pair, as "The Maze of Sleep" and "The Morning Pool." But he had a greater chance to display his power in the longer, more sustained poems, such as "Saturn," "The Star-Treader," and "The Masque of Forsaken Gods." They would have been accomplishments for a man of maturity, for one who had long written poetry, as the work of a youth they are remarkable achievements. The entire book has this note of maturity; it was a world-weary youth wise beyond his years who wrote these poems beautiful, fantastic, sometimes bitter and more than once inexpressibly terrible in their suggestion. "The Star-Treader" was published in 1912. Not for ten years did another book come from the poet. ("Odes and Sonnets" was privately issued by the Book Club of California in 1918. The odes are from "The Star-Treader"; the sonnets were included in "Ebony and Crystal.") What had he been doing those ten long years? Had the neglect of his first book compelled him to turn his mind into other channels? It is hard to say, but "Ebony and Crystal " is not a large volume for the work of ten years.

There is a great difference between the two, in imagery, in tone and subject, and in metrical skill. The first was, to some extent, experimental; the second, a fulfillment of the promise in the foreshadowing work. The craftsmanship of these later poems is well nigh flawless; the volume is rich in perfectly planned, perfectly fashioned jewels. It is jewel-cutting that he was engaged in those ten years. Here may be found "such stuff as dreams are made of," and the dreams themselves; here the utterance of god and witch, the harmony of the spheres, the strains of immortal music, the unveiling of an imagery unparalleled. The beauty of these poems is intoxicating, for the poet who wrote them was haunted and intoxicated by loveliness immaculate and incarnate, by all beauty. And the poems are couched, not in ordinary language, but in an English filled with curious and archaic forms, rare or obsolete words, unusual diction; and they have been given flowing rhythms and unforgettable melodies; and they move in measured intonation, and in cadence, and in musical sweep that are seldom found in poetry. They are whispers of the unearthly, rather than mortal work. They are enduring forms of unenduring dreams and ideals and desires. They are the unattainable, set in deathless words of gold. They are time-outlasting marble; they are lotus and poppy; they are fadeless amaranth and asphodel, pure, perfect shadows of the pure and perfect, eternal, aeonian. They are stardust and starshine, caught by a dreamer of the ages, fashioned in ebony and crystal. They are nectar and ambrosia, nepenthe, Lethean draughts to drown the world in forgetfulness and oblivion. They are the waters of paradise.

The poems are laden with a pagan, exotic beauty and imagery. Sometimes this takes the form of light and shadow, as in "Arabesque." Sometimes it deals with the lands of romance, as in "Beyond the Great Wall:"

Beyond the far Cathayan wall,
A thousand leagues athwart the sky,
The scarlet stars and mornings die,
The gilded moons and sunsets fall.
Across the sulfur-colored sands
With bales of silk and camels fare,
Harnessed with vermil and with vair,
Into the blue and burning lands.
And, ah, the song the drivers sing,
To while the desert leagues away-
A song they sang in old Cathay,
Ere youth had left the eldest king.
Ere love and beauty both grew old,
And wonder and romance were flown.
On fiery wings to worlds unknown,
To stars of undiscovered gold.
And I there alien words would know,
And follow past the lonely wall,
Where gilded moons and sunsets fall,.
As in a song of long ago.

Occasionally it reverts upon itself as in "The Melancholy Pool" and "Solution:"

The ghostly fire that walks the fen,
Tonight thine only light shall be;
On lethal ways thy soul shall pass.
And prove the stealthy, coiled morass.
With mocking mists for company.
On roads thou goest not again.
To shores where thou hast never gone,—
Fare onward, though the shuddering queach
And serpent-rippled waters reach
Like seepage pools of Acheron,
Beside thee; and the twisten reeds,
Close raddled as a witch's net,
Enuind thy knees, and cling and clutch
Like wreathing adders; though the touch
Of the blind air be dank and wet,
As from a wounded Thing that bleeds
In cloud and darkness overhead—
Fare onward, where thy dreams of yore
In splendour drape the fetid shore
And pestilential waters dead.
And though the toad's irrision rise,
As grinding of Satanic racks,
And spectral willows, gaunc and grey,
Gibber along thy shrouded way,
Where vipers lie with livid backs,
And watch thee with their sulphurous eyes,—
Fare onward, till thy feet shall slip
Deep in the sudden pool ordained,
And all the noisome draught be drained,
That turns to Lethe on the lip.

But usually it takes the form of a rich imagery, oriental in its profusion and splendour, unlimited in its concept and scope, imperishable by reason of its supreme, its unearthly, its ' alien perfection. "In Saturn"—

Upon the seas of Saturn I have sailed
To isles of high, primeval aramant,
Where the flame-tongued sonorous flow'rs enchant
The hanging surf to silence: All engrailed
With ruby-corode pearls, the golden shore
Allured me; but as one whom spells restrain,
For blind horizons of the somber main,
And harbors never known, by singing

prore
I set forthrightly: Formed of fire and brass,
Immenser skies divided, deep on deep
Before me,—till, above the darkling foam,
With dome on cloudless adamantine dome,
Black peaks no peering seraph deems to pass,
Rose up from realms ineffable as Sleep!

"The Kingdom of Shadows," "The Land of Evil Stars," "A Precept," "Chant of Autumn," Requiescat in Pace,"—but it is useless to try to select fine poems from a volume which has room for none other.

There is one long poem, however, that deserves special attention. It is "The Hashish-Eater," containing many hundred lines of blank verse. But it is far different from what is usually called blank verse, from what one knows as ordinary iambic pentameter. This has always been a stately metre, capable of impressive effects; and in his hands, with the aid of his boundless imagination and descriptive powers, besides his technical skill, it has become the implement of a poem—colossus, gigantic in theme and treatment, told in a heavy, sonorous English that sweeps onward in measured roll with an ever-swelling rhythm from the Imperial summons of the opening lines:

Bow down: I am the emperor of dreams:
I crown me with the million-colored sun
Of secret worlds incredible, and take
Their trailing skies for vestment, when I soar,
Throned on the mounting zenith, and illume
The spaceward-flown horizons infinite.

And at the very end of a volume which will one day be a prized literary heritage is the sombre and morbidly magnificent prose-poem, "The Shadows," a poem told with such care that no word is lost or wasted, and so well that it lingers in the memory as a sable fantasy enshrined, a rare perfume, darkly odorous and darkly poisonous, clinging to a bit of strangely shapen ebony.

III

In October, 1925, came the third of his published books, "Sandalwood," a volume which, though slender, contains more poems than his first. After "Ebony and Crystal," not much could be added to his laurels, but had that volume not existed, "Sandalwood" might have taken its place to a large extent. It is different from "Ebony and Crystal" in that the poems are less ambitious with regard to the depicting of strange, vast splendour, but more songlike, lyrical, and spontaneous, though the mastery of technique and the metrical skill displayed admit of neither spontaneity nor its attendant roughnesses. The poems may be divided into several classes, including nineteen translations from Baudelaire, and four songs from the uncompleted romantic drama, "The Fugitives," And there is a poem of six stanzas, "We Shall Meet," told in an original or very rare but very beautiful verse form. But to one who has read the early work of Clark Ashton Smith, his later poems remain beyond praise. One may go into ecstasies at a vision of glory; but the greater glory surpasses description. And he who has sate on the ramparts of Heaven and Hell is mute before magnificence and pageantry that shame the speech.

No critic and no criticism can do justice to the work of this poet. There are some things which are beyond the reach of both, and in this rare group belongs the work of Clark Ashton Smith. For there are books so distinctive, so excellent, that they can not be compared with others of their class, by reason of their perfection. For them, there is no standard of judgment, and one can only admire what one is helpless to censure or to sanctify.

To use homely language in estimating such work is to do it an injustice; and yet. superlatives are equally useless, for they have been so carelessly employed that nowadays they deprecate the work they are meant to extol.

Earlier in this essay, certain other poets of the romantic-imaginative group were mentioned. But Clark Ashton Smith can not be associated with any particular one. Each within that class was original, and by virtue of a similar originality, this modern poet deserves his rank. The great poets neither follow nor imitate; they create. And he has created, on a cosmic scale. The greatest indictment of contemporary verse is its lack of form, its deliberate exclusion of the most vital quality of a work of art, a quality which every book that aspires to greatness must have, above all else, if it is to endure. Substance-form; form-substance; of the two, form is by bar the most important. And this element—including, as it does, diction, style, presentation, euphony, craftsmanship—is present in the poems of Clark Ashton Smith to such an extraordinary degree that, had there been no substance, had he produced only rainbows and iridescent bubbles, he would still have deserved lasting attention. Indeed, the sole flaw in his poems is occasionally form in too great a degree. His gifts are so much beyond those of average poets, and his vocabulary is of such enormous content that the desired word is often an uncommon one. Yet even this lends a curious charm, a singularly effective atmosphere to the poem, at worst, it may only be considered what would be a god-send to the lamentably word-base verse of the Philistines. It is an example of his innate power of concentration, his ability to say best and to say beautifully the things that deserve to be clothed in costly raiment.

Just where the place of this emperor of dreams will ultimately be fixed in poetry can not, of course, be foretold, save that it should be very high. Nor can one prophesy the day he shall receive the recognition he has earned. It took the world forty years to appreciate Thomas Lovell Beddoes; it took longer for it to appreciate William Blake; Arthur O'Shaughnessy is still almost unknown; and few even of those occasional persons who have read "The Book of Jade" could tell the name of its author, Park Barnitz. And now, Clark Ashton Smith—

BEYOND THE VEIL

By Frank Coffman

Some few have journeyed out beyond The Veil.
Of those that venture, fewer still come back.
Dark tomes hold hidden spells to look, but lack
The black, archaic words that will not fail
To bring the seeker home to this our realm.
From this side, only shadowy shapes uncertain
Beckon and stir behind that tenebrous curtain,
And what waits there would quickly overwhelm.

Best not to look—but much worse that way to travel,
For its secrets are kept from no living soul forever;
There is time enough to wait for the Hand of Fate.
And those who return are changed. Their minds unravel;
Their rantings hold one theme: a wish they had never
Traversed a path so cursed…but now—too late!

Tales From The MAGICIAN'S SKULL

NO.3 $14.99

ALL-NEW SWORDS & SORCERY FICTION

STORIES BY KING, HOCKING, ENGE, MALAN, JONES, & OTHERS

GOODMAN PUBLICATIONS

ALL-NEW FICTION:

William King

Joseph A. McCullough

John C. Hocking

James Enge

Violette Malan

Howard Andrew Jones

Sarah Newton

GOODMAN •GAMES•

THE SKULL SPEAKS

Heed me, mortal dogs! I have fashioned a magazine like those from fabled days of yore! It overflows with thrilling adventures. There are swords, and there is sorcery. There are dark deeds and daring rescues. There are lands where heroes fear to tread. Dare you imagine it?

Picture this as well – maps to wondrous and terrible places. Electrifying art for every tale, and guides for bringing all these wonders to your own gaming table!

It may be that you have not yet heard of me, though it defies belief! I am the Magician's Skull, awakened from long years of slumber in the Chamber of Ages. I have returned from my deathless sleep with but one goal: to publish the greatest sword-and-sorcery tales in this or any other dimension. I have found modern tale-tellers steeped in the lore of the great ones – and I will share them with you!

I live again, and my magazine lives as well! Untold splendors await you! Join me!

www.goodman-games.com

DEAD RIVER REVENGE

PART II

By Chris Gruber

Illustrated by Timothy Truman

V. The Hunt

Billy had set a brutal pace in the hours since his escape from Fort Dearborn. That he had remained alive this long was as much a testament to his own iron constitution as it was to his legendary woodlands guile. He had used every trick of survival he had learned in his twenty-one years to evade capture, but he knew that Mukte'ksago and his human hounds would eventually reel him in. He had paused often to cover his tracks or to double back upon his own trail, deliberately avoiding the open expanses along the bluffs that overlooked the Great Lake to tramp through the shallow, rocky, creek beds. The dense, weed-choked wetlands swallowed all evidence of his passing; but the half breed Miami scout never allowed himself a moment's rest and remained on the move all throughout the day as afternoon melted toward evening.

While these tactics had proven effective in buying desperately needed time they had also taken a toll upon his pony. He realized that he must allow it to rest soon or risk the poor creature dying of exhaustion. Billy knew he must rest as well for a great weariness was beginning to exhaust his limbs. But each time he determined to stop some unseen force not entirely a product of his own determined nature would urge him to continue. Somewhere behind the curtain of his other senses, beyond his weariness, there pulsed a ghostly

voice that he knew belonged to his friend Wells. He heard it whisper the same word over and over, beating a staccato cadence in his mind that was horrifying and yet utterly compelling—*Revenge! Revenge!*

Nudging his tired steed forward he doggedly followed the pink clouds of the north as they melted like ice into the false light of twilight. The pony trembled now with each step and he knew, voice or no voice, that he must finally stop. Sitting heavily upon a rock he watched his pony drink deeply from a muddy creek, head hung low, and clearly spent. He wondered idly at his own plight and the strange events that had occurred after the battle. Billy was accustomed to hardship, born and bred upon the bloody legacy of the great lakes country, and was normally not one to assume the poetic melancholy so characteristic of the Native American during extended hardship or peril. But, he had never in his short, violent life, been so hard pressed by an enemy like Pesotum's human hound Mukte'ksago, a man who was as hard and unyielding as the northern winter and as relentless in pursuit of his sadistic desires as a starving wolf on the hunt. Billy realized he faced a deadly foe that would never quit the trail no matter how far north he fled and with this realization came reflection as he recalled the day's wild flight and wondered, not for the first time, if he had finally succumbed to the madness of battle.

After escaping the battlefield, he had had to negotiate the approach to Fort Dearborn with care to avoid detection by the families of the native warriors who had moved in after the attack to rummage through the smoldering ruins. Smoke had billowed from the fort's blackened timbers in dark, greasy, clouds as fire licked the remains of the slaughtered livestock still trapped within their pens. His lungs rebelled at the coppery smell of spilled blood and burnt flesh and he rode quickly beyond the fort to escape the stench. He heard the exultant shrieks of the women as they fought over the jewelry and bright clothes of the now dead or captured white women, and the pitiful wails of the native women who had lost a husband, brother, or son in the battle. Once beyond the fort he had been harassed almost immediately after crossing the She-ga-goy-nak River by Pesotum's scouts. He had stopped briefly to drink from a small creek when a brave had come upon him from the opposite bank.

The astonished brave had stopped short in mid stride, eyes wide, as surprised as Billy at the chance encounter. The Indian had thought to gain glory by taking the scalp of the Crafty Wolf for himself and so gave no warning cry as he attacked. Instead, he charged across the narrow creek, splashing water in his haste like a blood-mad buffalo, seeking to bury his tomahawk in Billy's skull. With a lithe twist of his torso Billy stepped quickly out of the way and struck the warrior a savage blow upon the head with his knife hilt. Not waiting for the other to regain his senses, he stooped down and drew his blade quickly across the exposed neck ending the attack in a crimson spray. His hand still gripping the tangled mop of hair Billy crouched low in the muddy water and listened intently, half expecting to hear the shouted alarms of discovery.

But the battle had lasted mere seconds and silence weighed heavily upon the creek. Even the birds that flitted through the trees had not been disturbed by the violent skirmish. Satisfied that no other scouts lurked nearby, Billy had taken the brave's scalp and pinned it to a tree with the other's tomahawk. He had dragged the corpse out of the creek and propped it beneath the bloody scalp to serve as a grim reminder that the Crafty Wolf was as much the hunter as the hunted. He knew the grisly message would strike fear into the hearts of Pesotum's band and this fear would breed caution, slowing their advance. Or so he had hoped.

With a start Billy shook his head to clear his mind of these memories and with an effort brought his senses to bear once again upon the present. The sun had sunk beyond the dark horizon leaving behind fiery javelins of crimson and gold that pierced the purple sky. It would be night soon and instinct warned him that his enemies were closing in. The voice in his head rose in urgent response, as if it, too, sensed their approach, and conveyed to him in some sort of ghostly transmission that the Dead River—and their revenge—was near.

With a weary sigh he glanced over at his pony and offered it an apology before hopping gingerly upon its broad back. He stroked its neck with a deft hand and murmured softly into its ears, "Carry me just a little further, nektoshe (pony), and then I will set you free and thereafter rest will be your only concern." The Pony's ear shot forward at the sound of his voice and it seemed to the half-breed warrior that despite the exhausting pace they had kept there was a proud and confident bounce in its step as they moved into the gathering darkness.

The dull glow of twilight gave way to the starlit glimmering of night. The vibrant hum and throb of the forest acted upon his nerves like a soothing remedy as he rode north. The rising cacophony of woodland insects mingled with the rocking sway of his pony's gait helped Billy relax somewhat, causing the hours to seemingly melt one into the other as he rode wearily north. Even the voice seemed content, murmuring quietly within his mind, mollified so long as he traveled north…ever north.

His contentment eventually turned to caution as the land began to change. The sparsely wooded bluffs gave way to more heavily forested land that cast night shadows across his shoulders like a heavy cloak. He made his way carefully, riding slowly beneath a thickening canopy of branches that threatened to envelope him in complete darkness. He was alone with his weariness and found himself struggling to remain awake. But Billy was a true son of the wild and knew that the aroma of the wilderness was as deadly as it was satisfying, and he resolved not to forget the danger that followed close at his heels nor give in to his weariness, for he knew that either choice would be his last.

Eventually, the impenetrable gloom began to work on his nerves, awakening that part of him that was the killer, the pragmatist, the ultimate survivor. Despite this, or perhaps because of it, he knew he still needed to rest, to calm the killer within. But he also knew that if he were to survive the night and reach the Dead River he could not stop to rest. In the detached way an animal knows it needs sleep and simply closes its eyes, Billy did the same. Without another thought he gave the pony free rein and allowed the gentle sway of the animal to lull him into a light sleep; the kind of sleep he had known countless times upon the trail, where his body relaxed but his mind remained active, sweeping the land in search of those hidden impressions that were out of place, unidentifiable, and thus a danger.

He did not dream. With the stoicism characteristic of men bred to the harsh life of the great lakes he knew that he would either end up dead, spitted upon the end of a native lance, or the sole survivor of this hellish escapade and arbiter of bloody justice, the violent herald of a dead man's revenge.

VI. Kegangizi

August 16th, 1812
48 miles north of Fort Dearborn, Illinois Territory

Billy was startled out of sleep by the snort of his pony and the spray of cold water upon his face. With a muttered oath Billy rubbed his tired eyes and tried to get his bearings. Small waves danced upon an immense body of water mere yards away and a fine mist dampened his forehead in a cool embrace. Drawn by the smell of fresh water and clearly on its last legs his pony had stumbled out of the surrounding forest and come to the very edge of the Great Lake. He jumped off the animal's back and let it drink lustily for a moment before leading it away from the water's edge lest it drink too much and become sick. It was too tired to protest and came meekly along despite the intense thirst it suffered from.

Billy stretched his aching muscles and looked about him in the pre-dawn glow, scanning the terrain for any sign of his pursuers. Sensing no immediate danger, he cast about in search of familiar landmarks and at once he realized that he had entered very near the country of the warlike Spring Bluff Potawatomi clan. They had for years successfully resisted white settlement upon their lands, resorting to violence when necessary to ensure the native integrity of their borders, and were fiercely protective of their tribal independence. They had also rebuked Pesotum's call to join Tecumseh's so-called red confederacy, resenting any alliance that might encourage encroachment upon their territory and thus were not amongst those Indians who had raided the fort.

In the east the sun had begun to dance and sparkle upon the waves of the Great Lake and Billy's gaze was drawn to the sandy stretch of beach to the north which was interrupted by more of the large dune formations that dotted the southern shores. He saw what appeared to be the mouth of a small river less than a mile away which drained into the lake from the east. He had never encountered this river in his many trips north into the Wisconsin territory as he had always skirted far to the west to avoid the Spring Bluff people and it took him a moment to realize that his pony had led him to the Dead River, the same river that Wells had described to him before the battle. The same river the voice had all but forced him to seek out.

Billy grabbed his musket and weapons and gave the pony a hard swat on the rump that sent it stumbling wearily south and west at a dead run. He silently thanked the hardy pony for carrying him so far without complaint and prayed to the Great Earthmaker that he would help it find its way safely back to its brothers. He then turned north toward the river, the voice in his head now a constant buzz, as if agitated by the proximity of the river. It demanded that Billy move toward the river's source, to the headwaters that harbored something he knew instinctively was evil, something monstrous that had roused itself from a timeless slumber to feed upon the fears and evil of humanity. Billy saw the land around him, the river, the trees, the dunes, as if through another's eyes, Wells' eyes, and he felt the other's spirit within him flare up in recognition at what he saw.

Twenty minutes after having spotted the river, Billy stood upon its banks and stared at the mouth which had been dammed by a great wall of sand. This wall prevented the river's water from draining into the Great Lake which lay mere yards away. Kneeling near the edge Billy could see that the water was dark, stagnant, and undisturbed by any current and though he could not see the bottom, he knew instinctively that it was very deep. The river gave off a fetid smell that choked and crawled down into his lungs like

liquid air, and he stood quickly, stepping away from the edge as he sought cleaner air to breathe. He cursed aloud, and wondered how bad the stench must be upriver, away from the cool sea breeze of the open beach as it snaked through the dense forest canopy toward its unholy source.

He decided to fill his water skin from the lake before heading inland when he heard the whinny of horses where he had left his pony earlier. He moved quickly toward a large sand dune and climbed quietly to the top, careful to keep his head and body concealed behind a clump of saw grass as he peeked over the edge. He saw seven men mounted upon ponies, their bodies painted red and black, shaven heads crowned by topknots and adorned with eagle feathers and porcupine quills: the headdress of the Potawatomi. A fierce thrill went through his body as he recognized Mukte'ksago, a man of mammoth proportions whose bulk and sinister features could not be mistaken even at a distance.

Mukte'ksago and the others had finally found him. They had trailed him over the many miles like a wolf pack trailing a swift deer. Billy knew that, like the deadly wolf packs that roamed the prairies and forests, Mukte'ksago had allowed Billy to run so that he might slowly reel him in, first letting weariness overtake his limbs and then allowing fear to work on his nerve and crush the spirit of survival long before the war party would finally sink their knives into his flesh. But Billy did not fear death. With a low growl of anger he quickly reminded himself that he was no deer to bleat in terror at the approach of the wolves; he was himself a deadly predator and the prospect of revenge beat like a savage drum within his heart at sight of his enemies. Whether that rage was entirely his own or an echo of Wells' bloodlust he neither knew nor cared.

He knew also that Mukte'ksago would not be fooled by the tracks of Billy's pony and had likely sent scouts to flush him into the open like a frightened rabbit to be feathered or filled with musket balls from a distance. Billy turned over on his back searching the sandy dunes and forest edge to the west for any sign of Mukte'ksago's scouts and instantly saw movement. He slid down the dune and into the sandy depression and prepared himself for what was to come.

Billy lay motionless within the sandy embrace of the tall dune, sweat running in tiny streams down his dust-stained face. His eyes strained to pierce the forest that bordered the great dunes, searching for movement, while his ears struggled to hear above the dull roar of the pounding surf. He listened intently for any sound that might alert him to the presence of his hunters . . . but he saw and heard nothing but the sharp cries of hungry gulls as they wheeled above his head.

Minutes crept by and still he did not move. His eyes scanned the dunes continuously, but no glimpse of an impatient head nor sound of advancing men arrested his attention. Then he heard it—a whisper of movement like leaves rubbing faintly against each other. Setting his musket aside, Billy listened again for the slight sound, knowing it to be the calloused feet of one of Pesotum's braves sliding awkwardly through the sand somewhere very near him. For a moment more he listened, attempting to gauge the direction from which the sound came.

Just then the morning sun began to burn through the lake mist that had risen near the shore causing Billy to squint in agitation, its glittering rays reflecting off the lake's mirror-like surface and directly into his eyes. Spurred to action by the hiss of the approaching Indian, Billy moved away stealthily, as sure of his footing as a mountain puma and as deadly confident. He had just placed the sun at his back when his keen eyes spotted the scarred, painted face of the Potawatomi scout as the

other moved hesitantly toward the very spot Billy had just vacated. Wild eyes grew bright as the native warrior looked upon the faint trail left by Billy just seconds earlier. The warrior moved forward recklessly, eager to be the first to count coup on the half-breed scout and wholly unaware that he had now become the hunted.

The glimpse of his enemy's scarred and painted face swept all thoughts of caution from Billy's mind. All that remained was an instinctive desire to eliminate his foe and he acted on that desire in a crimson fury. Thrusting forward from behind the dune wall Billy grabbed the wrist of the Potawatomi in one hand and the exposed throat in the other and drove his enemy's hapless body against the sandy ground, pinning his free hand as tightly as any vise. Not a sound escaped the lips of the scout as Billy's iron grip silently cut off the other's airway and only a quick and frantic thrashing gave evidence to the mad struggle of life and death that took place upon the sandy dune bottom. A fleeting moment passed before the Potawatomi scout relaxed in Billy's grip, his skin turning a ghastly shade of purple as the tongue began slowly to protrude between blood flecked lips. Billy lifted his head, certain that some sound of the struggle had escaped to betray his presence to Mukte'ksago and his human hounds. But he heard no shout of warning, no cries of discovery that would surely have followed if even the slightest noise of that desperate skirmish had been audible.

Yet, the silence that followed seemed suddenly to be charged with an all-consuming menace that he could not ignore. Almost instantly a wave of unreasoning fear engulfed Billy and he was nearly overcome with an urge to bolt from his hiding place and submit to the will of his pursuers. With mounting horror Billy realized that something was terribly wrong but his fear-mazed mind could not seem to comprehend what was happening to him. Billy did not fancy himself particularly valiant or heroic, but he knew that this sudden panic that had seized him was unnatural and was beating his normal iron resolve into submission. He could feel waves of powerful suggestions rolling over him like physical things. Even the ghost voice had ceased its relentless urgings, consumed for the moment by the surging tide of fear that had risen so suddenly to devour all resolve.

Billy cast about in confusion and terror and was for a moment overcome by an unnerving vision of hundreds of blood mad warriors, led by the hulking figure of Mukte'ksago, moving silently toward him from all directions with death in their hearts and fire in their eyes. He was suddenly certain that there was but one way to escape their relentless pursuit…run away! Yes, run away even if it meant revealing himself to the enemy. It was as if he were being commanded by some unholy force to flee and he felt powerless to deny the impulse. He realized in a detached sort of way that a feeling of abject terror was quickly stifling his sanity and he must break free from its grip or succumb to the madness of surrender.

His senses reeled with indecision as the powerful message of terror and fear beat a staccato cadence of submission into his brain. He struggled against the powerful emotions until his eyes started from his head in dread and his face became a mask of crazed fear. The origin of this sudden fear and anxiety he could not discern nor fathom and the helplessness which it generated maddened him. For a moment he could not move, his limbs frozen as if weighed down with colossal chains. He fought urgently against a new desire, unbidden, that demanded Billy throw down his weapons and run screaming across the dunes to prostrate himself before the twin evils of Mukte'ksago and Pesotum. The compulsion was so strong and without reason that he feared he had lost his sanity. It was as if something unnatural, some outside force, was attempting to break down his resolve, urging him to give in to his fear. His mind

rebelled weakly against the fear, an emotion he hated without end, and rather than give in to the hated fear he instead began to focus on the hate he felt for it. And the voice in his head, Wells' voice, so silent during the earlier killing roared suddenly to life! *Revenge! Revenge!* With a visible effort Billy pushed the fear-laced vision from his mind and at once felt again the master of his own body and emotions. He thought how strange it was to have bravely faced a thousand enemies with honor during his lifetime only to abruptly give in to his basest fears in the shadow of Mukte'ksago's villainy. It made no sense to the young warrior.

Frowning, Billy wondered breathlessly if the stories of Nau-non-gea were true. Was he an actual shaman capable of casting fear into the hearts of his enemies, sucking their courage and honor like some psychic vampire? He could find no other plausible explanation for his unexpected fit of terror. For the first time in his life Billy accepted the possibility that there might be a great many things about his native heritage that he could not explain away with the dismissive aplomb characteristic of his white blood.

Billy looked down at the purple corpse and an unquenchable anger built up inside him. He had been forced to suffer that emotion which he had refused to acknowledge even as a child growing up alone, loved by no one and despised by all. He felt again that same sickening sensation of weakness and vulnerability that had hovered over him throughout his lonely life like some impish companion, one he swore he would never again acknowledge; he hated that feeling more than any human enemy and had since his childhood refused to speak its name. The name was fear and he was not pleased at its appearance. He ground his teeth in frustrated rage and shame, his fists clenched into tight purple knots. Swearing to his gods a blasphemous oath he vowed he would make them all bleed for this affront.

He grabbed the dead Indian's tomahawk

and began hacking violently at the bruised neck until he had severed the head from its body, heedless in his rage of the sounds he made. He would send a message to the giant Winnebago Mukte'ksago, the significance of which the Winnebago would understand, one that would also strike fear into the hearts of the Potawatomi that followed him. Billy knew the Winnebagos were known amongst all the tribes as aggressive fighters and no man, white or red, allowed himself to be captured alive for it was well known that they would be tortured for days before having their heads cut off and their bodies eaten. Billy smiled as he hewed and hacked at the dead man's body. Now, let them fear what I will do to them for this outrage!

With a snort of disgust, Billy reached beneath the dead scout's loin cloth and hacked away at the other's genitals before placing them into the dead man's mouth. He poured sand into the gaping wound that had once been a neck and buried the tomahawk deep into the bald skull in an act of pure, unreasoning fury. Finally, he placed the ruined head upon a low dune, its lifeless eyes facing the Dead River, before moving silently away toward the sluggish waters of the river, no longer bothering to conceal his tracks.

"Let them come," he thought to himself before disappearing into the dark forest. "Let them fear."

Mukte'ksago looked down upon the mangled corpse and grunted.

The others held back, staring at the headless remains, each wondering if he would be the next to die. The half-breed scout had already killed two of their war party and the manner of their killing had driven a spike of fear into each of them. It was as if the half-breed were a ghost, an apparition that danced before their eyes and killed beneath their very noses. No one who had seen the man had

survived and now the shaman's magic had been broken. Dark, fearful glances were cast toward the thin ribbon of water that pierced the thick canopy of foliage like a spearpoint. No one dared look at Pesotum who fairly writhed in baffled rage at this latest insult.

It was clear to Pesotum that the others were quickly losing their appetite for the chase. He was puzzled by the half-breed's actions. He had thought the scout would have made a mad dash for the safety of Millioki or Fort Wayne to warn the whites of the uprising; instead, he had led them on a grueling chase that ended abruptly at this stinking, dead river. Moreover, he reasoned, this land belonged to the feared Spring Bluff clan and there were no whites nearby to rescue the half-breed scout. It made no sense, and his intuition warned him that the Crafty Wolf was leading them into a trap. "But," he asked himself. "What trap could possibly be laid within this desolate land?"

Pesotum looked intently at the ghastly skull before turning to his brother and demanding in a nervous voice, "I thought your magic was powerful. You said he would go mad with fear. Instead, we find . . . this." He kicked the dead scout's lifeless body violently. Nau-non-gea squatted in the shadow of the dune, the shaman's eyes staring in the direction of the skull's leering gaze which glowered upriver. He was as surprised as the rest that his fear magic had not worked. He had called upon the manidogs of this land and he was sure their spirits had answered. He could feel their presence strongly and he now feared that the half-breed must possess his own potent magic which he had used to counter his own. He looked up at his brother with haunted eyes.

"The stories are true, brother. He is a child born of white demons. My magic is useless against one like him."

"Bah!" spat the giant Winnebago as he searched the sand for Billy's trail. "We do not need magic. He taunts us and dares us to follow him. He is a man and nothing more. Let us kill the dog and fill our bellies with his flesh!" He snapped his jaw shut and began walking toward the smelly river not waiting for the others to follow.

Pesotum's band watched the broad back of Mukte'ksago disappear into the forest. Despite their growing concern, they were a hard lot, bred to the wild, the children of hardship and privation and they would not abandon the chase now that their quarry was on foot and so near that he might be watching them. Though they cast wary glances at their dead comrade, they nonetheless followed the Winnebago killer toward the river, each having privately resolved to continue the chase no matter what the cost.

Billy stalked along the river's edge as he moved deeper into the forest interior, moving with the supple grace of a hunting panther. His keen ears heard the screeching caw of a distant crow as it winged its way through the dark alleys of scattered tree branches, and he listened to the chatter of squirrels quarreling. But, most of all, he listened beneath the forest sounds, past the hoot of the owl and the rustle of leaves, searching with that part of him that was not wholly human for the signature, the aura of humanity, that alerted all the forest's creatures that man had come to their domain and death would soon follow.

The voice within his head had become little more than a whisper, humming contentedly as he wound his way through the marshy terrain, careful to avoid the river's foul water. All around him the vegetation was thick with weeds and wildflowers; vines descended from trees and slid into the black waters like the green fingers of a giant, and everywhere he looked the waist-high plants seemed to sway as if some large, unseen army of things were pushing their way through the dense undergrowth all around him. He was

sure the spirit of the place had been fouled by something monstrous whose malignant presence was mirrored in the rotting decay that seemed to taint everything. Even the trees seemed twisted and misshapen the further he traveled upriver. Their branches seemed to reach out, extending thin arms from trunks that oozed a greenish blue slime he refused to touch. And though he knew it was impossible, he nonetheless felt certain that the trees were alive; alive in the sense that he felt sure that they were animated with more than simple life, that they possessed within their barky armor a malevolent consciousness which watched him with hungry eyes and waited for him to wander too close.

He continued to follow the black finger of the Dead River as it cut its way through the forest, casting nervous glances at its stagnant waters now and then. Once, he repressed a shudder as he saw something huge break the scummy surface, too quick for him to be sure of what he had seen, but leaving him with a hazy impression of monstrous scales and only a trail of bubbles in its wake as evidence of its passing.

"This river is anything but dead," he said to himself, swallowing hard and willing himself to overcome his fear.

With a start he realized the voice in his head was gone. He knew then that this was where his friend had led him. This was to be the place where he made his stand. He stood within a small bowl-shaped clearing, little more than a soggy depression in the earth and ringed by black oak trees and cat tails. He looked around taking care to note the location of each tree, each clump of leaves, or tuft of tall grass, intently eyeing all approaches before deciding finally to lie alongside the river, partially hidden by large lichen-covered stones. He cradled his musket upon his shoulder and settled down to await his pursuers.

Time passed slowly as the day wore on. Now that the voice of his friend had departed, leaving him alone with his own thoughts,

Billy's only companions in this steaming bowl were the insects and the pervasive feeling that a malevolent force lay just out of sight but always close, gloating in silence, toying with his nerves, waiting to pounce. The moist heat of the bog combined with the fetid odor of the river to make a humid stew of the air and Billy resisted the urge to swat at the gnats and mosquitoes that swarmed around his sticky skin seeking to nest in his ears, nose, and in the crevices of his eyes. Their buzzing presence was a torment, but Billy had learned long ago that to yield to his body's complaints while hunting man or beast would yield failure…or worse.

Now and then Billy heard the soft *plop-plop* of bubbles breaking the surface of the river beside him and he felt rather than saw an evil presence glide beneath the surface, churning the water slightly as if agitated by his nearness to the river's edge. With an effort he put all thoughts of what might be in the water to rest and settled in to await the arrival of his enemies with the cunning patience of a stalking wolf. He did not have to wait long.

Suddenly, out among the cluster of trees to the east of his position, all sound ceased. Billy turned his eyes toward the thick black oaks facing him but otherwise made no visible movement. Satisfied that he remained hidden from the eyes of his stalkers he subtly raised his musket and waited though no sound came to his ears for a long time. He did not relax but waited silently with the patience of a starving mountain lion and was soon rewarded by a flicker of movement to his left. Though he could see the dim outline of the creeping brave he chose to hold his fire. He did not want to reveal his position to the rest of the war party before he had spotted Pesotum for it was the Indian chief that he most owed his revenge. Then, even as he lay in wait, he spied another dim form materialize to his right and he knew that the noose was tightening about him.

Long minutes passed and Billy lay absolutely still while he watched the two forms move toward each other, appearing to speak with their hands in mute communication. Their painted bodies limned against the dark trees, perfect targets for a crack shot like Billy but still he refrained from firing. More than once as they crept forward the Indians had looked directly at Billy without seeing him and he knew that he must eventually be discovered if they moved any closer. He was sure that the rest of the war party lurked nearby waiting for the advance pair to flush him from his hiding place. Frustrated, Billy knew the iron will of Mukte'ksago was what kept them hidden even when their every instinct likely was urging them to rush forward and make an end of it. He knew finally that he must act now or be spotted. Irritated at not having an opportunity to eliminate Pesotum he brought the musket up ever so slightly and took aim at the brave furthest from him before breathing deeply and pulling the trigger.

The musket cracked explosively, the ball tearing a red chunk of flesh from the hapless brave's shoulder, spinning him to the ground in a crimson spray. Billy moved quickly, taking advantage of the confusion to slip noiselessly into the river's inky waters. The water was ice cold and brought an involuntary gasp of pain from his lips as his flesh rebelled against the frigid embrace. The liquid was as thick as oil and where it touched him, he felt as if it were clinging to his exposed flesh with what felt like little hooks that caused him to shudder in revulsion. He moved awkwardly through water too deep for his leather boots to touch bottom, though he was only a few feet from the edge, and dog paddled with one arm while the other held his musket just above the surface. Though it felt like a lifetime, he reached a spot some twenty yards from his original ambush site in a matter of seconds. As he pulled himself silently from the river, he was certain he felt a powerful surge of water cruise past his submerged legs. His brain reeled at the thought of what lurked below the surface of that loathsome river and those thoughts helped him crawl quickly up the bank. Relieved to be out of the water, he took up a new position at the base of a twisted tree whose roots hung over the embankment and he listened intently for evidence that they had marked his escape and were moving toward him.

None came.

Quickly he reloaded the musket, ramming the ball, wadding, and powder with sure hands, all the while scanning the forest before him for his next target. The brave he had passed over had jumped behind a nearby tree for cover and was looking in every direction for his attacker, eyes wide with fear. He had not seen where the shot had come from nor could he see Billy who had moved almost directly behind him.

Another warrior moved carefully into the small bowl, moving quickly from tree to tree, heading to the spot Billy had vacated just seconds before. He leaped cat-like over the stones and thrust his lance violently between tree and stones seeking the flesh of his enemy but piercing only soggy earth instead. Billy rose up then and fired at the man who turned too late to avoid the blast that ripped through his body. Billy had already dropped the musket, useless now that his enemies had seen him, and drawing his knife he charged the bewildered Indian nearest him.

As the musket blast echoed loudly from the trees the Indian wheeled and rose to meet Billy's charge, chopping savagely at Billy's head with his tomahawk. In one fluid movement Billy ducked hard and crossed his knife, cutting edge out, from right to left across the Indian's exposed belly without stopping his headlong rush, releasing the Indian's entrails in a steaming flood while simultaneously driving his shoulder like a ram into the other's chest, knocking the brave hard onto the earth. Billy leaped upon the Indian and used his weight to pin the native scout to the earth as he plunged his blade deep within the other's neck.

Billy jerked his knife free and rolled across the dead man's body as arrows thudded into the space he had just occupied. He moved quickly from tree to tree, gauging the distance and direction from which the arrows had come, instinctively placing whatever cover he could between himself and the deadly missiles that whizzed about his head like angry bees. Billy dove behind a stunted black oak for shelter and immediately lowered himself below the broom sedge grass, all but invisible again to his enemies. He crawled quickly to a clump of Spikerush plants about a dozen yards away and peered at his attackers from between their long stems.

Billy heard Mukte'ksago's bull voice call out to the remaining Indians, ordering them to stop their advance before any more were killed. Billy cursed the patient Winnebago. He had hoped to cull their numbers before avenging himself upon Pesotum but the giant warrior was too wily, too much a product of the same ruthless life that had spawned the half-breed scout. Mukte'ksago, the man-ape, was a master of the hunt and, like the big cats, he was fond of cruelty and enjoyed toying with his prey.

"Half-breed! The crows gather above you. You are doomed," Mukte'ksago jeered from the protective ring of trees that surrounded the bog. "And soon I will eat your heart as I ate the heart of the great Apekonit!"

At mention of his friend's name, anger surged through Billy's veins replacing the weariness and caution that had been his constant companion throughout the chase. Seeing red, the bloodlust was upon him and he knew that Mukte'ksago and the others had him cornered like a frightened and desperate rat. It was merely a matter of time before he was surrounded and feathered like a wild hog and that image stoked his rage into a blazing tempest. He would run no more. Billy rose from his concealment deliberately and stood proudly exposed, head thrown back, daring his enemies to reveal themselves.

"I am here, dogs!" he called out to the dark forest at large. "Come and see what manner of man it is you chase! I will feed your brains to the ravens, Mukte'ksago! We two are at the end. You others are but meat for the forest and no concern of mine."

Moments passed before several shadows began to materialize out of the gloom like ghastly demons caught between this world and the next. They made no sound as they slowly approached their quarry, their blood-lust quelled by caution now that the long chase had ended, their courage dampened by the realization that it was the Crafty Wolf they had brought to ground and not some hapless white farmer and his defenseless brats. The remnants of the war party fanned out around Billy in a crescent formation, their bows knocked with arrows drawn tight and aimed at Billy's chest. With his back to the river he faced his hunters bravely and waited for Pesotum to give the order that would send him to the next life. He saw Pesotum emerge from behind his men, his sweat streaked face a mask of triumph, with Nau-non-gea close on his heels like some mongrel waiting for scraps. Billy could see the toll the past twenty-four hours had cost them, the strain of the hunt evident in the haggard looks Pesotum's men shot at him beneath brows furrowed in concentration, and he noted with pride that he had made them suffer during the long chase from Fort Dearborn.

"Half-breed pig," spat Non-non-gea from behind his brother's shoulder, "it is time to die. Brother, end this now. We have much to do before winter."

Whatever Pesotum had meant to say died on his lips as a giant form moved between Pesotum and Billy. "He is mine. I will kill any man," he looked at Pesotum, eyes blazing with volcanic fury, "that cheats me of his scalp."

Billy gazed up at the giant Winnebago, weighing his opponent with eyes that probed for any sign of weakness. Mukte'ksago stared back at Billy from under a shaggy black mane that hung to his shoulders and framed a face marred by scars. Small, piggish eyes glared hate at the half breed scout. Though he was taller than any Indian Billy had met, he did not possess the rangy hardness that was the Winnebago's birthright, giving off instead the impression of tremendous, lumbering, raw power. His mighty shoulders descended from a bull neck twice the width of an ordinary man's and his barrel chest was amazingly thick. His arms and legs were corded with bulging muscles and his hands, which seemed more like the paws of a bear than the hands of a man, gripped a massive war club as if it were a child's toy. His whole appearance reminded Billy of the monstrous anthropoids he had seen painted on the walls of caves in the deep southwest. For all his bulk, the man-ape moved toward Billy like a graceful hunting cat, eyes riveted upon his enemy with smoldering intensity.

"Pesotum! It is like you to let another die in your place!" Billy called out in a clear, derisive voice that pierced the veil of conceit which enveloped Pesotum like a dagger point. Pesotum stifled an angry reply as Billy and the man-ape came together with a thundering crash.

The Winnebago sprang forward in a flash and swung the heavy war club with astonishing speed. Billy lunged desperately to the side and was surprised to feel a numbing blow to the shoulder that sent him spinning through the reeds. Having missed his target, Mukte'ksago had stopped his rush and reversed the momentum of his swing with a powerful twist of his torso that brought the club into contact with Billy's exposed back. Billy did not wait to see what else the big man would do; he spun immediately away from the second blow and extended his arm inside the others reach with the speed of a striking rattler. As they came apart, circling warily, Billy noticed with some satisfaction a thin line of blood tracing its way across the man-ape's chest. His knife had drawn first blood, but the giant was not done. Though Billy had only been dealt a glancing blow, his shoulder ached all the way to the elbow, grim testimony of the power of the giant Winnebago.

Mukte'ksago rushed in again, swinging his war club in a deadly arc that would have shattered a tree had it landed. But Billy knew in an instant that there was no way to avoid the blow by moving back so he stepped inside the other's reach and locked his calloused hand upon the Winnebago's wrist checking the downward swing while he drove his knife point in a savage thrust toward the ape like face that leered above him. The blade skittered across the Indian's flesh ripping through the lips and laying the cheekbone bare before being knocked from Billy's grasp by a powerful blow from Mukte'ksago's free hand. They came together then, the weight of the larger man clearly an advantage as they each sought to leverage into a better position upon the soggy earth.

Once on the ground, Mukte'ksago manhandled the smaller man using his sheer size to effectively pin Billy to the earth. Mukte'ksago refused to drop his war club and could only pound Billy's face with one fist and elbow as he sought to wrench the weapon free from Billy's grip and deliver the death blow. Billy tried desperately to block the blows which landed with sickening thuds upon the side of his skull. He took a fist to the nose that brought the claret in a crimson flow down his face, and it seemed to Mukte'ksago that the Miami scout began to falter. He felt Billy's strength begin to waver as the scout flailed weakly against his own immense strength.

With an urgency born of desperation Billy stretched his free hand toward his fallen knife, still refusing to release his iron grip upon the other's arm, barely able to keep the man-ape's war club from pummeling him into oblivion. Mukte'ksago's eyes lit up with beastly glee as he watched Billy cough and gasp, choking on his own blood which drained down his throat faster than he could spit it out. He felt Billy sag for a moment, and he could not help but gloat as a look of despair passed across Billy's mangled features. He began to smirk and jeer at Billy's efforts to defend himself. Content that he had beaten his adversary into submission, he stopped the relentless pounding and reached into his belt to pull out a knife and make an end of it. He felt great pride at having dispatched Main'mwi, the Crafty Wolf, and he imagined the story of their battle being told around the fires of all the great lakes tribes.

As soon as the Winnebago pulled back to draw the knife Billy shot forward using the grip he had on the other's arm as leverage to extend upward and lock his free hand upon the man-ape's throat. Mukte'ksago's eyes grew wide in surprise as he realized he had been tricked and he could feel the awesome strength of Billy's hand as it closed off his airway in a grip as tight as a vise. Billy pressed his thumb deeper into the leathery flesh near the trachea as Mukte'ksago jerked violently back and forth in a mad effort to pull the hand from his throat which was already a burning agony.

The other Indians had moved close to the combatants and were shouting encouragement to the hulking Winnebago, urging him on, demanding that he end the struggle quickly. Their shouts rose above the river and settled upon the small bog like a violent blanket that covered everything with the spirit of their human madness; their emotions seemed to enhance the blind rage of the two warriors who had rolled free of each other, heaving and cursing in breathless gasps, pain coloring what might be their last moments on earth a ghastly hue that had in it the very essence of atavistic humanity.

They stood facing each other, eyes smoldering with savage intensity, oblivious to the howls of the warriors or to the danger that had silently invaded the bog. Their world had been reduced to its basic elements: survive or die. Billy snarled like a wolf and turned his wrath full upon the Winnebago who answered with his own wordless grunt, and the last remnants of humanity were shed from each combatant as the battle was renewed.

Standing slightly apart from the rest, Nau-non-gea was the first to feel the change in the atmosphere. The shaman felt as if some unseen presence had entered the bog and was observing the battle from some hidden lair, reveling in the confrontation, feeding off the waves of hate and fear like a bloated parasite. Nau-non-gea looked at the leering faces of his war party as if in a dream, seeing their features twisted in sadistic glee at the bloodletting, watching in horrible fascination as the two men continued stabbing and hacking at each other like animals in a pit, seemingly bound to each other by their mutual rage. He knew abruptly that something was very wrong, and he sensed also that they were not alone.

The shaman looked wildly about him as he began to finally guess the true meaning of Apekonit's curse. He had sensed the presence of powerful manidogs that morning and could now feel their pulsing power building as something began to stir in the waters of the river. It was as if all the fear, savagery, lust, and cruelty of the moment had somehow become substantial things that seemed to feed the very air itself, sealing a silent compact between a dead man's spirit and the evil thing that haunted the place. The Kegangizi had risen to feed.

VII. Revenge

Nau-non-gea shouted a warning to his brother as the first of the faces began to appear upon the trees. But Pesotum was focused upon the violent clash of the two titans, too keenly a part of the magic violence conjured by the curse to hear his brother's frantic cries. Like the others, Pesotum was held spell-bound by the bloody spectacle, having become a kind of emotional conduit that somehow allowed the forest to come alive around him. Nau-non-gea looked wildly about as the faces began to occupy the trees, animating them with the dead spirits of the slaughtered innocents of Fort Dearborn, their white faces burned hideously into the living bark, like fiendish caricatures of humanity.

Nau-non-gea began to run, screaming frantically as the trees seemed to move toward him, pulling their roots from out of the ground, reaching for him with grasping fingers and knobby limbs that were a mad parody of human arms. They were everywhere he turned, their dead faces writhing in agony, mocking him with mouths that gaped but issued no sound. The fresh turned earth released a foul stench that stank of the grave and suddenly the others became aware of their plight with soul shattering abruptness, as if they had been released from their role in the summoning of the manidogs and then cast aside as living refuse whose only use was as fodder for the Beast.

Pesotum fell to his knees, overcome with fear as the rest of the war party broke and ran toward the river. The small bog crawled with nightmare shapes that lurched after the fleeing Indians, a forest of dead faces that shambled on root legs and demanded revenge! While the Indians raced by, Mukte'ksago and Billy remained oblivious to the appalling transformation around them, aware only of the urgent need to kill. Mukte'ksago was tiring rapidly; his immense bulk heaved, struggling desperately for more air as he circled his adversary on legs that trembled from exhaustion. His face was a grinning mask of blood and his body was crisscrossed with red lines made by Billy's knife. He still gripped his war club, but he knew he faced a fresher, faster man, and he felt for the second time in his life the icy clutch of fear take hold in his gut.

Billy stalked outside the man-ape's killing zone, wary still of the giant's war club which had left his body a bruised mass of flesh, and still respectful of the speed with which the big man could move. He was dizzy from loss of blood and he could no longer feel his face and he knew that he must kill the Winnebago quickly or pass out never to wake again. He felt anew the thrill of fear as it coursed up his spine and hated with renewed fury the cause of that fear…Mukte'ksago. Billy broke the stalemate with a movement that would have shamed a starving wolf, slashing savagely at the Winnebago's knotty forearm that held the war club, cutting the skin to the bone and slicing tendons that forced the brute to drop his weapon. Billy ducked beneath the Indian's clutching grasp and thrust his blade deep into the giant's side before being dashed to the ground by a stunning blow to the head. He rolled to the side and barely avoided another headlong smash that would surely have crushed his skull had it landed.

Maddened by the pain and frustrated by the speed of his foe, Mukte'ksago bellowed in rage before twisting and pulling at the long knife with his good arm. His large calloused hand slipped repeatedly over the wet hilt, unable to remove the cause of the searing pain. Mukte'ksago's eyes glazed with fear as he realized he was dying. With an anguished cry the great man-ape turned and fled from his opponent, his mind unable to comprehend defeat nor reconcile the concept that he was about to face his own mortality. He had taken but a few steps before he was caught up in the crushing embrace of what Billy swore was a moving tree. Billy tried to shake his head clear of the maddening vision but fell to the earth instead, out cold from loss of blood and mercifully unaware of the manner in which Mukte'ksago left this life.

Fevered screams burst forth from quivering lips in a fear maddened stampede as, one by one, the Indians hurled themselves into the Dead River, thrashing desperately through the frigid waters to escape the nightmarish faces, heedless of the bubbling water that boiled and frothed beneath them, churned to a black stew by the passage of some colossal body.

Without warning, the black water erupted in an oily spray as a giant head broke the surface directly beneath one of the fleeing warriors. Slavering jaws opened wide revealing rows of sharp teeth that received the wretched warrior whole. It thrust its serpentine neck back like a gigantic snake as it choked down its meal and gazed at the rest of the doomed warriors with a baleful yellow eye that gleamed with a malevolent intelligence. Pesotum watched trancelike as the creature dived again and again beneath the Stygian waters, circling slowly beneath each Indian as they tried urgently to reach the other side. This action would induce in each man a panicked thrashing that seemed to excite the monster's appetite and one by one it consumed each of the ill-fated followers of Pesotum save Naunon-gea. The shaman had simply stopped swimming when he caught his first glimpse of the horrific monster and had begun screaming one word repeatedly, his sanity shattered by what he saw: "Kegangizi! Kegangizi!"

Pesotum watched in awful silence as the surface of the water rippled nearer and nearer his brother. Nau-non-gea noticed too and stopped screaming, looking instead for Pesotum and reaching a hand toward him once he had spotted his brother.

The shaman called out in a timid voice, the voice of a child as might call to an older brother in the darkness of night seeking comfort, "Save me brother!"

Pesotum was spurred into action, finally, and he rose up, lance in hand, and dove into the river to save his brother or die trying. He swam as fast as the oily water would allow but he knew he would be too late. With an awful cry Nau-non-gea was dragged slowly beneath the surface of the water, his eyes held his

brother's gaze as he disappeared, the gaze of a confused little boy who could not understand why his brother had not saved him; all his plans and strategies fled before the nightmare vision of his brother and it was then that Pesotum experienced a deep and intense sadness. The Kegangizi's physical hunger seemingly sated, it glared at Pesotum with eyes that seemed to gloat and revel in Pesotum's pain. With a contented hiss it descended into the inky black waters of the Dead River leaving Pesotum utterly alone with his grief.

Pesotum swam slowly to shore, holding back the choking sobs that wracked his body, and collapsed upon the muddy bank wondering if this was how the whites felt when they lost those they loved most. Deep in his heart he knew the curse of Apekonit, the white Indian called Wells, had been fulfilled.

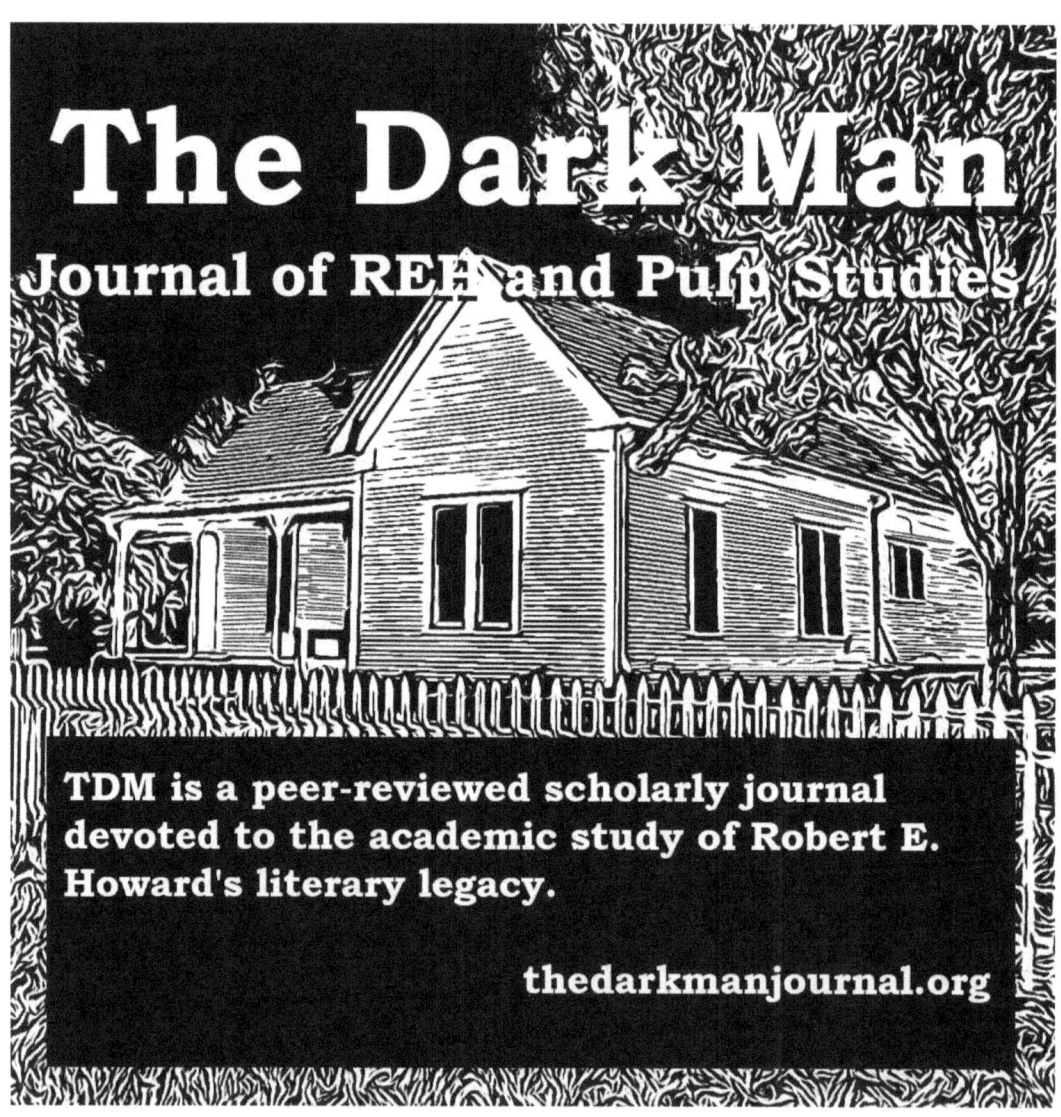

The Dark Man
Journal of REH and Pulp Studies

TDM is a peer-reviewed scholarly journal devoted to the academic study of Robert E. Howard's literary legacy.

thedarkmanjournal.org

Omari Ket Returns in Eda Blessed II!
Six new exciting stories from the world of Ki Khanga.
Available December 2020 from MVmedia!
www.mvmediaatl.com

Eda's Blessed is the perfect storm where setting, tone, character, and story all snap into place, creating something special.
-Steve Rosenstein and Rodney Turner, Microphones of Madness

FETCH

By Marshall Highet

The bathroom was done up in the chromes and cement of every other high end corporate bathroom Marisa had been in to date. And as of today—she glanced down at her cellphone: October 12th—she'd been in a lot of them.

"Number 26," she said to her reflection, sweeping dark bangs off her forehead with one damp hand. "Lucky number twenty-six." She grimaced and gripped the edge of the sink. Twenty-six doesn't sound very lucky. Twenty-seven maybe, or twenty-eight, but not twenty-six.

She straightened the collar of her crisp white button-down, one of ten she owned and the only thing she wore to work-related events. Her uniform. Same with the charcoal slacks she was wearing; identical to the other nine that hung straight as pins in her loft closet.

"Fetch isn't like any other app out there," she began, her game show host voice echoing off the hard surfaces uncushioned by carpeting or furniture. "You input your information into it at the outset and then Fetch is off and running in the digital universe."

Marisa's dark eyes bored into her reflection's, sparking feverishly. She wanted this badly. If this one didn't work, there would be the next pitch of course, but each rejection chipped away at her resolve, eroding her belief that Fetch was something special, an app like nothing else out there.

"What info, you ask? Great question." She glanced behind her to make sure that she was still alone in the bathroom. Still no one. "You input your personal information into Fetch: address, occupation, email, twitter handle,

instagram, likes, dislikes, to-do list… What's that you say? Why a to-do list? Another great question. Because that's what Fetch does. Like a digital butler, Fetch gets it done. Ooh, that's good. That could be a tagline." She whipped a slim cell phone out of her back pocket, tapping rapidly into its face. "Fetch, record note: Fetch gets it done." A muted ruff issued from the phone and Marisa slid her thumb across it, slipping it back into her pocket. She turned back to herself.

"For all the simplicity that the Internet has promised us, our lives are becoming increasingly more complicated with every new app that's launched. Fetch simplifies this, it curates your social media, calls in deliveries, ubers, schedules haircuts, dry cleaning. That photo calendar of the kids you've been meaning to create for your mom's birthday? Fetch has you covered. It'll get it to your mother before the big day, wrapped. Wondering what the show times are for the new Marvel movie coming out this fall? Fetch will tell you and show you the route to the closest theater. If Fetch knows that you like Indian food, your post-movie nosh will be mapped out automatically."

She grimaced. "God that's horrible. Note to self, never use the word 'nosh' in a pitch."

Turning back to the mirror, she cocked her head as if listening to an imaginary question. "Why not just use Siri? Because frankly, Siri isn't enough. Siri can do most of this but the thing that makes Fetch truly unique is that basically, at its core, Fetch is another you. A you that only exists in cyberspace. All of the digital imprints we make when we visit sites or make purchases online or google something, Fetch gets all of that: our past, our present, and our possible future. Then the app creates a digital prototype from this information, another you, the Internet you. An e-shadow." Her words rang in the metallic space. "For you, sir," she gestured at her reflection, "you would have a he-shadow. For me, a she-shadow." She tittered, then grimaced.

"Fetch sets that e-shadow loose on the digital world, solely for your benefit. Siri is helpful, but Fetch gets it done." Marisa nodded to herself in the mirror. "Siri is helpful but Fetch gets it done. That's good. Gotta remember that." She asked Fetch to amend the previous note and got a ruff in return.

Marisa turned on the faucet and wet her already damp hands under the streaming water. She patted her weirdly blotchy cheeks. Nerves.

"Showtime," she told herself, smoothing her dark hair one more time and turning away from her reflection.

After the pitch, Marisa shared the elevator ride down with one of the tech execs who'd been in the boardroom, which strung out her already-fraught nerves just that much more. She thought it had gone well, they hadn't laughed her out of the room or left early, always a positive sign. But she could never tell. Often, this felt like pouring her lifeblood into a black hole. She was lucky if she'd get an actual rejection in the form of an email. Mostly she never heard back at all.

The tech exec was a prototype of Mr. Smith from the Matrix movies, without the reflective shades, a relief. He had an impeccable nondescript suit on, short shorn hair, and was completely unmarked by any sort of distinguishing feature except for a pair of bright red socks, either his concession to his hidden individuality or his attempt at having one.

Marisa stared straight ahead, trying to calm her rabbit-jumpy heart. She could feel the exec's presence next to her like he was a banked coal. When he leaned forward to choose the second floor, she took in every crease and crinkle on his sleeve. Deliriously—for she did feel delirious, like she might break out sobbing or cackling or into song at any moment—she wondered if he used the same system that she did: same exact outfit times ten. It had cost her a bundle the day she'd bought her "uniforms," but it had been totally worth it. Ten designer suits and shirts? mucho dinero. Never having to think about what she was going to wear to work in the morning? priceless. She was about to ask him (was she really going to ask him?) but thankfully he spoke first.

"Fetch. Cute name." His voice was as nondescript as his suit, no hint of red socks in tone or accent.

"Thanks." She stared straight ahead, watching illumination move from behind one circular button to the next in descending order.

"Great tagline too: Siri is helpful but Fetch gets it done."

She inwardly leapt in the air, pumping her fist. Outwardly, she allowed herself a tiny smile. "Thanks twice over."

"Have you tried it out yet?"

Marisa chanced a glance at him. He stood with polished loafers equidistant apart, staring straight ahead at his own reflection in the polished elevator doors.

"I'm trying it out right now."

"Really?" In the reflection, she could see him cock his head minutely in her direction. "On whom?" He sounded genuinely interested.

Marisa paused, but she couldn't really see the harm in telling him. Even if he wanted to steal the idea, try and make his own app, she was already far out ahead of him with trademarks and a fully-manifested prototype.

"On myself." As if in response to this, her

back pocket vibrated and issued a soft ruff. Her Fetch was telling her she'd accomplished something. Good dog, she thought.

The tech exec turned to look at her full in the face. Their ride together was almost at an end, button number four was lit.

"Risky," he said. She noticed that the other distinguishing feature about him besides his socks was his eyes, bright green and insistent. And knowing. "You've got some cajones."

She shrugged, not breaking his gaze. What did she have to lose now? She'd already made her pitch. They'd either bite or not, and she hardly thought that this tete-a-tete in the elevator was going to make a difference. She glanced down as the elevator dinged on floor two. He was holding out a glossy black card. Just like the rest of him, it was sleek and forgettable. He held it between his pointer and middle finger, his hand a blade, ready to shake. He was like a lesser species of shark. Not as threatening as a tiger or a great white, but something equally as deadly, more insidious. A shark whose name was forgotten

as soon as it swam out of view. The doors slid open and still he stood there, offering his card. She took it and he stepped quickly out, pivoting so that he was facing her as the doors began to slide closed.

"Consider me very interested. Oh and Ms. Ponte, do take care." He grinned as the doors slid closed, leaving her with the imprint of a mouth full of professionally whitened, honed-to-a-razor-point teeth.

The air in the bar wasn't smoky, there hadn't been smoking allowed inside a building in this city in over fifteen years, but it somehow looked smoky. It was a combination of the muted lighting underneath the shelves of bottles behind the bar, the gaudy display of the pinball machine in the left-hand corner of the room, and the fact that it was still somehow midday. She scanned the bar for a half minute before she spotted Carl at the very end, staring at a TV set broadcasting another delirious moment from the presidential campaign. He saw her notice him and raised his beer in the air, she saluted in return and walked through the empty bar to take a seat next to him.

"How do, Maris, how'd that go?" Carl said in lieu of a greeting.

"It went tolerably," Marisa said as she slid her phone out of her pocket and put it face up on the bar. She considered for a moment, feeling the sharp corners of the tech exec's card in her pocket. "Perhaps better than tolerable. I got a bite."

"Well, well, that's something to celebrate." Carl raised his almost-empty beer to her in a mock-toast, draining it.

"Carl, with you there's always something to celebrate," Marisa said, noting the two other bottles lined up in front of him. Why didn't the bartender clean those up? Did Carl like to keep track?

Carl hmmphed. They'd known each other since high school, before either of them had escaped their personal heterosexual prisons. They'd escaped those only to find themselves in new prisons with stronger locks.

"And with you there never is." Carl raised an eyebrow in her direction, the little light in the bar glancing off his shaved head.

"Touche," she said and signaled the bartender. "Scotch, neat, water on the side." A trick she'd learned while living in Inverness, Scotland. Only non-Scotch drinkers drank their Glenn Gillian watered down with plebeian ice cubes. For shame. "And another of what he's having."

They were silent until the bartender returned with a heavy glass with two fingers of amber liquid in it, a shot glass of water, and a beer. She thanked him and turned back to Carl, who was looking at her expectantly.

"So you got a bite? Give." He scooted his newly-drained bottle towards the other empties and took up the new one.

"Well," she began, feeling oddly defensive about telling Carl about the man in the eleva-

tor. She pushed the feeling away. "I pitched it to them, and that was all good. But it was the guy in the elevator that bit."

Carl screwed his face up. "Did he work there?"

"What? Yes! He was in the meeting and we happened to be going down at the same time."

"I thought you'd gotten a bite from a food delivery guy," Carl chuckled.

"Not that desperate yet." Marisa poured a few drops of water into her Scotch and took a discerning sip. Lovely. Tasted just like damp peat off the moors. "He asked me how I was testing Fetch, and then gave me his card. Said he was interested. Very interested. Those were his words." She could feel the corners of the card still jabbing into her skin through her pants.

"Bravo." Carl began to peel the label off his beer. "How are you testing it? Grad student? Lowly intern at the company?"

"Erm, no."

"Who then?"

Marisa took another sip of Scotch, this one slightly bigger than was necessary. "I'm testing it on myself."

Carl's eyebrow cocked in full skepticism mode. "You're not."

"I am." She couldn't look at him.

"That's…unusual."

"I know, but I had to. I wanted to keep it to myself. Keep it close. It's personal."

A silence stretched between them, punctuated with the televised blathering of one candidate or the other, it was hard to tell them apart.

"Are you going to that thing tonight? The high school meet and greet at the Montage?" He pulled a green strip of paper off the bottle in one long curl and let it drop. "Fucking reunions."

"We are."

Carl turned to face her, all skepticism in his face gone. "We? You're bringing Lindsey? To the get together? How rash!"

"She really wanted to go. In her mind it's a way of making us official or something. But I'm going to try and keep the whole lesbian thing under wraps. If I can. Remember the A-ones?"

"Those assholes who made high school a living Hell? Despite the electro-shock therapy, I remember them."

"I'm sure they're, like, all grown up or whatever, but I don't want them to make a big thing about Lindsey and me in front of everyone. I don't want them to…I don't know." Marisa trailed off, swishing the Scotch around in her glass.

"You don't want them to ridicule you loudly about who you are, laugh hysterically about it while pointing, and then shove you in a locker or give you a swirly or some shit? Why ever not?" One corner of Carl's mouth turned up.

"Exactly. Grown up or not, asshole doesn't wash off." Marisa added more water to her drink.

"Cheers to that," Carl said, raising his half-empty beer to her. They clinked, glass on glass, and turned their attentions back to the shit show of the presidential debate.

"My first boyfriend, do you remember him?" Carl said after a while, apropos of nothing.

Marisa smirked. "Let me see, I'll have to flip through my mental rolodex for your ex-lovers. Man, it's chock full! What's his name?"

"Whats-his-name would have been a great name for him. His name is Gary, was. Pretentious prick. You were in grad school in Chicago so you probably don't remember him much. When we broke up, or right before I guess, he told me to pick up some photos at the one hour developing place. Remember those? Before we had digital everything and could print photos in our houses?"

Marisa nodded. She also remembered Gary, vaguely, from a Christmas party. She didn't remember him being particularly pretentious or prickish, but there you have it.

Perspective was everything.

"He must've had the plan in place for weeks, even before we took the photos, as well as the plan to dump my ass. I show up at the one hour photo develop place after work and there's a crowd in front of the counter, not a line. I go in and when they see me, they get this weird-ass look on their faces. All of them. Like a baby shoved a particularly sticky finger up their nostrils.

"In those days, I was always a little anxious about looking particularly gay, being a baby gay and all. So I thought I was exuding rainbows or some shit."

Carl paused for so long that Marisa wondered if that was the whole cautionary tale, and what the hell it meant. Or if it meant anything or if it was merely Carl on three beers on a weekday afternoon.

"Then I saw it. The printer was printing out its photos, one at a time, with the image facing the counter for the whole crowd to see. And there's a lot of pink flesh on those pics, I could see that straight off. That's when my stomach did a flippity-flop. The old punch in the gut. And sure enough, that asshole had sent the product of our drunken photo shoot to the developing place and then sent me to pick them up. Of course it was only my face in them. Prick."

"Damn, that's cold." Marisa added some more water to her Scotch. "What are you trying to tell me, don't ever take a nude? Cuz it's way too late for that."

Carl fixed her with very sober eyes over the pile of shredded beer bottle labels on the bar. "What I'm telling you is to be careful. Don't give away too much."

"Wow, dramatic Carl. I mean, I understand, you did have your naked bits and pieces shown to the world. That's traumatic. But I'm good, I promise you."

Carl stared at her for another moment and then grinned, his eyes crinkling up at the corners. "And it was one of those really slow old printers: errrrr-chickachick-errrrr," he mimicked the noise. "Like five minutes a shot. My face or bare ass, and sometimes both, slowly taking shape, pixel by pixel. Torture, having my junk out there. Absolute torture."

Before Marisa headed home, she had a list of errands to run. Even though Fetch could get most stuff done (or get Marisa's e-shadow to get stuff done) the app was non-corporeal, so she couldn't actually run the errands. While she and Carl had been enjoying their drinks (hers singular, his plural) Fetch had ruffed three times. The dry cleaning was done, Lindsey's dog needed to be picked up at the groomers, and for some reason Fetch was telling her that her video had almost been pulled together.

She asked Fetch to get her an Uber outside the bar. A few minutes later she was in the back of someone's civic, smelling overenthusiastic spearmint car freshener and listening to her driver, Dolly, blather on and on about The Great British Bake-Off. As if Marisa cared. She mmhhmmed when necessary and continued plugging information into Fetch.

Her favorite part of the app was the graphic she'd designed: the image of a dog with an uncanny resemblance to the one from Blue's Clues, her favorite childhood show. Except Fetch was brown with tan spots, not blue with navy spots. But in Marisa's mind, Fetch was female, just like Blue. Every time Fetch accomplished a task, the dog bounded across the lock screen to drop a bone at her paws and ruff. Too cute.

Fetch was cropping up a small hillock of bones this afternoon. Good dog, she thought again and looked up to see that she was at the dry cleaners.

Something had gone wrong. Apparently, the cleaners had gotten the instructions to use extra extra starch on her white shirts and now they were so stiff and grainy, they were almost unusable. Marisa could feel hives rising on her skin as she fingered the nappy cuff of one of her ruined shirts. And the worst part was that the dry cleaners was not going to refund her, it had been on the order, they said, not their fault.

Marisa took her clothes (now more like suits of armor) with her as she stomped out. She tried to slam the door but it was pneumatic with a cushioned close, so it whooshed shut almost silently. Not very dramatic. It was a three block walk to the dog groomers and she fumed all the way. Little did she know.

Mowgli, Lindsey's (and by association, hers) shih-tzu, usually got a standard cut. But again, the instructions had gotten stymied and Mowgli now looked like a, like a, well…

"He looks like a pygmy alpaca," Marisa told Matt, the groomer, in disgust as she looked at the poor dog's trembling naked body and the bouffant hair on his downturned head. "A really really ugly one."

Matt held up in his hands. "I know that. He knows that. But it was in the instructions. See?"

He spun his iPad around on a desk liberally sprinkled with dog hair: "Shave fur to look like a miniature alpaca. Leave some on tail and around ankles. Leave all on head. Tease."

There it was, plain as the snout on Mowgli's face, her email address showing as the sender.

Mowgli skulked all the way back to Lindsey's apartment, where Marisa dropped him off. After letting Mowgli and herself into Lindsey's apartment, Mowgli jumped onto the couch and stuck his head between two of the cushions as Marisa fumbled with her dry cleaning, trying to get to her phone. Now he looked like the love child of an ostrich and an ugly pygmy alpaca. She finally got the phone out and was about to text Lindsey when another ruff issued from it and Fetch bounded across the screen to drop yet another bone on what was becoming a large hillock. Practically a hill. She decided not to text Lindsey, not just yet. She had to think of the right wording for this…shit show. And maybe Linds wouldn't even notice? Marisa glanced back at Mowgli's frozen stance on the couch. He hadn't even pulled his head out for a treat. Lindsey was going to notice, no question. She had to think of wording, and fast.

She pondered the right way to tell Lindsey about Mowgli all the way back to her place. When the uber pulled up, she looked up and forgot all about the text she was supposed to send.

There were multiple cars at the curb outside her apartment building as if the newest Hollywood it-girl had just moved in and they were trying to get a shot. An inordinate amount of cars. Her neighbors were a social lot, Marisa figured, seems they were all headed out for a wild and crazy Friday night. Friday afternoon, she amended, glancing at her wristwatch. She held to the "all the neighbors are going out" theory until she had to fight through a small crowd to get to her own front door. This wasn't a mid-afternoon social jaunt by her neighbors. This was a throng specifically gathered around her doorway. A throng with one particular thing in common: they were all delivery people and they all addressed her by name as she approached.

"Ms. Ponte?" one asked as she began to push her way through them.

'Um," she hedged, and elbowed her way past him. From her back pocket Fetch issued another muffled ruff, undoubtedly dropping another bone on what was fast becoming a mountain of bones. That digital dog had uncanny timing.

"Sorry, I'm just a friend dropping off her…" She flailed. The too-starched shirts rustled in their plastic shrouds. "Her dry-cleaning!" Marisa's voice sounded false and tinny to her own ears. A smirk graced the face of the delivery woman closest to her. Right. Who knew how long they'd been waiting around for her. But she hadn't ordered all this stuff. Had she?

She broke through the remaining line of unfortunate people in their brand-emblazoned shirts and caps. She jabbed futilely at her lock, self-conscious of the familiarity with which she used the key. "Sorry," she said lamely and then she was on the other side of her door. She dropped the dry cleaning to the floor, where they didn't even have the decency to crumple like proper shirts, they just stood at attention like plastic wrapped headstones.

She took a couple deep breaths, trying to make sense of the whole afternoon. It had started off on such a high, with Mr. Smith in the elevator with his card. Like Clue. Mr Smith in the elevator with the card.

Her phone started chirping at her and it was relief to not hear Fetch's smug bark. Since when did she consider the audio she'd created smug? she wondered. Well, since Fetch wouldn't shut up, that's when. She pulled her phone out of her pocket and regarded the face of her boss on the front of her screen. She slid her thumb across his face.

"Hi Mr. Peyton, everything okay at the office?" She could hear the sundry delivery people milling around on the other side of the door she was leaning against. How could all that food have been possibly ordered? There was even an edible flower arrangement. She didn't think anyone actually ate those things.

"Everything's fine here, Ms Ponte. Although, thanks to you, I'm much more sparkly."

Sparkly? "I'm sorry, Mr. Peyton, why are you…sparkly?"

"You would know that better than anyone, wouldn't you, Ms Ponte."

As if this cleared things up. "Mr. Peyton. I'm confused."

Mr. Peyton didn't even address that. "Not only am I sparkly, I'm also pornographic. Again, thanks to you."

Marisa's mouth dropped open and she

pulled the phone away from her ear to stare incredulously at the image of her boss's face.

"And it's my fault that you're both sparkly and pornographic?" She stumbled over the last word.

"It seems so, Ms Ponte. And why you would think this is funny at all is beyond me." Mr. Peyton's voice was leaking anger all over her earhole. "A glitter dick bomb. Really. Frankly this calls your judgement into question."

"A glitter dick…"

"Yes, a glitter dick bomb. You open the box, it sprays dick-shaped glitter all over everything. I'll be cleaning these sparkly penises up for weeks. They're everywhere."

"No! I didn't…I would never do that, sir!" Marisa's hand was at her throat. She was mortified.

"Oh really? Then why was your name and address in the spot reserved for the sendee? You can explain that to me on Monday morning, my office, first thing. And bring a box."

"A box?" she squeaked.

"Yes, Ms Ponte, for your things. Perhaps I'll be able to save some iridescent cocks for you." The line went dead.

Marisa stood there for a few minutes, too shocked to move. She felt like she was in one of those carnival games where a person shoots bean bag projectiles at a line of ducks. Except she was the duck and each projectile exploded when it hit her, spraying (now that she had the imagery in her head) glitter dicks all over. She chuckled, she couldn't help it. This was ridiculous.

Her phone began to tremble in her hand again and she slid her thumb across its face without looking.

"Mr. Peyton, please, you have to believe me." Marisa's hands were sweating as badly as when she pitched Fetch.

"Maris, it's Lindsey."

Marisa rubbed her forehead, she couldn't tell if she was feeling relief or more dread. "Lindsey! Thank God, I've had the weirdest

fucking…"

Lindsey didn't let her finish. "Listen Marisa, I think I'm going to take a pass on tonight."

Jeez, what is it about today?

"But Linds, why? I mean, you were so excited for this! Remember, making it official?"

"Yeah, I know what I said. I changed my mind though." Marisa could hear a bark in the background. For a moment she thought it was Fetch again, but then understood that it was Mowgli. Lindsey was at home.

"You've seen Mowgli."

"Hard to miss him."

"I have no idea what happened, Linds. I did not ask Matt to make the dog look like a psycho alpaca."

"Well that is what he looks like. Or a really fucked up Muppet. How about I change his name from Mowgli to Muppet? How would you like that, Mowgs?" Lindsey asked him. "Oh shit, he's doing that thing with the cushions again."

"When he sticks his head in?"

"That's the one. Listen, sorry about tonight. But it'll be easier without me."

"Easier? How?"

"You won't have to navigate your past with your present hanging off your arm."

There was a long silence.

"Listen Maris, I've got to go." Then she hung up.

"Shit," Marisa opined, once again staring at her phone. She walked across her apartment and sank into her couch. There she stayed for the next two hours as the light drained out of the day and the room darkened pixel by pixel.

Marisa's high school get-together (not really a reunion, the email insisted, just a casual meet-up of long-lost friends) was in a former warehouse in the Pearl district. Three years ago the Pearl was on the brink of being the place to be. Now it had enjoyed its three months in the collective consciousness and was about to be passé. Post-hip, pre-passé. Marisa could relate.

The Montage advertised its presence with a single shingle, hung outside its decidedly still-warehouse-looking facade. It didn't even show the whole name of the joint, only a single M. It was the kind of place that if you weren't brought there, you wouldn't find it. And according to the pit of unease that was where Marisa's stomach used to be, she sure wished she hadn't been able to find it.

She was still wearing her work uniform from this afternoon's pitch and had barely run a comb through her hair. She didn't even know why she was still going to this stupid thing, only that it was something to distract her. She forewent asking Fetch to get her an Uber and walked the twenty blocks from her apartment on twenty-third to the warehouse district, craving fresh air and a sense of solitude, of which she got neither. The night was muggy, threatening rain but not delivering and as to being alone, Fetch wouldn't leave her be. Every ten seconds she ruffed, the macabre face of her lock screen showing a veritable catacombs at this point. It was as if Marisa had a new bizarre soundtrack to her life, one made of automated barks of her own creating.

It was Fetch's fault of course or, if Marisa was being straight with herself, her own damn fault for creating Fetch. For some reason she was trying desperately to work out, to salvage something of her creative aspiration, her e-shadow (she-shadow, she thought grimly) had gone loco. Something in the information she had fed the app had caused it to…to what? Get her girlfriend's dog a horrible haircut? Jeopardize her job by sending her boss the most juvenile prank it could think of? Was her-shadow really this self-destructive? Did that mean she was?

She wasn't quite ready yet to scrap what she had come to think of as her ticket out of the digital bump and grind that was her

day to day. If she gave up on Fetch, she was just another wage slave in the silicone forest. An e-shadow without a Peter Pan. Her e-shadow had gone berserk and it was up to her to salvage what was left of her career, her relationship, the sanctity of her home life. If only she knew how without completely killing the thing she'd been working on for the past six months. No, she couldn't be quite that straight with herself yet. Maybe tomorrow. But not tonight, the wounds were still seeping blood.

She came upon the Montage without realizing she'd arrived. She would've walked right by if it hadn't been for someone grabbing her by the upper arm and shaking her.

"Marisa? Marisa Ponte? Is that you?"

Marisa broke from her reverie to study the face swimming in front of her: red jowled, balding, and sweaty. But familiar. Achingly familiar. Like the wallpaper in her grandmother's house, something she'd lived with for years but couldn't describe if pressed. Smoke wafted up her nostrils from the cigarette clamped between the man's yellowed fingers still gripping her jacket.

"It's Louis! Louis Deangelis? From band?" He stared into her face with an open mouthed grin, waiting for realization to break over her. "Remember?"

She tried to muster the correct response to this. It would be good practice for when she got inside. She widened her eyes and smiled, hoping this signaled recognition to the complete stranger locked onto her arm.

"Louis! Great to see you." She tore her arm away from him and let him pump her hand up and down.

"Man, it's good to see you too! I would've been hard pressed to remember you except for the awesome video you put on. Talk about cajones." Louis waggled his eyebrows up and down. Marisa looked at him with genuine wide-eyed wonder. "It's all anyone is talking about. You sure know how to make an entrance."

The unease curdling in her stomach turned to outright fear mixed with a soupçon of deja vu. Why did this all sound familiar to her? And why was she suddenly very glad that Lindsey had decided to opt out?

"Everyone is going to love seeing you! Wish you had these steel-plated balls in high school. Video like this would've made that place so much more interesting." He placed his hands on her upper back, propelling her through the double doors of the restaurant and into the cavernous space beyond.

Oh shit. Marisa thought, trying to dig in her heels to stop their forward motion but to no avail, Louis's sizable girth impelled her across the slippery black and white parquet floor. The warehouse had ceilings at least twenty feet high and was about fifty by eighty. The air above her head was hung with large abstract art canvasses suspended by wires. A bar ran the entire length of the far wall and a group of about thirty people were gathered at one end. They erupted as Louis pushed her across the room towards their knot of waiting faces.

He used one hand to point enthusiastically at his catch. "This is her! It's her." Then he pointed up into the air with one finger as he maneuvered them around a smattering of tables. Marisa glanced up, catching a glimpse of the bottom of a suspended screen and the moving image on its face. Her dread deepened and she could taste bile in her throat. Then she was being absorbed into the group of vaguely familiar faces. Her back was thumped, a kaleidoscope of flushed faces moved through her field of vision, a mason jar with brownish liquid and a slice of lemon was thrust into her hand. This was more like high school than ever. She could almost feel the straps of her backpack digging into her shoulders and could hear the period bell behind the din.

"I can't believe you would…"

"Is it art? Are you an artist?"

"Who is she? She's beautiful? All of her."

The questions peppered her from all quarters as her mind assembled names to go with the faces. Most of these were the A-ones, annoyingly untouched by time or strife. They looked much like they had in high school, polished and smug. This time was different though, this time she was a part of their circle. She shook her head to clear it and scanned the crowd for Carl. She found him in much the same position she'd seen him last, seated at the bar with a host of empties in front of him. He caught her eye, shook his head, and moved off his bar stool. As he passed by the mob that was surrounding her, she could hear him say, inscrutably "errrr-chickachick-errrrr." Then he was gone.

When she turned to follow his passage, she was treated to the full view of the screen suspended in the middle of the restaurant. There was a lot of flesh. Pink flesh. Legs, arms, a flash of face. And hair. Blond hair. Lindsey's blond hair, periodically mixed with very familiar dark tresses. Her own. Before her vision funneled to a dark point and her knees gave out, she heard one last thing. Ruff.

Bad dog, she thought as her mind swam away. Very bad dog.

Saturday morning began as Friday night had ended: with a flurry of knocks and insistent doorbell ringing. She raised her head tiredly from her place lying on the floor and put it back down. It didn't matter. It wouldn't be any one she knew, but it would be for her all right. Just as every knock and ring had been for the last fourteen hours. She moved her foot, kicking one of the many pizza boxes as she did so. It was heavy, full of cold pizza. Same with the Chinese take out boxes crowding the coffee table. And there were three edible arrangements gracing the front hallway. These delivery people were very persistent, they wouldn't take no for an answer.

In fact, they were downright dogged.

ROMANCE

By Darrell Schweitzer

Ah, the moon! The brilliant sky

at midnight as bright as day, the landscape

revealed in exquisite detail for miles and miles,

rolling hills, white farmhouses gleaming,

trees swaying in the gentle breeze,

a brook like a band of silver, and here,

up close, swans asleep on a pond like cotton puffs

on a perfect, dark mirror.

I remember the overwhelming scent of honeysuckle,

and how we two climbed, giggling like naughty children,

through a wooden fence, and stumbled, and knocked

it down; and we laughed at that too until we came

to a secret place, and stood in awed silence before

a blank-eyed, stone god covered with vines.

You were already dead by then,

and had been for some time,

and I had grown so fat and stiff

I'd blundered through that fence like an arthritic ox;

yet you whispered such things to me that I could only wish

that it were some delightful dream that would go on forever.

Only it wasn't.

Your hand was so cold it burned.

I still have the scar.

POSTCARDS FROM LOVECRAFT

By Cliff Biggers

As always, the first thing that Tyler Markham did upon arriving home was to sort through the mail. It was a force of habit from decades of correspondence, mail order shopping, and magazine reading; even though he squandered hours on the internet every day, he always preferred the physical mail. Its tangibility made it somehow more important—and nowadays, it was all too rare for most people to take the time to physically mail a letter or a card . . .

Or a catalog.

Tyler recognized the return address immediately. A new catalog from W.W. Cummins, obviously. He'd been shopping with Cummins as long as he'd been collecting horror, fantasy, and science fiction books; Cummins was his go-to source for out of print material, particularly books, magazines, and ephemera related to the *Weird Tales* authors.

He tore the envelope open and removed the half-sized catalog, printed double-sided via mimeograph, collated, and folded to form a small booklet, complete with goldenrod paper for a makeshift cover. Who still uses a mimeograph? Tyler wondered. How do you even find ink and stencils and parts to keep it running?

As far back as he could remember, though, Cummins' catalog had always been mimeographed and mailed to his select clientele. No website, no email lists, no eBay auctions, no Paypal—the man was a Luddite, obviously. He mailed out catalogs, and he expected his clients to mail him orders, with payment by postal money order. No personal checks, no cash—just postal money orders.

Unless, like Tyler, you'd been a customer for more than a third of a century.

Tyler was one of the select few who actually had W.W. Cummins' phone number; he had shopped with Cummins for twenty years before he finally grew weary of ordering desirable first editions, only to find that someone else in a next-day postal zone had received the catalog before him and scooped up the rarities.

So he had written Cummins, expressing his frustration and pointing out that he had spent many thousands of dollars with him and hated to miss the opportunity to spend even more. Two weeks later, he got a slim envelope with a very familiar return address; he opened it and found his letter enclosed, with a phone number written at the very bottom.

He put the rest of the mail aside, picked up the phone, and called the hand-written number.

Six rings. He was about to hang up. Then a click, as if someone was fumbling with the phone, followed by a very soft-spoken "Hello?"

"Mr. Cummins? This is Tyler Markham—I just got your note."

"Mr. Markham? Yes, yes—we've done business together for quite a while, haven't we?"

"Yes indeed!" Tyler said with a bit of a laugh. "And now that you've been so kind as to give me your phone number, I suspect we'll be doing much more!"

"That's excellent, Mr. Markham—just excellent. I have a very select group of collectors for whom I like to offer this special level of service . . . customers who have been very supportive of my little business . . . customers who always seem to want very unique collectibles. I understand . . . you know, before I became a bookseller, I was one of those collectors, too," he said almost wistfully.

"I don't know how you do it," Tyler joked. "I'd look at all those great books, the Arkham House and Gnome Press and Fantasy Press, the *Weird Tales* and *Unknown* and all the rest, and I don't think I could stand to sell a single one of them . . . but I'm glad you do!"

"Oh, I understand; for the first few years, I held the best books for myself! After a while, though, I realized that if I continued to do that, I'd have to rent another apartment for me to live in, because this one would be full to the ceiling with books. Quit cold turkey, that day. Every book is for sale, every fanzine, every magazine, every manuscript . . . everything. Keep it all or sell it all—I had to make a choice, so here I am!"

"You're a better man than I!" Tyler replied with exaggerated drama.

"Well, I appreciate your business a great deal, so I wanted you to have my phone number. Anything you see that you want, you can call me and I'll hold it until your money order arrives. Oh, and one more thing—for special customers like you, I will from time to time include extra sheets with the catalog listing rarities of particular interest. Every now and then, I get particularly unique collectibles. Would you like for me to include you on that list?"

"You bet!" Tyler said—and the enthusiasm wasn't at all feigned. Tyler felt like he had been invited into an elite club that he hadn't even known about until now. Certainly, he looked forward to seeing the rarities—but it was the elite nature of the invitation that had him so

excited. It was as if he had joined some upper echelon of collectors.

Over the next several months, Tyler received catalogs on an every six week schedule—but he hardly ever looked at the catalogs. Instead, he went directly to the blue mimeographed sheet in the middle—the "special rarities" page. (*And wasn't it nice of Cummins to be so predictable?* he thought. *Cover on goldenrod, interiors on white, special rarities on blue—it never failed.*)

The first rarities sheet included, among other delights, an Arkham edition of Ray Bradbury's *Dark Carnival*, signed by the author, in near-mint condition with a nearly pristine Brodart-protected dust jacket. "Spine still tight," the description said. "does not appear to have been read." He picked up the phone immediately.

"Mr. Cummins, this is Tyler Markham. I was calling about—"

"Let me guess: the Bradbury *Dark Carnival?*"

"Exactly? How did you know?"

"Mr. Markham, you've ordered a lot of books from me, and I get to know the preferences of my better customers. As soon as I put that list together, I thought to myself, 'This one's for Mister Markham.' And here you are!"

"I'll get a money order out to you today!" Tyler said.

"That's fine—I'll package the book and have it ready to ship the day I receive your payment."

This is the beginning of a wonderful relationship, Tyler thought to himself as he hung up the phone.

As time passed, Tyler began to realize that he was, without thinking, cutting back on his frivolous expenditures in the two weeks prior to the approximate date of the next Cummins catalog. Once he became aware of the shift in his buying habits, he thought about it again and concluded that it was only rational; no other dealer with whom he did business could find such a high caliber of collectibles.

A Gnome Press *Return of Conan* by Robert E. Howard, signed and remarqued by illustrator Wally Wood. A pristine copy of *The Empty House and Other Ghost Stories* by Algernon Blackwood. A Sherlock Holmes collection inscribed by Sir Arthur Conan Doyle.

"I may not be able to afford food," Tyler said to Mr. Cummins after ordering the Kelmscott Chaucer book—the most expensive item in his collection, "but I'm going to have the world's best library!"

"That you are, Mr. Markham, that you are . . ." Cummins said with a chuckle. "And if our budget is up to it, I have something that I think you're going to find particularly interesting."

"What's that?" Tyler asked, his curiosity piqued. "The deed for 194 Angell Street? Robert E. Howard's pistol?"

"Oh, Mr. Markham, that would be quite the find!" Cummins laughed. "No, nothing like that. But it is something quite unique. Are you familiar with H. Riley Scarbrough? A member of the *Weird Tales* circle—not as important as Howard or Lovecraft or Smith, of course, but still—"

"I remember. He was a later addition . . . wrote 'The Outré Order' and a few other short pieces. Then he totally dropped out of sight—I remember reading that his editors couldn't even find out where to mail his checks. Strange guy. I've read his stuff, but I'm afraid I wasn't that impressed," Tyler said, a little disappointed. He had expected something more than a book by a second-tier writer (at best) who happened to know the A-team.

"It's not his *books* that I'm talking about, Mr. Markham—it's his *collection*. Mr. Markham and I had some mutual acquaintances, so

when he died, they contacted me regarding his estate. I've been offered a rare opportunity to acquire Mr. Scarbrough's entire collection—a very distinctive collection indeed. I've never seen another one like it. And it's not just books—he also has manuscripts, galley proofs, lithographs, prints, photographs . . . and epistolary ephemera."

"Letters?"

"Yes, Mr. Markham—letters. Mr. Scarbrough was part of the correspondence circle that involved all the major *Weird Tales* figures. He has original letters from several of them, including a number of handwritten Lovecraft items."

"You've got to be kidding! I've never seen any of that stuff reprinted, and I've read all the HPL collections—*Selected Letters*, Conover's *Lovecraft at Last* . . ."

"No, you're right—none of it has been released to the general public. Mr. Scarbrough was rather protective of his privacy and would not allow Mr. Derleth or anyone else to use any of his correspondence. He went one step further and threatened legal action if they even reprinted any of his letters to Lovecraft. As a result, none of their correspondence has been collected in any of those volumes."

Tyler was stunned. A chance to acquire an HP Lovecraft handwritten letter or postcard was almost unheard of—but the opportunity to own unpublished Lovecraft correspondence was something he never even considered.

"This is incredible . . . Of course I'm interested! What do I need to do? Can you get me a list? Do you need a deposit? Just tell me—"

"We'll work out the details, Mr. Markham. Now that I know you're interested, I'll send you a list. And since you've been such a good client, I'll offer you the right of first refusal."

"So no one else—"

"—will get a copy of the collection catalog until you've made your selections," Cummins said, completing Mr. Markham's statement. "I'll send you the first part of the catalog this week. It's going to take me a while to sort through the entire collection—it's quite voluminous, and my apartment is so small that it will take me awhile just to get the boxes in some sort of order so that I can determine what all Mr. Scarbrough has here."

Tyler Markham felt like someone had combined his birthday, Christmas, Easter, Thanksgiving, and Halloween into the best holiday ever.

The first list came in almost two weeks later. It was too early for a standard catalog, so Cummins had just printed up the pages on a pastel green paper—an old-looking, rather porous paper with small fibers throughout its surface, making it seem even older. Since the list was prepared especially for him, Tyler thought it odd that Cummins had gone to the trouble of printing up the listing. Perhaps he wants to have it ready to go out to his other clients once Tyler had made his selections.

The very first item was one of those dream finds that Tyler had hoped for but was afraid to actually imagine: a near-mint copy of the 1939 *The Outsider & Others* by Lovecraft, signed by both the illustrator and the editors. Tyler realized that he was picking up the phone even as he read the paragraph.

"Mr. Cummins?" He said as soon as Cummins picked up. "This is Tyler. I just got your list and . . ."

"Ah, yes, Mr. Markham! I prepared that list in the order that I anticipated you would rank the books—was I correct?"

"Yes sir!" he said. "*The Outsider*, signed by Finlay, Derleth, and Wandrei! I didn't even know that a copy like that existed!"

"As I told you, this was a very special collection."

"I will get payment out to you today, Mr. Cummins. Thank you so much! But I do have a question. I see some wonderful books here, but there's no mention of Lovecraft corre-

spondence. I was really hoping that . . .'"

"Oh, it's coming, Mr. Markham. There's so much of it that it's taking a while to sort through it."

Markham was speechless. An unpublished Lovecraft letter or postcard was an unheard-of find . . . but a collection so large that simply cataloging it was this time-consuming? . . .

"Mr. Markham, are you still there?" Tyler realized that the silence on his end was so prolonged that Cummins thought they might have been disconnected.

"I'm here, Mr. Cummins! I'm just amazed by the news. I may have to sell my house and my car to afford some of this, but I'm not going to let this get away from me."

"Excellent, Mr. Markham. I'll tell you what—why don't I include a sample with your Arkham House volume?"

"A sample? You mean . . ."

"A postcard, perhaps, just to help you gauge the quality of this collection."

Had his local bank branch offered him free samples of money in various denominations, Tyler would not have been any more surprised. "Mr. Cummins, that would be incredibly generous. I don't know what to say!"

"Say nothing more, Mr. Markham. I will prepare the package today, and will mail it out to you as soon as the payment is received.

Tyler found it impossible to focus on work for the next few days. Part of him wanted to tell everyone about his impending acquisition, but he realized that it would be meaningless to the people in his office. Even those who had heard of Lovecraft would have no idea why he would be so excited about an old postcard written by the man who wrote horror stories.

The package finally arrived on Thursday, one day short of two weeks from the time that Tyler had mailed his check. Tyler recognized the meticulous packaging, the careful handwriting, the array of miscellaneous stamps covering the front of the brown paper. He tore into the package.

The book was every bit as perfect a copy as Cummins had said—perhaps even better. Tyler had seen straight-from-the-printer new copies that lacked this book's sharp, undamaged edges, its perfectly aligned dust jacket. He opened the book carefully, and heard a creak to the binding that told him the book had been opened very rarely, and very carefully. The signatures were there, just as Cummins had said.

Tyler expected to get a whiff of the mustiness that sometimes accompanied older books, but there was no such smell. For the briefest moment, he detected a smell that seemed to hint of the sea, although Tyler couldn't explain exactly what that would smell like. His mind knew, however. *Perhaps Scarbrough lived near the ocean*, Tyler thought . . . but any further speculation left his mind as he realized that what he had thought to be a bookmark was actually a postcard.

A postcard covered in tiny, meticulous handwriting.

Even before he read the card, he knew the penmanship to be Lovecraft's; the elegant wording and the many references contained in the card's message only confirmed it.

H.P. Lovecraft actually touched this card, he thought. *He wrote these words!*

Tyler wondered if, when he first found this card in his mail many decades before, Riley Scarbrough had experienced even an iota of the exuberance that Tyler was feeling right now.

The book, once a holy grail of his horror want list, sat on the table all but forgotten. Cummins had opened his eyes to a whole new vista of collecting—one so intellectually intoxicating that any book seemed positively insignificant by comparison.

Weeks passed, and each week brought more updated lists. Issues of *Weird Tales* with marginalia notes and typescript pages from Howard, Lovecraft, and Smith, all with handwritten notes and corrections; signed Clark Ashton Smith volumes complete with sketches on the title page; a complete set of Unknown magazines featuring Leiber's *Fafhrd & Gray Mouser* stories, each signed by Leiber, even a Visionary Press edition of *The Shadow Over Innsmouth*. The prices should have made many of these collectibles beyond the means of Tyler Markham, but for some reason Cummins' prices were well below the money he could have gotten in an auction or an open sale. And tucked neatly into each book was a lagniappe—a postcard from Lovecraft to Scarbrough. It made no sense for Cummins to give these away—these "bonus items" were worth far more than any of the books or magazines—but Markham wasn't going to jinx the deal by questioning it.

If Tyler had been amazed at the rarities he had thus far been offered, he was positively stunned by the latest mailing from Cummins. It contained only two books: *The Story of the Glittering Plain* and *The Wood Beyond the World*, both from William Morris's Kelmscott Press. Vellum binding. Cloth cases. Green and blue respectively. Not only seminal fantasy works, but some of the finest examples of the bookmaker's art.

And with editions of 200 and 350 respectively, incredibly rare.

But here they were, in a matched pair, for a price that was only a fraction of their value. He called before he had even completed the descriptive copy.

"Mr. Cummins—"

"Yes, Mr. Markham?" He obviously recognized Tyler's voice now—in fact, Tyler felt almost as if he knew exactly when the mail would be delivered, that Cummins took his station by the phone to receive the inevitable phone call.

"I want them both. I'll get the money order out to you first thing tomorrow—"

"I felt relatively certain that you'd be interested, Mr. Markham, so I've already boxed them for mailing. I'll post them tomorrow; you've been such a good customer that I have no doubts as to your honesty."

Tyler was flattered and confused; just a few months before, Cummins had been an enigma, almost an early 20th Century book dealer in a 21st century world. But in the course of the past few months, he had moved from regular customer to preferred client to trusted regular whose word was sufficient for books to be shipped out. Apparently he didn't know Cummins as well as he thought!

"Oh, and one more thing, Mr. Markham—"

"Yes?"

"For a purchase of this significance, I'd like to include something special as an added value. I think you'll be quite pleased with it."

Tyler started to ask for more information, but the phone clicked as Cummins hung up.

This was one of those times when Tyler wished that Mr. Cummins would give up his antiquated ways and use express mail or FedEx overnight. As far as Cummins was concerned, however, there was only one method of delivery that was acceptable: first class mail. With the shipment not going out until Friday, that meant a wait of three days, minimum.

When the package didn't arrive on Monday, Tyler alternated between frantic and furious. What if the package was damaged? What if it was lost in the postal system? What if it was stolen?

Tyler had flashbacks to his teenage years as a collector, when the mailbox was his first stop as soon as he got home from school, and it seemed that his whole life revolved around the postal schedule.

As soon as he finished his work on Tuesday, he rushed home. As he was pulling in the driveway, he could see the carefully wrapped brown paper that was becoming more familiar to him with each passing week. He parked the car sloppily and rushed to the door, grabbed the package, and fumbled with his keys. At last, he unlocked the door and rushed straight to the kitchen counter with the package, leaving his keys dangling from the lock.

The packing tape was so meticulously applied to every edge and corner that Tyler couldn't get the paper to tear. He opened the drawer, pulled out a pair of scissors, and started to use one of the blades as a knife to pierce and then slice the paper. *Wait a minute*, he thought. *The last thing I want to do is slice the book when I'm trying to open the package.* Tyler forced himself to stop for a moment, then he began to cut through the tape more carefully, focusing on the packaging rather than its contents.

Finally the end was loose. He pulled the protective box from the packaging, opened the flap, and gazed upon two of the finest examples of the art of book making that he had ever seen. The condition was superlative; other than some slight yellowing the books were near mint.

But it was the volume that was packed between the two Morris books that captivated him. He recognized the familiar design that mirrored the look of the five Arkham volumes he already had. But it was the title on the spine that startled him.

Selected Letters Volume 6 – HP Lovecraft.

But there *was* no *Selected Letters Volume 6.*

He opened the book and flipped to random pages. The style, the cadence, the vocabulary, the structure, the friendly in-jokes . . . all of them read exactly as if they had come from hitherto-unseen postcards and letters drafted by HPL through the years. There were even letters to familiar correspondents—Robert Bloch, Alfred Galpin, R.H. Barlowe . . . all known HPL acquaintances whose correspondence was known and documented.

Then he found the first letter to Riley Scarbrough. It was a lengthy letter, discussing metaphysics, a bit of astronomy, and the mundane problems of maintaining the condition of a personal library in an oceanside home. In every regard, it seemed genuine and legitimate.

I get it, Tyler thought. *Cummins said that Scarbrough had corresponded with various members of the* Weird Tales *circle over the year. He must have put this book together himself, having it bound to look just like another Lovecraft* Selected Letters *volume.*

With that in mind, he began to read further. The Scarbrough-correspondence began in late 1935, and continued from there, interspersed with postcards and letters from HPL. The more he read, the more he admired Scarbrough's attention to detail. If he didn't know better, he would swear that this was actually a long-missing volume in the Arkham House *Selected Letters* series.

The letters from late 1936 and early 1937 were particularly intriguing—a fascinating back and forth between Lovecraft and Scarbrough about the eternal nature of the soul and the psyche, and about the nature of death.

Before he knew it, he had skimmed ahead to the final pages of the book. The last letter in the book, a brief note from Lovecraft, was dated March 16th, 1937.

The date startled Tyler.

Lovecraft died on March 15th.

That's a little bit sick, Tyler thought. *He's forging letters from a dead man.*

But he had to admit, the letter was absolutely perfect in every regard. It was a lengthy missive, discussing horror, weird fiction, philosophy, and other topics with which Lovecraft was exceedingly familiar. It was at times jocular, at times serious, and always fascinating. Finally, he reached the end of the letter; its last line caught his eye. "I hope the extreme length of my letter isn't an imposition on your time, but I find myself strangely energized. All the impediments to my writing suddenly seem to have dissipated; I am writing constantly, almost as if I can't get the words on paper with sufficient speed. I have so much to share with you . . ."

And there, the book ended.

Could the date be wrong? Tyler thought to himself. *A typographical error, perhaps? Or is the final letter a fake, a forgery? Perhaps this whole book is a fraud? . . .*

Tyler put the book on the shelf, both intrigued and disturbed. The posthumous date of the final letter clearly indicated that it was a forgery. But if it was a fraud, then he had to wonder about the authenticity of some of the rarities from the Scarbrough collection that Tyler had purchased from Cummins . . .

Disillusioned, he decided to take a break for dinner and investigate this more fully later in the evening.

Normally, he'd celebrate an acquisition like this with a special meal—a sort of celebratory feast. The lingering questions about the book's authenticity had taken the edge off Tyler's enthusiasm, however, so he just grabbed a couple of slices of pizza from a nearby restaurant instead. Good, plain food. Pizza doesn't pretend to be something that it isn't. Crust, sauce, cheese, pepperoni, sausage, a few spices . . . no pretensions.

When he got back home, he undertook the routine household chores that usually went undone on the day that a rare tome arrived. After sorting through the remainder of the mail, washing the coffee pot so that it would be ready for the next morning, and doing some superficial house cleaning, he took a shower.

I'm avoiding this whole book thing, he realized. Obviously the nagging questions about the book were bothering him more than he had initially realized.

Out of a sense of duty, he picked the book up once again. *I guess I'm going to have to contact Cummins and find out what's going on.* This is going to be a very unpleasant conversation. As he began planning what he might say, he idly

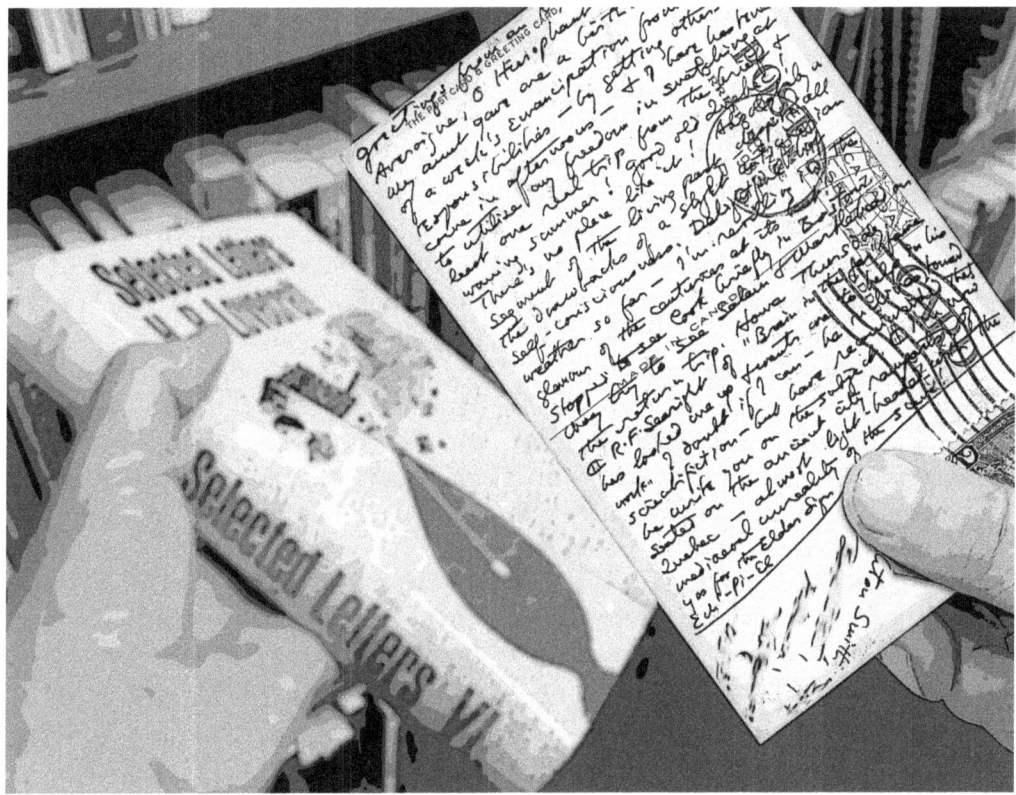

flipped to the back of the book again.

All plans were suddenly put on hold, however, as Tyler looked at the final letter in the book.

It was dated March 27th, 1937.

Had he misread the letter's date earlier? He flipped back a few pages . . . and found the end of the letter that he had read earlier that day. The letter that had brought the book to a close.

But now there was another letter, dated more than a week later, that hadn't been there before!

"My health issues seem mostly to have passed," the letter mentioned. "I find myself returning to my writing with a rediscovered vigor, and am quite determined to catch up on my neglected correspondence. I hope the delays haven't caused you too much concern, my dear R'lyeh!"

But that letter hadn't been there earlier . . .

With that, he closed the book. Tyler had

already seen far more in its pages than he had ever anticipated. He laid it on the table for a moment, looking at its cover. He turned to walk away, then reconsidered; once again, he looked at the book. Slowly, he reached to pick it up. His motions were slightly hesitant, almost as if he expected it to do something once he touched it. Nothing happened, however, so Tyler picked up the book, looked at its cover once again, and walked over to his bookshelf.

He placed it on his bookshelf next to the other *Selected Letters* volumes; it looked like it belonged there—same trim size, same dust jacket design, even the same degree of age-related shading here and there. In spite of everything, he felt a small bit of satisfaction to see the books together on the shelf . . . Then he walked to the door without looking back, turned off the light, and went to bed.

That night, Tyler's troubled mind struggled to find logic in the day's events. His thoughts kept returning to the book, to the impossibility of it. He was convinced he'd never go to sleep, but eventually he dozed.

And he dreamed. Disturbed dreams filled not only dark, fetid places and cool, clean libraries. Sallow-complexioned strangers with sepulchral faces and rheumy eyes, and familiar figures from the past with welcoming smiles and knowing looks. Books everywhere—some new, some older, and some positively ancient, bound in blood-red leather and greenish-black buckram. And every time he would look away and look back, there were more shelves filled with more books—an infinitely long library that was populated by every book that existed . . . and many that didn't. And always in the alcoves, in the nooks and corners, shadowy figures of those who had read these books alongside those who wrote the books . . . and interspersed, those unfamiliar figures that he somehow knew were the ones who made the books happen. And just as he seemed to know them, they seemed to know him.

Tyler awoke with a spasmic jerk. *I can't stay awake, but I can't sleep*, he thought. It felt like he had only gone to bed an hour or two before, but a glance at the clock showed that he had been in bed for nine hours.

Normally, his thoughts would turn to breakfast—Tyler always woke up hungry—but this time, food was totally forgotten. No matter how he tried to turn his attention to anything else, his mind went back to the book; it was unpleasantly irresistible, like a broken tooth that simply can't be left alone.

Selected Letters Volume 6 was still there. It looked like it was taking up a bit more shelf space than it had occupied the night before. As he picked it up, he noted that the paper felt thinner, less substantial . . . but there were so

many more pages now. The letters from Lovecraft went on for hundreds of pages.

Curiosity and apprehension conflicted, but it was curiosity that won out. Tyler picked up the book, opened it to the end . . . and there were indeed new letters, letters that had not been present the day before. Scores of letters and postcards from Lovecraft to Scarbrough, correspondence purportedly composed over a period of decades.

The book fell open to certain places so naturally that it was as if the book wanted him to read those pages. *Scarbrough must have left the book open at these spots for a while*, Tyler thought . . . that had to be the explanation.

My good friend R'lyeh, I was surprised you hadn't told us of your move. Relocating from Massachusetts to Virginia—I would never consider such a relocation. I hope this letter is the first to wish you well in your new home . . .

He let the book open to another page . . . and he saw a similar note.

Arizona now—you are quite the pioneer! I no longer have the spirit for travelling . . . the more time I spend here, the more I feel rooted to this place. I fear that if we are to meet at some point, I will have to convince you to make the pilgrimage.

He flipped the pages again. Another mention of a move. And another. But the moves apparently hadn't interrupted an endless stream of letters and postcards.

Without consciously thinking about it, Tyler first sat down, then stretched out on the sofa as he read through page after page of correspondence, forgetting for the moment the impossibility of it all. He was drawn into the text, unable to put the book down. It seemed like he had read for hours . . . but it wouldn't take that long to read a book of this size, would it?

It wasn't uncommon for Tyler to nod off on the sofa while reading. But this time, his nap was far from restful.

Once again, he was in that eerie library . . . but at the end of the long row of shelves was a door, slightly ajar. Beyond the door, a cluttered room lit by a kerosene lamp and the dull glow of fireplace embers. On the rustic wooden desk, an old Underwood. In the boxes that lined two walls, there were stacks of books. Not so much a home as a last refuge. And standing next to the wooden desk was an old man, slightly hunched, paunchy, and unkempt. His weary expression hinted at both fear and panic, but it was obvious that these emotions had long ago made themselves at home in this husk of a man. And in his hands, a postcard. The handwriting was scrupulously small, meticulous in its penmanship—Tyler knew that, even though he couldn't really see it. He also knew whose handwriting it was. The man looked at the card for longer than it would take to read it. Finally, he mumbled two words, then let the card flutter to the floor.

"Not again."

Tyler woke from his restless nap. He felt even more tired than before; neither the attempt at a night's sleep nor the subsequent dozing had been at all restorative. Looking at the book now lying face-down on his chest, he saw that he had nodded off just a page or two prior to the end of the book. His compulsive nature demanded that he finish the volume, so he resumed reading.

The final card in the book was a brief one. *I can't tell you how much Two-Gun Bob and Klarkash-ton and I are looking forward to meeting you at last*, the card concluded. *There is so much we have to discuss . . .*

And with that, the book ended.

He closed the book, preparing to put it back on the shelf. Then he noticed for the first time a yellowed newspaper clipping barely visible below the lower edge of the dust jacket.

He gently pulled it out, and saw that it was a newspaper article about the mysterious death of one Riley Scarbrough.

The article, from a local newspaper in Wagner, South Dakota, reported that Scarbrough had been found dead in his home. He lived in a remote house, totally isolated, with no electricity, no phone, no internet . . . absolutely off the grid. No one could explain though how he had drowned, since his house wasn't near any lakes, ponds, creaks, or streams nearby. And he wasn't found outdoors; he was found in his bed. Even stranger, the autopsy had determined that he had drowned in salt water . . . ocean water.

The phone rang seven times. Tyler was just about to hang up when he heard the distinct click of someone picking up on the other end.

"Mr. Cummins?"

"Yes, Mr. Markham? I had thought I might be hearing back from you. The package arrived in good shape, I presume?"

"What? Oh, yes–yes, it was perfect. But I need to know—"

"There's no charge, Mr. Markham. This is a gift—the minute I saw it, I knew that you would be able to appreciate the unique nature of this . . . rarity."

"That wasn't what I was going to ask, Mr. Cummins. I need to know . . . what is it? It doesn't make sense."

"Things don't always make sense, Mr. Markham . . ."

"This is some sort of a hoax, right? Dead men don't write letters."

"Dead men don't write letters?" Cummins scoffed, then half-laughed. "I assure you, the provenance of the volume is indisputable. I have it on the best authority that this unique volume is from the collection of Mr. Scarbrough—it was one of the few books he simply couldn't get rid of through his many relocations."

Tyler's curiosity and apprehension was gradually being displaced by annoyance and anger. "Quit playing games—you know what I'm talking about. The book . . . it's different now."

"Yes. I know. I understand your concern, but don't worry . . . everything will be clear soon."

"What do you mean?"

"Just check your mail, Mr. Markham. Just check—" And with that, the line went dead; had Cummins hung up, or had the call been dropped? Tyler immediately pressed redial, but Cummins didn't answer.

As he pressed the button to end the call, Tyler noticed the small stack of mail on the counter.

I don't remember getting the mail, Tyler thought. *I didn't get the mail. I haven't been outside of the house at all.*

He picked up the stack and began to go through it. Catalogs, credit card offers, a coupon mailer . . . it appeared to be the usual stack of junk mail that went unread into the recycling bin.

Then he saw it, near the bottom of the stack.

A postcard, covered front to back in tiny, meticulous handwriting. It was a script that he recognized immediately.

And it was addressed to him.

The phone rang twice, then ended abruptly. A recorded message began to play. "The number you have dialed is not in service. Please check the number and try again." He dialed again, certain he must have mis-entered the number. Once again, same message.

But I just talked to Cummins, Tyler thought. *Why would his phone not be in service?*

He tried three more times, while in the back of his mind he kept remembering that old saying, "Insanity is doing the same thing over and over again, expecting different re-

sults."

He finally gave up—not on contacting Cummins, but on calling that number. Cummins might not use the internet, but Tyler certainly did! He did an address search, and within a minute he had a number for another occupant of the same apartment building—a Lizbeth Webber who, he suspected, would be Cummins' neighbor across the hall if it was a typical apartment building. Another few seconds and he had a phone number for Ms. Webber. He dialed; it rang three times before someone picked up.

"Hello?"

"Hello-is this Ms. Webber?"

"Yes, it is—who's calling?" Ms. Webber sounded about ten years past middle age, and she seemed a little suspicious to be receiving a phone call from someone whose name she didn't recognize . . . assuming she had caller ID at all, of course.

"Ms. Webber, my name is Tyler Markham," he said. "I'm sorry to bother you, but I'm trying to reach a friend of mine, and there seems to be some problem with his phone. I think he lives near you."

"Well, I don't . . . who are you trying to reach?" she said hesitatingly, unsure whether to dismiss the stranger or not before her curiosity surpassed his suspicion.

"I'm trying to get hold of Mr. Cummins," he said. "I've been a customer of his for a long time, and I usually called him with special orders. When I tried to call today—"

"I know—it's sad, isn't it?" She said. "He was here when I moved in, and he was always such a nice neighbor." Tyler noted that she said *was.*

"What do you mean, Ms. Webber? Has something happened?"

"It was in the papers, Mister—I'm sorry, but I forgot your name."

"Markham—Tyler Markham."

"Mister Markham. It was in all the papers. Mister Cummins is dead. The paper said it was a combination of pneumonia and congestive heart failure . . . the paramedic said it looked like he drowned in his own juices," she said in a conspiratorial tone, as if it were somehow irreverent to speak at all about causes of death. "Must have been sudden. The paramedic said there was a postcard in his hand—like he was reading his mail when it hit him. Who even sends postcards nowadays?"

There was more conversation after that, but Tyler was only half-listening. At the same time, he was busily typing on his keyboard, doing a search for Cummins and death and pneumonia and Pickman, Georgia. There it was—a link to the Pickman Tribune.

"Wallace Whately Cummins," the obituary said, "passed away from complications related to congestive heart failure on February 11th . . ."

He quit reading immediately. February 11th was nine weeks ago. He had spoken to Mr. Cummins less than an hour ago!

"Are you there, Mister Markham?"

"Yes—yes, I am, Ms. Webber," he said. "I was just googling his obituary while we were talking. There must be something wrong, though—the newspaper said he died on February 11th."

"That's right, Mister Markham."

"But that can't be—I just spoke to him . . ."

"Oh, I'm sure of it," Ms. Webber asserted. "It was just before Valentine's Day. It was so sad. Do you know that he always gave me an old-fashioned Valentine Card with candy every year? He died just before Valentine's Day, I'm sure of it. After they took him out, I even looked in his apartment to see if he'd already bought any candy. I knew he would have wanted me to have it. But there wasn't anything there."

"What about the books, Ms. Webber?"

"The books? I don't know anything about accounting, Mister Markham . . ."

"Not accounting books, just the books. I bought a lot of books from him, and he had been a bookseller for forty years. What hap-pened to all of the books?"

"There were no books, Mister Markham. No books at all. The apartment was almost empty. A table, two chairs, a sofa, a radio, a bed and a nightstand and a dresser, some junky old printing machine, and an old aquarium that didn't work—it was positively filthy! I took the radio and one of the chairs when they threw it all out, but the rest of it was so old that nobody wanted it, so the garbage man took it away."

Any further questions that Tyler might have asked suddenly faded from his mind. For while he had been talking to Mrs. Webber, he had once again picked up the copy of *Selected Letters 6*, turning idly to the final page.

And on that final page was the text of a postcard. A postcard to Tyler Markham. The same postcard that was sitting on his counter, covered in a handwriting that he knew quite well.

He hadn't read the card in its entirety before trying to contact Mr. Cummins, but now his eyes were drawn to the final paragraph of the *Selected Letters* text.

"We are all anticipating your arrival, Tyel'rr. New members of our rather esoteric order are exceedingly rare—in fact, we have not welcomed a new guest since R'lyeh joined us. He wanted us to warn you that your journey here will be laborious and quite possibly discomfiting—but once you're here, there is so much that we must convey to you!"

He looked up from the counter, towards his living room, with its bookshelves filled with his rare and exotic volumes. But the room now looked dark and distant, filled with shelf after shelf of tomes, some positively ancient, bound in blood-red leather and greenish black buckram. And in the gloom at the far end of that library were shadowy figures, including a long-faced man whose visage Tyler recognized . . . but behind him, there were writhing things, things that he knew from his reading. And just as he seemed to know them, they seemed to know him . . .

THE BONE YARD

Reviews by Divers Hands

Earth, Air, Fire & Water
Brian Lumley (writer), James Pitts (illustrator)
Fedogan & Bremer 2017

H. P. Lovecraft gave short shrift to Paracelsus. The assignation of various entities in the Cthulhu Mythos to the classical elements was the invention of August Derleth, who introduced the concept in "The Thing That Walked on the Wind" (*Strange Tales* Jan 1933), as well his own contribution, the "air elemental" Ithaqua. The "elemental" classification

system was perpetuated by Francis T. Laney in his article "The Cthulhu Mythology" (*The Acolyte* Winter 1942), and by those authors that chose to follow Derleth's lead—and by the nature of Derleth's handling of the publication of Lovecraft's fiction, his posthumous collaborations, and his being almost the sole arbiter of published Mythos fiction until his death in 1971—the "elemental" theory remained largely unquestioned until 1972, when Richard L. Tierney pointed out in "The Derleth Mythos" (*Crypt of Cthulhu* #24) that this "elemental" business had been the creation of Derleth, not Lovecraft.

Which does not make the elemental approach any more or less valid when it comes to writing Mythos stories; whatever Lovecraft or Derleth conceived, it is the talents, skill, and imagination of the other writers that is applied to their creations to make something new, to put their own spin on the old ideas. Brian Lumley is one of the great British writers "discovered" by Derleth, and who has contributed profoundly, throughout his long career, to expanding on and elaborating the Mythos in his own way. Yet the nature of the title for this collection demands at least this much historical background. Readers dismissive of the elemental theory may be assured that this is not a collection that directly seeks to resurrect or reaffirm Derleth's elemental theories, but neither do they ignore Derleth's contributions.

The collection itself consists of two novelettes, a short novel, and a short story. The novelettes are older pieces, republished here to fit the theme, and essentially the price of admission; the short story is fairly recent but obscure, and the novel entirely new. The collection is without an introduction per se, but Lumley offers brief thoughts to preface each piece.

"Lord of the Worms" (1983) is an episode in the life of Titus Crow, one written after Lumley's initial spate of stories starring his Lovecraftian adventurer, much as Michael Moorcock has done with his later Elric stories and novels. It's a bit of an odd choice for the 'Earth' entry, given Lumley's creation of the Cthonians in "The Cement Surroundings," but again, the collection was not being too literally-minded. There is a good deal to like about this story, as it depicts Crow in what is essentially occult investigator mode the central crux of the novelette, which involves numerology, is perhaps less exciting.

"Born of the Winds" (1975) is a sequel to Derleth's "The Thing That Walked on the Winds," and because it involves Ithaqua ties somewhat into Lumley's novel *Spawn of the Winds* (1978), although a reader need not have read either of those to appreciate the novelette. The story is written in the relatively classic mode of the Mythos pastiche—not one where Lumley tries to ape the diction or style of Lovecraft, but a Mythos tale written in a kind of metanarrative, with many direct references to old familiar stories. Readers need not have a library of Mythos volumes to appreciate the tale on its own, but the way Lumley presents the connections is unsubtle. Then again, neither was "The Thing That Walked on the Winds," which was written in essentially the same style, so perhaps it fits.

"The Gathering" is the original Mythos novel of this collection, and represents the element of fire—although not the blazing heat of fire vampires or Derleth's elemental Cthugha. Rather, it is a sort of sequel and recapitulation of Lovecraft's "The Shadow over Innsmouth" and the cold fire of "The Colour out of Space," with Lumley adding "The Hamlet" to the register of Lovecraft Country,

and delving into the mysteries of Deep One hybrids that take a little too much after their human side. Novels are a tricky format for the Cthulhu Mythos; most writers have difficulty sustaining a mood over so many pages, and while the story is original and interesting enough, it is hard to say that Lumley couldn't have improved this novel with judicious cutting. Partially this is because Lumley chooses to expand upon parts of "The Shadow over Innsmouth" that Lovecraft either covered only briefly, or neglected to cover, and Lumley in turn develops that with regard to his own characters and mythology—and not without real skill, for Lumley knows his craft. The novel is worth the price of admission.

"The Changeling" (2013) is not a weak story, but after the preceding novel and novellas it feels the least substantial. Representing the 'Water' element, the story recapitulates some of the mythology that Lumley had built up in "The Gathering," which makes me wish that the two had been placed as polar opposites in the book rather than right next to each other (although I suppose that would make it *Water, Earth, Air & Fire*, which doesn't have quite the same ring to it). The effectiveness of the story lies in boiling down the essential final revelation of "The Shadow over Innsmouth" into what is essentially a single very compact, brief, personal dialogue—again, the master at work.

Earth, Air, Fire & Water is not the best Mythos collection; I wouldn't even say it is Lumley's best Mythos collection (which is *Haggopian & Other Stories*), but it is a solid collection, at least for "The Gathering" and "The Changeling." James Pitts' illustrations are very handsome and fitting to the material, being reminiscent of Stephen Fabian's Mythos work.

Bobby Derie

Time Burial
Howard Wandrei
Fedogan & Bremer, 2017

Modest as the fame of his older brother Donald is—better recognized for co-creating Arkham House with August Derleth than for his own fiction—Howard Wandrei is even less well-known. The new *Time Burial* from Fedogan & Bremer, featuring Howard Wandrei's collected fantasy stories, should help remedy that situation. (As should accompanying books devoted to Donald Wandrei by the same publisher.)

In this handsomely produced trade paperback, an engrossing and well-researched biographic introduction by Dwayne H. Olson makes clear why Howard Wandrei's reputation did not match his substantial talent. Most stories appeared in pulp magazines, written under pseudonyms, in varying genres, with little interest by the author in pursuing book collections of his work. Those eroticized "Spicy" pulps were a favorite outlet for his stories. Even if tame by modern standards, they were considered even more lowly in that era than other pulps. That his personal life was frequently in turmoil and a substantial batch of published and unpublished manuscripts ended up burned among other papers by an unscrupulous editor seeking to cover evidence of his chicanery didn't help.

Yet, what a fascinating man Howard Wandrei was! A youthful burglary-for-thrills spree ended with serving time in a reformatory. He'd "met Lovecraft a number of times and corresponded with him for a number of years"; was a gifted and award-winning artist; had collaboratively written Superman scripts for radio; his tales of weirdness and mystery had appeared in pulps ranging from those risqué *Spicy* magazines to the revered *Black Mask*, *Weird Tales*, and *Unknown*.

The Howard Wandrei art that adorns the covers and interior of *Time Burial* is a foretaste of what to expect in Wandrei's stories. There is sophistication, intelligence, technical mastery, and much that is unsettlingly odd. In his cover painting, under the arch of a bridge biomorphically distorted forms, some utterly alien, some warped parodies of humanity, inhabit a landscape saturated with exceedingly detailed strangeness. While other art pieces here are not as impressive and ambitious, even in more mundane scenes there can again be something disquietingly "off."

Howard Wandrei's stories are more accessible. Varying in tone from breezily pulpish tales to those more artfully styled, whether in the turn of a phrase or writerly approach, Wandrei's substantial intelligence, aesthetic merits, and inventiveness are evident. His "The Hand of the O'Mecca," where a rustic goes a-wooing, features its own peculiar tone. It begins thusly:

It was Elof Bocak, large and unmistakable. Like the two figures which waited for him in the lane, he most nearly resembled an erect shadow. His formidable stature alone identified him. Unlike those two shadow-figures, which were still, his body gyrated remarkably above his feet. Elof had that in him tonight which was stronger than himself. In John Colander's kitchen behind him the whiskey ran . . .

It is a werewolf story; yet rather than the predictable description, with odd details Wandrei delineates his lycanthropes:

. . . each [had] a short, broad tail like that of the fallow deer . . . tails that flicked and frolicked in the fog in a rhythmic dance of their own. When Elof saw the tails frisking, he howled like a wild dog that has newly discovered the moon.

Besides its own pleasures, *Time Burial* also leaves me wanting to search out a collection of Howard Wandrei's mystery stories, a field he had an affinity for, and where he found substantial success. Here, "Master-the-Third" stars Lieutenant Stan Rawls, and though the story is very much in fantastic fiction territory, we get a taste of how superlatively well Wandrei does hard-boiled.

The introduction mentions how some of Wandrei's stories were too "hot" for the Spicies, and here we are given uncensored versions of those tales. Even if not explicit, they are nonetheless quite steamy. The elegance and style of the author's touch elevates them far above the standard Spicy fare; actually, of most modern erotica.

An added bonus is that though the overall focus is on male protagonists, women characters, whether in small roles or major, are far from cardboard cutouts. One ferociously battles the aforementioned Lieutenant Rawls—no pushover—into submission, then "Her slim, steely fingers worked and she systematically dislocated two fingers of his left hand, kept grinding the bones together until he fell in a half faint to his knees. Even then she didn't relax that maiming, inescapable grip."

Ouch! Hard-boiled, indeed.

In "The Monocle," library worker Constance Ydes, formidably learned main protagonist of the story, while brushing up on her Latin reads aloud a portion of a donated book and inadvertently summons up a sorcerer from olden times. This is one method he has set up by which his immortality is assured. He has a bit of a time adjusting to the 20th century, giving Wandrei a chance to mock modern sociopolitical mores, and deftly detail the mage's culture-shock, such as when he "picked up the watch, and listened to it tick, curious. 'Is there an insect inside? It is trying hard to get out.' ' In return for Constance's help, he gives her an emerald monocle; which, when you look through it, shows the instant of your death.

"O Little Nightmare" is another story where a woman figures prominently. The tale begins when an artist and his model engage in, well, extracurricular activities after a session. The painter, Rodney Quist, has a feeling they're being watched. As it turns out, "They were being watched, and by his wife Ursula, who had once been a model for him . . . Ursula's friend Cicely Bourne had an apartment across the way, unknown to Rodney; further, she owned high-powered binoculars . . ."

A lengthy dialogue between the women ensues. After griping about the "double-standard," Ursula bemoans she'd not want a divorce "on New York grounds," apparently onerous at the time; and is worried about Rodney's sanity. Cicely, "a hard-headed, athletic English girl," suggests "a careful, genteel, foolproof murder at moderate rates"; and tells how:

"I killed two men on that last hunting expedition in Africa . . . There was no sign of a trail but they went through the motions of following one. When they had lured me far enough from my party, believe it or not they turned on me just like wild animals. One of them—Well, anyhow, they were listed as hunting accidents by the authorities."

Later, Ursula tells Rodney, "[Cicely's] awfully strong . . . If you made any passes at her, she could give you the beating of your life if she felt like it."

(Cicely is no villain—she plays but a minor part in the story—and suffers no punishment for her actions or attitudes. Besides showing Wandrei's regularly off-the-trail approach, this reminds how pulp magazines in actuality could feature stories, characters, and writing styles far from the stereotypes for which they were condemned on aesthetic and ideological grounds, then as now.)

As it turns out, no mayhem is necessary. A bizarre creature roughly resembling a deformed, hairless rat, vividly realized with a repugnantly convincing physicality, which zips about with uncanny speed to escape attack, appears in Rodney and Ursula's apartment and begins to bedevil him.

Though Howard Wandrei did not much pursue science fiction, here stories like "The Missing Ocean" and "The God Box" show how his talent imparts a unique flavor to even tropes that are not particularly unusual. For instance, in "The Other" the being in particular is a strangely copper-hued woman of an ancient, advanced species; flash-frozen mid-gesture with a strange tool wielded in an upraised arm. She is beautiful, though not of our variety of humanity. But with all her appeal—the enraptured captain who discovered her body in solid ice near the North Pole killed to keep possession of her—she also exudes menace. And when she is thawed out, the results are horrifying, the last line utterly chilling.

Time Burial is a fascinatingly varied showcase of the splendid talent of Howard Wandrei. His refreshingly unique style and imagination makes these stories of horror, science fiction and fantasy a delight to discover.

Mike Hunter

Some Notes on a Nonentity—The Life of H.P. Lovecraft
Sam Gafford and Jason C. Eckhardt
PS Publishing, 2017

Sam Gafford and Jason C. Eckhardt's graphic biography *Some Notes on a Nonentity—The Life of H.P. Lovecraft* is an extraordinary achievement. Even if one had no more than a passing interest in the Gentleman from Providence, this book would prove a fascinating and highly enjoyable reading experience. For admirers of Lovecraft, it's a feast of delights.

A truly remarkable amount of detail and information is smoothly folded into the book. The Dickensian travails and reverses in Lovecraft's lifetime are movingly conveyed in story and art; yet there is much warmth, liveliness and wit as well. The person in all his complex and contradictory facets, his journeys and friendships, difficulties in publishing (and painful rejections of) stories that would become recognized as classics, the creative milieus of amateur journalism, pulp magazines, the "Lovecraft Circle" and much, much more appear between these covers. There are substantial appearances by Robert E. Howard, R. H. Barlow, August Derleth, and cameos by many, such as the maddeningly fickle Weird Tales editor Farnsworth Wright.

Kudos to Sam Gafford for a script that so fluidly and touchingly encapsulates a remarkable lifetime. A longtime weird fictionist—I've a copy of his new collection, *The Dreamer in Fire and Other Stories*—as well as expert on Lovecraft and William Hope Hodgson, Gafford's experience in critical and biographical writings about both authors makes him an ideal co-creator for *Some Notes*.

HPL's family background, with array of positive and negative influences shaping the man and author, is thoroughly covered. In childhood, for instance, we see a young bibliophile who became successively enraptured with the magical Middle East of *The Arabian Nights* and mythologies of Ancient Greece; a science-fascinated youth who experimented with his own chemistry set before moving on to a great love of astronomy. But he was not simply a recluse: Lovecraft recalled how he and a group of boys—the Providence Detective Agency, headquartered in a deserted house—". . . enacted and solved many a gruesome tragedy. I still remember my labors in producing artificial bloodstains . . ."

Here's one example of the superbly deft economy with which so much biographical detail is imparted. In a caption, HPL recalls how "My mother attempted to socialize me by enrolling me in Sunday School and violin classes. These activities soon ended, although for different reasons." A narrow panel devoted to that Sunday School experience might well be titled "The Budding Atheist." Seen from behind, one student—we can imagine who—raises his hand for a question. From

the "What's he going to say now?" reactions of other students, scowl of the clerical-collar-wearing teacher, that query will surely be dogma-challenging.

Was there ever so sadly ill-starred a marriage as that of H. P. Lovecraft and Sonia Haft Greene? She is warmly and sympathetically depicted (in panel-count, probably the second-most-important character in the book); the intellectual and emotional factors attracting them are charmingly, touchingly expressed. His gentlemanly treatment of women, friendships where he treated their persons, intellects and creativity in the exact same fashion as he did that of males, rather than simply seeing them as objects of conquest or silly frothy things to be guided into stereotypical "ladies' interests" impressed many of them favorably. (Of the slings and arrows aimed Lovecraft's way these days, that he was a "misogynist" is the most grotesquely unjust.)

Some women wished that friendship could be turned into a more intimate relationship, but found romantic overtures were passed by because of his cluelessness or entire lack of interest towards connections of that sort. That utter shock was the reaction among Lovecraft's friends upon hearing of Sonia and Howard's marriage did not bode well. In Some Notes, one recalls, "I had a feeling of faintness at the pit of my stomach and became very pale."

His emotionally-damaging childhood was but the first of the punishing blows to What Might Have Been. Consider Sonia's loss of her high-paying job in New York; Howard's inability to find work; the grinding hellishness of his worst New York experiences culminating in the burglarizing of his apartment, with almost all his clothing stolen; Sonia's frustration as she futilely tried to make the relationship work despite his stubborn adherence to antiquated ideas of how a Gentleman behaves (progressive in some areas, he could be reactionary in others) and the intransigence of his aunts (whose ideas were even more antique), to whose authority he deferred. Any one of these might have killed a marriage; put together, well . . .

Illustrators, no matter how talented, rarely do well as comics artists; one may as well expect a still photographer to segue into being a movie director. Judging from *Some Notes on a Nonentity—The Life of H.P. Lovecraft*, one would mistakenly think that Jason C. Eckhardt had years of comics-creating experience behind him. For here, like Athena born full-grown (and armored!) from the brow of Zeus, Eckhardt enters the graphic-novel stage brilliantly creative, with complete mastery of the art form.

I've previously only known Eckhardt's artwork from a late-in-life passion and plunge into Lovecraftiana, acquiring books such as his heavily-illustrated version of "The Colour Out of Space" from Necronomicon Press. Topnotch, serious work. Yet some on-line searching revealed that he is a gifted cartoonist and children's book artist as well. His mastery of realistic rendering gives a solid foundation for the stylization of cartooning, which adds liveliness and nuance to his characters' expressiveness.

The narrative verve and variety of panel layout are exceptionally fine. The book's "Lovecraft on Broadway" format serves as a unifying image for the various "offstage" scenes from HPL's life and fiction. Not simply a gimmick, it's superlatively deployed to dramatic effect. As, for instance, while Howard remains at the podium from which he speaks, the increasingly alienated Sonia heartbreakingly appears as an isolated figure, seated off to the side of the stage.

On the page which covers his return to Providence after that New York exile, featuring a drawing of a train and a map, expressive, varied lettering enhances the rhapsody in Lovecraft's words as his excitement mounts upon approaching the beloved city

with which he so wholly identified. Befitting one who is at the very least one of the foremost Lovecraft illustrators, scenes from the Master's fiction are also powerfully embodied. Cthulhu, Nyarlathotep, Keziah and Brown Jenkin are but a few of the fearsome figures who appear. Countless tales from the modestly-scaled "The Picture in the House" to the epic *At the Mountains of Madness* are gloriously illuminated, the better part of three pages allotted to the last.

We feel the tragedy, frustration and melancholy as well as scenes of fun: the liberating exuberance of an all-day electric-car trip across several states on Lovecraft's twenty-first birthday; his wobblingly bicycling on the cobblestoned streets of Nantucket, while delightedly taking in the old architecture; the conviviality of parties and gatherings of the Kalem Club. A splendid attention to period detail, likenesses of those sharing his world, environment, and architecture in all its richness of form, make us feel we're not simply reading about Lovecraft, but are right there as he lives his life.

One page shows, despite his reclusive tendencies, the vital importance of friendship in Lovecraft's life, as well as more of Eckhardt's rendering prowess. Lovecraft was hypersensitive to dropping temperatures; the opposite number of his Doctor Muñoz in "Cool Air," for whom cold was life. In the first panel ("February of 1934 saw the coldest winter on record in Providence . . ."), HPL peers out of a window in his rooms like a trapped revenant, while sleet slashes by. An invitation by youthful admirer and devoted friend R. H. Barlow for Lovecraft to visit and stay for a while with him in Florida leads to scenes with the pair in glaring sunshine; as backlit figures (feather-fine strokes gracefully shading their forms) with lush tropic greenery in the background, delightedly discussing mutual interests on the Barlow porch, glass of iced tea handy, a clowder of cats providing amiable company. At night, dim lighting, expressions, body language make for a conspiratorial atmosphere as Barlow and Lovecraft gleefully plot like kids in a treehouse, concocting "The Battle That Ended the Century," their anonymously-published satire of amateur journalism politics and personalities.

It might be added that *Some Notes* is no hagiography; Lovecraft's unworthy aspects, resolutely out-of-touch attitudes, denigration of the worth of his work (he did, after all, call himself a "Nonentity"), self-defeating behaviors leave one either shaking one's head in dismay or wanting to grab him by the shoulders and give him a good shake: "Get REAL!" Yet his positive parts—childlike enthusiasms, infinitely giving capacity for friendship, artistic and intellectual brilliance, dedication to Art above any commercial considerations (embodying that ideal of the Romantics: the artist starving in a garret, unwilling to compromise his creativity), and oh, yes, love of cats—by far overwhelm them. For all the acknowledgment given his failings, it's self-evident that Sam Gafford and Jason C. Eckhardt have great affection for Lovecraft, "warts and all."

I've been reading graphic novels since before the term was coined; a substantial portion of which have been biographies. Many of these were fine indeed; at least one (Art Spiegelman's "Maus: A Survivor's Tale") deservedly acclaimed as a masterpiece. But Some Notes on a Nonentity—The Life of H.P. Lovecraft is in a class by itself. In its astonishing written and visual richness and depth of characterization, narrative and detail, it towers above the rest, just as the peaks in At the Mountains of Madness dwarfed even Everest.

Mike Hunter

Selkie Summer
Ken MacLeod
NewCon Press, 2018

This is an interesting one. The publisher's blurb hints at paranormal romance, which isn't really one of my go-to subgenres. While that's certainly an element of this novella, it's also heavy in Celtic lore and political intrigue, which actually makes for a fast and very entertaining read.

We're very much in an alternate universe—such mythological/crypto-zoological creatures as vampires, kelpies and selkies are known to actually exist here. That's not to say that this is a world steeped in magic and the supernatural. For the most part it's just like ours, except for the fact that there's a treaty with the selkies; some of them work with the Navy, and indeed were a huge help to the United Kingdom during the second world war.

Siobhan Ross is a student, come to the Isle of Skye for a summer job in a bed and breakfast establishment. Partly to get out of Glasgow for a while, partly to escape a persistent ex-boyfriend, but mostly because she left it too late to find anything locally.

On the ferry, she catches sight of Cal and is immediately besotted. It's no spoiler to reveal that Cal is a selkie. One of the abilities of a selkie is that they cast a glamour, which brings humans under their spell. It also tends to work both ways, and it isn't completely under their conscious control.

The story starts to get really interesting when a Royal Navy nuclear submarine runs aground where it shouldn't have, which turns out to have been an orchestrated protest by a group of selkie dissidents. Siobhan soon finds that her presence on Skye at that time was more than mere happenstance. She has a natural affinity for the selkie, and they need her to negotiate on their behalf. The otherworldly origins of the selkie, so ancient that even they don't really know the details, almost hints at the Lovecraftian notion of strange races inhabiting this planet long before us.

I've come to trust publisher/editor (and accomplished author in his own right) Ian Whates' judgement, even when he offers me Something that looks a bit like a paranormal romance book to read. Obviously this novella has a far wider scope than that term suggests, but, in any case, I do admit to having previously read several books I really liked in that genre. Sturgeons Law: that 90% of everything is garbage, does presuppose that the other 10% is good after all.

In summary, this is a short book, only 39,000 words in all, which allowed me to read it in just a couple of sittings. Once I got into it, it was hard to put down. You know you've enjoyed a book when you find yourself musing on possible future storylines for the characters. As to whether, or not there will be sequels, or indeed if the author has used the same setting for prior work, I have no idea— but I shall keep my eye open.

I encourage people to not be put off by the use of the word 'romance' here, which after all was a major factor in so many great books, not written expressly for the female market, including those of Edgar Rice Burroughs, whose books were actually termed 'romances' back in the day.

Dave Brzeski

CONTRIBUTORS

Cliff Biggers read his first Lovecraft book in 1964, and was forever enthralled. He has written Lovecraft-influenced tales for various anthologies, along with folk horror, occult detective fiction, and heroic fantasy. He is currently co-editing (with Charles R. Rutledge and James Ray Tuck Jr) an anthology of original weird fiction for the Yuletide.

Dave Brzeski is an editor and book reviewer. His reviews appear in *Occult Detectives Quarterly*, *FEAR Magazine* and on the British Fantasy Society website. He's a consulting editor for *Occult Detectives Quarterly*. He also edits books for Pro Se Productions. *The Spirit of the Place & Other Strange Tales: The Complete Short Stories of Elizabeth Walter*, due later this year from Shadow Publishing, will mark his first front cover credit as editor.

Frank Coffman is a retired professor of college English, Creative Writing, and Journalism. He has published speculative poetry, fiction, and scholarly research in a variety of journals, magazines, and anthologies, including *Black Veins* I, *Eldritch Tales*, *Test Patterns*, *Hell's Empire*, and elsewhere. His poetic magnum opus, *The Coven's Hornbook & Other Poems* has been followed by his rendition into English Verse of 327 quatrains of Khayyám's *Rubáiyát*. A second large collection of poetry, *Black Flames & Gleaming Shadows* was published in 2020. A collection of seven of his occult detective stories, *Three Against the Dark*, will be published in early 2021 as will his third poetry collection, *Eclipse of the Moon*. A member of the Horror Writers Association and the Science Fiction & Fantasy Poetry Association, he established and moderates the Weird Poets Society Facebook group and his blog can be found at https://www.frankcoffman-wordsmith.com.

Adrian Cole is a native of and lives in North Devon, England. His first published work was a ghost story for IPC magazines followed by a trilogy of sword & planet novels, *The Dream Lords*. He has had more than two dozen novels and numerous short stories published over the years, including science fiction, heroic fantasy, sword & sorcery, horror, pulp fiction, and Mythos as well as two young adult novels. His best known works are the *Omaran Saga* and *Star Requiem* fantasy quartets. *Nick Nightmare Investigates* (Alchemy UK), Adrian's first arc of stories about the hard-boiled occult private eye, won the 2015 British Fantasy Award for best collection. His other works include the 3 volume *Voidal* sword and sorcery saga and *Elak, King of Atlantis*, out now from Pulp Hero Press.

Scott Connors is an independent scholar living in northern California who specializes in the life and work of Clark Ashton Smith. He edited the five volume edition of Smith's *Collected Fantasies*, as well as the essay collection on Smith, *The Freedom of Fantastic Things*. His most recent books are *In the Realm of Mystery and Wonder*, a collection of Smith's artwork and prose poems published by Centipede Press, and a bibliography of Smith published by Hippocampus Press (with S. T. Joshi and David E. Schultz).

Bill Crider (1941–2018) was, among many things, a teacher, a singer, a writer, a family man, knowledgeable speaker on books and writers, and a good friend to many. He taught college students at Howard Payne University and Alvin Community College. He had a PhD in English literature. He wrote mysteries, westerns, horror, YA novels, comics, non-fiction, erotica, and more. He loved talking books, collectibles, Jim Thompson, and Harry Whittington, among others. He won two Anthony Awards from BoucherCon (one for First Novel and one for short story which he shared with his wife Judy). He passed away in 2018 after a battle with cancer. For more insightful information, see the Skull Session section of this magazine starting on page 6. He is sorely missed.

Scott Cupp is a John W. Campbell Award-nominated short story writer from Texas. He was the editor (with Joe R. Lansdale) of the World Fantasy nominated anthology *Cross Plains Universe: Texans Celebrate Robert E. Howard*. His short fiction has appeared in a number of anthologies, such as *Razored Saddles*, *Obsessions*, and *Freak Show*. His REH-inspired story "Hell in a Boxcar" appeared *Weirdbook* 32 in 2016.

Milton Davis is an award winning Black Fantastic writer and owner of MVmedia, LLC, a publishing company specializing in Science Fiction, Fantasy and Sword and Soul. Milton is the author of twenty-three novels and editor/co-editor of seven anthologies. Milton's work had also been featured in *Black Power: The Superhero Anthology*, *Skelos: The Journal of Weird Fiction and Dark Fantasy Volume 2*, *Steampunk Writes Around the World* published by Luna Press and *Bass Reeves Frontier Marshal Volume Two*. Milton's story 'The Swarm' was nominated for the 2018 British Science Fiction Association Award for Short Fiction. His screenplay, *Ngolo*, won the 2014 Urban Action Showcase Award for Best Screenplay. Milton Davis can be reached via his website, https://www.miltonjdavis.com.

Bobby Derie is the author of *Sex and the Cthulhu Mythos* (2014) and *Weird Talers: Essays on Robert E. Howard and Others* (2019), and helped compile *The Collected Letters of Robert E. Howard - Index & Addenda* (2015). His essays have been published in the *Lovecraft Annual*, *The Dark Man: Journal of Robert E. Howard and Pulp Studies*, *Occult Detective Quarterly*, and *Skelos,* as well as *The Unique Legacy of Weird Tales: The Evolution of Modern Fantasy and Horror* (2015) and *Representing Kink: Fringe Sexuality and Textuality in Literature, Digital Narrative, and Popular Culture* (2019).

Atlanta author **Amanda DeWees** received her PhD in English from the University of Georgia and wrote her dissertation on 19th-century vampire literature—the perfect training, although she didn't know it at the time, for writing Victorian gothic romance novels. Her books include *With This Curse*, winner of the 2015 Daphne du Maurier Award in historical mystery/suspense, and the Sybil Ingram Victorian Mysteries series. Visit her at AmandaDeWees.com to learn more.

Called "one of the grand old men of horror comics" by comic art historian and journalist Stephen R. Bissette, **Mike Dubisch** has been publishing art and stories in horror comic anthologies since his teens in the 1980's to the present day. Dubisch was a student of the legendary cartoonists Will Eisner and Walter Simonson, and has worked for DC, Marvel, Image and Dark Horse comics. Dubisch's illustrations have appeared in the magazines *Weird Tales*, *Science Fiction Age*, and the *H. P. Lovecraft Magazine of Horror*, as well as the animated film *Howard Lovecraft and the Undersea Kingdom* and many independent productions. His art has been used in toy design and illustration for *Star Wars* and *Dungeons and Dragons* role playing games, covers for *Aliens vs. Predator*, and graphic adaptations of children's literature and pulp fiction. Dubisch is an instructor in the illustration undergraduate program at The Academy of Art University in San Francisco, California. Mike lives in Mazatlan, Mexico with his wife, Carolyn, and three daughters.

Mark Finn is an author, actor, essayist, and playwright. His biography, *Blood and Thunder: The Life and Art of Robert E. Howard*, was nominated for a World Fantasy Award in 2007. He writes comics and fiction, dabbles in magic, acts as a creative consultant for media companies, and produces and performs community theater. He is currently producing *Monty Haul*, and old school RPG fanzine for 5th Edition D&D, available on DriveThruRPG. He lives in North Texas with his long-suffering wife, too many books, and an affable pit bull named Sonya.

Darrell Z. Grizzle is a horror, dark urban fantasy, and thriller writer. He is the author of "I Never Meant to Start a Murder Cult" (2018) and a featured author in "Pink Triangle Rhapsody" (Lycan Valley Press, 2020), an anthology of pulp fiction by gay writers. His stories have been published in *Shotgun Honey*, *Daily Science Fiction*, *Mad Scientist Journal*, *Eldritch Tales*, *Near to the Knuckle*, and *Story & Grit*. Darrell is a former parole officer who now works as a counselor in Marietta, Georgia. His home on the web is www.ShadowHaunted.com and on Facebook, Goodreads, Twitter, and Instagram as dzgrizzle.

Chris Gruber was the editor of *Boxing Stories* by Robert E. Howard, published by the University of Nebraska Press, and is the co-editor of the four-volume collection *Fists of Iron* by the REH Foundation Press. He was the co-editor of the anthology *Dreams in the Fire* and recently co-authored the Kull source book for the new Conan RPG from Modiphius Games.

Chad Hensley is a Bram Stoker Award-nominated author. His fiction and poetry have received honorable mentions in various best of anthologies including *The Year's Best Fantasy and Horror* and *The Best Horror of the Year*. His most recent book of horror poetry, *Embrace the Hideous Immaculate*, is available from the publisher Raw Dog Screaming Press and Amazon.com. His horrific non-fiction has appeared in the last four volumes of *Weird Fiction Review* published by Centipede Press ("Visceral Visual Wizardry", an interview with 1970s *Dungeons and Dragons* artist Erol Otus in volume #8 and his article "The Horrific History of H.R. Giger's Alien Toys" in volume #9 were both lauded by *The Washington Post*). Look for more of his poetry in *Weirdbook* issues #43 through #47, and in the last several volumes of *Spectral Realms* published by Hippocampus Press.

Marshall Highet is a professor and writer. Her YA sci-fi novel *Spare Parts* was published in 2014 and *Hold Fast*, a YA historical novel, came out in 2019. She enjoys reading, writing, walking, talking, and world domination. Hailing from the chilly climes of the Northeast, she now lives in Pittsburgh with her family, two rescue dogs, and a chinchilla who is a master escape artist.

Mike Hunter is a lifelong aficionado of genre fiction who first read Lovecraft and Robert E. Howard close to 50 years ago, yet somehow managed to miss delving into the pulp magazines which brought them fame until recently. The Surrealists awakened an interest in the visual arts. He did much volunteer book reviewing and illustration for *Morbid Curiosity*, and makes his living as a graphic designer. He has contributed his editing and design talents to *Skelos*.

Rachel Kahn is an illustrator with a love of heavy metal, megafauna, and mighty-thewed barbarians. She has her BFA in Visual Art from York University, studied in the Concept Art program at Max the Mutt College of Animation and Design, and currently illustrates and creates concept art for indie and small-press games and fiction. She has a passion for diverse characters.

Karen Joan Kohoutek, an independent scholar and poet, has published about weird fiction and cult film in various journals and literary websites, and received two Robert E. Howard Foundation Awards for scholarship. Recent and upcoming publications have been on subjects including August Strindberg's *Inferno*, Howard's women protagonists, Marvel's *Black Panther*, and the film *Nude on the Moon*. She writes regularly on vintage horror films for the website The Haunted Cinema, and, through Skull and Book Press, has published a New Orleans cemetery guide, along with *The Jack-o-Lantern Box*, a novella about a small-town Halloween. She lives in Fargo, North Dakota.

Allen Koszowski is one of the most prolific artists in his field, having published more than 2,500 illustrations for hundreds of genre publications, including *Isaac Asimov's SF* magazine, *The Magazine of Fantasy & SF*, *Cemetery Dance*, *Whispers*, *Fantasy Tales*, *Weird Tales*, *The Horror Show*, *The Robert Bloch Companion*, and many others.

Matthew Gregory Lewis (1775–1818) was an English novelist and dramatist, who is considered one of the pioneers of Gothic horror. He was frequently referred to as "Monk" Lewis, because of the success of his 1796 Gothic novel *The Monk*. He also worked as a diplomat, politician and an estate owner in Jamaica.

Will Murray is a lifelong Lovecraftian, the author of many Cthulhu Mythos stories, and a contributor to innumerable Cthulhuvian journals. Stupendously prolific, he has penned nearly eighty novels in classic adventure series ranging from The Destroyer to Doc Savage. He is a recognized expert on all things pulp. His latest published novel is *Tarzan, Conqueror of Mars*, teaming Tarzan of the Apes and John Carter of Mars in an historical crossover. Currently he is writing *The Spider: Fury in Steel* for Altus Press. He is also threatening to collect some of his Cthulhu Mythos stories in a collection called *The Wild Adventures of Cthulhu*. The Marvel Universe celebrates him as the creator of The Unbeatable Squirrel Girl, whom even the Great Old Ones justifiably fear.

Legendary fantasy artist **Jim Pitts** first published artwork appeared in David Sutton's horror magazine *Shadow* back in 1970, along with Jon Harvey's magazine *Balthus*. Jim's cover for *Balthus* won the Ken McKintyre Award for best artist at Novacon the same year. Over the past five decades Jim has continued working in the fantasy and horror genres, winning the British Fantasy Award twice, in 1992 and 1993. His artwork has seen print world wide, and appeared regularly in publications such as *Fantasy Tales*, *Whispers*, *Kadath*, *Shadow*, and *Nyctalops*. His work has been used by publishers such as W. Paul Ganley's Weirdbook Press, Fedogan & Bremer, Centipede, Puffin, Granada, Star, Phantasmagoria and Parallel Universe Publications. In 2017 Parallel Universe Publications published a hardback collection of Jim's work from 1970 to 2017 entitled *The Fantasical Art of Jim Pitts: Rolling Back the Years*. Jim has worked extensively with his friend, author Adrian Cole, illustrating many of his stories including The Voidal tales, Nick Nightmare and of course his Elak stories. His forthcoming work includes illustrations for *After Nightfall*, a collection of of stories by David Riley, and the anthology *Swords & Sorceries*.

Michael H. Price is lead author of the *Forgotten Horrors* books—longest-running film history franchise in commercial publishing (since 1979)—and author-artist-editor of such anthology projects as *Comics from the Gone World* and *Deep in the Horrors of Texas*, as well as a curatorial contributor to the Library of American Comics project at IDW Publishing. Price is founding president of the original Fort Worth (Texas) Film Festival and a board member of the Fort Worth Public Library Foundation.

Peter Rawlik is the author of more than fifty short stories, the novels *Reanimators*, *The Weird Company*, and *Reanimatrix*, as well as *The Peaslee Papers*, a chronicle of the distant past, the present, and the far future. As editor he has produced *The Legacy of the Reanimator* and *The Chromatic Court*. His short story "Revenge of the Reanimator" was nominated for a New Pulp Award. He is a regular member of the Lovecraft Ezine Podcast and a frequent contributor to the *New York Review of Science Fiction*.

Andrea Rushing studied at the Academy of Art in San Francisco. He has had one man shows at San Diego State University, San Marcos State University, and at the San Diego Museum of Art. His is a distinctly European sensibility, driven by a profound interest in the human condition and by the insights humanity displays in response to that condition — sometimes as in studies of rich symbolism; other times in straightforward portraiture, where his brushwork reveals the sitter's truth and destiny. Currently his work hangs in the Michael J. Wolf Gallery in San Diego, and in the Heritage Art Gallery and the Reginald Ingraham Gallery in Los Angeles.

Charles R. Rutledge is the author of *Dracula's Revenge*, and co-author of three novels in the Griffin and Price supernatural suspense series, written with James A. Moore. His short stories have appeared in over twenty anthologies. He owns entirely too many editions of the novel *Dracula*, keeps actual soil from Transylvania on his desk, and is seldom seen in daylight.

Darrell Schweitzer is the author of four novels, *The Dragon House*, *The Mask of the Sorcerer*, The *Shattered Goddess*, and *The White Isle*. He is a former editor of *Weird Tales* (1988-2007) and an active anthologist. His most recent anthology is *The Mountains of Madness Revealed* (2019). In 2020 PS Publishing issued a two-volume retrospective of his fiction, *The Mysteries of the Faceless King* and *The Last Heretic*. As a poet he may be better known for Cthulhuvian limericks and T*he Innsmouth Tabernacle Choir Hymnal*, but he actually does have two volumes of serious poetry in print from Wildside Press, *Groping Toward the Light* and *Ghosts of Past and Future*.

Jeffrey Shanks is an archaeologist and pulp scholar and he served as co-chair of the Pulp Studies area for the Popular Culture Association from 2012 to 2018. He has written numerous popular and scholarly articles on Robert E. Howard, H. P. Lovecraft, Edgar Rice Burroughs, and other topics. His work has appeared in *The Dark Man*, *REH: Two-Gun Raconteur*, *Lovecraft Annual*, *The Pulpster*, *Blood 'n' Thunder*, *Comic Book Quarterly*, *Foreign Comic Collector*, *Conan Meets the Academy*, *Undead in the West II*, and many others. He is the co-editor of the Bram Stoker Award-nominated essay collection *The Unique Legacy of Weird Tales: The Evolution of Modern Fantasy and Horror*. In 2018, he risked unearthing unspeakable horrors by leading an archaeological excavation of the buried cellar in Robert E. Howard's backyard.

Dacre Stoker is the great grand-nephew of Bram Stoker and the international best-selling co-author of *Dracula the Un-Dead* (Dutton, 2009), the official Stoker family endorsed sequel to *Dracula*. Dacre is also the co-editor (with Elizabeth Miller) of *The Lost Journal of Bram Stoker: The Dublin Years* (Robson Press, 2012). His latest novel, *Dracul*, a prequel to *Dracula*, released in October 2018 co-authored with JD Barker, published by Putnam in North America, Penguin Random House in the UK, and various publishers internationally, with film rights recently acquired by Paramount Studios. A native of Montreal, Canada, Dacre currently lives in Aiken, SC, and together with his wife Jenne manages the Bram Stoker Estate. His website is DacreStoker.com.

Anthony Taylor is a writer and the licensing & brand manager for the Bram Stoker Estate. He is the author of *Arctic Adventure!*, an official Thunderbirds™ novel based on the iconic British television series by Gerry and Sylvia Anderson. He has written episodes of the animated series *Paddle Pop Adventures*, as well as *Voyage to the Bottom of the Sea: The Complete Series – Volume 2*, which includes reprints of the classic Gold Key comic book stories, and *The Future was FAB: The Art of Mike Trim*, chronicling artist Mike Trim's career designing models and special effects for Thunderbirds, Captain Scarlet, UFO, and other works. Anthony was a monthly columnist for *Toy Shop Magazine* for twelve years and a regular contributor and editor for the British magazine *Sci-Fi & Fantasy Models International*. His articles have appeared in *SFX*, *Video WatcHDog*, *Fangoria*, *Screem*, *HorrorHound*, *Famous Monsters of Filmland*, *FilmFax*, *Amazing Figure Modeler*, *Effects Special*, *Modeler's Resource*, and many other magazines. He is the force behind the film and disc review column, *Apes On Film* for ATLRetro.com. His website is online at Taylorcosm.com.

Timothy Truman has worked as an professional illustrator and writer since since 1981, doing artwork for role playing games, comic books, magazines and books, as well as CD covers, merchandise and comics for such musicians as the Grateful Dead, Santana, and Rory Gallagher. He is the creator of *Scout* and co-creator of *Grimjack* (with John Ostrander) and *A Man Called Hawken* (with Benjamin Truman). His work includes, *Jonah Hex* (with Joe R. Lansdale), *Hawkworld*, *Conan*, and many more. To learn more about Timothy and see further examples of his work, visit timothytruman.com.

George E. Turner (1925-1999) provided Mike Price with an apprenticeship in film scholarship and cartooning during their newsroom association of the 1960s and 1970s. Turner's seminal film-history book, *The Making of King Kong* (1975; revised in 2018) is a Standard Desk Reference of the American Film Institute, as is his long-term collaboration with Price, the *Forgotten Horrors series*. An alumnus of the Art Institute of Chicago, Turner spent the 1980s-1990s as editor of *American Cinematographer* magazine.

Donald A.Wandrei (1908–1987) was an American science fiction, fantasy and weird fiction writer, poet and editor. He was the older brother of science fiction writer and artist Howard Wandrei. He had fourteen stories in *Weird Tales*, another sixteen in *Astounding Stories*, plus a few in other magazines including *Esquire*. He was the co-founder (with August Derleth) of the prestigious fantasy/horror publishing house Arkham House.

Cynthia Ward has published stories in *Analog*, *Asimov's*, *Nightmare*, *Weird Tales*, *Weirdbook*, and other anthologies and magazines. She edited the anthologies *Lost Trails: Forgotten Tales of the Weird*

West Volumes One and Two. With Nisi Shawl, Cynthia co-created the groundbreaking *Writing the Other* writers' workshop and coauthored the diversity fiction-writing handbook, *Writing the Other: A Practical Approach*, which were honored with the 2020 Locus Special Award. Her latest short novel, *The Adventure of the Naked Guide: Blood-Thirsty Agent Book 3*, is available from Aqueduct Press.

Bill Willingham never fought a desperate and losing battle in a good cause, never contributed to society in a meaningful way, and hasn't lived a life of adventure, but he's had a few moments of near adventure. At some point in his life Bill learned how to get paid for telling scurrilous lies to good people, and he's been doing it ever since. He is best known as the creator of *Elementals*, *Coventry*, and the Eisner Award-winning *Fables*. His latest novels include *Just Another Ranker* and *Hammer of the Gods*. He lives in the wild and frosty woods of Minnesota.

Shannon Connor Winward is an American editor and writer of manifold things. Her work appears widely in places like *Fantasy & Science Fiction*, *Analog*, Pseudopod's *Artemis Rising*, T*he Pedestal Magazine*, *Lunch Ticket*, *Eye to the Telescope*, and *Flash Fiction Online*. Shannon is an erstwhile recipient of honors and awards including an emerging artist fellowship from the Delaware Division of the Arts. Her debut poetry collection, *Undoing Winter* (Finishing Line Press, 2014) earned the SFPA's Elgin Award for best speculative chapbook. Her first full-length collection, *The Year of the Witch* (Sycorax Press), was published in 2018.

ON SALE NOW FROM SKELOS PRESS:

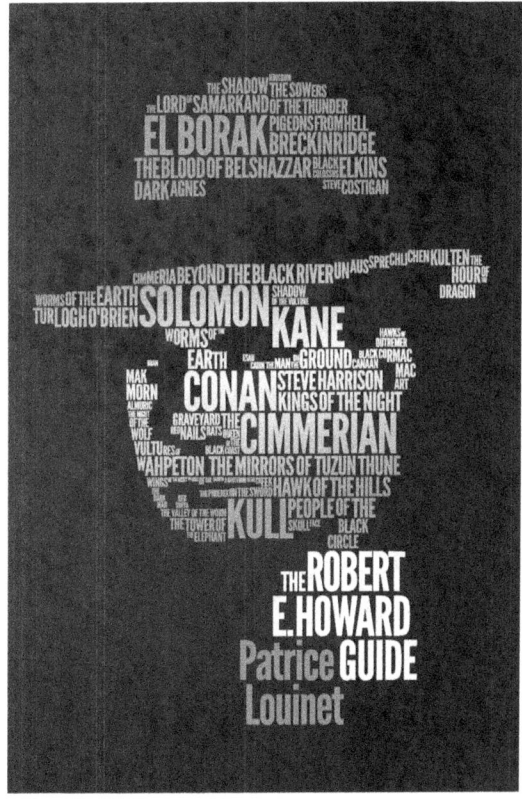

OCCULT DETECTIVE QUARTERLY

TALES OF SUPERNATURAL SLEUTHS & STRANGE INVESTIGATIONS

Stories by Ted E Grau, Adrian Cole, Joshua M Reynolds, Amanda DeWees and more, plus reviews, articles and fantastic art - coming Fall/Winter 2016

order at - electricpentaclepress.bigcartel.com
detailed info at - greydogtales.com

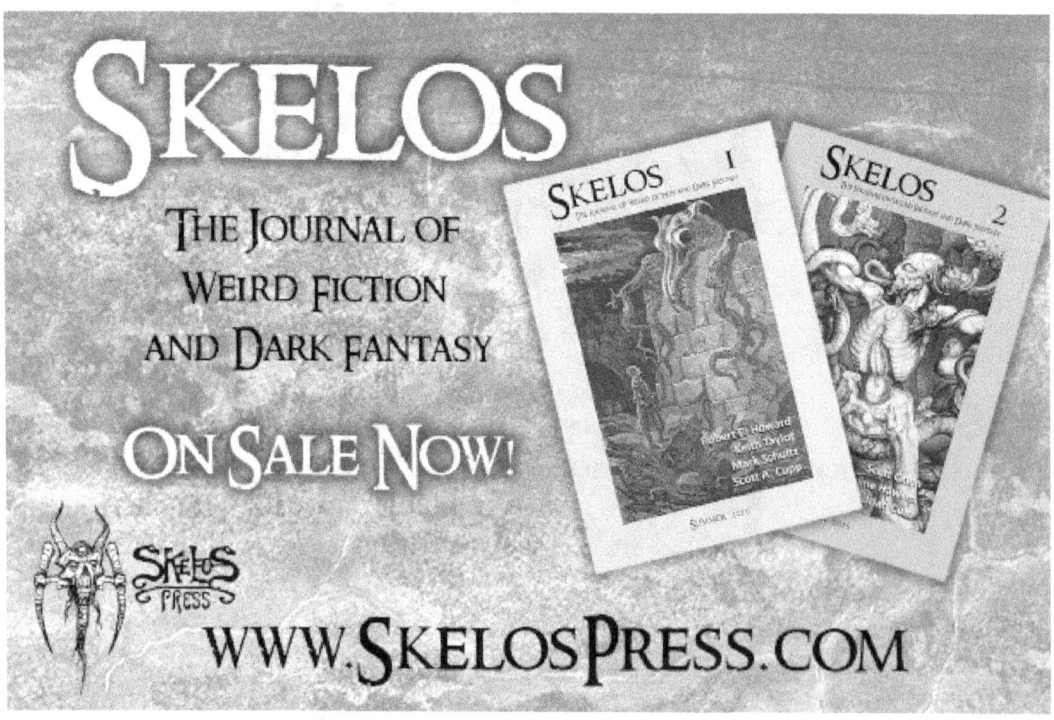

SKELOS

THE JOURNAL OF WEIRD FICTION AND DARK FANTASY

ON SALE NOW!

WWW.SKELOSPRESS.COM

SKELOS
FOUNDING PATRONS

Michael Adams
Jason Aiken
Charles C. Albritton III
Anonymous
Christopher Joseph Antony
Roger Beckett
Valdenor Monteiro Brito Júnior
Mark Buckley
John Bullard
Rusty Burke
Douglas Candano
Ben Cartwright
Chainsaw
David Lars Chamberlain
Sandy Chidester
Anthony Conrad Chieffalo
Cirsova Publishing
Frank Coffman
Blake Aaron Coleman
Adrian Coombs-Hoar
Eddie Coulter
Scott A. Cupp
Vincent N. Darlage
Tony Den
Bobby Derie
Louis Downs
Zeb Doyle
Christopher Dunnbier
Jeff Fournier

Mick Gall
Phil Garrad
David Gentzel
Lee Greenberg
Diana Griffin
Ståle Gismervik
Dierk Günther
Gus Gyde
Peggy J. Hailey
Andrew Hatchell
Morgan Hazel
Alvin Helms
Jason B. Karns
Jim "DC Books" Kirkland
Karen Joan Kohoutek
Oskar Elenäs Landström
Christopher La Pierre
Richard Lemon
Randall R. Logan
D. C. Lozar
Ian Magee
Martin Metzler
Paul Niedernhofer
Alexander Nirenberg
Nicholas Ozment
Michael J. Pacheco
Frank Parsche
James Reasoner
Tom Reinhart

Stuart Rimmer
Richard "Bluddworth" Sellati
Daniel Sharpe
Stickfight
William Thom
Eric Tighe
F. Scott Valeri
Joseph Harley Vaughan
Todd B. Vick
Amedeo Scottie Vidaic
Kit Walker

Bill Ward
Todd Warren
Bill Webb
Chris Wegner
Jeremy D. Weinstein
Keith West
A. Wilder
Jason A. Woods
Todd A. Woods
James Wolff

BENEFACTORS

Adam T. Alexander
James Estes
John Hannan
Mike Hunter
Thomas Krabacher
Steven Ladas
William Lampkin
Daniel M. Look
Ryan McMahon
Paul O. Miles

Brian Murphy
JB Murphy
North Wind Adventures
Alan Pinion
Sandor Silverman
Andy Sommerville
Fletcher A. Vredenburgh
Charlie J. Wall
Jake van der Weide

SUPPORTERS

Sanford Allen
Chad Bowden
John Burchill
Wesley D. Clifton

Philip Glass
Michael Myers
Juan Luis Perez

www.ingramcontent.com/pod-product-compliance
Lightning Source LLC
Chambersburg PA
CBHW080822250626
47160CB00008B/2835